TENNESSEE BRIDES

THREE-IN-ONE COLLECTION

DIANE ASHLEY
AARON MCCARVER

BARBOUR
PUBLISHING

Dear Reader,

 We want to thank you so much for taking this journey with us through Tennessee history. We were thrilled about doing these stories of three generations of one family living in the exciting years of the nineteenth century in the Volunteer State as it is my (Aaron) home state. The events of this period provide great backdrops for the spiritual and romantic struggles of our characters. We hope that you learn a little about this great state as its people fought with Andrew Jackson in the War of 1812, watched the tragedy of the Cherokee Trail of Tears, and struggled with their own divisions in the Civil War. We especially pray that God touches your heart through our characters as they strive to follow God's leading through the tough situations life has to offer.

 As any book is a true team effort, we want to thank the wonderful team at Barbour Publishing, including our editors—JoAnne Simmons, Becky Fish, and Rachel Overton—and the fantastic people who design our books and covers. We also want to thank our families and our friends—especially our writing support, the Bards of Faith—for keeping us grounded and sane. . .most of the time. Most importantly, we owe everything to our heavenly Father. All that we do is for His glory and honor!

Diane Ashley & Aaron McCarver

These things have I written unto you that believe on the name
of the Son of God; that ye may know that ye have eternal life,
and that ye may believe on the name of the Son of God
1 JOHN 5:13

UNDER THE
TULIP POPLAR

Dedication

From Aaron:
To Gilbert Morris, a true legend: None of the wonderful
opportunities that have come to me in the Christian publishing
industry would have happened without your special help and guidance.
Thank you for all you have done for me, for your special friendship. . .
and for finally redeeming the name "Aaron."
With special love to Johnnie and Lynn, too.

From Diane:
To Vicki Tyner Joyce and Mitchell Harry Tyner: No one could have better
siblings. Together we have faced many challenges, and I deeply appreciate
the times you were there for me to lean on. Daddy was right, you know—
blood really is thicker than water

In loving memory:
Weldon Harry Tyner, Jr.—September 12, 1933–September 26, 1995
Dorothy Gene McKinley Tyner—April 16, 1934–April 30, 1997

Prologue

Taylor farm outside Nashville, Tennessee,
Mid-September 1813

Rebekah, send Eleanor out to gather the eggs this morning. I need you to help your pa with the corn. He got behind when he went to that rally last week."

Rebekah Taylor watched as her ma plucked little Donny out of his crib and cradled him in her arms. She could understand her ma's happy expression. Donny was an adorable bundle. They all spent time cooing over him to get him to show his tiny dimples.

Like her, he took his coloring from their pa—light blond hair and eyes as brown as a hickory nut. Eleanor looked more like Ma with her curly brown hair and hazel eyes. Rebekah often wished she had inherited a few curls of her own, but her hair only curled if they applied a hot iron to it, and then only for a few hours before stubbornly straightening out again.

"Hurry up now. The weather is getting cooler, and we don't need to risk losing our crop to an early freeze." Martha Taylor smiled as Donny gurgled, one tiny hand swinging through the air as if he were waving good-bye.

"Yes, ma'am." Rebekah tried to keep the disappointment out of her voice. If she was out in the field with her pa, she might miss seeing Asher if he came for a visit. And she had the feeling he was planning to stop by. The weather was gorgeous, and besides, it had been nearly a week since his last visit. She didn't know how much longer she could keep their news secret.

Not that her parents didn't suspect the truth. She and Asher had been sitting together in church for almost a year now. Everyone knew that the two of them had been keeping company since last spring when he came back from the College of William and Mary in Virginia. But how was he supposed to see her if she couldn't even stay home and wait for him? She would have asked the question out loud except for the distracted look on her ma's face. Pastor's words from last Sunday rang in her ears: *"Every Christian has the duty of putting the needs of others first."* Pastor taught that was the way to make certain all needs were met according to God's plan.

Rebekah placed the egg basket into the waiting hands of her six-year-old sister. Eleanor's eyes sparkled, and she grinned widely, showing the gap between her front teeth. She was nearly dancing with the excitement of her new responsibility. The basket dangled from one hand, and she held her skirt up with the other as she fairly skipped out of the cabin.

Rebekah sighed and carefully removed the apron she'd donned that morning in an attempt to look more dignified in case of a caller. It would never survive a day of field work. She folded it and placed it in the chest at the end of her cot. Another sigh. How could she manage to be where Asher could find her and still do as her parents wished?

Slow footsteps took her to the door. Rebekah sighed once more.

"Whatever is the matter with you? You sound like one of those fancy Scottish musicians. Remember? What did they call those big instruments?"

Rebekah thought back to the magical night. Her whole family had spent a long weekend in Nashville while her pa bartered with the local merchants. How excited she had been when her pa had allowed Asher's parents to pay for all of them to attend a special concert. She remembered the way Asher's azure eyes looked in the dark theater and the feel of his strong arm under her hand as he helped her to her seat. A blush suffused her cheeks. "I. . .they were bagpipes."

"That's right." Her ma turned to look at Rebekah. "And why are you blushing? Could it be thoughts of a certain young man. . . ?"

Rebekah ducked her head and reached for the door. She was outside and halfway across the yard before her ma could finish the gentle teasing. It was so good to be alive on a beautiful day like today, even if she might have to miss seeing Asher. Maybe he would come looking for her. She halted for a moment as another thought struck her—maybe that was the real reason Ma had sent her out to work in the fields with Pa. Maybe it would be better if Asher had to come looking for her.

࿏

Asher Landon, Esq., encouraged his horse along the rutted track toward the Taylor homestead. The long, fifteen-mile trip from Nashville had seemed easier today because he was anxious to share his news with Rebekah. She would be so excited. At least he hoped so.

After the rally in Nashville last week, he and his pa had debated Andrew Jackson's plan day and night. The general was very convincing. And he had a lot of experience, even if President Madison did not want to give the man a chance.

It was a shame how those pompous windbags back East tried to control things they didn't understand. Like how they'd sent General Jackson to defend New Orleans last year, then changed their minds when he got to Natchez and told him to disband the militia. But the general had showed them. He'd refused to abandon his men so far from home. He'd brought them all back, even giving up his own horses so that the wounded and sick would have easier transportation. No wonder they called him Old Hickory. That march had shown everyone how tough General Jackson was.

How Asher wished he could have been part of that campaign. But he'd been off at college. Now he was a man. He was ready and eager to do his duty for his country.

General Jackson had spoken long and hard about that very thing last week. Asher agreed with everything the man said. If they did not all stand against the English and their Indian allies, they would end up losing their hard-won independence. He was not about to stand around and let his home and family be threatened. Especially after the horrific massacre down at Fort Mims. Those Creek Indians needed to be trounced, and General Jackson was the man to do the job.

Asher pressed his knees together, urging his horse to hurry a bit as he spotted Rebekah's cabin. From amble to canter to gallop, he hurried to reach the cabin and the girl he hoped would one day become his wife.

When he reached the yard, he dismounted and looped the reins around a sapling. Always aware of his appearance, Asher took a moment to dust off his trousers and straighten his jacket. He glanced longingly toward the stream that gurgled between leafy poplars to one side of the cabin. Maybe he could coax Rebekah into dipping him a cool drink. It would give him an excuse to get closer to her. The very thought made his heart speed up a bit. He couldn't remember a time when he had not loved Rebekah Taylor and planned to make her his wife. But sometimes, personal desires needed to be set aside for greater ideals. There would be time for them to marry and start a family as soon as he got back.

❧

"Good afternoon, Mr. Taylor, Miss Rebekah."

Asher's familiar voice brought a gasp to Rebekah's throat. She straightened and tugged her bonnet back onto her head, tucking strands of hair under it with an impatient hand. She should never have let it slip and hang down her back. No matter that the late-morning sun had made her face as hot as a bed of coals. Now she would probably have a dozen new freckles she would have to bleach with lemon juice. She wanted to cry in exasperation. Why did she have to look so. . . so frowsy?

Asher dismounted, looking every inch the dapper young businessman. Just seeing his straight shoulders and easy smile made her heart beat faster. She never grew tired of looking at him. He was the one who held her heart and occupied most of her thoughts.

Growing up near him, she had admired Asher's honesty and integrity as well as his innate kindness. She had turned to him with every problem, and he'd always managed to find a solution. Her heart had broken when his parents insisted on sending him away to college. But now he was back, and they could begin their life together.

As he strode across the rows toward Rebekah and her pa, her gaze drank in his snowy white neckcloth and stylish blue coat. These days, Asher always looked like a fashion plate—as if he were ready to attend a society picnic or a tea party. The color of his coat was reflected in his eyes—eyes that sometimes reminded her of a cloudless summer sky, and at others of a picture of the Atlantic Ocean she had seen hanging in Aunt Dolly's parlor in Nashville.

Her pa's dry voice caught Rebekah's attention. "I wonder what a young man might be doing this far from Nashville on a fine autumn day." His right eyebrow rose up as he glanced from Asher to Rebekah.

Asher cleared his throat and thrust out a hand. "My pa sends his greetings, sir. We missed seeing you at the rally last week." As the two men shook hands, Asher looked over Pa's shoulder, and his smile widened ever so slightly.

Rebekah could not keep from returning his smile. Suddenly, it did not matter as much that she was hot and tired from working beside her pa all morning. It only mattered that Asher had come. And he was smiling. The world seemed to fade away.

As if from a distance, she heard her pa's voice and recognized the gentle humor in his tone. "I believe I'll go back to the house and see if your ma still has one of those biscuits left over from breakfast."

"Do you want me to come with you, Pa?" Rebekah held her breath, hoping he would turn down her offer.

"Seems to me that you need to finish that row, Rebekah. Perhaps Asher could help you gather the rest of the corn."

"It would be my honor, sir."

"I'll not be very far away. So be certain to mind your manners, you two." Her pa hummed a lilting melody as he turned to leave.

Asher reached for the half-empty basket at the end of the row. "Thank you, sir. We'll only be a few moments."

Rebekah could feel the color rising in her cheeks. Why did Pa have to be so old-fashioned? He knew Asher was a gentleman and could be trusted to treat her with respect. Blindly, she grabbed the nearest stalk and stripped an ear of corn from it.

Silence filled the air between her and Asher for several minutes as they worked side by side. Then it happened. They both reached for the same stalk. Their hands brushed against each other. Rebekah caught her breath, and then when she tried to draw her hand away, Asher wrapped his fingers around hers. Her heart stuttered to a halt and seemed to lose its rhythm. Her breathing grew ragged, and she had a difficult time concentrating.

"We have to talk, Rebekah. There's something I have to tell you."

This was it! She was about to hear the words she'd been dreaming of for weeks. What would she say? Should she pull her hand away? Or leave it in his? But the feel of their hands tenderly clasped together felt so right. There had been very little private time between them. Only whispered compliments and tender glances. But she had known for several weeks that Asher wanted to ask her to marry him.

She wondered if he had talked to her pa yet. That might explain why Pa had been willing to leave them alone for a few minutes. Had Pa given his permission? But when could Asher have spoken to him? She would have known if he'd come to their home.

Rebekah tugged the hand he had captured, disappointed when he allowed her to pull it away without resistance. His eyes narrowed, and he turned his head up. She noticed his square chin and the way his Adam's apple bobbed up and down in the folds of his neckcloth before she allowed her own gaze to sweep the midday sky.

The sun had bleached most of the color away, leaving the sky pale. A flock of geese winged a southerly path across the sky as she waited for Asher to continue. Should she say something? Had he changed his mind? Should she have let him keep holding her hand? Had he lost his courage?

Asher ran a finger around the collar of his shirt and looked at her once again. "It's quite hot for September."

"Yes, I suppose so." Rebekah turned back to the corn, somewhat surprised to realize they had completed the row. It was time to go back to the cabin. "How are your parents doing?"

"They're fine, thank you. They send their compliments and told me to ask you to consider visiting again in the near future."

Rebekah held her breath. If his parents were sending messages like that, they must have given their blessing. "I will see. I'm not sure when Ma and Pa will return to Nashville. But please tell your family I miss them and would love to visit."

"Yes, well. . ." His voice drifted off, and he looked over her shoulder. "Let's go sit under our tree."

Her heart turned over. How she loved Asher. He was such a romantic. "Their tree" was the tall, shady tulip poplar that towered over one end of the field. They had often played there as young children.

As they walked toward the broad-leafed tree that's leaves had just started to turn yellow-gold around the edges, Asher continued their conversation. "Did I tell you that Pa has talked with General Jackson about his idea for a new kind of banking system?"

Rebekah twisted a hand in the skirt of her dress. What did she care about banking?

But Asher apparently did not recognize her frustration. He continued talking about his pa's plans and the economic challenges faced by the nation as it struggled to define itself apart from the English Crown.

Rebekah nodded as her mind wandered to the familiar visions that occupied most of her waking hours. She could see Asher entering the front door of their comfortable home and giving her a quick hug before being swamped with loving hugs and kisses from their children. She would stand back and smile, waiting until their eyes met and his hand reached for hers. They would walk together to a dining table filled with fresh vegetables, meat, and a heady assortment of fruits. After dinner, she would darn clothes by the fireplace while he spoke of his challenging job. They would gather the children together, and Asher would read to them from God's Holy Word. Then they would all pray for God's blessings and thank Him for leading them safely through another day. . . .

". . .has such a vision for our country. And I think it's time for me to fight for our freedom. Don't you agree?"

Rebekah drew her mind away from her daydreams. "What did you say?"

"I said I've joined the Tennessee militia. We're in the middle of a war, and General Jackson says it's our duty to help keep this country safe. He has so many great ideas. If all of the members of Congress would listen to him, I have no doubt the British would already have been routed."

Rebekah's dreams crashed around her as the meaning of his words sank in. Asher had not come to ask for her hand in marriage. He had come to tell her good-bye. She shook her head in denial, backing away from him. "You're. . .going away? How could you do this to me—to us?"

Asher's eyes darkened. "I know you don't mean what you're saying, Rebekah. My pa fought for our freedom, the same as yours. You and I both know I owe a duty as an American citizen to heed the call to arms. Our very lifestyles are at risk. Everything that you and I have was wrested from English tyranny only a few decades ago. If we ignore the needs of our nation, how can our country survive?"

Tears flooded her eyes. It was fine to talk about patriotism and sacrifice until it became personal. What Asher was talking about was not just some fine ideal to be discussed and argued by the menfolk. This was *her* love, *her* life, *her* future. And it was being destroyed before it could even begin. In an instant everything had changed. All of her dreams and hopes lay shattered. Rebekah balled her fists and pressed them against her eyelids. She would not cry.

She felt his hands on her shoulders, and she lost the precarious control over her emotions. Hot tears pushed their way past her knuckles. On some level, she knew his arms had wrapped around her. Asher was rocking her like a baby and whispering words of comfort and endearment into her ear. But mere words could neither fill the emptiness nor calm the fear that had settled in her heart.

Chapter 1

Rebekah waved to Eleanor and Ma as Pa clucked his tongue and Old Bess ambled forward. The wagon jerked, marking the beginning of her exciting adventure. So why did she feel like crying along with her little sister, whose face was hidden in Ma's skirts? For a minute, Rebekah wanted to tell Pa to stop. No matter that Aunt Dolly was sick and needed help. She could not go through with leaving. She stretched a hand out toward his arm. But then, looking up at the taut expression on his face, she let the hand fall back to her lap.

She twisted in her seat as the wagon turned a curve on the track. "I'll be back before you know it." She forced the words past the large lump that had wedged itself in her throat.

"Are you all right, Becka?" Pa's brown gaze, so wise and gentle, made her want to weep even more. He looked sad, infected with the same sorrow that had flooded every member of the family.

"Yes, sir."

"Your ma and I discussed this at great length over the past week. We're going to miss you dreadfully, but your aunt Dolly needs our help. Since your uncle George passed away, she has no family but us. She's been quite sick for a month, and now, one of her maids quit to move to Knoxville with her husband." He shook his head. "My sister-in-law does not trust that anyone else is capable of hiring competent help, so she has asked if we would allow you to come stay with her for a while."

Rebekah nodded. Her whole life had turned upside down since last fall. First, Asher had not asked her to marry him. Then he'd left. He was gone—still fighting the Indians, or the British, or whoever it was they thought they had to defeat. She prayed for him every day.

Before the beginning of the new year, there had been little news, only the report from Mr. Partain, who owned the farm over the rise, that there had been a large group of volunteers. Nearly twice as many as expected. But not to worry; they had sufficient provisions to last for a considerable length of time. When they learned of the need to send more supplies, she and Ma had contributed baskets of cornmeal and flour, as well as jars of honey and canned tomatoes.

She sure wished she could tell Andrew Jackson a thing or two. He was the reason everyone had gotten so riled up. She had seen the famous general once while they were in Nashville, but her parents had not sought out his acquaintance. He was a good-looking man, tall and proud, even if he was old. Probably as old as her pa. But no matter his age, the man undoubtedly had a silver tongue. One rousing speech from him, and Asher had decided to answer the call to arms instead of wrapping his arms around her.

A sigh filled her chest, and Rebekah let it escape quietly. No need to upset Pa. She already knew he didn't really want her to leave to stay with Aunt Dolly. Last week, she had heard her parents arguing late into the night. But Aunt Dolly was sick, and Ma could not go tend to her. Eleanor was too young, and Pa had to work the land, so Rebekah was the logical choice. Ma had explained the situation to her two days ago during breakfast.

At first, Rebekah had been excited. Staying in Nashville would be a dream come true. All of the shops, the people, the excitement of being in the midst of things. She would know all the news well ahead of her parents. Everyone in Nashville heard about current events from the traffic along the river. Unlike at home, where news came weeks late, if at all, the newspaper would likely be delivered to Aunt Dolly's home the day it was printed.

What would life be like at Aunt Dolly's? She remembered visiting her aunt last year and being awed by the luxurious furnishings and modern conveniences that her ma's sister enjoyed. She even had running water in the house—a long-handled pump that could make water gush out faster than a river during the spring melt.

No more buckets to be filled at the creek. Rebekah flexed her hand. Even with a cloth wrapped around the handle, a heavy bucket could raise blisters when it had to be carried into the cabin several times a day. That was a chore she would not miss.

She would miss other things, however. She would miss sleeping next to Eleanor and teasing her younger sister. She would miss playing with the baby and practicing her reading and writing with Pa's guidance. She would even miss sewing and cooking and making jams and jellies with Ma.

But how silly she was being. Aunt Dolly most likely sewed. She might even have some new patterns Rebekah could use to embroider a pair of pillowcases for Ma and Pa. If she could barter something for material, she could also make a pinafore for her little sister and stitch Eleanor's initials on it. What a grand scene it would be when her family arrived to fetch her. Aunt Dolly would be recovered from her illness and doting on her. Everyone would be very impressed with her skills, and Aunt Dolly would be reluctant to let her return home.

The front wheel of the wagon hit a rut, forcing Rebekah to abandon her daydreams and grasp the edge of her seat.

"I want you to mind your manners while you are staying with your aunt Dolly. I do not want to hear reports of your acting like anything but the most gently bred young lady in Nashville. Always get one of the servants to accompany you when you leave the house, no matter how close your destination. There are dangers around every corner when you're staying in a bustling city like Nashville. You cannot imagine the types of characters who would love to prey on an innocent country girl."

"Of course, Pa. I'll be very careful." Rebekah couldn't keep the note of surprise from her voice. She'd seen no evidence of troublemakers when they'd traveled to Nashville last year.

Looping the reins over his left hand, her pa reached his right hand under her chin and raised her face toward his. "I know you mean that. But you're very young and innocent, my dear. I don't know if we did you a service to keep you so insulated from the dangers of city living."

Rebekah put her hand over his larger one and squeezed it. "You and Ma have done an excellent job of raising me. You've taught me to rely on God and His instructions in the Bible. I won't let you down."

"You could never let me or your ma down, honey. We love you and only want the best for you. Your ma thinks this visit may be an excellent opportunity for you, as well as a boon for her sister. Aunt Dolly has apparently decided it is time for you to think of marriage and raising a family of your own."

Rebekah blushed at his words and looked away at the rolling hills, dotted here and there with the remnants of last week's dusting of snow. "I'm nearly seventeen years old. Wasn't that how old Ma was when she married you?"

Pa nodded and returned his attention to the road ahead of them. "But I didn't realize then quite how young she was. I guess you'll always be my baby."

"You don't have anything to worry about. You know I'm waiting for Asher Landon to return from fighting. I'm not likely to have my head turned by anyone in Nashville. Besides, I'll be spending all my time nursing Aunt Dolly back to health. If she gets better soon, I might even be traveling back home within a month. And if I'm not, maybe you can bring everyone for a visit."

"We will see. . . ." His voice faded away as they topped a hill.

The sun's weak winter rays made it hard for her to make out the gray shape some distance ahead of them. "What's that?"

"I don't know." Her pa reached under the seat for his musket and swung it across his knees.

Rebekah could feel her heart racing as their wagon slowly gained on the dark shadow. When it was a couple of hundred yards away, she giggled her relief. "It's only an empty cart."

"Yes, but where is its driver? The horses? Why is it sitting out here unattended?" Pa slowed their wagon to a crawl. "I want you to get in the back. Get under the blanket, and don't come out unless I tell you to."

"But, Pa—"

"Don't argue with me." His curt tone got her attention.

Without further protest, Rebekah gathered her skirts and climbed over the seat. She shifted her baggage and the crates of corn around until she had made an opening she could squeeze into.

"Are you hidden?"

"Yes, sir." Rebekah pulled a horse blanket up and over her. It was warm and stuffy under the woolen material. She fought the urge to sneeze and strained her ears to hear over the creaking of the wagon wheels. After a few moments, she heard the unmistakable thunder of several horses racing toward them. Why didn't Pa speed up? If *she* were driving, Old Bess would be halfway to Nashville by now.

The hoofbeats drew closer until Rebekah was sure the riders would run right over Pa. Then the sound changed to stomping paws and whinnies. The wagon came to a complete stop and shifted slightly, indicating her pa had stood up to face the horsemen. She heard his calm voice question the riders about their intentions. The answer was a series of staccato syllables. Indians!

Her scalp tingled with remembered stories of Indian braves and their trophies. She could not make out exactly what was said because the flaps of her bonnet had been mashed against her ears by the blanket that covered her. Rebekah wished she had the courage to pull the bonnet off or even stand up and face the Indians. But she dared not move an inch.

After what sounded like a heated exchange, the Indians rode away. Her pa clucked to the horse, and they ambled down the road.

"Stay where you are. I don't want them to know you're here." His voice was gruff with repressed fear. She recognized the tone from past incidents. Out on the untamed frontier, danger lurked at every bend of the road.

Rebekah gritted her teeth and remained hidden for what seemed an eternity. The road grew rougher, causing the wagon to lurch uncontrollably and throw her against the rough edges of the wooden baskets at her back. By the time this was over, she would be a mass of bruises and splinters. Finally, Pa brought the wagon to a halt. She felt the blanket being pulled away.

"Are you all right?"

"What happened? What was that all about?"

Pa's face was creased with worry. "A group of Cherokee braves claimed the travelers who drove that cart were ambushed and left for dead by a band of Creek Indians."

Rebekah could feel the blood draining from her face. Since the massacre at Fort Sims near Mobile, there had been more and more stories of Indian attacks on innocent farmers and traders, although the area around Nashville had remained relatively peaceful. Rebekah prayed that was not changing. Some of the Indian tribes had joined forces with the English and, some said, the Spanish. All three groups seemed determined to crush the expansion of the United States.

Rebekah knew God was in control, but sometimes she thought how wonderful it would be if He would just step in with a few miracles and stop all the terrible killing. With a shake of her head, she looked around, only now realizing that she did not recognize their surroundings. "Where are we?"

"The Cherokee warned me to get off the road and make haste to Nashville. You'll have to get back up here and look out for trouble."

Taking a deep breath for courage, Rebekah gathered her skirts and clambered back onto the seat. "It's a good thing you taught me how to use your musket."

*

Asher was on guard duty again. He marched wearily forward, turned, retraced his steps, and then turned back once more. Evening was beginning to darken the landscape. Another day in the unforgiving wilderness. At least it was no longer as bitterly cold as it had been. After the desertion of so many of the troops in January, it seemed that Jackson's command was doomed to failure. But the warmer weather had brought provisions, new soldiers, and defeat of the enemy.

After the resounding victory over the Creek Indians at Horseshoe Bend, the talk was that the Indians no longer had the weapons, support, or manpower to mount an attack against innocent settlers. They had been decimated. Remembering the carnage that followed the battle still tended to make him feel ill. Six months of fierce battles and forced marches without sufficient rations had hardened him so much that few things had the power to make him queasy anymore. But the savagery that had been visited upon the Indians had been beyond vicious—as brutal as the attack on Fort Mims that had precipitated this campaign. It proved to Asher that any man, white or Indian, could be overcome by bloodlust. He was thankful that his faith in God had helped him resist the temptation to take revenge on the hapless survivors.

"Do you see that man?" The quiet voice of a nearby soldier distracted him from his somber thoughts.

Asher looked at the soldier before turning his attention in the direction indicated. Two soldiers were escorting an Indian across the center of the camp. "Who is he?"

UNDER THE TULIP POPLAR

"Someone said he's Chief Red Eagle come to surrender to General Jackson." Asher looked curiously at the tall, fair-skinned man being led toward General Jackson's tent. He wore his hair long in the style of an Indian and was bare from the waist up, but somehow, he didn't fit with Asher's idea of an Indian chief. "He's the one who led the massacre at Fort Mims? Except for his dress, he doesn't even look like an Indian, much less a chieftain."

"They say he's only half Indian." The soldier spat at the ground next to Asher's boot, obviously to show his disgust and contempt for the chief. "His pa was a Scots trader."

The Indian walked ahead of his horse, on which a deer had been strapped. For some reason, he stopped and looked toward them, his piercing gaze seeming to see right through Asher. With a gasp of dismay, the gossiping soldier slipped off into the gathering gloom.

His gaze caught by the stranger, Asher refused to look away. He would not be cowed by an Indian, no matter what title he might hold.

Another soldier confronted Red Eagle, and after a brief altercation, the two entered General Jackson's tent.

Asher sighed and once again began his slow walk back and forth across the camp. Sixty-four paces to the tall oak. Turn. Sixty-four paces to the edge of the pine forest. Turn.

A tiny sliver of moon appeared on the eastern horizon, and Asher's stomach rumbled. Given the amount of noise it was making, he probably wouldn't hear an Indian attack until an arrow pierced his chest. He should have brought a biscuit to assuage his hunger. A bead of sweat trickled down his back. Turn.

"You're being summoned to the general's tent." The voice of his captain interrupted the monotony of Asher's measured paces. "I've brought Johnson to relieve you."

Asher didn't know whether to be excited or worried. Why would General Jackson want to see him? He didn't even know the general knew his name. Had he done something wrong? He tried to be so careful to meet and even exceed every order he was given. He'd volunteered to remain with the troops even when his tour of duty had officially ended in January. Many had chosen to return home, and Asher had wanted to see his family—and Rebekah—again, but he was here to serve a purpose for God and his country. He would not leave his duty incomplete, even for the chance to be reunited with his love.

His mind went back over the events of the day. He'd risen from his pallet at first light, made up his bedroll, and dug out the battered coffeepot that his pa had sent with him last October when this campaign began. He'd been lucky enough to trap a rabbit yesterday and had traded part of the fresh meat for a double handful of chicory-laced coffee grounds. The coffee he'd made this

19

morning was wonderfully delicious. And he still had enough to stretch out the luxury for a week or more.

Then it had been time to drill with the regulars. Even though they had defeated the Creeks, General Jackson said it was only one battle in the war. They had to stay sharp and ready. Their countrymen were counting on them.

"Are you asleep, boy?" The captain's voice prodded him forward.

Asher shook his head. Apparently thinking about Rebekah had led him to daydreaming, as he teased her about doing. He saluted and hurried to the tent into which the Indian chief had disappeared earlier. He pulled back the flap, surprised at the tableau in front of him. Maps had been rolled and stacked in one corner. Neither of the guards was inside, but several high-ranking officers were present, most of whom he recognized. He nodded to Lieutenant John Ross, who sat next to General Jackson, a quill poised in his hand as though he was ready to pen whatever words his commander might utter. Jackson was talking and nodding at the Indian whom Asher would have thought would be kneeling at Old Hickory's feet instead of being treated like an honored guest.

As he snapped a salute, Asher couldn't help but notice several similarities between the general and the Indian chief. They were of comparable height and age and shared intense blue eyes that seemed to see right through a man's skin to his soul. While General Jackson's distinctive mane contrasted with the darker hair of the stranger, there was something about them—some attitude or stance—that made them appear more like distant cousins than deadly adversaries.

Both men bore the scars of many battles, but those scars only enhanced their charismatic appeal. Even though the general had undoubtedly lost weight during the six months since they'd left Nashville, no one could say he had lost an ounce of his steely determination. It was that strength of will coupled with his genuine concern for his men that had won the love and admiration of both volunteer and regular soldiers.

"Soldier, I want you to meet a man who has seen the inevitability of defeat and decided to act with honor. This is William Weatherford, formerly known as Chief Red Eagle."

Asher controlled his features with some difficulty. What was going on here? Why did General Jackson call his enemy an honorable man?

"Thank you, sir." He turned to the stranger. "Mr. Weatherford." Asher observed the man's eyes narrow as he and Weatherford studied each other.

With an abrupt nod, Weatherford returned his attention to Jackson. A wordless message seemed to pass between the two.

"Mr. Landon, your commendable loyalty and devotion to duty have been many times brought to my attention. So I have a special assignment to offer you. Mr. Weatherford, here, needs an escort out of the area. He has expressed his willingness to work toward the absolute and peaceful surrender of any holdouts there may be among the Creek nation. You will accompany him for the next two months before returning here to report the success or failure of his efforts."

General Jackson turned back to Weatherford. "And if any harm comes to this man, or if you should change your mind and decide to once again take up arms against this sovereign nation, your life will be forfeit. Do we understand each other?"

Weatherford nodded. He was obviously a man of few words.

"You'll leave at daybreak." General Jackson nodded in his direction, and Asher thought for a moment he saw a smile of encouragement. "Dismissed."

Chapter 2

As Rebekah and her pa drew closer to Nashville, they began to see homesteads here and there, as well as other travelers. They topped a hill, and the city lay before them as if it had sprung from the banks of the river that twisted through it.

Even though she'd traveled to Nashville before, Rebekah was amazed at the beehive of activity. Carriages, horses, and pedestrians filled every street. On the main thoroughfare, dozens of people scurried along as if they were on important errands. She wrinkled her nose at the multitude of smells. An unpleasant odor of hot iron and horse leavings emanated from the livery stable they passed. But a little farther down the street, the smell of fresh bread made her want to stop and visit the bakery.

They passed a millinery, its windows filled with hats ranging from simple bonnets to wide-brimmed, feathered concoctions that looked much too heavy to wear. "How will you ever find Aunt Dolly's home?" Rebekah's head was spinning with the hustle and bustle around them.

"See the mercantile?" Pa pointed at a two-story building on his left. "You need to go one block past it and then turn down the next street to the right."

"There it is." She clapped her hands, excited to have recognized the tall windows and portico of Dolly Quinn's three-story brick home. Then her spirits plunged. "Everything is so different from home."

"You'll be fine, honey." He winked at her and drew back on Bessie's reins, bringing the wagon to a halt. A young boy ran up and offered to hold the horse. Pa hesitated only a moment before nodding. Then he climbed down and helped her alight from the hard seat.

Rebekah pushed the folds of her cloak back and shifted her weight from one foot to another as she waited for someone to open the front door in response to her pa's knock.

The door creaked on its hinges, revealing a shocking sight. Gone was Aunt Dolly's elegantly appointed entry hall. Family portraits hung askew, and a mop leaned against one wall. The rug was bunched haphazardly under a window. Dust could be seen on every surface, from the floor to the furniture to the windows. She even spied a cobweb swaying gently in one corner of the hall. "Oh, my. I believe Aunt Dolly does need my help."

The black woman who had opened the door looked as rumpled as the rug behind her. There were dark circles under her eyes, her cap was askew, and her apron was covered with stains. "Oh, thank the Lord you're here, Mr. William."

"Hello. . .Harriet, isn't it?" Pa had the oddest expression on his face. Like he wanted to run away from the chaos inside Aunt Dolly's house.

For a brief moment, Rebekah wanted to run away, too. Could she take care of her aunt and see to the house at the same time?

Harriet curtsied and waved them inside. "I know it looks bad, but since Maude moved with her husband to Knoxville and left me with all the work, I'm a little behind. Now that you and your daughter are here, I'm sure we can get everything back in order."

Rebekah followed Harriet toward the parlor, her eyes taking in the general air of neglect. But after the first shock, she realized things weren't as bad as they initially appeared to be. With a bucket of water and some rags, this room could look pristine in an afternoon. The thought gave her courage.

She turned to reassure her father and realized he was still in the hallway. "Pa?"

"I'd better get your stuff from the wagon."

Harriet reached back to untie the strings of her apron. "I can help."

"No, no. There's not much to unload. You take Rebekah upstairs to see her aunt. Tell Dolly I'll be up in a minute to visit with her before I go back home."

Harriet's smile was a broad, white slash that eased the worry from her face. She nodded and led the way upstairs. "It's good that you're here. Your aunt will rest easier and recover her health faster."

Rebekah followed her reluctantly. She would much prefer to stay on the first floor and delay seeing her ailing aunt. It would be hard to see a loved one so weak. But that was the reason she was here, so she raised her chin and stiffened her resolve. Everyone was counting on her—she would not let them down.

Harriet opened Aunt Dolly's door and led the way into a seemingly cavernous room. Draperies covered every window, leaving the bedchamber dark and gloomy even at midday. A large rice bed stood in the center of the room, its tall, thin posts drawing Rebekah's gaze upward to the ornate carvings on the ceiling. Anyone lying down could spend hours looking at the fascinating patterns above.

A series of hacking coughs indicated her aunt's presence in the large bed. "What is it? Who's there?"

"It's me, and look who has arrived." Harriet plumped a pillow and helped Dolly to a sitting position. "It's your niece, Miss Rebekah. And Mr. William will be up after unloading her things."

Another fit of coughing ensued, and Rebekah wondered what to do.

"Come. . .closer. . .child." Each word was punctuated by another cough.

"Don't speak, Aunt Dolly. You need to rest." She bent over and placed a quick peck on the older woman's cheek.

"That's right." Harriet added her support as she smoothed the quilt covering Aunt Dolly. "You're going to get better soon now. Just you wait and see."

Rebekah sent up a fervent prayer that Harriet's words would come true and, after a quick glance around, that God would give her strength to tackle all that lay ahead.

&

Rebekah ran loving fingers across the oak dining table. Her brown eyes stared back at her from its rich surface. She noticed a spot of dirt on her nose and rubbed at it impatiently, turning it into a streak. Her wheat-colored hair, drawn back with a ribbon, had pulled loose from its binding. It would be nice to cut it short like a boy's instead of having to deal with the tangles. But Asher might not like that. If Asher ever returned.

She looked around the room, satisfied with its appearance. After several weeks, Aunt Dolly's house sparkled with cleanliness. She had interviewed and engaged another maid, making it possible to get caught up with all of the household tasks. But the greatest blessing of all was Aunt Dolly's returning health. Her chronic cough had finally yielded to the broths and teas Rebekah and Harriet had concocted, as well as to the many prayers they sent heavenward. Rebekah knew that had been the true cure.

A knock on the front door interrupted her musings. Rebekah was glad to hear it. While Aunt Dolly was not fully recovered, she was able to come downstairs and have short visits with the guests who came by to check on her. Seeing her friends always seemed to cheer her up.

From the dining room, Rebekah could not see who was at the front door, but she could hear Harriet's booming tones and a feminine voice answering. After a minute, she heard Harriet climbing the stairs to fetch Aunt Dolly.

Rebekah decided she'd stay hidden in the dining room as long as possible. She didn't want anyone to see her with her hair all messed up. It was hard enough making conversation with strangers when she was tidy. The time passed slowly while she waited. When she judged it safe, she slipped out of the room. . . and ran into Aunt Dolly and her guest in the hallway.

"Oh, good. There you are." Her aunt put a hand on Rebekah's arm and turned to the dark-haired woman next to her. "I have someone you'll enjoy meeting, Rachel. This is my sister's oldest daughter, Rebekah. Rebekah," she continued, "this is Rachel Jackson, the wife of our illustrious military commander, General Andrew Jackson."

Rebekah could not believe her ears. She'd expected a famous personage like Andrew Jackson to be married to a stunning beauty—not a short, matronly woman dressed in a plain calico dress. She looked like she'd be at home on Pa's farm.

"I've heard good things about you, my dear."

Rebekah blushed. She didn't deserve any praise, given her unchristian attention to Mrs. Jackson's looks rather than her heart. She bobbed a quick curtsy, her eyes on the floor. She hoped God would forgive her for her earlier thoughts.

"She's a wonderful help." Aunt Dolly patted her arm. "Not only does she supervise Harriet and the maids, but she also reads and sings to me, and she has even prepared several medicaments that have made my recovery possible."

Rebekah's cheeks grew even hotter as the praise continued. She was so unworthy. She'd not known how to do much of anything when she arrived. Harriet knew more about running the household than Rebekah. She'd have been overwhelmed without any help.

"Rebekah." Dolly's tone sounded different, like she had a wonderful secret to impart. "I mentioned your young man to Mrs. Jackson. She hears from Andrew quite regularly, so she's going to ask him for a report on Asher. Won't that be lovely?"

Rebekah's heart stuttered. She looked toward Rachel. "C–Could you?"

"I'd love to do that for you, Rebekah. I know how worried you must be." She patted Rebekah's hot cheek. "I'm certain he's fine, but we all know how men sometimes don't have a mind to do as they ought."

"Thank you so much. I'll be forever in your debt." Tears pricked at the edges of Rebekah's eyes.

"It's not any trouble." Rachel turned back to Dolly. "I'll let you know as soon as I hear something."

Rebekah sent a quick prayer upward that Rachel would hear good news and hear it very soon.

Chapter 3

I insist, my dear." Aunt Dolly's voice gained a slight edge.

Six months of living in her aunt's home had taught Rebekah that it was best to acquiesce when that raspy edge appeared. Failure to do so could result in a relapse or a fainting spell. Once, her aunt had been so distraught, that she had taken to her bed for a week, refusing to eat or allow anyone to visit her.

Rebekah nodded and took the dress her aunt proffered. "You're too generous, Aunt Dolly."

"Now, now. Do remember to call me Dolly. There is no reason to remind others of my advancing age."

Rebekah smiled. "No one would think you're a day over twenty, Au—Dolly. You are full of energy now that you've recovered your health. And your complexion. How do you keep it so clear and smooth? I'm always fighting freckles."

Dolly sighed and patted her cheek. "You're such a sweet thing. I don't know how I ever managed without you here." She shooed Rebekah toward the door. "Go on. You must try on the dress. I have the feeling we'll need to make some alterations."

Rebekah hurried down the wide hall to her bedroom, which never failed to cheer her with its pink beribboned drapes and four-poster bed. The canopy that topped it made the bed seem like her special refuge. Double doors on the far wall opened out onto a small balcony overlooking the street. When she'd first arrived, the noise from the street often woke her at night, but now she was used to it.

She laid the dress on her bed, its pale yellow fabric reminding her of spring daisies in the meadow back home. She sighed. It was not that she was unhappy staying with Aunt Dolly. . .no. . .Dolly. She really needed to remember not to call her *Aunt*. Even though her father had come to check on them a couple of times, she missed her family. She hadn't seen her mother and siblings since spring. Little Donny was probably through teething, and there was no telling how much Eleanor had grown between March and June. Rebekah knew this was a busy time on the farm. She wondered how well they were getting along without her help.

A wave of homesickness swept over her, but Rebekah refused to give in to the melancholy. She had much too much to be thankful for. Including the gorgeous dress lying on her bed. Used to homemade dresses woven from cotton or wool and often handed down from her ma, Rebekah had never owned anything half so beautiful. Her fingers traced the delicate lace outlining the neck and sleeves of the dress. The bodice was high, accentuated by a golden length of ribbon that would fall gracefully toward the wearer's ankles after it was tied in the back. The skirt was quite narrow and looked too revealing to Rebekah's eyes. There was not much room to wear petticoats or pantaloons beneath the dress. It would almost certainly reveal a lady's limbs if she had need to hurry across a room. She was sure it was the latest fashion and just as sure Pa would frown on her wearing it.

What would Asher think if he saw her in such attire? Would his eyes light up with admiration, or would he be shocked? Her eyes closed as she imagined the scene. A dress like this would be worn for a fancy party. Asher would be wearing formal clothes, his thick chestnut hair falling just so against his brow. His broad shoulders and proud bearing would be shown off to advantage in his evening dress, and his boots would gleam in the candlelight as he walked across the room to greet her. All of the other ladies in the room would follow his progress with hope, and they would be filled with envy when he stopped at her side. He would bow, and she would curtsy. And he would take her hand in his, maybe even press a kiss against it in the European manner. . . .

Her aunt fluttered into the bedroom, ending her daydream. "Whatever are you doing, Rebekah? Are you not anxious to see how the gown looks?"

"I'm sorry, Dolly. I was—"

"I know. You were daydreaming again. Really, you have got to rid yourself of that habit. What if you were attacked by a bear or Indians?" Dolly paused and shivered. "When you begin daydreaming, you lose any awareness of your surroundings. You would not recognize the danger until it was too late."

Rebekah hung her head in shame. It was true. She did spend too much time imagining the future. It would be better to spend her time dealing with the present.

A knock at the bedroom door interrupted the women, and they turned to see Harriet peeking at them. "Excuse me, ma'am. You have a guest."

Dolly brushed the skirt of her day dress, smoothing the blue material with practiced fingers. "Who is it?"

"Mrs. Jackson."

"Oh, my." Dolly clapped her hands and turned to Rebekah. "Perhaps we should leave the dress for now. We'll adjust it later. Let's go find out what news Rachel has of the fighting."

Rebekah wanted to leap over her aunt to get downstairs and hear the news, but she forced herself to take her time and mimic Dolly's tiny steps. Her aunt always appeared to float into a room, a technique Rebekah would like to acquire so she could impress Asher once he returned home. Wouldn't he be surprised at her cosmopolitan polish when she approached him, resplendent in her new yellow dress?

"Good morning, Rachel," Dolly's warm tones welcomed her friend.

Rachel's smile was wide, transforming her face from plain to angelic. Her expression was a reflection of her disposition—gentle and sweet. There might be some in Nashville who would condemn her for her past, but not Rebekah or Dolly. Rebekah didn't understand the complaint people made against Rachel and Andrew Jackson. Something about Rachel having been married before.

The two older ladies chitchatted about the weather and the latest Indian sighting while they waited for Harriet to serve refreshments.

Rebekah had learned many rules that were observed in the city, but today she could have cried with frustration as they exchanged social niceties. She would have much preferred the country way of going straight to the point. Clenching her teeth, Rebekah balanced on the edge of Dolly's settee and picked up the embroidery she had been working on for the past week. It would give her hands something to do besides twist themselves into a knot.

Harriet brought in the silver service, and Dolly handed round, delicate china cups filled with tea. Rachel helped herself to one of the maple cookies that were piled on a china plate, but Rebekah shook her head. There was no way she could choke anything down right now. Not until she knew the reason for Mrs. Jackson's unannounced visit.

"I have very important news, ladies. And I knew you would want to learn of it as soon as possible."

Dolly dismissed Harriet with a nod. "Whatever can it be?"

"Ouch." Rebekah jerked her thumb from the needle that had pierced it, dropped her handwork, and quickly wrapped a handkerchief around the tiny wound.

Dolly and Rachel looked toward her.

"I'm all right. I'm just anxious. *Please* go ahead and tell us your news."

Rachel opened her reticule and pulled a sheet of stationery from it. "Andrew has sent for me to join him in New Orleans at the beginning of the year. And I want the two of you to travel with me."

Rebekah squealed, then caught herself and coughed. She would get to see Asher! She could wear the yellow dress! She could almost hear his voice greeting her, his surprise overtaken with joy as they were reunited. Oh, how romantic! Her mind's eye revised the scene she had created earlier, putting Asher in his dashing uniform instead of evening wear.

Aunt Dolly was saying something about plans and dangers, but Rebekah pushed those aside. She had six long weeks in which to convince her aunt and her parents that she should go. She wanted to hug Rachel Jackson, who was beaming at both of them. She would allow absolutely nothing to prevent her from making this trip. If the men could not return to Nashville, why shouldn't their ladies go to them?

≈

Asher strode under the graceful, wrought facades supported by cast-iron columns. This part of New Orleans had been carefully laid out, its streets forming squares within squares. He had to admit that the uniformity of its design made the area very easy to navigate. Much easier than navigating the political situation of the city.

He had nothing but the greatest admiration for General Jackson, even though he might not agree with every decision the man made. Like trusting the Baratarian pirates. There was no telling if they wouldn't decide to switch sides in the middle of the looming battle.

His musings were interrupted by a feminine scream that seemed to issue from within a knot of soldiers ahead of him. Putting a hand on his pistol, Asher quickened his pace. "What's going on here?"

A man he didn't recognize answered the question. "We wasn't doing nothin'."

"Stand aside. I distinctly heard a lady."

"Oh, please, kind sir. Save me from these ruffians. They've trapped me."

Asher's anger soared. How dare they accost a woman in the streets in broad daylight? "You should be ashamed of yourselves." He drew himself to his full height and met each man's gaze separately. Only one of them seemed disposed to challenge Asher's authority, but one of his buddies pulled on his arm, and they all drifted away.

Once they had disappeared around the corner, Asher turned his attention to the young woman he had rescued. She was slender, with hair as dark as coal. From her expensive clothing, he guessed she was from a wealthy family. "Where is your attendant?"

She looked up at him, her brows drawn together over eyes that shone like glass. She was so frightened he could see her shoulders shaking. "I shouldn't have come alone. It's just that my slave, Jemma, has yellow fever. And the day was so pretty. I thought I would walk to the *Place d'Armes* and watch the soldiers march. I didn't think it would be. . .dangerous."

Asher let his frown deepen. The girl had probably learned her lesson, but he would not condone her actions. He shivered to think of Rebekah doing anything so precipitous. But that was foolish, as his Rebekah was a model of modest behavior. She would never go out alone in a big city, especially not on the eve of battle.

"Where do you live, Miss. . ."

"Lewis. I'm Alexandra Lewis. Papa is part of the militia. My mama and I came down to visit with him. Our rooms are only a block away. I can—"

"No, you cannot. As your papa is fighting with General Jackson, I consider it my duty to see that you are returned safely to the bosom of your family." He held out his arm, annoyed when she hesitated. Did she think he would rescue her from a mob only to attack her himself? "Allow me to introduce myself. Asher Landon, at your service."

When she laid her hand on his arm, he could feel it shivering even though the temperature was quite warm for a December afternoon. Immediately his conscience smote him. Alexandra Lewis was clearly still overcome by the attentions of those men. Not surprising for a young lady of such obvious gentility. He patted her hand and gave her an encouraging smile. She had nothing to fear from him.

His reassurance must have been effective. They had hardly walked a full block before she began talking to him as if they were old friends. Her exuberance reminded him of Rebekah.

"Are you going to the Richelieus' ball, Mr. Landon?"

"If we're not battling the British." As an officer, he was expected to attend. The general thought it was good policy to socialize with the local gentry.

"Papa is taking Mama and me. But I'm so worried no one will dance with me."

"I doubt a pretty girl like you will have to worry about that. The men will likely line up for the honor."

"But what about you, Mr. Landon? Would you dance with me?"

Asher frowned. Miss Lewis was somewhat forward, but maybe it was only a bit of naïveté. With his experience in the military, perhaps he should take her under his wing and protect her a bit.

"I would be honored, Miss Lewis."

❧

Rebekah wrapped her arms tighter against her waist, burrowing into the layers of her cloak for comfort. A damp, gray mist wound its way around tree trunks as the muddy Mississippi River swept their flat-bottomed boat southward toward their destination. Rachel and Dolly had already retired for the evening to their shared cabin, but Rebekah was not sleepy.

What would this year bring? Last year, she'd wondered the same thing. And she'd been filled with the same optimism that currently kept her from seeking sleep. If someone had told her that she would go another whole year without Asher, she'd have refused to accept the possibility.

But that was exactly what had happened. She had marked his anniversary date with abiding hope, knowing that he would soon be released from service.

But he had not appeared. Then in the spring when other men returned from the war, faces hardened and gaunt from their experiences, she'd awaited his return patiently. She'd been ready to nurse him back to excellent health with kind Christian concern and loving care.

Still no Asher.

Then the victory over the Indians had been reported in Nashville, and she had waited to welcome her returning hero. She'd sewn a sampler to commemorate the date and the valorous deeds of the Tennessee militia. Many was the night she'd knelt by her bed and prayed earnestly for his safe return.

Her spirits had dipped to a new low when it became apparent he would remain with General Jackson. Finally, *finally*, her opportunity had arrived the day Rachel Jackson burst in on her and her aunt with her marvelous, daring proposal.

So here she stood gazing at the sky and trying to imagine what her family was doing. She'd missed getting to see them at Christmas, but that was a sacrifice she'd been willing to make as she and Aunt Dolly prepared for their trip. The desire to return home paled in comparison to her desire to see Asher.

It had taken several letters from Mrs. Jackson and Aunt Dolly to convince her parents that Rebekah should accompany them on their trip. They had finally yielded, unable to withstand Dolly's assurances that their daughter would be safeguarded and her pleas to them to remember how they had felt when they were courting.

A creaking board alerted her to someone's presence on deck. She smiled at her new friend. Despite the disparity in age, she had grown very close to Rachel Jackson during their trip.

"Isn't it time for you to come inside?" Rachel's skirt billowed gently in the humid evening breeze. "I have already sent my son to bed, and Dolly and I are about to retire. We don't like leaving you out here alone."

"I get more excited with every day. How long do you think it will be before we get to New Orleans?"

"The captain said we'll get to Natchez tomorrow. Then he'll need to drop off some of his cargo and load new provisions for the last leg of our journey. We'll likely be there within the week."

"I cannot wait."

The two women stood side by side for several minutes, watching the dark water swirl around the edges of the boat. Then the older woman put an arm around Rebekah's shoulders and hugged her tightly. "Me, either."

Chapter 4

"Victory!" The whole world seemed to breathe it. General Jackson had done it! He had routed the British against all odds. Rebekah felt like a part of the triumph as her friend, Rachel, fairly beamed her happiness and pride in the accomplishments of her husband. He was a real American hero. Everyone agreed the battle had been instrumental in proving to the world that Americans would not be defeated. Nearly every plantation they passed sent heartfelt messages of thanks and praise to be delivered to General Jackson. And now they had arrived in New Orleans, eager to end their journey and join the celebration.

Rebekah picked every step with great care. She didn't want to end up falling off the debris-strewn wharf into the muddy currents below. Was it always so dirty here? In Natchez, the wooden platform used for loading and unloading goods and passengers had been freshly swept and its planks uniformly spaced and flat. Here the gaps between boards looked huge, and some of them were splintered and lying at odd angles. She had avoided one that looked too rotten to hold the weight of a baby, much less one of the tired passengers.

She reached for Aunt Dolly's hand when they came to a spot where the barricade had been removed so they might enter the town. Her nose wrinkled at the sight before them. The streets were mud-choked, rutted canals that grabbed at horses' hooves and the wheels of the carts they dragged. Thank goodness there were raised walkways for people, but what Rebekah could see of them showed them to be barely cleaner or in better repair than the wharf.

"This way, ladies." Neither Rachel nor her adopted son, Andrew, seemed perturbed by the mayhem or the general state of decay around them. She waved a hand toward an open carriage.

"However did you secure such an excellent conveyance?" Dolly smiled at the ebony-faced driver who offered her a helping hand. "I was sure we would have to walk or at best ride in the back of a wagon."

Rebekah waited for Dolly to pull in her skirts somewhat before settling herself next to her aunt, their backs to the driver's seat. Rachel smiled widely as she and her son took the seats on the opposite side of the carriage. "The boat captain arranged it. He apparently told someone that the hero's family had arrived."

The driver closed the door and clambered nimbly onto his wooden seat. He said something to the horse, but Rebekah could not understand his words.

"What language is he speaking?"

"In his last letter, Andrew told me that the inhabitants here speak more French than English. It makes sense when you think about it. France, through her Acadian settlers, built the town."

"Humph." Dolly raised her brows. "I've heard French all my life, but I didn't understand him any better than Rebekah. It must be some local dialect."

Rebekah nodded her head and looked around at the people they were passing. Everyone seemed excited, if a little forward for her taste. Strangers waved at them—men in rough buckskins reminiscent of home, as well as uniformed men who made her ache to see Asher.

A loud noise made all four of the occupants turn their heads. Telltale wisps of smoke trailed from a raised pistol. Had the man killed someone or just shot into the air? His dark face looked dangerous, and Rebekah noticed that the stranger wore gold jewelry around his neck like a woman. Her breath caught when their eyes met. He smiled, and her heartbeat accelerated. What a handsome—

"Rebekah." Aunt Dolly's voice was sharp in her ear. "Do not look at him."

She jerked her head away and focused on her hands in her lap.

"Don't be too hard on the girl." Rachel's voice was choked with laughter. "He was a charmer, and I doubt we'll see him again."

"Still, she must be aware of the dangers. You or I might not always be around to protect her."

"True, but I can understand her curiosity."

Several minutes passed before Rebekah dared to raise her gaze, and by then, the bold stranger had been left behind. As they got farther from the waterfront, the townspeople seemed even odder. She was beginning to see more women strolling along the walkways, but her mouth dropped open when she realized that several were allowing men to clasp them around their waists. Some were even kissing men! Right out on the street!

Would Asher expect her to allow him that freedom in this debauched setting? Well, he had better not. She had been raised properly, and he would have to respect that. But maybe she would allow him to hug her. A blush heated her cheeks at the thought. It had been more than a year since they'd seen each other. Surely she could allow him to show some delight at their reunion with a brief hug.

It would be so different from the last time. She wouldn't be distraught, and he wouldn't be trying to comfort her. No, this time it would be completely romantic. She could almost feel his arms around her waist, hear his heart beating against her cheek. . . .

The carriage stopped, and the pleasant thoughts ended. "Is this our hotel?" Rebekah asked.

The building was at least three stories high, but it leaned somewhat to the right, as though it had been wounded in the recent battle. Tantalizing odors of spicy meat and stews, however, emanated from somewhere nearby. She squared her shoulders. It would not be so bad. And it was worth it to see her beloved Asher.

The women disembarked and entered the shadowy front room of the hotel. The innkeeper was a short man with a bald head and round stomach, who bowed over and over again while wishing them a "*bonju.*" Even with her limited French, Rebekah knew the word was *bonjour*, but she smiled and waited behind the older women as they arranged for a suite of rooms and to have an early dinner brought up.

Her gaze wandered to the dining room, where a more sedate group of citizens sat at long wooden tables to eat and converse. She could tell from their dress that they were higher class, but still, they were unlike any other people she'd ever met in her life. Their voices drifted out of the room, the words melodic if incomprehensible.

A new couple entered from the street, and she could not tear her gaze away. The woman was stunning—tall and graceful with the most beautiful skin she'd ever seen stretched across high cheekbones. She had a generous mouth and dark eyes that hinted at exotic mysteries. The woman laughed at something the gentleman said, and they entered the dining room, greeting the other diners and being hailed in return.

"Come along."

Her aunt's words snagged Rebekah's attention, and she followed her aunt to the room they would share, while Rachel and her son retired to the adjoining room.

Dolly and Rebekah hardly stopped for the next hour, getting their trunks emptied and instructing the chambermaids as to the placement and care of their clothing. Between commands, her aunt continually bemoaned having left Harriet at home.

Rebekah was too glad to be off the river and finally in New Orleans to quibble about who helped them unpack. She lovingly pulled out a cloth-wrapped bundle and placed it on the table next to her Bible.

The sounds of drums and marching feet caught her attention, and Rebekah flew to the window facing the street that had brought them to the hotel. Pushing open the wooden shutter, she gazed at the street, now turning orange under the rays of the setting sun.

As Dolly joined her at the window, a battalion turned the corner and marched with rough precision down the street. Their uniforms were streaked with dirt and mud, but their faces smiled as the onlookers cheered and clapped.

"Do you see him?" her aunt asked.

After frantically searching the men's faces, Rebekah sighed her disappointment. "No, I don't think so." Still, they watched until the battalion disappeared from view.

Aunt Dolly leaned forward and pulled the shutter closed. "Even though it's not as cold here as at home, I imagine the air will be quite cool tonight."

Rebekah nodded and turned away from the window. "Would you like to see the gift I have for Asher?"

She looked toward the older woman, who frowned. "Do you think it's seemly for you to give him a gift? You are not betrothed after all."

Rebekah grabbed the cloth bundle and held it to her chest. "It's only a handkerchief with his initials stitched on it. Remember when you had the parlor draperies replaced at home?"

Dolly nodded.

"The old linings still had some wear left, so I used them to make scarves and things. I even used some squares on the back side of the quilt we were working on."

"How practical of you, dear, but there is plenty of nice cloth stored away at home." Dolly patted her on the shoulder. "I sometimes forget that you were raised without the luxuries I take for granted. I suppose it will be acceptable for you to give the handkerchief to Asher. We will call it a congratulatory gift because of the victory."

Rebekah breathed a sigh of relief at her aunt's decision. She wanted to see Asher open her gift. Would his long fingers trace the outline of his initials? Initials that her very hands had stitched. And then would he place it in an inner pocket next to his heart? She sighed again. It would be perfect. She could hardly wait.

A knock on the door that separated their room from Rachel's room signaled that dinner was ready. Before joining her companions for dinner, Rebekah took a moment to carefully tuck the white cloth into the top drawer of her bureau.

"Your aunt and I have had the most inspired idea," Rachel greeted her as she took her place at the table. "I have discovered that there is going to be a victory ball at the Beaumonts' tomorrow evening. I will be expected to arrive in time to partake of the dinner with my husband, but what if we surprise your young man by allowing you and Dolly to appear unannounced in the middle of the ball?"

Rebekah's breath caught, and she could not stop herself from smiling. Perhaps she would finally be reunited with her love tomorrow.

Chapter 5

Asher straightened the cuff on his uniform and turned to face the window. The setting sun cast enough light on the pane to allow him to see his reflection. He practiced a smile and straightened his neckcloth. It wouldn't do to appear slovenly at the victory celebration.

His smile widened. The politicians in Washington would have to give General Jackson his due now that he had soundly whipped the British forces. There was no doubt America owed her freedom to the intelligence and perseverance of one man. Asher was thrilled to have played a small part in the exciting events.

His smile dimmed a bit in the windowpane. There was only one small wisp of disappointment in his life these days. He missed his home. He closed his eyes and imagined his parents' house, the walk swept clean of winter snow, a roaring fire in the parlor. He could almost taste his ma's apple pie.

And Rebekah would be there, too, with her sparkling brown eyes and worshipful smile. How he ached to talk with her. No one understood him better than Rebekah.

He wanted to tell her about the friends he had made—white men, Indians, and French Acadians. He had been promoted several times and now held the rank of captain. And surely he would move even higher as his career followed General Jackson's. Why, by the time he got home to Rebekah and his parents, he might even be a colonel. How surprised and proud they would be.

Rebekah would forgive him for postponing their future when she realized how much his decision to remain with the militia for the past year would benefit them. His pay would provide a nice home for them, while his connections would give them entrée into the finest circles of Nashville society. His Rebekah would be the best hostess in the whole country—charming, sweet, and talented. Together, they would make a name for themselves. There was no telling what all they would attain once peace had been declared.

Asher nodded at his reflection and drew a deep breath. He swept his palm across the hair that tended to fall down over his forehead, only to feel it fall forward once again. With a grunt, he strode to the tall bureau that stood on the far side of his bed and grabbed the pomade. As he returned to the window, someone knocked at his door.

"Time to leave!"

Asher subdued the lock of hair and turned to the door, joining the other young officers who were making their way down the stairs and across the French Quarter. They walked up St. Ann Street to the two-story mansion where the ball was being held.

Their arrival caused a bit of a stir as the society dames whispered behind their fans. He was reminded of the chicken yard back home. The older women were the laying hens, full of clucking and posturing to attract the attention of the rooster. The more timid "hatchlings" peeked over their chaperones' shoulders but quickly hid their dark glances from the interested gazes of the soldiers.

Asher leaned against a column and watched the scene unfold before him. His ears were tickled by the accents as the guests mingled together. Several couples danced to the strains of a minuet, while dozens of people stood around talking. The parties he had attended with his parents in Nashville were as dull as a rusty saber in comparison to this glittering ensemble.

"That's him, Papa. He's the one I told you about—the one who rescued me that afternoon." Asher turned to see the young lady whom he had found wandering the Quarter two weeks earlier. Amazing that they would run into each other so quickly in the press of guests.

A heavy hand slapped the gold braiding on his shoulder. He turned to face a short man with a gray fringe of hair and mustache to match.

"I'm Colonel James Lewis, Captain. And I'm pleased to finally get to say thank you for the mighty fine thing you did."

Asher shook the man's hand and introduced himself, noting the colonel's navy blue uniform with wide lapels and an impressive number of colorful medals. He wondered if Colonel Lewis was a seasoned soldier or a politician who had only recently donned his uniform. Either way, it had taken all of them to route the British.

A slight movement brought his attention back to the pretty girl standing to the right of the colonel. "It is my hope that you will formally introduce me to the lovely lady, sir."

"Of course it is." The colonel puffed out his chest. "All the young men want to meet my daughter."

Asher was again reminded of the chicken yard, this time of the strutting pride of a rooster.

"Captain Landon, I would like you to meet my daughter, Alexandra Lewis." He drew her forward. "Alexandra, Captain Asher Landon."

Asher bowed and reached for her hand, holding it gently as he kissed the air some two inches above her elbow-length glove.

"Captain Landon, thank you so much for saving me that day. I have told Mama and Papa that I would surely have perished if not for your gallantry."

Asher straightened and patted her hand. "You exaggerate, Miss Lewis. I did nothing more than any other gentleman would do when in the same circumstances."

"I beg to differ." Colonel Lewis reached into the breast pocket of his coat and withdrew a square of white. "Here is my card. Come see me at the general's headquarters in a few days. I believe I may have use for a young man whose heart is in the right place."

"Thank you, sir. It will be my pleasure."

"Yes, good. But for now, you young people enjoy yourselves." He shooed his daughter in Asher's general direction.

Asher held his hand out to her. "If you would be so kind. . ."

Alexandra put her hand in his, and he thought it trembled slightly.

He smiled to alleviate her discomfort. It was easy to understand why such a young miss should feel a little overwhelmed. "It is good to see you recovered from your. . ." He hesitated, searching for the right word.

"Stupidity." Alexandra's gaze dropped toward the slender skirt of her gown.

Asher stood opposite her on the dance floor, wondering how to alleviate her embarrassment without condoning her behavior that afternoon. Of course, it wasn't his place to chastise Alexandra, but he thought how he would like for his younger sister, Mary, to be treated in a similar situation. Or Rebekah. But what foolishness. Even though Rebekah and Alexandra were probably about the same age, his Rebekah would never be so imprudent as to wander city streets alone. What would she say to Alexandra? She would be gracious and kind, of course.

"I was going to say 'adventure.'" He was rewarded when her sparkling gaze swept upward to meet his. It felt good to know he was responsible for the tentative smile that curved her lips. Rebekah would be proud of him for easing Alexandra's discomfort. He bowed to her curtsy as required by the French contra dance and concentrated on presenting a polished appearance on the dance floor.

The gossamer material of Alexandra's rose gown swept his legs as they turned in unison. He placed a hand on her waist and stepped forward, then took two steps back. They faced each other again. "I cannot believe how many people have come tonight."

"Yes, and they are still arriving."

Asher followed the direction of her gaze. A press of people stood at the top of the staircase. He wondered if the ballroom would be able to hold all of them.

❧

Candles lit every corner of the ballroom, their light reflected on the mirrored walls. Rebekah's eyes drank in the sight of the graceful dancers. The twirling dresses of the ladies looked like a multihued rose garden swaying in a gentle wind.

Even the men on the dance floor were colorful. Some wore evening dress—long coats and starched white shirts—but many were in uniforms from the different battalions who had come together to fight under General Jackson's leadership. Some of the uniforms were green, some blue, and she even saw one man in a white uniform. It was nearly more than she could comprehend as she descended the grand staircase with Aunt Dolly.

The musicians ended their song as she reached the bottom of the staircase, and she saw Asher standing tall and handsome in his uniform. Her Asher. The man who loved her. How blessed she was to hold his affection. Happiness, pride, excitement, and anticipation all burst open inside her like fireworks in the nighttime sky.

Rebekah moved toward him as if drawn by an unseen hand. It might not be seemly, but she wanted to feel his embrace. She looked for the same feelings to be mirrored in his expression, but instead she saw confusion on his handsome face.

"Asher?" She stopped a few feet short of him, suddenly uncertain of herself, of him, of reality. Instead of rushing toward her in excitement and wonder, he was still standing in the same place.

And who was the woman standing right next to him? She was everything Rebekah was not—tall, poised, and exotically beautiful. She looked very womanly and very certain of herself. Her hair sparkled like polished mahogany in the glow of the candles. Her pink ball gown was cut low across her chest, showing far too much skin to be considered respectable back home in Nashville.

Rebekah could not believe how she had fretted over the fit of her own gown. It was about as revealing as a flour sack when compared to the straight skirts of the other woman's gown. Why the dress was so short, she imagined that the other woman's *ankles* could be seen if she dared to dance. Did Asher now find that sort of woman attractive?

Her gaze searched his face. Was he even the same person she'd fallen in love with? He looked so different. His face was tanned from exposure to the Southern sun, and his shoulders looked twice as wide as they'd been the last time she saw him. That day at the farm might as well have been more than a decade ago rather than a little over a year.

Rebekah drew a deep breath. "Excuse me. I. . .I thought you were s—someone I knew." She turned on her heel and pushed her way through the crowd. She refused to let him see how he'd torn her heart in two.

"Rebekah! Rebekah, come back."

She heard his voice, but she could not turn back. After all of her dreams and expectations, she wanted nothing more than to leave. She wanted to leave this house, this town, this foreign world, and travel back to a place and time where everything had been right.

Her blurry vision led her into the wide hallway. To her left, incoming guests crowded the entryway, so Rebekah turned right. She had only gotten a dozen paces away from the ballroom when a hand clamped itself onto her shoulder.

"Rebekah." It was Asher's voice. He spun her around and pulled her shoulders against him.

Rebekah felt like the rag doll she'd played with as a child—floppy with no backbone. Hot tears burned her eyes and trickled down her cheeks. She could feel one of his hands patting her on the back, while the other smoothed the material at her shoulder. After a few minutes the tears slowed, then ceased entirely. The crushing disappointment was still there, but it had turned into a block of winter ice and frozen around her heart. "How could you?"

"How could I what?" His voice was the same as she remembered, but the man in front of her seemed more a stranger than her dearest betrothed.

Of course they weren't really betrothed. They had an understanding between them, but Asher had never approached her pa. Maybe now she knew why.

"We are as good as promised. How could you betray me with that. . .that woman?"

The face that had once been more familiar to her than her own lost its frown. One corner of his mouth turned up in the crooked smile that she remembered so well. "Don't be silly, Rebekah. She's just a girl I met and shared a dance with."

"Just a girl. . ." Rebekah could hear the tremble in her voice. She took a deep breath to steady it. "You were so focused on her that you didn't recognize me. She is obviously more—"

"Oh Rebekah, you're exaggerating the whole thing. It's a simple misunderstanding. I helped her a couple of weeks ago, and she told her pa, who insisted that we dance. Of course I recognized you, but it was such a shock to see you here that it took me a moment to react."

He seemed earnest. Rebekah searched his eyes for some clue, some hint of deception. This was not how she had imagined their reunion at all, but suddenly her heart began to thump wildly. It was a giddy feeling, being so close to him after all this time. And he might have changed, but he was still the same where it counted, wasn't he? He did still love her—she could see it in his face.

Asher reached into his coat pocket and produced a handkerchief that he used to gently dab at her cheeks. "All better now?"

Rebekah nodded. She stood still and let him minister to her. It felt so wonderful, just the way she had known it would. Everything was going to be okay. They were together now, and she would not allow anything to come between them again.

"Asher? Asher, what's wrong? Why did you leave the ball—"

Rebekah sprang away from her beloved as if he had suddenly sprouted porcupine quills. Asher turned to face the woman, shielding Rebekah as she composed herself.

"Alexandra, I didn't mean to worry you. It's just that I saw someone I had not expected to see. Please allow me to introduce someone very special to me. In fact, she is the woman who holds my heart. . .Miss Rebekah Taylor."

Rebekah stepped to one side and looked at the woman who had started the whole thing. Now that she saw her up close, she realized that the woman was even more beautiful than she had first thought. Although Asher's words should have reassured her, she couldn't help wondering what he could see in her if a woman like this was pursuing him.

"Rebekah"—Asher's voice wrapped around her like a blanket—"I want you to meet the daughter of one of our officers, Miss Alexandra Lewis."

"Hello, Miss Taylor." The woman's voice had a curious twist. Wonderful. Even her sultry voice hinted at hidden secrets.

"Miss Lewis." Rebekah nodded her head in acknowledgment of the introduction.

"I don't believe I've ever seen you around here, Miss Taylor."

Asher cleared his throat. "Rebekah, I've never been more shocked than when I realized you were in New Orleans. When did you arrive? How did you get here? Who is chaperoning you?"

Rebekah felt like the two of them were attacking her. Her head was still trying to sort out the facts while her heart had been wrung out like laundry. "I. . .we. . .Aunt Dolly. . .I mean Dolly and Rachel. . .yesterday. We got here yesterday. We came down by boat because General Jackson sent for his wife and son."

She intercepted a glance between Asher and the other woman. What did it mean? She put a hand to her head. "I'm afraid I'm overwrought. Perhaps—"

"Rebekah," another voice interrupted her, "where have you gotten off to, child? Your parents would skin me alive if I didn't keep an eye on you and your young. . ." Dolly's voice trailed off as she took in the three of them.

Rebekah handed Asher's handkerchief back to him and lifted her skirt slightly. "I'm coming, Dolly." She turned to go, but Asher held his arm out. She had to either ignore him or accept his escort. And if she didn't accept his arm, would he offer it to *her*?

Rebekah's hand virtually flew to his arm, and she allowed Asher to lead her into the ballroom, while *she* was left to follow behind.

Chapter 6

Dolly sat at the window seat, her fingers tracing the dog-eared edges of the magazine in her lap. "It's so difficult to keep up with the latest fashions since *The Lady's Miscellany* stopped publication."

"I know, but perhaps they will resume printing their magazine now that the war is over." Rebekah didn't think her aunt's complaint had anything to do with clothing styles. "How are you feeling?"

Dolly smiled, but it was a weak gesture. "I must be getting too old for all this gadding about."

"I'm glad we turned down the invitation to breakfast. It gives us time to rest." Rebekah folded a blouse and placed it on top of the skirt. The past weeks had been filled with activities. Fancy breakfasts drifting into fancier luncheons. Afternoon soirees on the banks of the Mississippi. Then quick naps to keep up their strength and off again to attend a ceremonial ball or formal dinner party.

It was no wonder her aunt looked so worn out. They both needed to get back to Nashville where life made more sense. The Jackson family had left several days ago, but Aunt Dolly's cough had been so bad that they had decided to remain an extra week in the hopes that the weather would be more salutary during their journey.

"Rest? You're working harder than most maids I've hired."

"I don't mind, Dolly. Not if it means we'll be able to leave soon."

Paper crinkled as Dolly flipped the pages in her magazine. "I know our accommodations are not the best, but are you so miserable here?"

"Not miserable. . .but I do miss home. And I have to admit I wouldn't care if I never saw another lady's fan again." Rebekah rolled her eyes, pleased when her aunt laughed. In their months together, they had forged a friendship she treasured. Sometimes she had to remind herself that Dolly was her ma's sister—she seemed closer to Rebekah's age than her ma's.

"I know what you mean." Dolly's voice interrupted her musings. "It is amazing, though, how much use we get from them." She fanned her fingers in front of her mouth and fluttered her eyelids as if flirting with an imaginary beau.

Rebekah giggled at her aunt's posturing. "That's precisely my point."

"Are you sure your displeasure is with all the ladies we've met?" Her aunt sent a pointed gaze her direction. "Or is there one particular miss who has gained your ire?"

Rebekah could feel the blush heating her cheeks. Was it so obvious? She could have happily pulled out every dark hair on Miss Alexandra Lewis's head for spending so much time trying to capture Asher's attention. Rebekah had tried and tried to bury her resentment, but it was beyond her ability to do so. "It's just that I hardly ever get to see Asher. And those Lewises seem to be at every party we attend."

"They are very well received," her aunt agreed. "You must know that Captain Landon only has eyes for you, no matter how much that young lady throws herself at him."

Rebekah shook her head. "Asher says he only spends time with her family because her pa is close to the general and has promised to help him attain a promotion."

"I see nothing wrong with that. He is obviously looking out for the future, a future that he wishes to share with you."

"If that is the real reason, then it seems he would also spend time with us. After all, Rachel is the general's wife. Winning her admiration would probably advance him faster than the efforts of some pretentious local planter."

Dolly tsked her disapproval. "You are not very charitable toward Colonel Lewis. He and his wife are well connected by all accounts. I understand that their families own land up and down the river."

Heat filled her cheeks again. "You are right, but I cannot help thinking that Asher is ashamed of Rachel Jackson. You know how all these people whisper about her and make us all uncomfortable with their barbed words. If Asher were not influenced by people like the Lewises, perhaps he could have led the way to showing all of them Rachel's true worth. And then she might have convinced the general to wait an extra week so we could all travel home together."

Silence fell in the room. When her aunt failed to comment, Rebekah returned to her work. "Are you sure you feel all right?"

Dolly's eyes regained their focus. "Perhaps it is because he does not want to use a woman's influence to further his career."

Rebekah's brows drew together in a frown. "Do you think so?"

Dolly nodded. "I am sure of it. And besides, you need to remember that all of your worries will soon be groundless. Since the general arranged to send us home with a whole host of strong soldiers, including your Asher, Miss Lewis will soon be nothing but an unpleasant memory."

The knot in Rebekah's stomach seemed to diminish at her aunt's assurances. Once they were headed back north, Asher would forget all about Alexandra Lewis and her connections. Then things would get back to normal. Finally she and Asher could continue planning their future together.

A knock drew the ladies' attention.

Dolly got up and went to the door. "Yes."

The words of their visitor were inaudible, but Rebekah heard her aunt's response. "I see. Tell our guest we'll be down in a few moments."

When her aunt shut the door and turned around, Rebekah sighed. She didn't know if she could continue being polite to the local gentry. They were too different from the folks at home. "I can finish the packing while you go downstairs."

"Nonsense. You'll want to see this visitor." Dolly seemed more animated, her eyes twinkling as if she knew a wondrous secret.

Rebekah's heart leaped upward. "Asher?"

Her aunt nodded, and Rebekah instantly reached to check that her hair was not mussed. She smoothed her calico skirt, wishing she'd worn something prettier and not quite so practical this morning.

"You look fine, dear." Dolly's voice calmed her nerves.

Rebekah stopped fussing with her appearance as an idea occurred to her. "Do you think it would be okay to give him his gift now?"

Dolly nodded. "I think this is the perfect time to do so!"

Rebekah smiled, retrieved the package, and followed Dolly to the parlor downstairs. Asher had finally come to see her! She pushed back her discontent; she was determined to enjoy his visit.

The broad window that took up one wall of the parlor outlined her beloved's straight shoulders. He turned and smiled as she entered the room, and Rebekah's heart fluttered. He was so handsome. She sent God a quick prayer of thanks that Asher loved her. And a request that He would smooth the pathway for their marriage. She couldn't wait until they were husband and wife—then they could talk every day.

Dolly greeted Asher before taking a seat in one corner of the room and turning her attention to the magazine she'd brought from their suite.

Asher took Rebekah's hand and enveloped it gently. "How have you been, sweetheart?"

Rebekah smiled at his endearment. "Fine."

Dolly cleared her throat, causing Rebekah to pull her hand out of Asher's warm grasp. "I have something for you." She held out the gift.

Asher took it from her and unwrapped the cloth with a quick motion. "Look! What a fine handkerchief. And you stitched my initials on it, too. What a talented seamstress you are."

"I hope you like it."

"How could I not, when you made it especially for me." He smiled, and her heart did a little jump. "Thank you so much, Rebekah."

"You are most welcome." She sat gingerly on the edge of the striped sofa that was stationed at the far end of the room from Dolly. The sun outside was brighter, and she felt like laughing out loud. Her whole world seemed to have changed in a matter of moments as she had gone from worrying about Asher's preoccupation to basking in his admiration. Asher's love and approval were the only things that mattered.

"I missed seeing you at the Dupree breakfast." Asher settled himself beside her on the sofa, but he left a respectable distance between them.

"Dolly and I decided to stay here and begin our packing." Rebekah realized she was twisting her hands together and consciously relaxed them in her lap. A lady was not supposed to broadcast her feelings. Another of those silly society rules.

Asher cleared his throat, and she turned her gaze up to his face. "I'm certain you ladies are exhausted with all the social occasions. And you will need all of your strength for the journey home. In fact, that's one of the reasons I was looking for you this morning. I have news to share."

Her heart became an icicle. "From home?"

Asher shook his head. "No, but I'm sure everyone is fine back home. This has more to do with our upcoming trip. It seems you will have a traveling companion. Someone of your own age."

Rebekah tried to hide the disappointment that rose in her as she realized this might hinder her time with Asher.

"The Lewises and their daughter." Asher paused and glanced down at her. "Do you remember Alexandra Lewis?"

Surely he couldn't mean. . .

"She's a sweet thing. I'm sure you will be the best of friends."

His words brought a gasp of dismay that she covered with a cough. She knew he was watching her, so she pinned what she hoped was a convincing smile on her lips. No need to tell him how she felt about Alexandra. He might even try to defend her rival, and Rebekah could not abide that. What could she say? "How. . .nice. I'm sure we will. . .find something. . .in common."

Asher patted her hand. "You are the sweetest girl in the world."

She didn't feel very sweet. She felt as deceitful as Delilah. A burning sensation made her blink her eyes rapidly. She would *not* deceive the man she loved. In that instant, Rebekah decided to do everything she could to deserve Asher's praise. She would find something to like about Alexandra Lewis—no matter what it cost her.

Chapter 7

The next morning, Rebekah's vow was immediately put to the test when she found out they would be sharing their wagon with Alexandra and her mother. Was God trying to test her? She had never dreamed that the Lewis family would not have their own wagon. Instead of having to put up with Alexandra during meals, she would be subjected to her every day, all day long, for the entire trip.

She looked at the wagon, trying to decide whether there was any chance for privacy. It was nearly twenty feet long from the tip of the tongue to the gated back, but the area where the four women would travel facing each other for the next month was the bed of the wagon—a space of some five by eight feet. It was topped with bent poles that would be covered with heavy, oiled canvas for most of the trip. The inside was fitted with two long benches that had been covered with padding for their comfort. Underneath the benches was room to store a few bags containing basic necessities, but most of their clothing would follow in the provisions wagon.

Rebekah glanced longingly toward the men on horseback. Why did she have to be relegated to the wagon like a sack of meal? She could ride as well as Asher and would have been glad to show her ability if not for the ridiculous strictures placed on women by society's conventions.

Alexandra and her mother had already made themselves comfortable on one side of the wagon. Rebekah forced the corners of her mouth up and waited as Aunt Dolly was helped into the wagon.

"Bonju," Mrs. Lewis greeted them with the accent so prevalent in New Orleans. She was an older version of her daughter—a slight woman with dark hair and eyes and an air of sophistication that Rebekah wished she could emulate. "I am so happy to see you both again. I think we met at one of the victory celebrations. We are honored to travel north with you to your home."

Aunt Dolly stowed her leather satchel and held her hand out to Mrs. Lewis. "It is a pleasure to see you again, also. We look forward to becoming the best of friends before we arrive in Nashville."

Best of friends? Rebekah had serious doubts whether she would be able to maintain the appearance of civility.

But Aunt Dolly did not seem to share her misgivings. As the wagon

46

headed north, she chatted with Mrs. Lewis about everything from the defeat of the British to the latest reports of bandit gangs on the northern route to Nashville.

Rebekah turned slightly to watch as the riverfront gave way to forest, wishing they were at the end of their journey rather than the beginning.

"Miss Taylor. . ." Alexandra's whisper drew her attention away from the scenery.

"Yes, Miss Lewis?"

"I hope you don't mind our company on your trip to Nashville. Surely you are not envious because Asher has been visiting my home so much."

What could she say? She did not want to be rude, but she could not lie either. It was obvious to her that Alexandra was interested in having more than a casual friendship with Asher. A shrug was all she could manage.

"That Asher. . ." Mrs. Lewis's comment was a welcome interruption. "The colonel believes he will make an excellent officer."

"Yes, he has been very loyal to his country, staying past his original obligation." Aunt Dolly leaned forward and smiled toward her. "Our Rebekah has proved herself to be the perfect mate for Asher by the way she has patiently awaited his return and traveled into the wilderness to see him when he couldn't come home."

The topic of their conversation must have heard his name. He pulled his horse even with the wagon. "Are you ladies comfortable?"

Aunt Dolly answered for them. "We are quite content. Thank you for arranging this large wagon we can share."

Asher's shoulders straightened. "We have a cover to protect you from the weather, too."

Alexandra opened her fan. "You've thought of everything, Captain Landon."

"Thank you, Miss Lewis, but your father deserves part of the credit, too."

"Yes." Mrs. Lewis nodded. "The colonel is a good husband. He is always thinking of our comfort."

Asher saluted the ladies before riding to the front of their cavalcade to scout the pathway ahead.

As Mrs. Lewis continued to sing the praises of the colonel, Rebekah played with the fringe of her bonnet. Until they put the cover up, it would protect her skin from the sunshine. She peered upward through the thick canopy of pine trees. Of course, if the forest remained this dense, she would have little need for either. But what would shield her from watching Alexandra Lewis flirt with Asher?

≈

"I would really like to reach the Natchez Road before day's end. Our journey from New Orleans has been uneventful so far, but I'm not sure if it's a good idea to take a detour. How many days would it cost us?" Asher watched Colonel Lewis sharpen his razor on a strip of leather.

The colonel frowned as he began to shave in the reflection of a mirror he had propped on the low branch of a dogwood tree. "We could be there by midday, and we'd resume our journey in a day or two, as soon as everyone is rested. Our ladies need a respite from these primitive conditions."

Asher looked around at their campsite, ringed by leafless, moss-hung oak trees. Alexandra and the older ladies, all of whom were accustomed to the modern conveniences of city life, could not be comfortable sleeping out in the open with only the underside of a wagon for shelter. His Rebekah, of course, thrived in any conditions, but she would probably enjoy a little extra pampering as well.

He brushed the sleeve of his uniform with a fond smile. Rebekah had done a good job mending the tear in it. "If you think the ladies would like it, I suppose we could take a side trip."

"Excellent." Colonel Lewis trimmed his mustache. "I know you're anxious to be home, but I think we will all enjoy staying with the Tanner family. My wife has received several letters from her widowed mother, but she'll be elated to see her again."

Asher realized he actually looked forward to the respite as well. Just as he'd enjoyed many times in New Orleans, he delighted in seeing his Rebekah ensconced in the society in which he dreamed they would one day belong.

Chapter 8

Y ou're a handsome young man, and as mannerly as you are good looking. I imagine half the girls in the territory are trying to turn your head." Mrs. Althea Tanner's voice was strident and forceful, her words drawing a snicker from the assorted relatives who were seating themselves at the formal dining table.

Asher could feel his ears heating up from her comments as he helped Alexandra's grandmother to the table. She leaned her hickory cane against the arm of her chair and grabbed his sleeve. Asher was anxious to get to Rebekah, but he had no choice except to lean over the older lady. Her skin was so thin it was almost translucent, but he did not make the mistake of thinking her senile. Although her brown eyes had faded to the color of buckskins, they were as sharp as a hunter's.

"Don't be embarrassed. When you get as old as I am, you learn to speak your mind and accept whatever compliments come your way."

"Yes, ma'am."

Mrs. Tanner pointed to the seat on her right. "Sit here next to me." She waved away the son who most likely considered the seat his and looked at her granddaughter, who was hovering in the background. "You may sit on his other side, Alexandra."

Asher threw an apologetic glance toward Rebekah. Dismay was plain on her face, but what could he do? They should be sitting together farther down the table. The seats next to Grandma Tanner should be occupied by Alexandra and her parents, followed by the host of Alexandra's relatives who lived on the extensive plantation. But in the hours since their arrival at Tanner Plantation, he had quickly learned that Mrs. Tanner ruled her family with all the authority of a royal queen. Etiquette did not matter—only the wishes of the matriarch. He pulled out a chair for Alexandra on his right and took the seat between her and her grandmother.

Colonel Lewis offered a gruff blessing, and the unobtrusive slaves began to serve the food.

The first course was a thick, white soup. Asher picked up his spoon and tried it, his smile deepening at the wonderful flavor of fresh corn. "Delicious."

"Thank you." Mrs. Tanner inclined her head, reminding him again of royalty. "We grow all the ingredients right here on our land, from the spices to the corn in that chowder. In fact, I am proud to say that we either grow, raise, or catch nearly everything we eat. There's little we need to barter for. Not like those who live in the big cities and rely on others to supply their needs. But then, we are not quite so hard-pressed for our survival as those of you living on the frontier."

Asher nodded his agreement and looked down the table toward Rebekah. He was relieved to see she had been seated next to her aunt. He would have liked the opportunity to converse with her, tell her how proud he was of her efforts during their journey. Even though they had both been very busy on the trip—he with securing their safety, she with making the travelers as comfortable as possible—he felt like they had been working in tandem. It was like practice for being married.

Once they were man and wife, they would have different responsibilities, but it would take both of them to become successful. He had such hopes that he could make a contribution to the development of the United States. These were confusing days, and he knew it would take men with boldness and clear vision to make the important decisions that would secure America's future. He wanted to be one of those men. And with a woman like Rebekah by his side, he could succeed.

Alexandra's voice brought him out of his reverie. "That's a terrible frown you have on your face, Captain Landon."

"I'm sorry. I was thinking of home."

Alexandra put her spoon down beside her bowl. "Tell me about Nashville."

"It is certainly not an important metropolitan center like New Orleans, but the land there is breathtakingly beautiful. I'd venture to say it is the most beautiful part of the world with its majestic trees and sparkling streams. The Cumberland River that flows around Nashville is narrower than the Mississippi, with clear, swift water and fish that are longer than my arm."

"You make it sound wonderful."

Nostalgia tugged at Asher's heart. The past year and a half had been eventful—and he would never trade the experience those months had brought him—but he was glad to finally be going home. "My favorite time of the day is early evening when the sun drops down on the far side of the hills. The stars begin to appear one by one until the whole sky looks as bright as that chandelier. Even the trees seem to whisper that God is greater than man can conceive as the wind blows across their branches in the evening. When I look at the forests and realize that God put them there years before I was born and that they will be there long after I am gone, it puts my problems into perspective."

"You are quite poetic, Captain."

Asher laughed, a little embarrassed that he had allowed them to see his love for home. "It's been a long time since I've been there, Miss Lewis."

જ

Rebekah lost count of the courses that were served at the Tanner dinner table. It seemed there was more food than would be needed to supply General Jackson's whole army for a week—including the Baratarian pirates. She picked at the meat on her plate and wondered if the interminable dinner would ever end.

Things could not be worse. Asher was sitting at the head of the table, laughing with their hostess and *that woman*. How dare he enjoy himself when she was trapped next to some portentous old man who did nothing more than burp and belch his way through dinner.

With a sigh, she turned her attention to Aunt Dolly. "How are you feeling?"

"Much better." Dolly yawned behind the cover of her hand. "But I am still quite ready for a return to that comfortable bed."

Rebekah was relieved that her aunt was looking much less wilted. At least she could be thankful for that. The last thing she wanted was for her aunt to suffer a relapse. "I wonder if we should stay here a day or two before we resume our journey."

Dolly rolled her eyes. "I'm ready to get home. It's taken so much longer than I'd thought. And I'm not an invalid, you know. Sometimes you are too solicitous of my health. I'll be ready to go as soon as your Asher says it is time."

Rebekah would have challenged her aunt's characterization of Captain Asher Landon, but the scraping of chairs against the dining room's pine floor alerted them that dinner was officially over. She could not resist a glance toward the head of the table to see if Asher would come to escort them to the parlor, but he seemed to have all of his attention taken by a certain dark-haired temptress.

Rebekah pasted a smile on her face and laughed as if Aunt Dolly had said something terribly funny. Aunt Dolly and the old codger were both looking at her oddly, but she shook her head and proceeded to the parlor.

There was a fireplace in the room, and Rebekah was thankful there was no fire lit. Sometimes people as old as Mrs. Tanner liked to keep fires burning no matter how warm the weather. In front of the fireplace stood a tall-backed chair that resembled a throne. Instinctively, she looked toward Asher, catching his eye. It was as if they could communicate without words.

He tipped his head slightly toward the chair, and she nodded. They both smiled. It felt wonderful. Maybe he had not changed so much after all. Maybe there was hope for her dreams.

More relatives kept coming into the room. The Tanner household was certainly extensive, which explained why they lived in such an enormous house.

She was sure she would get lost and never be found again if she wandered away from the parlor on her own. The house was even larger than the hotel in New Orleans and must be three or four times the size of Aunt Dolly's home.

She thought back to the day when her pa had first taken her to Nashville to care for her aunt. She'd never imagined she would spend the night in a home that made that house seem small in comparison. It was odd how things changed one's perspective.

Mrs. Tanner took her seat and waved a hand toward her granddaughter. "Alexandra, why don't you play for us?"

"I would be happy to, *Grand-mère*. But I will need some help with the pages."

Rebekah watched as Alexandra turned toward Asher. Surely he would not. . . . But he did. He walked over and helped Alexandra at the piano as she fussed with everything—her skirts, the music, the stool. Finally, it seemed she was ready to perform.

Rebekah clenched her teeth. Things had certainly gone from bad to worse. She tapped one foot and wished the evening would end so she could go to bed. Then it would be morning, and they could leave.

Mrs. Tanner's strident voice cut across the polite applause after Alexandra finished her piece. "Why don't you play something for us, Miss Taylor?"

Rebekah's attention jerked back to the older lady. "Oh, no." She could not believe the suggestion. She looked around to see that she was the center of attention. Her heart pounded so hard she thought she might pass out. There was no way she could push any more words past her frozen throat.

"Perhaps Miss Taylor is shy." Alexandra's sultry voice quieted the hubbub of speculation from her relatives. "But we are all friends here." She stood up and took a vacant seat on the sofa next to her grandmother. "Perhaps she needs some of you to encourage her to perform for us."

Aunt Dolly raised her hand to get their attention. "Rebekah is not shy." Her voice remained calm and assured. "She does not play the piano."

Someone gasped. Rebekah heard one of the women talking. "How can any young lady's parents so neglect her education?"

Rebekah desperately wished she were somewhere—anywhere—else. She wished she'd never heard of Tanner Plantation, much less met any of Alexandra's relatives. This is what came of trying to pass herself off as a society miss when she did not possess the right accomplishments. She shook her head, wishing the nightmare would end. She wanted to crawl under her chair and never come out again. Perhaps she should lose herself in the mansion.

Aunt Dolly came to her rescue again. "I know it's different here, but in Nashville, we don't spend as much time worrying about teaching our young ladies how to sing or play the piano. We think it's more important that they know how to survive and how to help others in need. Rebekah Taylor has nursed me back to health with her loving care and medicinal potions. Furthermore, she has spent the last year keeping an entire household running smoothly. And if you could taste one of the apple pies she bakes, you would understand the meaning of real talent."

Gasps and titters followed Aunt Dolly's words, and the elder Mrs. Tanner harrumphed her obvious disapproval of such plebeian accomplishments.

"Come along, dear." Dolly's hand felt warm around her fingers. "I think I need a bit of fresh air."

As they left the parlor, Rebekah thought she heard Mrs. Tanner saying something about manners and hospitality, but she was too distraught to make sense of it. She followed her aunt onto the wide porch.

"Breathe, Rebekah," Dolly said.

Rebekah nodded and concentrated on filling her lungs. After a few moments, her heartbeat returned to a more normal rhythm. "Thank you, Dolly."

"Silly girl, you can't let people like that affect you so."

The words were said with so much love that Rebekah felt some of her shame easing. She was not happy she'd had to rely on her aunt for defense, but at least Aunt Dolly had come to her rescue. Asher, on the other hand, had remained silent. Didn't he love her enough to protect her reputation?

As if her thoughts had summoned him, Asher stepped onto the porch. "Are you okay, Rebekah?"

"I believe I hear someone calling me." Dolly squeezed her hand and placed it on the rail. "I'll be right inside if either of you needs me."

Silence filled the night as Rebekah concentrated again on her breathing. She gripped the railing so tightly that she wondered if it would break under the pressure. "I want to go home."

He was standing right behind her, so close she could smell his pomade. She wanted to turn and bury herself in his arms, but she could not. Not until they talked about the matter of his attraction to Alexandra.

"I know you do, sweetheart. And I want to get you home. Get back to where we were before this war started. You have only been away from Nashville for a few months. It has been nearly two years for me."

His words sparked another point of contention. "Yet you passed up the chance to come home earlier."

"It wasn't like that, Rebekah. General Jackson gave me a special assignment. I was proud to serve him and our country. But because of that assignment, I had no real choice."

His words melted away one of the resentments she had held against Asher.

She turned and looked up at him. "What kind of assignment?"

He put a finger on her nose. "The secret kind, my curious girl."

Rebekah pushed away his hand. She supposed she would have to accept his answer. She knew there were things men could not talk about in regard to their military service. The same had been true of her pa. Her ma had told her years ago that there were some things it was better to leave alone.

But Alexandra Lewis was another matter entirely.

"Do you still love me?" She was glad that her eyes had adjusted to the darkness around them. She could see every expression on his face, the face she loved more than any other.

"What?"

The first thing she saw was confusion, followed swiftly by disbelief and then humor. What she did not see was shame or deceit. So maybe he was still in love with her. . .and not Alexandra. But that still did not appease her. "You know she is trying to entrap you."

"Who? Alexandra?" He laughed. "She's like a little sister. Always getting into trouble and needing someone to guide her. She does not feel anything toward me except the love a sister feels toward a big brother."

Rebekah pointed a finger at his chest. "That's where you're wrong. You mark my words, Asher Landon. Alexandra Lewis does not think of you as a brother. She thinks of you as a suitor. And if you're not careful, she'll get you into a compromising position and rely on your chivalry to trap you."

"I cannot believe you, Rebekah. I thought you knew me better than that. You are the only girl who interests me at all. Ten Alexandras could not hold a candle to you. You're the only girl I've ever asked to marry me."

"And yet we are not married."

"As soon as we get back to Nashville, that will change. I'll go to your parents the very first day and procure their blessing. Then as soon as I can buy or build us a home, you will become Mrs. Asher Landon."

Rebekah longed to embrace his words and cling to their promise, but even though she forced a smile to her face, her heart hid a cloud of concern for the future.

Chapter 9

Rain drenched the canvas sides of their wagon, bringing a steady, cold breeze that chilled the travelers and made Rebekah wish for an early summer. Mrs. Lewis and Alexandra were sleeping on the bench opposite where she cuddled close to Aunt Dolly.

Rebekah stretched her right hand to push back the heavy cloth covering the wagon's back gate and peered out at the tall pines standing like silent pickets on both sides of the muddy track. The separate wagon holding their clothes and provisions trundled into view around a bend.

A flash in the underbrush drew her attention. Out of the corner of her eye, she saw another swift movement. She jerked her head around but spotted nothing. Was someone hiding behind one of the large tree trunks, or was she imagining things? "Wake up, Dolly."

"What, dear?" Aunt Dolly's voice was slow and thick. She stretched her arms forward and yawned.

"I'm sorry to disturb you, but I thought I saw something in the woods."

Neither of the Lewis ladies roused, but the soldier who was driving the wagon turned around and placed a silencing finger over his lips.

Rebekah's heart began to thump heavily. Only a few days of travel separated them from Nashville, and the trip thus far had been uneventful. The dreary weather had been their greatest trial. It had rained on them nearly every day since leaving Tanner Plantation, turning the road into a muddy path and placing an extra burden on the men and horses.

Rebekah held her breath and prayed for safety. A bird whistled in the distance, answered by another that sounded closer to their wagon. A bush alongside the road trembled as though caught in a strong wind. She looked upward, but the branches of the tall pines were still.

She was nearly thrown to the floor when their horses were brought to an unexpected halt. Both Alexandra and Mrs. Lewis woke abruptly, their voices sharp inside the wagon.

A small scream escaped Aunt Dolly, but Rebekah refused to give way to the panic building inside her. Instead she looked around for some type of weapon to use. Her sewing basket and Aunt Dolly's jewelry box were the only items she saw.

Mrs. Lewis put one hand over her heart and grasped Alexandra's arm with the other. "What's happening? Is it bandits?"

"Could be." Their driver reached back for the musket leaning against the seat and laid it across his knees. "All I know for sure is someone wants us to stop."

Rebekah looked from one lady to the other, her mind grappling with the implications. Was the situation that desperate? She hoped not. Yet who had not heard of travelers meeting their demise along the road to Nashville?

The sharp report of gunfire punctuated her thoughts. The horses whinnied and fought to get away from the noise, making the wagon rock back and forth violently as the driver tried to calm them. Something thudded against the side of the canvas wall. Another *thud*. Rebekah realized it was the sound of arrows striking the sides of the wagon. Indians!

Aunt Dolly slid to the floor and gestured for the rest of the women to join her. "Lord, protect us." Her voice was calm, as if she were sitting in a church pew at home rather than on a dusty wooden floor in the middle of a forest full of dangerous Indians.

Were they about to be scalped? Burned to death? Rebekah squeezed her eyes shut and tried to pray along with Aunt Dolly and the others, but her mind was in a dither. The noise was horrendous—she could hear screaming from the servants in the other wagon, wild cries from the Indians, and the men shouting back and forth to each other. *Lord, save us.*

Rebekah opened her eyes. She had to see what was going on outside. She thought about the empty cart she and her pa had seen when he first took her to stay with Aunt Dolly. Would some other traveler come across their empty wagon in a few days and wonder what had happened to them? She could not hear any more thuds against the sides, but that was because the rushing noise of her pulse was blocking out all other sounds.

She watched as Aunt Dolly lifted her head slightly to gaze over the wooden back of the driver's seat.

"What's happening?" Rebekah wished her words sounded as calm as Aunt Dolly's had. She took a deep, calming breath and released it slowly. The noise outside had definitely abated.

"They're talking to the Indians. Something about a storm. I can see Asher shaking his head, but I can't hear what he's saying."

A heartfelt praise lifted the worst of the fear from Rebekah's mind. At least he'd not been harmed. And she had no doubt he could calm the situation. She rubbed her aunt's cold hand. "Everything's going to be all right."

Their horses began to quiet as if they also sensed that the greatest danger had passed.

The minutes seemed to stretch out as the four women waited for the confrontation to end. Aunt Dolly pushed herself up onto the seat. "I'm going to see exactly what's going on. The rest of you stay here."

"Do you think that's wise?" Mrs. Lewis's question echoed Rebekah's thoughts.

"It may not be wise, but I cannot cower in here any longer." Aunt Dolly clambered onto the driver's seat before climbing down and disappearing from Rebekah's view.

Rebekah and Alexandra helped Mrs. Lewis back up onto the seat now that the most immediate danger had passed. The men's voices moved around to the back of the wagon, and Rebekah scooted down the bench to the gate. She separated the heavy, wet material protecting them to watch the confrontation.

Asher had dismounted and was standing next to his horse, his rifle held loosely in one hand. His stance seemed odd, but maybe it was only her imagination.

A slight sound behind the wagon to her right made her wonder if they were completely surrounded by Indians. Rebekah leaned against the wooden gate, trying to understand what was being said.

When an unseen hand pulled the bolt free on the gate, it fell open and she fell with it, tumbling out and landing on the muddy road with a jaw-cracking *thump*. Rebekah was so surprised she didn't even cry out. Someone grabbed her arm and jerked her back onto her feet. She twisted her head and looked into the darkest brown eyes she'd ever seen—eyes that mirrored her own fear.

He was an Indian brave, but he couldn't have been more than twelve years old. Her shocked gaze took in his buckskin attire and straight black hair. Somehow, when she thought of the danger of Indians, they were full-grown adults, not boys who were young enough to be in short pants.

Rebekah's fear melted away. This was not some faceless danger. This was a person, someone who had hopes and dreams and fears, just like she did. Her thoughts were cut off, however, when he jerked his head to indicate that she should join the others who were still having a somewhat heated debate.

". . .no food." Asher's words were clipped, and his voice sounded harsh to Rebekah. He turned and saw the Indian brave guiding her forward. "Don't you put your filthy hands on her."

"It's okay, Asher. He's not hurting—"

Aunt Dolly's voice cut off her protest. "I thought you were going to stay inside."

"I thought so, too." Rebekah glanced down at her muddy dress. "But I sort of fell out."

Asher strode to her and pulled her from the Indian's grasp. "Are you hurt?"

"Only my dignity."

He smiled his crooked half smile, and the others faded to nothingness. She forgot the cold and the danger. Asher was the only thing that mattered. But then he turned his attention back to the discussion at hand, and reality returned in the form of cold raindrops sliding down her back.

She listened to the debate between the men, her sympathy roused as the Indians' desperation became apparent. It had been a difficult winter made harder by the influx of white settlers who competed for the wild game in the area. At first, this tribe had tried to trade with the newcomers, but they had been met with distrust and hatred. Unable to overcome the settlers' fears, they had turned to other means to provide for their families.

"Maybe the hatred was earned." Colonel Lewis pointed at the Indian. "Maybe you took a few scalps along the way."

The man who seemed to be the spokesperson for the band of Indians shook his head. "We want peace with you." He was tall and straight, with shoulders as wide as her pa's and with the bearing she associated with military men such as Asher and General Jackson.

Aunt Dolly let out an unladylike snort. "I might find that easier to believe if you had not attacked us today."

"Do you see dead white men?" The Indian raised his chin. "If we really attack, all the men die, and we take you back to our village."

Rebekah could not help the shudder that passed through her. The Indian's words painted an awful picture in her mind—Asher lying on the ground with an arrow piercing his heart, his lifeblood staining the ground as she was dragged away to face unimaginable hardship. She grasped Asher's hand.

"If you want peace, return to your village." Asher squeezed her hand before releasing it. "Don't you see that stopping people and stealing from them will bring nothing but more death and hatred?"

"And what do we tell our starving women and children? Do we tell them to suffer so the white man will be our friend?"

Rebekah could hear the pain in his voice. There must be something they could do to help his people. "Don't we have some extra provisions we can give them?"

"Have you lost your mind, girl?" Colonel Lewis frowned at her. "Do you want to take the chance of starving yourself by giving away our food?"

"Rebekah is right, Colonel." Aunt Dolly's voice was as calm as it had been in the wagon. "We have more than enough to last for the final week of our journey. There is a full wagon of canned vegetables and flour sacks traveling with us. I think we can share our bounty. It is our Christian duty to do so."

"Christian duty? Where does the Good Book say we should feed the heathens who attack our farms and kill innocent women and children?"

"I believe it's in the book of Matthew. Jesus said, 'But I say unto you, Love your enemies, bless them that curse you, do good to them that hate you, and pray for them which despitefully use you, and persecute you.'"

The colonel's face turned as red as an autumn sunset. "The next thing you'll say is that we should give them all of our food and let God provide manna like He did for the Hebrews in the wilderness. This is men's business. You should both get back to the wagon."

Rebekah wished she could remain as calm as Aunt Dolly, who managed to keep a smile on her face as she answered the colonel. "I am not accustomed to bowing to the 'wisdom' of belligerence and intimidation."

Asher cleared his throat and stepped in front of Colonel Lewis. The Indians raised their bows in response, but he ignored them. "Why don't we see if we can share our provisions? It's obvious we are outnumbered, and it would be wiser to share rather than provoke these men into taking everything." His voice dropped so low that Rebekah could barely make out the quiet words he directed to the colonel. "There will be a better time than today to show our strength."

A tense moment passed while the colonel and Asher stared at each other. Then the colonel nodded. "Do what you must." He turned on his heel and pushed his way past the braves, who still held their weapons ready.

The Indian who had spoken to them turned back to the rest of the raiding party and addressed his men in staccato words. They lowered their weapons and stepped back, but Rebekah had the feeling they were still poised to attack if anything went wrong.

Asher and the Indian leader went back to the wagon that held their provisions.

Aunt Dolly turned to Rebekah. "You're shivering, Rebekah. And no wonder. Standing out here in the rain is beyond foolish."

"You must be cold, too."

Aunt Dolly nodded. "I believe your Asher has everything under control. Let's get back into the wagon where the wind will not cut us in two. We'll be none the worse for helping the Indians and on our way again soon."

Once they were inside, Aunt Dolly told the other ladies about the encounter.

Half-listening to her aunt's story, Rebekah's mind wandered to the young Indian lad. What would happen to that boy who had pulled her from the wagon? Would he grow into a hard man filled with hatred for the white man? Was there any chance to forge a bond between his people and her people? Surely there was enough room in this great country for both to coexist.

She thought about the argument she had sparked between Colonel Lewis and Aunt Dolly. He apparently had little understanding of Jesus and His love for others. Then another thought struck her. What about the Indians? Were they saved? Her personal considerations were swept away in a flood of concern. They needed the chance to know Christ as their personal Savior. If caring Christians didn't share the gospel with them, who would? And if they didn't have Christ in their hearts. . .

Rebekah shuddered. Distrust and fear were rampant these days, but with patience and love she prayed it would be possible to bring the two worlds together.

❧

Asher shaded his eyes from the rays of the late-afternoon sun. They would have to set up camp immediately. He wished he could count on Colonel Lewis to help, but the man seemed to have little understanding of the amount of work to be done. Instead of gathering wood or rubbing down the horses, he would spend his time talking to the womenfolk and leave all the chores to Asher and the soldiers driving the wagons.

The ferry bumped against the bank, and he led his horse off of its bobbing surface. Then he dismounted and tied his reins to a convenient branch. Striding back to the ferry, he grabbed the leads of the horses pulling the first wagon to calm them as they negotiated the transition between rushing river and dry ground. By the time both wagons were safe on dry ground, the sun was hanging low in the sky.

The bearded ferryman pulled against the rope that guided him back and forth across the river. "Keep a sharp eye out for Injuns," he shouted across the sound of the rushing water. "I been seein' a lot of them thievin' braves up and down the river last week or so."

Asher waved at the man. It was too bad he couldn't have stated his warning privately instead of shouting it out so all the women would hear. There was no need to cause them undue alarm. They were under his care, and the Good Lord had given him the ability to watch out over them.

A quick survey of the area led him to a pretty meadow about two hundred feet from the bank of the river. He went back to collect the rest of the party and start getting everyone settled in for the night. He had almost finished checking the horses for thorns and stones that might delay their travel when Rebekah walked up.

"Would you like some hot coffee? I brewed it strong the way you like it."

He blew on his frozen hands and reached for the tin cup. "Perfect." He hoped she understood that he wasn't only referring to the beverage she'd brought.

Rebekah's head dipped. He would have liked to continue looking into her eyes. There was so much he wanted to tell her. How thoughts of her had sustained him during their many months of separation. How wonderful it was to be near her now and see her every day.

He also wanted to tell her that he looked forward to building a big home for her right in the center of Nashville. He had big plans that would almost certainly make her the wealthiest woman in Nashville. Once they were married, he would make certain she never had to work hard again. She could spend all of her time in the company of the most prominent citizens of Nashville.

"I guess I should get back to the fire." She peeked up at him for a brief instant before looking away. "Aunt Dolly will need help preparing supper."

Was she teasing him? Asher gulped down the rest of his coffee and reached for her hand. It felt cold, and he wrapped his fingers around hers to impart some of his warmth to her. "I have a better idea. Why don't we collect the canteens and walk down to the river together?"

"I. . .I don't know if we should."

"Please, Rebekah. We'll be back in Nashville in a few days. . . ."

His heart sped up when she smiled and nodded. "But you have to promise to be a gentleman."

He put a hand over his heart and staggered back a few steps. "You wound me."

They kept up a lighthearted conversation as he led her down the path to the river. In the fading light, the water began to take on a silver sheen. It was wild and beautiful, a fine example of God's handiwork. They filled the canteens and stood quietly enjoying the sounds of nature.

Asher's breath condensed in the cool air. "I've missed home."

Her small hand touched his arm. "I prayed for you every day. I was so afraid you would be killed or maimed. And then after a year when you didn't come home, I thought maybe you'd found a reason to stay away. . . ."

His Rebekah was almost too beautiful for words. He reached out a hand to push back a tendril of her moon-kissed hair. Her eyes closed as if she, too, was overcome by the moment. Her lips parted slightly. She was so close he could feel her breath on his cheek. If he leaned forward just a few more inches, their lips would meet. But he would not ruin this special moment they shared. He backed away.

"Is something wrong?" Her voice, so warm a moment ago, sounded lost.

"No." He turned toward the forest in an attempt to control his turbulent emotions. "You should go back to the others."

"Asher, what is it? Did I say something wrong?" Her voice caught. "Or did you really find a reason to stay away?"

A scream interrupted his thoughts before he could form the right words. He turned and ran into the line of trees while reaching for his pistol. "Who's there?"

"It's me. Alexandra!" Her voice ended on a wail.

"Where are you?" He ran forward until he could make out her shape in the gathering dusk.

"There's something out there." She pointed to a willow tree that was indeed shaking in a most odd fashion.

Asher crept forward, his pistol cocked and ready, his mind filled with images of Indian braves and wild animals. He was a few yards away when the tree tilted toward him. He jumped back, nearly landing on top of Alexandra.

In the clearing where the tree had stood was a large, furry, brown shape standing on its hind legs. As soon as he saw the animal's flat black tail, Asher laughed. "It's only a beaver trying to build a new home."

Alexandra's throaty laughter joined his, and Asher found himself overcome with mirth. He doubled over with large, loud guffaws. It must have been relief that made her laugh with him, but whatever the reason, her giggles were contagious. His chest shook, and his stomach clenched, but he could not control the laughter. He pointed at the confused-looking beaver, which seemed unable to decide whether or not to claim his willow tree, and chortled again.

That's when Rebekah found them laughing together like a couple of demented geese. She shot him a look of pain and pushed past them.

The laughter dried up as suddenly as it had come. He had not meant to hurt Rebekah. He took a step toward her retreating figure, but Alexandra put a hand on his arm.

"Thank you for coming again to my rescue."

Asher nodded and turned away from Alexandra to watch Rebekah until he was sure she was safely back in the camp. He knew he ought to catch up to her and explain things—from why he had turned away from her to why he was laughing with Alexandra. But he had no idea how to put his feelings into words. He reholstered his pistol and returned with Alexandra to the river for the canteens.

As they climbed the pathway through the darkening woods, Asher's vague guilt hardened into a sense of injustice. Did Rebekah expect him to ignore a cry for help? Of course not, but instead of rushing back like an impetuous, spoiled child, she should have stayed with him and Alexandra. They could have explained their laughter, and then all three of them could have traveled together rather than returning to camp separately.

The thought of them traveling separately in life flitted through his mind, but he pushed it away, assuring himself Rebekah wanted the same things he did. *Didn't she?*

Chapter 10

Rebekah shifted on the hard wooden bench as the new pastor looked out over the congregation. When Brother Lawrence had died last fall, Aunt Dolly's church, as Rebekah distinguished it in her mind from her home church, had been led by a series of elders. All of them were good men, but the church needed its own shepherd. In response to the church members' prayers, Roman Miller had arrived in Nashville at the beginning of the year, and he and his wife, Una, set to work immediately to serve God's purpose.

Pastor Miller called for a prayer, and Rebekah reined in her attention, focusing on the blessings he asked for the congregation. She added her own prayer for a happy future with Asher. He had not attended service this morning, and she was worried he was ill.

When the prayer was over, the pastor issued an invitation to all new believers to come forward, and the congregation sang the closing hymn. As the last notes died away, Rebekah and Aunt Dolly gathered their cloaks and rose to leave.

Alexandra Lewis and her mother waved to them from across the sanctuary, and Rebekah forced a smile to her lips as she nodded. The dashing young woman seemed the embodiment of every problem in her life. She dropped a glove and slowly picked it up, hoping to avoid a conversation with Alexandra. After all of those weeks in close company with her, Rebekah had failed to find they had much in common. Except Asher, of course.

"How are two of my favorite ladies this fine Sabbath morning?" Pastor Miller's cheerful voice welcomed them at the door to the church.

Aunt Dolly laughed. "You are quite the diplomat, Pastor Miller. I suppose that all of the ladies in Nashville are your favorites."

He beamed at them. "Only the ones who are or may become members of the church."

"How are you feeling today, Una?" Aunt Dolly directed her words to the short woman who was beginning to show signs of her pregnancy and who stood next to the pastor.

Rebekah peeked over her aunt's shoulder at the dark-haired, green-eyed beauty who stood with one hand on the small of her back. Rumor said she was from a wealthy family, but her face glowed with humility and love for others. She was a talented baker as well. While her husband ministered to people's souls, she soothed their taste buds with delicious homemade pies and cakes.

Una shook her head. "I tire before I can get through a day's work."

A pang of remorse hit Rebekah, and tears threatened to overwhelm her as she watched the pastor and his wife. She wanted to start her own family, but would her dream ever come true? It seemed everyone was moving forward except Asher and her. When had it all started to go wrong? Was it that night at the river, the night he had pushed her away? Or had it started in New Orleans when she caught him dancing with Alexandra Lewis?

Her mind went back to the day Asher had told her he was going to war. The time between then and today had changed both of them. He was no longer the boy who wanted to live the simple life.

"I hope your frown is not an indictment of my sermon."

"No. . .no, sir." Rebekah shook her head for emphasis. "I was thinking of something else entirely."

"Hmm, I'm not sure it's much better to learn my sermon had so little effect that you've already forgotten it. It has always been my hope that God will use my sermons to make a difference in the congregation's lives, not be forgotten before they pass through the exit."

Aunt Dolly came to her rescue. "You must forgive my niece, Pastor. She is pining over her young man, who was apparently unable to attend this morning."

Maybe it would be better if no one tried to rescue her. Rebekah's cheeks burned, and she glanced down, unable to bear the sympathetic expressions of the pastor and his wife.

Pastor Miller reached for her hand, placing it in both of his. "Perhaps you will allow me to bring my wife to visit with you and your aunt this week."

Aunt Dolly raised her parasol to shade her face. "I have an even better idea. Why don't you and Mrs. Miller come by today for dinner? Rebekah and I would welcome your company."

"If you're sure it's no imposition. . ."

"I insist. Please say you'll come. I know Rebekah agrees, don't you?"

Rebekah looked at the earnest face of the pastor. She'd rather have had her dinner alone, but she knew her duty. She forced a smile to her face. "We'd love having you join us."

Pastor Miller helped them enter their carriage. "Then we would be delighted."

"Excellent. We'll look for you within the half hour."

As the carriage rumbled away, Aunt Dolly turned to her. "You may remove that grimace from your face, Rebekah."

"I thought I was smiling."

"If that's a smile, I would hate to see what your face looks like when you are in pain."

Rebekah dropped her gaze, ashamed of her sour disposition. What would Asher think if he could see her right now? But that was exactly the problem. Asher was nowhere around. And he'd apparently forgotten his promise to approach her pa as soon as he returned to Nashville. Well, she was not going to pine for him. She would smile and converse as if her heart were not breaking apart. What did it matter if everyone, even God, had abandoned her?

Aunt Dolly cleared her throat. "I have an idea I'd like to discuss with you, Rebekah."

The tone of her aunt's voice was light, but Rebekah twisted her gloves between her hands. Was her aunt about to chastise her for some other shortcoming? "Is something wrong?"

"Oh, no, dear. Not at all. But it is a rather delicate matter, and I am concerned that I may hurt your feelings."

Rebekah smiled brightly even as she steeled herself for yet another blow. "You could never do that, Dolly. Please tell me what's wrong."

"I was thinking about that weekend we spent at Mrs. Lewis's family home in Natchez."

Rebekah shifted on the seat. "I'd just as soon forget that weekend."

"I know, dear, but it made me think of that piano in the drawing room. I used to play it for my dear husband, but since his death, I simply don't have the heart for it." Aunt Dolly paused for a quick breath. "I was wondering about arranging piano lessons."

Piano lessons? What an intriguing idea. Her jaw muscles relaxed, allowing her smile to become more natural. "But wouldn't that be expensive?"

"I wouldn't have suggested it if I couldn't afford it."

A sudden scene flashed in Rebekah's mind. She and Asher were sitting on a piano bench, their shoulders touching as he turned the pages. Beautiful music was pouring from the piano as her fingers swept up and down the keyboard. Somewhere in the background, Alexandra wept into a handkerchief. . . .

"Rebekah? We're home, dear."

The carriage had stopped in front of Aunt Dolly's home.

Rebekah climbed down and followed her aunt inside, her feet practically dancing to the sweeping melody playing in her mind.

❧

Rebekah's fingers seemed to tangle as she tried to sort out the notes on the paper in front of her nose. She leaned forward and stared at the sheet, but the little black marks made no sense. Whoever thought to write down music in dots and slashes that had no relevance to the black and white keys under her fingers?

From behind her, the quick footsteps of Mr. Smothers, the piano teacher for many of the young ladies of Nashville, approached the stool. "Let's try again, shall we?"

His squeaky voice irritated her further, but Rebekah bit down on her lower lip. It wasn't Mr. Smothers's fault she had no talent. "It's hopeless. I cannot even master the simplest of tunes. I will never be able to play a real song." She twisted on the piano stool to face him.

Mr. Smothers pursed his lips, looking as if he had bitten into a crab apple. "Anyone can learn the basics, my dear. But you must apply yourself if you wish to excel. I believe the problem may be your advanced age. Most of my students are a great deal younger. Their fingers are likely more nimble and their minds not so cluttered with. . .with whatever it is that clutters your mind."

A knock on the front door interrupted them.

Rebekah pushed back the piano stool. "I think we've both suffered enough today."

Mr. Smothers did not have to look quite so relieved to be done with their lesson as he gathered his music sheets and overcoat. Rebekah saw him to the door, pondering whether or not to free the poor man from future trials by dispensing with his services. She would mention it to Aunt Dolly tonight. It was obvious she would never learn to play well, and there was no sense in spending Aunt Dolly's money for a lost cause.

They were met at the front door by Pastor and Mrs. Miller, who had dropped by for a visit. Much to her surprise, Rebecca had enjoyed having lunch with them after church last week. They seemed to find such joy in reaching out to the community, and their love for one another was evident in every glance they shared.

Rebekah trailed them into the parlor and sat in one corner, listening as they discussed the Indian attack at a settlement only a few miles north of Nashville. The people living there had not been killed, but their livestock was stolen, and several barns burned to the ground.

"Our wagons were stopped by a group of Indians on the Natchez Road." Aunt Dolly smiled at her. "But thanks to the quick thinking of my niece, we were able to come to an agreement to share our food with them and thus avoid disaster."

Una Miller shuddered, making her teacup teeter. "I fear for all of our lives if we cannot find a way to live together in Christian love."

Aunt Dolly passed a tray of pastries to her, but Rebekah could not concentrate on them enough to choose one. Her mind raced with questions. "How can the Indians practice Christian love if they don't even know Christ?"

Pastor Miller nodded. "That is an excellent question. Since coming to the frontier, Una and I have been burdened by our concern for these Indians, and we've prayed for God to show us how we might help them."

"Has God answered your prayers?" Rebekah asked.

"Indeed, I believe so." A smile of delight wreathed his face. "I think we were called to this area to found a school for the Indians. I understand an Indian couple has bought a farm about fifteen miles away. Una and I are planning a trip to visit them next week."

Rebekah listened as the pastor and his wife expounded on their ideas, but inside she felt they were taking on a task too great for two people. It would take more than one earnest couple to help the different Indian tribes adapt.

Her mind wandered to a recent newspaper article describing General Jackson's position on the Indian problem. His argument against the Indians seemed based on his belief that they could not live inside the sovereign territory of the United States. He proposed that those Indians who did not wish to become subject to American law should be moved to land outside the United States, land on the far side of the Mississippi River.

While she admired the general's bravery and military accomplishments and dearly loved his placid wife, she was appalled at his stance on the subject of Indians. It was too easy to put herself in the place of the Indians. Would she want to be told to leave her home just because someone with different beliefs had moved into the area?

". . .near your family, Rebekah. Would you like to join us?"

Rebekah's head jerked up. "I beg your pardon."

A frown from Aunt Dolly made Rebekah cringe inwardly. "I'm sure my niece would relish the chance to visit her family."

For the first time that afternoon, Rebekah felt a genuine spark of happiness. How wonderful it would be to see her family. "May I?"

Pastor Miller winked at her before turning to Aunt Dolly. "We'd love to have both of you join us."

"No, thank you." Aunt Dolly shuddered. "I find the country singularly depressing."

"If everyone thought as you and I, Nashville would be a very crowded place." Mrs. Miller laughed and rose to her feet, and her husband followed suit.

Rebekah practically bounced to her feet and trailed her aunt and their guests to the door. She could almost see her parents and siblings as they were reunited. Maybe she and Eleanor could even have a picnic under the shady leaves of the tulip poplar.

Pastor Miller adjusted his hat. "I will let you know the details in a day or two."

As soon as they closed the door on the Millers, Rebekah threw her arms around her aunt.

"My goodness. It seems someone is yearning for home." Aunt Dolly laughed. "If I didn't know better, I'd think you were unhappy here."

"Not at all. You are the sweetest aunt any girl could imagine, but I do miss home."

"I'm flattered." Aunt Dolly patted her cheek. "In the meantime, I will need your help with our ball."

All of Rebekah's excitement melted away like an early frost. She looked at her aunt in horror. "You're going to host a ball?"

⁂

"Please, Lord, heal Asher's heart." Hot tears seared Rebekah's cheeks. She gripped her hands more tightly together and rested her aching head against the side of her bed. "You know how much I love him, but something seems to be terribly wrong between us. Should I stay here and wait for Asher to change into the man I once loved? Do I remain patient with him and pray for him? Or should I give up and go back home? Lord, it was so much better back then. Maybe if I go back home, we can rediscover the love we once had. Please, Lord, show me what to do."

Rebekah ended her prayer and climbed into bed. She was not looking forward to tomorrow evening's ball. But once it was over, there would be no real reason for her to stay in Nashville. Aunt Dolly no longer needed her assistance. In fact, she had very little to do with herself during the day, especially since she had convinced Aunt Dolly to cancel her music lessons.

Every day, she hoped Asher would come by and tell her he'd been out to ask Pa for her hand in marriage. Every time the knocker sounded on the front door, her hopes had risen along with her heartbeat—and every time, she was disappointed. The only time she saw Asher was a social occasion. Never alone.

She turned over and sighed. She no longer paid much attention to the sounds of the city outside her window, but she would gladly exchange them for the melodic song of crickets and bullfrogs. More tears slipped free of her eyes and dampened the pillow beneath her head. What if God didn't send her an answer she could understand?

Rebekah closed her eyes, but sleep would not come. She slipped out of bed once again and returned to her knees. No words formed in her mind as she tried to pray, but a feeling of love and comfort enveloped her. The tears stopped, and she could feel a smile turning up the corners of her mouth. This was the touch of the Lord. She knew it deep in her heart. No matter how things worked out with Asher, Jesus would always love her.

Chapter 11

But I don't want to be a teller." Asher's voice had risen in volume as he tried to explain to his pa why he wanted to continue working for the militia. His parents were frustrated with his refusal to change his mind, but he was equally frustrated with their inability to grasp his desire to launch a challenging, interesting career that would keep him in close contact with General Jackson. They wanted him to embrace a boring future with a steady income that offered no chance for fame or fortune. They did not understand the importance of what he was involved in.

"It makes a lot more sense than hanging around that braggart, Colonel Lewis." His pa took a deep breath and released it with a grunt. "You are letting that man draw you into questionable schemes without a thought to the consequences."

"It's not like that, Pa."

"Then tell me what it is like." Pa's eyes narrowed. Asher could almost feel the flashes of lightning coming from them.

He hated arguing with his pa, but this was too important an issue. The way to convince his parents was through calm and rational discussion. He tamped down his anger. "I cannot. I've sworn an oath."

"To whom? The United States Army or to that New Orleans fop?"

"Pa, I've never heard you cast such aspersions. Colonel Lewis is a respected officer in General Jackson's militia."

"Isn't he the one you report to? Or do you have another reason for spending so much time at the Lewis home?"

Asher could feel his anger building again. First Rebekah and now his own family. Didn't anyone trust him anymore? "What kind of son do you think you raised?" He turned away and looked out the window.

After a moment, he felt Pa's hand on his shoulder. "I'm sorry. You're right. Your ma and I raised you to be an honest, God-fearing man. We have to allow you to make your own decisions."

Asher wanted to turn around, but he could not. It was time for his family to realize that he was fully grown. Maybe when he and Rebekah got married . . .as soon as he asked Mr. Taylor for permission to propose. And why was he taking so long to do that?

Somewhere along their journey from New Orleans, Rebekah had changed.

He hardly knew her anymore. At first he'd thought she was worried about her aunt or maybe overtired from the hardships of traveling, but they'd been back in Nashville for nearly a month and there had been plenty of time for her to recover. Mrs. Quinn seemed to be thriving, so that wasn't the problem.

He was beginning to think Rebekah didn't love him anymore. She was distant and cold the one time he called on her. Of course, the reason he hadn't been by more often was because he was busy preparing for their future. But had she understood that? No. Instead of being glad to see him, she seemed to be waiting for him to make some confession of wrongdoing. Asher never knew what to say anymore to bring a smile to her face. It was impossible to talk to her about anything other than the weather or her aunt's health. What had happened to the sweet girl he'd fallen in love with?

He felt Pa's hand fall away and listened as retreating footsteps indicated that he had given up.

Asher wanted to bridge the gap between them, but he had no idea how to do that. At one time he would have talked to Rebekah about his quandary, but now that option seemed out of the question. His sister was available to listen, but he didn't want to draw her into the middle of this. She would feel torn between her loyalty to her parents and her love for her big brother.

He pulled his watch from the front pocket of his waistcoat and popped it open. It was nearly time to leave for tonight's ball. He had promised Alexandra he would attend to help ease her introduction to local society. . .even though he doubted she would have any trouble. But perhaps she could give him some sage advice. Women always seemed to understand these things better than men.

❧

Rebekah put a hand on the balustrade and slowly descended the staircase. How different things looked since that long-ago afternoon when she and Pa had first arrived at Aunt Dolly's house. Gone were the grime and disarray that had greeted them that day. The whole house literally sparkled this evening, with dozens of candles lending a warm glow to the staircase and entry hall. Harriet and the maids had done an impeccable job getting the house ready for tonight's ball.

The afternoon Rebekah had learned Aunt Dolly planned a soiree in her niece's honor, she had been appalled. She felt so uncomfortable in social settings. All of those parties in New Orleans had been difficult because she had so little in common with most of the people who attended. And then the debacle at Tanner Plantation. . . It was enough to make a person want to avoid society for the next twenty years or so.

After her initial response, however, Rebekah had been unable to withstand her aunt's obvious desire to throw a party. And she had to admit the planning had been fun—the invitations, menus, and decorating. But now, half the city would be coming to judge whether or not she was a worthy relative of her dashing aunt.

Something smelled delicious. The new cook Aunt Dolly had hired was outdoing herself for tonight's event. The aromas of roasted meat and zesty sauces made her mouth water.

"You look absolutely stunning." Aunt Dolly's voice floated up from the foot of the stairs. Rebekah thought her aunt was the one who looked stunning in a brand-new aqua gown that enhanced her natural beauty.

"You're the real reason everyone's coming. All of your friends are anxious to see you again now that you've fully recovered your health. I doubt anyone will even notice me, which is a perfectly acceptable state of affairs."

Aunt Dolly wagged her finger at Rebekah. "You'll be turning heads and collecting compliments from all of the eligible men. Especially a certain dashing young captain."

Rebekah felt her smile fading away. If only that were true. But Asher had been so distant since they'd returned. Was he regretting his promise to her? Did he yearn for a more sophisticated wife? Someone with all the accomplishments of a lady? Someone named Alexandra?

She shook her head in an attempt to silence the needling suggestion. But the evidence was overwhelming. Whenever she tried to find out why Asher was distracted, he pushed away her concern. Something elemental had changed in him. He was as charming as ever but. . .

Tears stung her eyes. Rebekah missed those quiet afternoons back home, sitting under the shade of "their" tulip poplar while they made endless plans for a future together. A future that seemed more distant now than ever before.

Rebekah had wondered if she should stay in Nashville and wait for Asher to reaffirm he still wished to marry her as he had promised that night at Tanner Plantation. How well she remembered his assurance that he would approach her pa the very first day they returned. Yet the first day had become the first week. And then two weeks. Now it was nearly a month since their return, but Asher had made absolutely no mention of asking for her hand in marriage.

There was no getting around it. After the tearful hours she had spent last night on her knees talking to God about her dreams, hopes, and fears, Rebekah felt she could not ignore the tug on her heart. There was only one thing to do. She loved Asher more than life itself, and she did not want him to feel trapped by the promise he obviously regretted making.

Tonight she would release him. She was determined to do the right thing and tell Asher he was free to pursue others. His feelings for her must have faded. He would be happier if she told him he was free to move on without her.

A knock on the door indicated the arrival of the first guests. As predicted, they laughed and chatted with Aunt Dolly and paid Rebekah very little attention before moving to the ballroom. Soon the steady stream of townspeople made it clear the ball was going to be a success—in sheer numbers of attendees if nothing else.

Alexandra and her parents arrived, gushing over Aunt Dolly's house and complimenting her on the large number of people attending her party.

Rebekah breathed a sigh of relief when they moved on.

The next group entering brought a genuine smile to her face as they included some of her favorite people in Nashville—Rachel Jackson, Pastor and Mrs. Miller, and Mr. and Mrs. Landon, Asher's parents. Asher, however, was conspicuously absent in spite of the fact he had accepted Aunt Dolly's invitation.

Rebekah stood beside her aunt and greeted the arriving townspeople for two more hours and wondered why she had ever agreed to a party. She had smiled for so long that her mouth actually hurt. And her feet. She should have worn her sensible day shoes. But they would not have complemented her new periwinkle blue gown, so she had sacrificed comfort for appearance. But what good would her sacrifice do if she were crippled from wearing the high-heeled brocade shoes dyed to match her dress?

"You're the most beautiful girl in the whole of Nashville." Asher's voice pulled her from her thoughts.

Her heart fluttered when she looked up and saw his face. He was the man she would always love. "Asher." Her heart raced so that she barely forced the word out.

He bowed over her hand and straightened. "I've missed you so much. It's hard not getting to see you every day. I almost wish we were back on the Natchez Road so I could talk to you all day long."

She studied his face. Was it her imagination, or did Asher look tired this evening? There were dark circles under his eyes and lines on either side of his mouth. It made her want to draw his head down and stroke his hair until he was rested.

"I would like to see you alone before the evening is over, Rebekah. There's something very exciting I want to tell you about."

She searched his face for a hint of what he meant. Had he been out to the farm as he'd promised? Was all of her soul-searching for naught? And if he had secured her parents' blessing, was that enough proof that he truly loved her and only her?

But what if she was jumping to conclusions again? Wasn't this exactly what Asher had said to her the day he'd announced he was going to war? That he had "something" to tell her? Why should she assume that his idea of good news would match hers? It certainly had not all those months ago. Besides, she had already made her decision, hadn't she?

"Just a moment." Rebekah turned to her aunt and hesitated. She was very aware of Asher watching her, so she chose her words with care. "Would it be permissible if I step away for a few minutes?"

"Go on, Rebekah." Aunt Dolly took Rebekah's hand and placed it on Asher's arm. "I'll stay here and greet any late guests. You two can stand right down there at the door to the parlor. That way you can have some privacy and still satisfy propriety."

Rebekah allowed Asher to draw her away from the entry hall. "What do you have to tell me?"

"It's the best of good fortune! Pa has been trying to coerce me into taking a job at the bank, but I cannot see myself working in a dingy office for the rest of my life. Now that the war is over, Colonel Lewis has secured me a position working directly for General Jackson. His popularity has only continued to grow since the victory in New Orleans. I believe he's a man destined for great things, and as a key member of his staff, I will have the chance to be part of them."

She looked at the crisp coat of his uniform. No words would form in her mind.

"Don't you understand what this means? I'll soon be making enough money to buy us a home. We'll finally be able to make our dreams come true."

Rebekah could not bear to hear any more excuses from him. "I'm going home."

"What! What do you mean?"

"Pastor and Mrs. Miller are going out to the country to visit, and I'm going with them." She looked at the wall behind his shoulder. "I may not come back."

"What are you talking about?"

Rebekah wanted to pour out her heart to him, but she could not. He was not the same man who had once shared her dreams and helped her solve her problems. He had become a stranger. She closed her eyes for a moment and sent a prayer heavenward for the right words. "I think we need some time apart."

Asher shook his head slowly. "Haven't we had enough time apart?"

"I. . .Asher, I don't know what to say or think. You seem reluctant to speak to—"

"I'm not reluctant. I've been busy. A lot has happened since we got back from New Orleans."

Rebekah sighed. She was so tired of hearing his empty excuses.

"What do you want me to do?" His brows drew together. "Do you want me to resign from the militia and take a job in the bank like my pa?"

"I don't care what profession you choose."

His frown eased a little. "I'm glad to hear that. Please be patient, Rebekah. Soon you'll have the whole city at your feet."

He still didn't understand her. A tear escaped from the corner of her eye. "I don't want the whole city."

"Exactly what do you want then?"

She looked at him, longing to touch him. "I want a man who is eager to marry me, not one who feels trapped by a promise he made when he was an idealistic youngster."

He put his hands on her shoulders. "Rebekah, don't be preposterous."

She twisted away and moved back into the hall, her heart breaking as his words and tone showed how little he valued her feelings. Didn't he realize how long she had agonized over this? "It may be preposterous to you, but you asked what I want, and I have told you."

"I should have known this would happen." Asher's mouth became a straight slash and his eyes hardened. "You are becoming quite adept at manipulating people."

Rebekah's head jerked as if he had slapped her. She doubted she could have been hurt more by a physical blow. "I think you should go now, Captain Landon."

"If that's what you *want*."

His emphasis on the word made her cringe, but she didn't try to defend herself.

Asher pulled a pair of snowy white gloves from the belt of his uniform and jammed his fingers into them. "Don't think this scheme of yours has me fooled. I love you, Rebekah, and I want to marry you. But I have too much respect for you to rush into a marriage when I don't know if I can support you."

He left her standing at the parlor door, her heart lying in pieces around her fancy shoes. She lifted a hand as if to stop him but let it fall to her side. What more could she say?

❧

Asher stalked away from Rebekah, wondering if he shouldn't leave Mrs. Quinn's home right away. But his parents would be disappointed if he did not make at least a brief appearance. A pang of remorse pierced his anger as he thought of the scene with his pa earlier. He needed to put the argument with Rebekah aside for right now.

Pa had taken the news of his decision to work with Colonel Lewis hard. Asher did not like hurting his pa, but this was *his* life, and he had to make his own way to success. Everything he'd dreamed of was within his grasp. Well, almost everything.

Asher stopped for a moment and concentrated on taking deep breaths. He would not allow Rebekah's immaturity to spoil his evening. When had she become so. . .he searched for the right word. . .so *backward*? Why had she set her heart on living way out in the wilderness? He might understand her feelings if she had not been living in Nashville for more than a year. But she had experienced the luxuries of town life. It made no sense to shun progress.

She must know how much he liked the hustle and bustle of city life. Years ago, he and his family had left behind the dull and thankless world of farming. He was no longer the type to break his back to provide the bare necessities for his wife and children. There were so many more opportunities here for a man to make his mark on the world. Why couldn't Rebekah see that?

He pulled his gloves off and tucked them into his belt. Nobody was going to stop him from succeeding.

He stepped into the ballroom and looked around. The orchestra was playing, and several couples were swaying in the center of the room while other guests lined the walls, spreading the latest gossip and showing off their fancy clothes.

He spotted Alexandra across the room. Her warm smile was like a balm to his lacerated heart. He eased his way through the crowd. Why couldn't Rebekah be more like her, pleasant and welcoming? Alexandra didn't seem to think he was deficient in some ridiculous way. She accepted him for the man he was.

"Bonju, Captain." She pulled out her fan and fluttered it in front of her face. "Congratulations! Papa told me of your new position."

Asher bowed. "I am flattered to be selected."

"You need not feel flattered, Captain. Papa is lucky to be able to rely on your strength and intelligence. The general keeps him so busy he barely has time to eat a meal with his family."

A hand fell on his shoulder, and Asher turned to see Colonel Lewis. "Sir, we were just talking about you."

The man looked from Asher to his daughter, his bushy eyebrows climbing toward his hairline. "In my day, there were other topics more interesting for a young couple to discuss than work and parents."

Alexandra's cheeks brightened to the hue of a summer sunrise. "Papa!"

Even though the colonel had made several comments during their journey from New Orleans about a suitable match for his daughter, Asher had always brushed aside his rather clumsy hints.

But tonight was different. Tonight he was seeing things with greater clarity. "Don't be embarrassed," he told Alexandra. "If I had as pretty a daughter as you, I would be equally surprised."

She tapped his arm with the end of her fan. "You are quite a smooth talker, sir."

"It is nothing but the truth, Miss Lewis." He bowed slightly. "May I have this dance?"

"That's more like it." Colonel Lewis beamed at them. "Don't let one of these other Nashville beaus turn her head. I happen to know that Alexandra thinks you are quite the dashing war hero."

Asher drew her onto the dance floor before the colonel could embarrass them further.

She curtsied, her gaze on the floor.

Asher took her hand as they followed the dance steps. "Don't worry. Parents have a decided talent when it comes to discomfiting their children." He nodded his head toward his own parents who were watching them circle the dance floor. "They are probably talking about us right now."

She glanced toward them and then at him. "What do you think they're saying?"

"What else but that I am the luckiest man here to have such a beautiful young lady as my dance partner?"

Alexandra's smile rewarded him. "Thank you for your sweet compliments. Since we arrived in Nashville, not everyone has been so welcoming."

Now this was more like it. More like what he had expected the evening to hold. Pleasant company and gentle flirting rather than accusations and manipulative ultimatums. "The young ladies are probably jealous to have such a sophisticated newcomer competing for the attention of our local men."

Her hand squeezed his. "Me...sophisticated? But I was raised on a plantation. Surely the ladies here have the advantage since they have grown up in the center of Nashville. I am very much the outsider."

Asher looked to the doorway in time to see Rebekah entering. Good. Let her see exactly how much it would affect him if she left Nashville. He returned his attention to his dance partner. "But you have something none of them have."

"What is that?"

"You have an air of mystery and intrigue. None of the local gents knew you before you attained the full flower of your beauty." He nodded at a tall, graceful blond dancing a few yards away. "You would never think it to look at her tonight, but I remember when Dorcas Montgomery was as thin as a sapling and more clumsy than a newborn colt."

Alexandra was so easy to talk to, and he had only to look at her expression to realize that she did seem to admire him. He ignored the whispery voice of his conscience. Alexandra was only being friendly, and there was nothing wrong with letting her kindness soothe his bruised heart.

Chapter 12

Watch out for that rut." Una Miller, perched next to her husband, pointed toward the road. "I'm sure Rebekah is tired of being bounced around."

If she had not been taught better, Rebekah would have voiced her agreement. She was beginning to wish Pastor Miller was driving Pa's wagon. It was a bit disturbing to be pitched about when they were sitting so high above the ground. But at least she was going home.

Away from Asher. Away from heartache.

Yet when she considered a future without him, Rebekah wondered if there would ever be joy in her life again. She only knew she could not stand to watch him dance and flirt with Alexandra.

Anxious to drive the uncomfortable pictures from her mind, she leaned forward. "Thank you so much for letting me come with you."

Pastor Miller's hands slackened on the reins as he glanced back at her, causing the buggy to increase its speed. "You've already thanked us three times."

"We've been planning this visit for weeks," his wife added. "Having your company only adds to our pleasure."

Rebekah's stomach clenched as the landscape rushed past them. Would it be rude to ask Pastor Miller to slow down a bit? Although she was anxious to reach her parents' home, she had no wish to risk life and limb in the process. She leaned back to escape the dizzying sensation, but it was no use. Even closing her eyes did no good.

"I promise Roman is a very competent driver."

Her eyelids flew open and a blush heated Rebekah's cheeks. "I'm sure he is. It's a bit disconcerting though. We must be covering more than a mile every ten minutes."

When the pastor looked back over his shoulder once again, she wanted to beg him to keep his attention fixed on the road. Perhaps she should ask the couple about something that had been bothering her for a while. "Will there be Indians in heaven?"

Pastor Miller's hands jerked convulsively on the reins, slowing the buggy considerably. "Of course there will be."

Mrs. Miller turned in her seat, and Rebekah saw a hint of tears in her eyes.

"We are concerned all the time about those who have had no chance to ask Jesus into their hearts. It's our hope and prayer that all men will soon heed the words of our Lord and choose everlasting life."

Rebekah leaned forward again. "What about those people who don't believe the Indians can be forgiven?"

This time, Pastor Miller answered her question. "We are all people in the eyes of God, and we have all sinned and need a Savior. Including me. Whether it's killing or stealing or even telling a lie about someone."

"I know, Pastor. 'For all have sinned, and come short of the glory of God.'"

"That's right." Mrs. Miller's pink bonnet moved up and down as she nodded. "But don't forget the next verse in Romans: 'Being justified freely by his grace through the redemption that is in Christ Jesus.' The Bible promises that anyone, not just this group or that one, can be saved."

"How will the Indians get to know about Jesus?" Rebekah's fear of the buggy ride began to subside. "Pa and Ma always read to us from the Bible when I was growing up. And we'd get to hear sermons from traveling preachers who stayed over and preached in the little church Pa and some of the other men built. But who preaches to the Indians?"

"That's exactly why we want to start a school," Mrs. Miller answered. "We feel the Lord wants us to share His message with them."

Rebekah played with the strings of her bonnet. "Remember when Aunt Dolly told you about the Indians who stopped us on the Natchez Road?"

She waited for them to nod before continuing. "There was one Indian, a boy really, who made me stop and wonder about what future he had."

Pastor Miller tossed a smile at her over his shoulder. "There's no telling what ramifications your decision to share your food may have had. A light shower falls and, when joined by other rains, becomes a flood that carries everything before it."

Rebekah felt another stirring of the excitement that had gripped her the day they met the Indians. A whisper echoed through her mind. Was it a sign? Was she meant to do something about teaching the Indians? But what did she know about such things?

A movement caught her attention, and Rebekah shaded her eyes, straining to see who it was. Had their conversation brought Indians down on them? The harder she looked, however, the more familiar the figure seemed. She watched him raise an arm up and swing down on what looked like a fence post. His head raised, and she recognized him. "Pa! It's Pa! Please stop!"

Pastor Miller pulled up on the reins, and Rebekah scrambled past the Millers, heedless of the great height that had terrified her earlier. She was home!

"Pa!" she yelled as loudly as she could and had the satisfaction of seeing the man's head turn toward her. She barely noticed the second figure, who'd been hidden until her pa turned. All she could really see was Pa's familiar face. She ran across the wide field and was caught up in his arms and swung around like a girl of four instead of the young lady she was supposed to be.

"My Becka." He hugged her as tight as a corset bone and kissed her on the cheek before setting her back on her feet. "Aren't you a sight!"

His smile was as warm as summer sunshine. It melted the lump she'd been carrying in her chest since the argument with Asher. She was home, and everything was going to be all right.

"I want you to meet someone very special, Becka." He turned to the man who had been helping him mend fence posts. This is our new neighbor, Wohali. He owns the land we're standing on."

Her eyes widened as Rebekah took in the stranger's long, black hair, dark eyes, and swarthy skin. An Indian! This must be the man the Millers had come to meet. But why was Pa working with him? If the ground had opened up underneath her feet, she could not have been more surprised. No matter what else changed in her life, she'd clung to the belief that everything at home would remain the same. How unsettling to find even bigger changes here than in Nashville. "How do you do?"

The tall man nodded his head. "I am pleased to meet you."

Would wonders never cease? Not only was the Indian a landowner, his grammar and diction were impeccable. She realized her mouth had dropped open, and she shut it with an audible *pop*.

"Now it's your turn." Her pa nodded toward the Millers, who were waiting in their buggy.

Rebekah, Wohali, and Pa made their way across the field toward the road, and she performed the introductions.

"Why don't you go on up to the house with the Millers? Wohali and I will be there in a few minutes. I don't want to waste a minute of your visit." Pa turned to the pastor. "I hope you can stay overnight with us so we'll have more time to hear all about Rebekah's adventures before she returns to Nashville."

"I'm not going back, Pa." The lump returned, larger than before. She turned away to hide the tears that had sprung to her eyes.

"I see." He squeezed her shoulder gently. "We'll talk about it at home. Your ma and your siblings are going to be thrilled to see you."

Rebekah blinked her eyes rapidly to force the tears back. She did not know if she could talk about her feelings. Better to remain silent and stoic. She concentrated on climbing safely into the buggy as her vision blurred.

❧

"Hurry up, Rebekah. We're going to be late for church." Eleanor was practically jumping up and down in her impatience.

"What do you mean? There's plenty of time to get to the church before the service begins."

Ma unpinned her apron and folded it neatly before placing it on the kitchen shelf. "Your sister is right, Rebekah."

"What? We've never left for church this early."

Ma sighed. "Eleanor, go get your brother. Rebekah, sit down. There are a few things we need to discuss."

When Eleanor left the cabin, Rebekah looked toward her ma with some apprehension. Was this yet another change? Since coming home last week, she had discovered many things were different than she remembered. Of course, she expected Eleanor and Donny to be more grown up, but so much else had changed. Ma looked older, her brown hair liberally streaked with gray. And Pa, who once prided himself on his independence, was working with Wohali nearly every day.

Even the crops had changed. Pa still planted corn, but he also had several acres of wheat. Here at home, he and Ma had added an extra bedroom so she and Eleanor would no longer have to sleep in the loft. Although she knew the changes were indications of progress and prosperity, Rebekah would have much preferred that everything stay the same.

"There have been some who are not happy about Wohali and his family moving into our community."

Rebekah nodded. She did not personally mind having Indians for neighbors, but her imagination boggled at the idea of Wohali's wife joining a quilting bee or exchanging recipes with the ladies in the area.

"Your pa and I have prayed about the tense situation since they moved here, and we believe we received an answer when Wohali asked whether or not he and Noya—that's his wife, who has become a dear friend—could attend our church. We decided we would help them get established by escorting them for the first few Sundays."

"Why didn't he go to the preacher?"

Ma smiled and patted her hand. "We've grown fairly close to Wohali and Noya. I guess they feel more comfortable talking to your pa than some stranger down the road."

Someone, probably Pa, had brought in a handful of wildflowers and laid them on a cloth in the center of the table. Rebekah picked one up and twirled it between her fingers. "How did they come to buy their place?"

"Wohali was educated by a missionary who came to share the gospel with his tribe. He's a Christian and very eager to be a part of our community. It took a long time, but he and his wife managed to save enough money to buy some land."

"They left their tribe?"

Ma placed a calming hand over Rebekah's fingers to keep her from destroying the delicate wildflower. "I'm sure it was a difficult choice, but Noya told me they prayed for guidance and were led to move away."

The front door swung inward, and Pa stepped inside. "Are my girls ready to get going?"

"I'll just be a minute." Rebekah hurried into the bedroom and rummaged through her bags to find her hairpins before twisting her braid into a knot and quickly pinning it into place. What an amazing story. She was glad God didn't expect her to leave her home. . .or did He?

Her hands fell to her sides as a sudden question struck her. All the times she and Asher had planned for their future, it had never occurred to her to pray for God's guidance. She had prayed for an answer before she broke things off with him last week. But had she prayed for His will, or had she only prayed for her own plans to be fulfilled?

❧

Asher wiped his hands against his dress trousers and watched for the Taylors to arrive in their buckboard. He greeted his former neighbors, many of whom wanted to hear of his exploits with the Tennessee militia. He was well into describing General Jackson's canny strategies when he realized that none of the men were paying him any attention. They had all turned to look at the latest arrivals.

Asher turned to see what had caused the commotion, and his eyes nearly jumped from his head. Rebekah and her family were pulling up to the church—with a couple of Indians on their buckboard.

One of the men who had been standing in front of Asher grabbed his wife and escorted her back to their wagon. Another was pulled away by his wife and into the church. A third man spat at the ground and rubbed a suggestive thumb on his holster.

Asher wondered what he should do. Ignore the Taylors? But that was why he had made the trip out here. He wanted to patch things up between him and Rebekah. Now that a few days had passed, surely she had begun to see reason.

He stepped forward. "Mr. and Mrs. Taylor. It's nice to see you this fine Sabbath day."

"Hello, Asher." The older man did not smile, and Asher wondered if Rebekah had mentioned their argument.

Mrs. Taylor, however, smiled broadly at him and put her hand on his arm. "What a lovely surprise. Rebekah did not tell us you might visit today. I hope you will stay for dinner. We are having our new neighbors over, also."

Asher assumed a pleasant expression as she introduced Wohali and Noya.

The man's posture reminded him of a large cat, sleek and dangerous, a formidable adversary. He inclined his head in a slight nod. "How did you come to meet the Taylors?"

"They are our neighbors." The dark-skinned man nodded at Mr. Taylor. "We work well together. What one man cannot accomplish, two often can."

Asher could not argue that logic. "I'm sure Mr. Taylor and his family are happy to have you living so close by."

Wohali described the work he and Rebekah's pa had accomplished over the past season. Asher was impressed. Not only was the Indian articulate, but he was also obviously a hard worker and interested in making a comfortable home for his family. Just like Asher wanted to do. With Rebekah. For a moment he felt the pull to move back out here and farm. But what was he thinking? He was much better suited to work in Nashville.

He followed the Taylors into the little church, his mind in a whirl. It was hard to pay attention to the pastor's sermon about Jesus' warning to store treasures in heaven.

The church felt warm, and Asher found himself sliding down in the pew. He cleared his throat and pulled himself upright. It would not do for these people to see him sleeping in a public place, especially in a church. He was going to have to learn better discipline if he was going to keep his position with General Jackson.

He tried to catch Rebekah's attention, but she was totally engrossed in the sermon, following along in her Bible and nodding as the pastor described the pitfalls of focusing on wealth and position. Asher didn't see why good Christians couldn't have those things. The Bible didn't say that one had to be poor and miserable to make it into heaven.

Finally, the service ended. Everyone stood and sang an invitational hymn.

Asher half expected the Indian couple to approach the pulpit, but they didn't. In fact, the whole morning seemed to have been wasted.

Somehow he ended up escorting Eleanor out to the front of the church instead of Rebekah. She let go of his arm the minute they stepped outside, dashing off to say hello to some of the other young people from the area.

He looked around and caught sight of Rebekah standing near her pa's wagon. He hurried over and offered her a hand, relieved when she accepted it. "It's good to see you looking so well, Rebekah. I don't have much time—I have to be back in Nashville this afternoon for a meeting—but I wanted to tell you that I'm sorry about our. . .discussion. . .the other night." He also wanted to tell her how much he missed her, but they only had a few seconds before the older adults would reach the wagon. "Please forgive me."

"Of course I forgive you, Asher." She said the words he wanted to hear, but Asher could see from her expression that something was still wrong. He wanted to say something more, but there wasn't enough time. Her parents had nearly reached the wagon.

He made his excuses to the Taylors and climbed back on his horse, wondering if he had accomplished anything by coming all this way.

❧

Rebekah ignored the teasing of her younger sister on the way home. Eleanor simply didn't understand the situation. She was full of romantic notions, exactly as Rebekah had been at her age.

Whether she should marry Asher was a matter of faith, not romance. If she and Asher were going to repair their relationship, they would have to spend more than a few seconds talking about their problems. She could not withhold forgiveness—the Lord's Prayer said Christians should forgive others if they wanted to be forgiven for their own transgressions. But forgiveness was one thing. Deciding what to do about marriage was another thing entirely.

Rebekah could tell that Asher had not changed much, if at all, since she'd come home. He apparently thought that an apology was sufficient to bridge the distance between them. She knew better.

Somehow she felt older than Asher now, more mature. While he was still chasing ephemeral dreams of wealth and fame, she had come to realize what was important in life. A sigh filled her, and Rebekah's heart ached for Asher to return to the Lord. All she could do was continue to pray that he would allow God to change his heart.

They dropped Wohali and Noya off at their home and continued to the cabin.

"You seem awfully quiet for a beautiful Sunday morning." Ma patted her knee. "Did you and Asher have time to talk?"

Rebekah shook her head.

Pa pulled up to let everyone off at the front door to the cabin. "Perhaps we can remedy that. Wohali mentioned that he and Noya need to get some things in Nashville, and I was thinking of going along with him. You can join us, Rebekah. I'm sure Noya would appreciate some feminine company."

"But shouldn't we all go?" Rebekah asked.

Ma laughed. "Didn't you notice how crowded it was with all of us in the wagon? I think I can wait until another time. And I have the feeling you need to work out some problems." She put an arm around Rebekah and squeezed her tightly. "Hiding out here with your family is no way to resolve whatever it is that stands between you and Asher."

While Rebekah agreed with her mother, she wasn't sure if anything could bridge the widening rift between her and the man she had once shared future dreams with.

Chapter 13

Asher hated the waiting that seemed to go along with his new position as special liaison for Colonel Lewis. For nearly two weeks, he'd been expecting a directive from General Jackson. He'd been thrilled to finally receive a note from Colonel Lewis instructing him to attend a meeting in his home.

He pulled out his watch and glanced at it. He'd been alone in the colonel's study for nearly an hour. What could be keeping the man? His bored gaze again traveled around the handsomely appointed room. The luxurious furnishings testified to the importance of the Lewis family—deeply padded leather armchairs, a huge mahogany desk, and heavy drapes the color of a dark forest. One wall was lined with floor-to-ceiling shelves, partially filled with leather-clad books.

He'd spent at least fifteen minutes looking at the pristine volumes. The colonel took great care when he was perusing his books, just as he did with everything he was involved with—obviously one of the many reasons he had all the right connections.

A clock in the hallway chimed two more quarter hours. Asher was beginning to wonder if his host would ever appear when the door finally opened.

The colonel trundled across the room and gave him a perfunctory handshake. "Sorry to keep you waiting."

"I was wondering if I had the wrong time. . . ."

"Oh, no, no. I was up late last night escorting my ladies to the Purnell ball. They have to go to all of the parties, you know."

Asher noticed the man did look tired. His coat was creased and dusty. His mustache, usually waxed and shaped into an upward curve, had drooped until it brushed his chin.

"And then it was up early again for an emergency meeting with General Jackson," the colonel continued. "I barely had time to get a note to you before I had to go right back out for yet another conference—this time with the local politicos. These Indians. . .I don't know what the general's going to do about them. I've been encouraging him to go forth with his removal plans even if those idiots in Washington haven't given him their blessing. What are they going to do to the Hero of New Orleans?"

Asher didn't know how he felt about the issue of Indian removal. While it seemed heartless to force them to leave their homes, it was equally obvious the quarrelsome Indians would never peacefully accept the land-hungry white settlers who arrived every week. However, he knew what response the colonel expected to hear. "Probably give him another medal when they realize he's single-handedly solved all of their problems."

The colonel slapped his back. "Exactly. Have a seat, boy." He walked to the far side of the polished mahogany desk in the center of the study.

Asher hesitated for a moment before taking one of the armchairs in front of the desk.

"I invited you here to ask for your help with a rather—"

The door swung open with a loud *thump*, and Alexandra hurried inside, her attention on the wall of books to Asher's right.

Asher jumped up and bowed to her. "Good afternoon, Miss Lewis."

"Captain Landon, what a pleasure." An eager smile lit her face.

Her father rose more slowly. "I'm holding an important meeting."

"Excuse me, Papa. I didn't realize you and Captain Landon were here."

Her smile should not have suggested duplicity, but Asher wondered if she was as unaware of his presence as she claimed. He could not help being a little flattered that she would risk her father's censure for a chance to see him. If only Rebekah was as anxious to spend time with him.

"I am so sorry to disturb you. I promised Mama that I would find the collection of William Shakespeare's sonnets."

Asher stepped toward her. "Perhaps I can help you find the volume you need."

Colonel Lewis sighed. "I guess we can postpone our meeting for a while, daughter. After the amount of time I've had this young man waiting, I imagine he could use some refreshment"—he winked at Asher—"and some refreshing company, too, eh?"

While Asher and Alexandra looked for the elusive volume, the colonel rang for refreshments. After a few minutes, a tall, slender slave brought in a silver tea service and quietly disappeared.

Alexandra took the seat next to Asher's and poured for the gentlemen, prattling on about how different things were out in the frontier than what she had seen in New Orleans. As she talked, she waved a lacy fan in front of her face. It was warm enough that Asher wished she would waft a breeze in his direction.

A noise from the far side of the desk turned his attention to the colonel.

After lowering his hand from attempting to cover his yawn, Colonel Lewis apologized. "Please forgive me. I guess the long working hours are catching up with me."

Alexandra put the tip of her fan against her bottom lip. "Staying out so late hasn't helped either, Papa. I woke up sometime during the night as I was a bit warm. I got up to open my window and saw you riding up—"

"Well, Captain Landon doesn't want to hear unimportant details about work. I guess I should just go upstairs and take a nap. Asher, could we finish our business at another time?"

"No problem, sir." Asher put his napkin on the tea tray and stood. "I shall take my leave."

"Please don't." Alexandra put a hand on his arm. "We can go down to the parlor. There's something I need to ask you about."

Asher raised an eyebrow. "Wouldn't it be more seemly to remain here?"

"Don't be ridiculous." She slid her hand under his elbow and pulled him into the hall. "No one will think a thing of it. You're like the big brother I always wanted. I truly value your opinion."

Asher allowed her to pull him to the parlor but stopped her from closing the door. It would be disastrous for them to be found closeted alone. Both their reputations would be in shambles.

"I saw Rebekah in Nashville yesterday."

Her words wiped out other considerations. If Rebekah was back in Nashville, it could only mean one thing—she was over their tiff. "I thought she would be back soon."

Alexandra's eyes narrowed. "And did you know she was in the company of an Indian couple?"

Surprise stiffened his back. But then the explanation dawned on him. They must be her Indian neighbors. Probably her whole family had come to Nashville, and she had agreed to escort the couple around since she would be the most familiar with Nashville. What a thoughtful deed. But he would have to remember to tell her to be careful. Not everyone would be so generous toward Indians, regardless of their aspirations.

"I didn't know what to say. Mama and Papa do not like the uppity ways of some of the local Cherokees. They say that by befriending them we are only asking for trouble. The Indians are wild heathens with no idea in their heads but to stop us in any way they can."

Asher had to agree with that sentiment. The Indians he'd seen while serving under General Jackson had been bloodthirsty and dangerous. Of course, the same could be said of some of the soldiers. But the couple he'd met a few days ago at the Taylors' farm had seemed different. They had been well-spoken and appeared to be hardworking individuals who wanted to be regular American citizens.

"I'm worried about Rebekah, Asher. She is so naive and trusting. She hasn't had the same advantages to help her properly judge people. But you and I both know the Indians would like nothing better than to wipe out all traces of white settlements. Trying to force people here to accept the Indians will make her many enemies."

Asher looked down into her earnest face. It was sweet of Alexandra to be concerned about Rebekah's welfare, but she had misinterpreted the situation. This was not New Orleans. He often saw Indian families doing business with local merchants. "I hardly think taking a stroll with her neighbors would have such disastrous consequences."

"I'm worried about you, too, Asher. Papa says you have a brilliant career ahead of you, but your association with Rebekah could bring everything crashing down."

Now she was being downright foolish. Women had such a tendency to overdramatize. "I think you are making much ado over a very minor incident and drawing conclusions when you do not understand all the circumstances."

Alexandra turned her back to him and stared out of the window. "Please don't be angry with me. I have only your best interests at heart."

When Asher realized that her shoulders were hunched forward, he felt like a villain. She was as young and as easily misled as Rebekah, but her heart was in the right place. "Don't worry, Alexandra. I'm not angry. But I do think you're assigning too much import to one instance."

"I pray you're right." Alexandra turned back toward him, her eyes large with unshed tears. "I only want to see you succeed."

As Alexandra looked up at him with such sincerity, Asher couldn't keep from wondering if Rebekah wanted success for him as well. Maybe it was time he found out.

༄

Fearing that his frown was tensing the muscles between his eyebrows, Asher consciously forced a smile on his face as he looked around at the small group in Dolly Quinn's parlor.

Rebekah perched on the edge of the settee, one foot tapping a staccato rhythm beneath the folds of her skirt. Mrs. Quinn looked much more relaxed on the other end of the settee, sipping tea and nibbling at a strawberry scone. Rebekah's father stood with his back to the fireplace as he described yesterday's visit to the local smithy with his Indian friend, Wohali.

Asher nodded and tried to focus his attention on what the man was saying, but all he wanted to do was draw Rebekah away and talk to her. He had to be sure she had really forgiven him, even though he still wasn't certain what he had done. He wanted to have the right to pull her into his arms and tell her how much he loved her.

Asher kept his smile relaxed. It wouldn't do to let Rebekah know how hard his heart pounded. Was she ready to resume their plans for a future together? He could not bear the thought of her falling in love with someone else. She *had* to be reasonable and agree to remain in the city, where he could earn enough to support her.

Mr. Taylor ended his story, and silence filled the room. Asher turned his attention once again to the girl he loved. "Rebekah, I hope you will dance with me at the Davis ball on Friday."

Her cheeks flushed, causing him to wonder if she was embarrassed by his statement or pleased at his attention.

"I'm sorry, but I doubt we'll still be here."

"Nonsense." Rebekah's aunt frowned and put down her teacup. "Your father knows how much I need you here. If you leave so soon, I will have to conclude that you no longer care for my company."

Rebekah's cheeks grew even redder, and Asher wished he had never opened his mouth. He had to rescue her. His mind searched frantically for a new topic. Something that would bring a smile to her face. "Have you heard that General Jackson has been given command of the southern division of the United States Army?"

Rebekah shook her head.

Excitement and pride filled Asher. "He's finally getting the recognition he deserves. He's a great man."

A commotion at the front door interrupted the conversation. Asher was surprised when Pastor Miller came rushing into the parlor.

"You have to leave. Quick!"

"Whatever is the matter, Pastor?" Mrs. Quinn asked. "Is something wrong?"

Asher had not been around the pastor much, but he recognized the man's perturbation in the way he glanced over his shoulder and wrung his hands together. He didn't even have the presence of mind to remove his hat.

The pastor shook his head and took a hurried breath. "There's been another Indian raid! Last night! They stole cattle and horses from the Marshall farm and burned down their cabin. No one can find the family. They're presumed dead."

His announcement was greeted with a small cry from Rebekah's aunt, who fell back against the settee. Rebekah grabbed a small brown bottle sitting on a table next to the settee and uncorked it. She sprinkled a few drops of pungent oil on her handkerchief and waved it below her aunt's nose.

As soon as Mrs. Quinn appeared to be recovering, the pastor continued. "I'm sorry for barging in with such distressing news, but I fear you are all in danger if we do not take quick action."

Asher turned his attention to the older man. "Why would Mrs. Quinn or her family be in any danger?"

"The townspeople seem to believe that Mr. Taylor's neighbor may have been involved." Pastor Miller finally remembered to remove his hat.

"But why would they think that?" Rebekah asked. "Wohali and Noya had nothing to do with any raid. They've been right here with us."

Asher left the other two men and came to where she sat with Aunt Dolly. "A mob won't be logical. They will want to hang any Indians they find."

The pastor nodded his agreement. "They're looking for scapegoats to bear the guilt for all the Indians."

Mr. Taylor stood and beckoned to the women. "I guess we should load up the wagon. We can hide both of them in the bed like we did when I first brought Rebekah here."

Asher pictured them meandering through Nashville on the lumbering wagon. "Do you think you can get away safely in a wagon?"

Pastor Miller crushed the brim of his hat with nervous fingers. "I think it would be better to take my buggy. It's much faster and has a fresh horse hitched to it. Five passengers will be a squeeze, but comfort is not our biggest concern."

"We can saddle a horse and tie it to the back of the buggy." Mr. Taylor looked out the front window while he considered the pastor's offer. "Then as soon as we get out of Nashville, Dolly or Rebekah can ride the horse."

Mrs. Quinn pushed herself into an upright position. "I'm not leaving my home."

Rebekah's father turned to her. "Don't be silly. A single woman is an easy target for an angry mob. We won't leave you to face them alone. You'll have to come with us."

Asher raised a hand to get Mr. Taylor's attention. "I'll stay behind and make sure no one hurts Mrs. Quinn or her home."

"I'll be here, too." Pastor Miller's mouth quirked upward. "After all, you'll be in my buggy."

"Thank you, Asher, Pastor." Mrs. Quinn nodded and sent a smile in his direction.

Asher straightened his shoulders. It was time to take charge. "We'll need to get that buggy out of here before there's real trouble. Mrs. Quinn, would you go and tell Wohali and his wife what's happened while Mr. Taylor and Pastor Miller get the buggy and the horses ready?" He hesitated a moment before turning to Rebekah. "Maybe you can show me where to find some extra blankets. We're likely to need something to help hide your passengers."

Rebekah's brown eyes had rounded, and he thought he could see a hint of admiration reflected in them. Good. It was time for her to understand that the boy she'd fallen in love with was a full-grown man, capable of dealing with any situation that arose. He followed her into the hallway, hoping to get a moment to tell her how much he still cared for her.

She opened a closet door and pulled at a tidy stack of wool blankets. "Will this be enough?"

As she turned to see his answer, Asher reached past her to help her hold the stack of blankets. Her forehead was barely an inch from his mouth. How he wanted to press a kiss against her soft skin—

A sound behind them jerked Asher's head up. He stepped back and turned to find Wohali and his wife standing at the foot of the stairs. Their faces were expressionless, but he could feel heat burning his cheeks.

Rebekah shoved the quilts toward him. "Wohali, Noya, I'm so glad you're here. Did Dolly tell you what's going on?"

Asher could see the confusion in Noya's eyes. "We had nothing to do with the Indians who attacked those poor farmers. Why are they trying to hurt us?"

He felt Rebekah's gaze on him. Did she think he could explain the situation? The suspicions on both sides were deep and unyielding. But what answer could he give? He shrugged his shoulders.

Wohali looked down at his wife. "They are angry and frightened people who would not listen to us. It is the same with those of our tribe who blame all white men for the evil behavior of a few."

"Rebekah!" Mr. Taylor called to them from the back stairs. "Hurry up. We have to leave now."

Asher shifted his pile of blankets to one arm and held the other out for Rebekah to take, relieved when she rested her hand lightly on his forearm. Maybe she didn't realize how close he'd come to embarrassing both of them.

He led the way to the back door and the alley where Pastor Miller's buggy awaited them. Mr. Taylor was already seated in front and held the reins. Asher assisted Rebekah into the buggy beside her father before helping Pastor Miller tuck several quilts around Wohali and Noya, who had climbed into the back among sacks of potatoes and flour. They were fairly well concealed from a cursory glance, but he didn't know if it would fool anyone who came looking for scapegoats.

Pastor Miller stood to one side of the buggy, his head bowed. Asher could see his lips moving. He wished he could conjure up the words to a prayer, but nothing came to mind, so instead he watched mutely as Mr. Taylor prodded the horses and the buggy careened around a corner.

As they disappeared from sight and Asher heaved a sigh of relief at their escaping in time, the full extent of what he had done struck him. What if

Rebekah's Indian neighbors had been involved in the massacre? Should he have encouraged Rebekah and her father to wait for the townspeople and turn Wohali over to them? He may have helped a murderer escape justice. If Colonel Lewis or General Jackson found out what he had done this afternoon, he would not be pleased.

But in the same instant, he acknowledged he would gladly risk a bit of their ire to have Rebekah look at him again with respect—and hopefully renewed love—in her eyes.

Chapter 14

Rebekah carried a heavy basket of wet clothing to the ropes Pa had rigged between two tulip poplars. The strong smell of Ma's lye soap made her nose wrinkle as she hung sheets and quilts to dry in the warm sunshine. She hummed as she wrung out a pillowcase and tossed it over the rope, enjoying the time alone.

She loved Eleanor, but her younger sister asked a lot of questions. What was it like in Nashville? Had she seen pirates in New Orleans? Was it fun to dance the night away in ballrooms? Was she going to marry Captain Landon? Ma had finally taken pity on Rebekah, sending her around to the side of the house to start drying the laundry while she and Eleanor finished the boiling and scrubbing.

The creak of a wagon turned Rebekah's attention from her task. She shaded her eyes, trying to make out who was coming to visit. She hoped it was not someone with more bad news. The trip from Nashville to Wohali's farm had been tense yesterday. She had been worried the whole time they would be attacked by either bloodthirsty Indian braves or enraged white settlers. It had been a relief to finally get home and stow Pastor Miller's buggy in the barn.

As the wagon drew nearer, she realized it was Pastor Miller returning her father's wagon. What a relief! He would be coming for his buggy and to report on what had happened yesterday after they escaped.

Rebekah picked up the last piece of wash and flung it over Pa's rope, making a note to herself to straighten it later. She then hurried to the front of the cabin, where the pastor was dismounting. "Welcome, Pastor Miller. What news do you bring?"

"Your aunt Dolly is fine. There were a few tense moments when the townspeople realized that all of you had left, but they dispersed after Captain Landon warned that their actions could put them in jail."

"That's wonderful news. So Asher. . .I mean Captain Landon. . .wasn't hurt either?" She could feel warmth in her cheeks at the mistake. It was one thing to refer to him by his given name when she was talking to her family—they all knew she and Asher had grown up together—but Pastor Miller might think she was being forward. He couldn't know that she and Asher had an agreement. Or at least they used to have an agreement. Maybe she should stop thinking of him as Asher. Their future together was no longer certain.

"The captain wasn't hurt." Pastor Miller smiled and put a hand on her shoulder. "He is a good man, Rebekah."

Rebekah realized the pastor might be able to help her with her confusion. "Yes, I think he is. But sometimes I worry about the other people in Nashville who seem to be influencing the way he thinks. He is always listening to that Colonel Lewis, and I don't know if he is a good example."

"I have seen the Lewis family in church upon occasion and have spoken with them. They seem to be nice folks who are close to General Jackson. Do you have some reason to worry about them?"

"Not exactly. Although they seem to support the removal of the Indians to the Western Territory." She looked up at him. "I don't like the idea of taking away their lands and homes."

"I applaud you for your sentiment, but I am afraid that there are many who would disagree with you. They point to events like the raid on the Marshall property to prove that we cannot allow the Indians to continue living among us."

"What do you believe, Pastor Miller?"

"I believe that we Christians have a duty to spread the gospel. God has given us a wonderful opportunity to show love and charity to a people who have never been exposed to His plan for salvation."

"I don't think Ash—Captain Landon would agree with you. He seems to be focused on advancing his career rather than his Christian duty."

"Why do you say that? He helped us get Wohali to safety, didn't he?"

Rebekah looked down at her apron. "Yes, but he often quotes Colonel Lewis and talks about the big fine house he wants to build. He won't listen to me when I tell him that a simple cabin will be sufficient."

"I think he is like most men." Pastor Miller rubbed his chin. "He wants to provide the best for the woman he loves."

"But what if that's not what I want?"

"Have you taken your worries to Jesus?"

Rebekah nodded. "I've prayed so hard that Asher would change back to the man he was before the war. Everything was easier then. He and I thought alike, and he listened to my hopes and dreams instead of telling me that I am being foolish or tenderhearted."

"Are you sure you thought exactly alike, Rebekah? Or did you misinterpret his dreams to make them match your own?"

She wanted to protest Pastor Miller's words. But what if he was right? Had she been mistaken about what Asher wanted? "I. . .I don't know." Her breath caught on a sob.

"You can never go back, but I believe you and Captain Landon can still have a future together if that's what God wants for you. Remember that you are God's beloved child. He wants the very best for you, and as long as you are willing to follow Him, you will find more blessings than you can imagine."

Rebekah wondered how this man could sound so sure of himself. He must have suffered disappointments and setbacks like anyone else. Yet faith flowed from him like a mighty current, sweeping all doubt away.

A small ray of hope broke through her confusion and worry. She would trust God to work it all out.

⇛

Asher followed Colonel Lewis into the two-story log building that was General and Mrs. Jackson's home. The general had named his farm Rural Retreat but now called it The Hermitage, which meant the same thing. Asher had expected something more ostentatious for such a wealthy and important person, but this house was nearly as plain as the home in which he'd been raised and quite rustic when compared to the houses in Nashville.

The black house slave led them past a dining room that held at least a dozen chairs around a long plank table. They followed her to the door of the parlor to find the Jacksons engaged in prosaic activities, their chairs bracketing a bright window. He was perusing the newspaper while she embroidered a colorful design on a snowy white cloth.

Asher noticed the parlor walls had been covered with decorative paper that he supposed was nice. A round rag rug divided the room into two main parts—one side for leisure activities, the other side for business. The business side held a slightly smaller version of the dining-room table. On it stood a pair of candelabra, a scattering of maps and papers, and several haphazard stacks of books. A wooden armchair was situated on the far side of the desk, and a couple of simple stools on the other side stood ready for planning strategies.

General Jackson stood when they entered. "Rachel, I believe you know Colonel Lewis and his companion—"

Rachel Jackson interrupted her husband with a raised hand. "There is no need for you to introduce the dashing Captain Landon. How pleasant to see you and Colonel Lewis. I trust our mutual acquaintance, Miss Rebekah Taylor, enjoys continued health."

Asher crossed the room and bowed over her hand. "She was in a bit of a hurry the last time I saw her, but I believe she is doing well."

"Yes, we heard about the commotion yesterday." Jackson frowned. "That's the main reason I invited you and the colonel over."

Rachel put away her needlework. "I believe I will take a short walk while you gentlemen have your discussion."

They waited until she left the parlor before taking their seats on either side of Jackson's desk. He pushed the candelabra and books to one corner and spread a map before them. "This is the location of an Indian village that may be hiding our culprits."

It took Asher a moment to get his bearings. The area outside Nashville was mostly wilderness, with small communities spread around it in an arc that followed the course of the Cumberland River. Jackson had his finger on a large longhouse shape that had been drawn at a curve in the river, indicating an Indian village. He moved his hand across an uninhabited area toward the land where Asher's parents had raised him. The hair on his neck stood on end when Asher realized the victims lived so close to the area in which he'd grown up. That meant they were very close to where Rebekah was right now.

"Everyone in Nashville is terrified, and the local authorities have asked for our help. You'll be working with the sheriff, but it will probably be up to you to find the culprits and bring them to justice."

Asher looked into Jackson's blazing eyes. "We'll find them, sir."

He held the older man's gaze for a minute or two before Jackson nodded. "Good. Colonel Lewis said you were a true patriot."

Asher looked toward Colonel Lewis, who was still studying the map. "The colonel is very kind, sir. I was privileged to escort him and his family along the Natchez Road."

"You look familiar. I know you were a Tennessee militiaman, but have you performed some other service?" asked General Jackson.

"Yes, sir. You assigned me to be the liaison for William Weatherford."

"Ah, yes. Chief Red Eagle. Now I remember you. Good job you did on that assignment." Jackson rolled up the map. "No wonder the colonel speaks so highly of you. I can always use a man who quietly attends the business of his country. This is a matter of gravest importance. There are not many men who can accomplish the task I've set for you."

Asher's face heated as though he'd been outside farming. "Thank you, sir."

Colonel Lewis twirled his mustache. "Something has to be done about these Indians, Andrew."

The general's intense gaze left Asher's face and turned to the colonel. "Something is being done. I have already begun the process of drawing up a treaty between the government of the United States and the Cherokee Nation. While I sympathize with their wishes to retain their heritage and culture, it cannot be tolerated within the bounds of United States territory. They will either pledge their allegiance to our country, or they will leave it."

Asher's heart thumped in his chest like a drum. He realized he did agree with every word. This was an exciting time, a time when American supremacy was unquestioned. They had bought the right to expand westward with both their assets and their lives. Failure to demand absolute compliance from the Indian peoples would be nothing less than treason. God had smiled down on them by giving them this fertile land, and Asher would do everything in his power to ensure that his countrymen were allowed to fulfill their destiny.

"When I was about your age, Captain, I came west with little but the sense God gave me and a determination to succeed no matter the cost. I have never bowed to tyranny. Nor do I believe that our government should be controlled by the rich to the detriment of all free men. It is my duty and yours to uphold the words of America's Constitution."

"Quite right," said Colonel Lewis.

"Haven't we bled for our country?" Jackson banged his fist on the table. "Why then should we sit back and allow shortsighted politicians in the East to dictate how and where we shall govern ourselves?"

Asher snapped a salute, his back ramrod straight. He was in the presence of greatness. General Jackson was a man of integrity and a force of will that would never bow down. He was lucky to be able to work for him and hoped he could measure up to the general's expectations.

Rachel Jackson came back into the parlor. "I could hear you thundering all the way outside, husband. I thought surely you were being attacked by one of your visitors."

The fire in the general's eyes softened to admiration when he looked at his wife. It reminded Asher of the way he felt whenever Rebekah walked into a room. But he was glad she was not with him today. She might not have appreciated the general's words. Not that she wasn't a patriot. She was just tenderhearted.

He remembered when they were barely more than children and she had discovered a mockingbird that had fallen out of its nest. She had convinced him to help her nurse the bird back to health. When he'd been certain the mockingbird could survive on its own, Asher had met her at their tulip poplar, and they had set the bird free. He had comforted her while she cried, not exactly understanding her emotional outburst. Then he had shared her joy when the mockingbird returned in a few weeks to build a nest in their tree.

Even though she was now a full-grown woman, Rebekah was as compassionate as ever. She would never understand the necessity of freeing the Indians by sending them to a place where they could safely follow their heathen nature. He rubbed his hand on the back of his neck to distract himself from the voice whispering that there were Indians, like those he'd met at Rebekah's church, who could not be labeled heathens. Should they be forced to leave their homes, too?

Asher tried to force the voice to be silent, but its echo remained uncomfortably fixed in his heart even as he knew he must go forward to maintain his sought-after position.

Chapter 15

The next morning, Asher was up with the sun and anxious to get to Colonel Lewis's home. He dressed with haste and hurried through breakfast with his family. He would have liked to discuss with his pa how to proceed in the investigation, but given Pa's attitude about his new job, he decided to say nothing.

The streets were relatively quiet this early in the morning, and he made his way to the Lewis home without incident. Half expecting that the colonel had gathered a posse of angry men, Asher was thankful to discover no one awaiting his arrival.

He took the steps two at a time and banged his fist on the front door. An elderly black woman answered and led him toward the colonel's office. As he followed behind her, he wondered if the colonel would keep him waiting for long this morning.

"Come in, Captain." The colonel's voice answered his unspoken question. "I'm glad you arrived so early. I have been brought some evidence that will make our job much easier."

Asher shook the older man's hand. "That sounds promising. What kind of evidence?"

The colonel walked to his desk and picked up a brass-accented wooden writing box. "I considered sending a message to you last night when this was brought forward, but I decided it would be better to wait since we could not act upon it until daylight anyway."

"Who brought it?"

"Apparently the Marshalls had a farmhand who lived above the stables and helped Mr. Marshall. As he knew I work for General Jackson, he came to me with this box."

Asher could hardly believe it. Someone had seen the raid? What wonderful luck. Now they would have descriptions of the culprits they were seeking. "How did he escape the attack?"

"He wasn't there. He'd been sent to Nashville for some provisions and decided to stay the night."

His explanation dashed Asher's hope for an eyewitness.

The colonel put the box in his hands and nodded at him to open it. Asher removed the wooden top and looked inside. His gaze registered the blood-stained Cherokee tomahawk while his imagination supplied the screams and pleas of the Marshall family before they died, as well as the coppery scent of their spilled blood.

"Where did he find this tomahawk?"

The colonel tapped his chin with one finger and looked toward the ceiling. "He went back the next morning to find the farmhouse and barns burned. He found the bodies of the Marshall family and decided to bury them. While he was working, he discovered the tomahawk lying on the ground near the place Mr. Marshall died. I can only surmise that it was dropped in the struggle."

Asher wanted to drop it right this minute. He had done his share of killing, but that had been his duty to his country, and it had been against men on the battlefield. He could not abide the images in his head of Mrs. Marshall and the children screaming in the night as they were mercilessly attacked by cold-blooded killers.

The colonel took the box from him. "There's one thing you may not have noticed."

Asher didn't want to have to look at the weapon again, but he steeled himself. "What's that?"

The older man reopened the box and withdrew the tomahawk. "This is a fine piece. Not made by an Indian."

Asher was confused. "Indians didn't raid the Marshall farm?"

"I didn't say that." The colonel threw a smug look his way. "See the carved handle and steel blade? This is no crude weapon. It was probably made right here in Nashville by a white man."

"Then how did it—"

"I'm not sure, but my carriage has been brought around while I showed you the weapon. We're going to visit the craftsman this morning and find out." The colonel closed the writing box and locked it with a key, which he then pocketed. "And that information will likely lead us directly to the murderer."

It took the two men the balance of the morning to discover the designer of the tomahawk. He was a woodcarver who had a shop on the north end of Nashville. When they pulled up, the owner was sitting on a crude bench in front of the shop, whittling a large piece of white oak.

"Good morning, gents." The man smiled at them, exposing dark teeth with several gaps. "What can I do for you?"

Colonel Lewis stepped out of the carriage, his writing box tucked under one arm. "We're here to ask you about a tomahawk."

The man stood and leaned his work against the bench. "Come on in then. I've got plenty to choose from."

Asher walked inside, his gaze swinging around the room. Hundreds of handles hung on pegs all around the shop—some were smooth, while others had intricate designs carved on them. There were painted handles, leather-covered handles, and handles decorated with beads and feathers. Asher was amazed at the variety of styles to choose from.

"Are you looking for something fancy?"

"Not exactly." Colonel Lewis turned the key in his writing box and withdrew the bloody tomahawk. "We need to know if you carved this one."

The owner turned as pale as fresh snowfall. "Yep, it's one of mine. See the eagle's head I carved into the handle here? I. . .I sold this very tomahawk to a tall Indian who come in here with his squaw last week. He said he done broke his tomahawk and wanted somethin' special."

A look of satisfaction briefly replaced the man's alarm. "He came to me because he heard I'm the best there is. And he picked out this here one." He nodded at the weapon. "Said he 'specially liked the eagle on it."

Asher could barely contain his excitement. It had taken time and perseverance—and a bit of good fortune—but they had traced the weapon back to its source. Now all they had to do was find the Indian who'd bought it. He mused over the woodcarver's words, wondering if he should ask about a bill of sale. There had to be a clue. And then he knew. Like someone lifting a curtain to let bright sunshine into a dark room, the answer exploded into his consciousness. The Cherokees had a special word for the eagle—*wohali*. The woodcarver had to be describing Rebekah's new neighbor—the man he had helped escape justice. What had he done? Would his actions make her the next victim?

❧

Rebekah's ma laughed as she watched Noya punch her needle through the layers of her quilt patch, the force of her action nearly catapulting her from her rocker. "That's better, but you have to remember it's not as tough as a tanned hide."

The Indian woman smiled at her, pushing herself back before she overbalanced. "I know, but it seems to fight my needle."

"That's exactly why we came over." Rebekah stitched as she spoke, her needle moving up and down through the material. She loved sewing, watching as something came into being under her fingers.

That was especially true of quilts. Each square represented a memory. Here was a square fashioned from an old dress of Ma's; there was one of Pa's wool vests. When they finished piecing all of the squares together, this quilt would tell a story about her family. And Noya's family as well, since several of the squares contained scraps donated from their old clothing.

Making the quilt had been Ma's idea. After the near disaster in Nashville earlier in the week, she had wanted to do something to show Wohali and Noya they were part of the community. And what better way than to work together on a project that both families had contributed to?

"You've made your home so charming." Ma squinted a little as she looked around the homey cabin. "I'm glad you bought it from Mrs. Winter's family after she passed away. She was a sweet lady, but we never seemed to have much in common. In the short time you've been here, we've already shared more recipes and stories than I ever did with Mrs. Winter."

Rebekah's gaze wandered around the small room. It was dominated by the kitchen area, complete with a wooden counter, a table with two benches, and a fireplace for cooking. In the far corner from the kitchen was the sleeping area. Someone had attached a raised sleeping platform to the wall and covered it with a colorful blanket. She wondered if Noya, who couldn't be five feet in height, had to use a stool to climb into it.

Much like her parents' cabin, there were windows on both sides of the door. They allowed sunlight and a fresh breeze into the cabin by day while their wooden shutters kept out the damp night air. A black bearskin rug had been placed in front of the door to prevent dirt and leaves from being tracked into the cabin. Dried apples hung from pegs that had been driven into the timber wall, along with berries and summer squash that would be used to supplement meals.

The hours flew by as the women sewed and chatted. After taking naps, Eleanor and Donny intermittently played inside and outside the cabin, carefully watched by the adults. When Pa and Wohali came in from the fields, it signaled the end of their party.

Before they could gather up their sewing notions, however, someone started banging on the front door of Wohali's cabin.

Rebekah looked at her parents. "Who can that be?"

Wohali snatched up his rifle and trained it on the door while placing himself between his wife and the disturbance. "I doubt it's good news."

"Open up."

Rebekah's heart leaped into her throat. She knew that voice. "Please wait! That's Asher." It must be a misunderstanding. She ran to the door and pulled it open.

Asher's jaw dropped when he saw her. "What are you doing here?" He grabbed her by the elbow and pulled her to him. "Have they hurt you?"

A part of her wanted to rest against him and listen to his heart beat, but she pushed herself away. "Of course not. Have you lost your senses? Ma and I came over to show Noya how to quilt while her husband and Pa were out digging a well because the creek has nearly dried up."

Pa pulled her back and faced Asher. "A better question would be what you are doing banging on the door like you're being chased by bandits."

Asher pointed past them at Wohali. "I've been sent to take Wohali into custody for the murders of the Marshall family."

Rebekah gasped. Had he been infected by the madness in Nashville? Or was this evidence of the very kind of influence she had worried about from the Lewis family? "What do you mean? You know they didn't have anything to do with that raid. They were with us at Aunt Dolly's house that night. How could he have been out at the Marshall place?"

Asher turned his gaze on her. Never had she seen him look so hard. His face seemed chiseled from stone, and his eyes looked straight through her. "A witness has come forward. We have enough evidence against Wohali, and you should be thankful for my arrival. You and your family may have been his next targets."

Rebekah's hand flew to her mouth. She glanced back at the Indian couple, who were standing close together. For an instant, she wondered if they could be capable of murder. But it was not possible. There was no way she would believe the woman she had spent the morning with could be in any way involved with the violent deaths of an innocent family.

She shook her head and turned to Pa. If Wohali harbored any evil intent, he would have seen evidence of it. "Pa, you can't let this happen."

Pa looked as shocked as she felt, but he shook his head. Was there nothing he could do to stop Asher from taking their neighbor?

Noya leaned up and whispered something to her husband, who turned his black gaze on Asher. "Who is this witness?"

"A farmhand. He got there too late to do anything to help the family. But the evidence he has is very convincing."

Rebekah could not, would not believe it. This was a gross miscarriage of justice. "There has to be a mistake."

"I wish there was, but you don't know all that I know—"

"I don't care what you think you know. It's simply not possible."

"Stay out of this, Rebekah. Someone found Wohali's tomahawk at the farm the next morning. There's no way it could have gotten out there unless he was a party to the murders. I know you have a soft spot for Indians, but you're allowing your feelings to cloud your judgment."

"At least I still have feelings." Her words fell into a well of silence. If possible she would have stuffed them back in her mouth. But it was too late.

Asher looked at her for a moment before shrugging. "I have to do this no matter what you think of me." He shouldered his way past the others to face Wohali. "I'd like you to come peaceably. If what Rebekah says is right, we'll soon find out. But in the meantime, I have to take you to Nashville."

The Indian pried his wife's hands from his arms and nodded. "Do not worry, wife. God is in control." Without another word, he followed Asher into the yard.

Rebekah went to the short woman and hugged her tightly. "He's right, you know. Take heart. We'll straighten everything out in no time." Rebekah hoped to reassure herself with these words, but she knew she sounded much more certain than she actually felt.

Chapter 16

Asher took his prisoner to the jail. He was not happy with the way things had turned out. First, Rebekah's accusation that he was being heartless. Then Wohali's stoicism on the way back to Nashville.

The man had not put forward the least resistance, practically offering himself up as a sacrifice. Who did he think he was? Jesus? Asher's conscience pricked him. Was Wohali's silence an indication of innocence or guilt?

It was dusk, but he wanted to talk to Colonel Lewis about a couple of things. He hoped the man was at home, not escorting Alexandra and her ma to another ball. As his horse cantered across Nashville, Asher searched his memory for any invitations that his ma had mentioned, but he could not recall anything.

The Lewises must be at home, as nearly every window glowed against the deepening gloom. It was a very welcoming sight.

A stableboy came running to take care of his horse, and Asher climbed the front steps. How different the day had turned out than what he had been expecting when he first arrived at this very same doorway.

The same slave let him in. "I need to see the colonel again."

"Yes, sir." This time, she led him to a different part of the house, opening the door and announcing him to the people inside.

Asher entered the parlor, squinting at the sudden brightness. Alexandra was the first person he saw. She and her parents were enjoying tea in the parlor. Her smile was as wide and appealing as always. As she rose to meet him, Asher squelched a comparison between her and Rebekah. The last time he and Rebekah had disagreed, he had made that mistake, and he was determined not to repeat his error. Alexandra was nice, but his heart belonged to a stubborn, backward girl who was determined to rescue the world while dragging him away from a lucrative position in Nashville.

"To what do we owe this pleasure, Captain Landon?" She put out her hand for his kiss.

He bent and pecked at the air above her hand. "I have business with your father."

She pouted at him. "Is that the only reason you've come?"

"Alexandra!" Colonel Lewis's voice was sharp with censure. He left his easy chair and came over to stand next to his daughter. "You should mind your manners, young lady. It is unseemly of you to fish for a compliment."

Asher wondered why his shirt collar suddenly felt so uncomfortable. Although he agreed with the colonel, he did not like to witness Alexandra's discomfiture.

She looked down at the floor. "I'm sorry, Papa. I did not mean any harm."

Colonel Lewis's face lost its angry glower. He patted her shoulder. "No harm done, dear. Eh, Captain?"

Asher nodded his agreement and tugged at his collar. He turned to Alexandra's mother, who had remained seated on the sofa. "How do you do this evening?"

Mrs. Lewis sighed and waved a lacy kerchief. "As well as possible, I suppose, given the uncivilized nature of our surroundings."

Colonel Lewis cleared his throat. "Please remember that Captain Landon is from here, my dear. He probably doesn't agree with your disapprobation of Nashville."

"I would not dare to disagree with you, ma'am. I know you are more used to the comforts of a big city."

"Good answer." The colonel winked at Asher. "Perhaps we should retire to my study."

They left the ladies to their tea and headed down the hall.

"How did it go? Did you get the vermin?"

Asher winced at the colonel's choice of word. Before the evidence had been brought forward, he'd thought Wohali was an honorable man—hardworking, God-fearing, and honest. When he'd looked into Rebekah's eyes earlier, he had remembered that opinion. Had there been some mistake? "I'm worried about Wohali."

"Why? He murdered that poor defenseless family. He deserves whatever punishment we decide to mete out."

Asher sat down in one of the leather chairs. "I'm not sure he is guilty."

"Not guilty?" The colonel lifted a finger. "First, there's the bloody weapon, and then the description from the woodcarver of the man who purchased it. What more do you need? To see his hands coated with innocent blood?"

Asher leaned forward. "But can we be sure Wohali is the man who purchased the tomahawk? There are a lot of tall Indians around."

The colonel held his gaze for a moment. "If you're that worried about it, why don't you and I take this Indian to the woodcarver tomorrow and see if we've got the right person?"

Asher felt as though a weight had been lifted from his shoulders. "That's a good plan." Asking the woodcarver to identify Wohali would clear up his doubts, and he would be able to report to Rebekah that no mistake had been made. Surely then she would see the truth.

❧

Asher threw his pillow on the floor, relieved that the sky outside his bedroom window was finally beginning to lighten. It had taken him a long time to fall asleep last night, and he had not enjoyed his normal restful repose.

Haunting dreams had featured a disappointed Rebekah shaking her head and calling him heartless right before she was attacked by a wild-eyed Indian brave. No matter how hard he'd tried to save her from harm, by the time he reached her, she was dead. And when he turned to wreak vengeance on her attacker, the Indian faded into the shadows and disappeared.

He pushed back the bedcover and got up. One thing was for certain. Once all of this mess about the Marshall farm had been settled, he was going to Rebekah's home and ask for her pa's permission to marry. He had been foolish to put the matter off. That was the real reason Rebekah was unhappy with him. Never mind that he felt it was rushing things. If his Rebekah wanted to have their relationship formalized, he would do it.

So what if they had to live with his parents for a few months until he could put together enough resources to buy or build a home fitting the position they would hold? Look at Alexandra's relatives. Several married children lived with her grandmother at Tanner Plantation.

As he dressed, Asher got more and more excited about the idea of approaching Mr. Taylor. He couldn't think now why he had not done it sooner. He bounded down the stairs to tell his parents the exciting news before going to collect Wohali and Colonel Lewis. When he reached the first floor, however, he realized something was wrong. Several people were talking in the parlor.

He opened the parlor door to find the main participant in last night's dreams staring straight at him. "Rebekah! What's wrong? What are you doing here? Did someone attack your pa's farm?"

She was sitting between his parents on the sofa, her gloved hands clenching her reticule as though it held priceless treasure.

His ma stood up and gestured for Asher to take her place on the sofa. "Miss Taylor has some important information I think you should hear." She smiled at Rebekah. "Mr. Landon and I will be in the dining room, dear. Call for us if you need anything."

As his parents left the parlor, Asher took the seat his ma had vacated. "What's wrong, Rebekah?"

Rebekah moved away from him a little. "What's wrong? Everything is wrong, Asher. The whole world has gone mad, and you with it. Pa brought me

106

to town last night to try and avert disaster."

"What are you talking about?"

"I'm talking about you invading Wohali's home and dragging him away from his wife on some trumped-up charges that you know are not true."

Asher stiffened. "You don't know what you're talking about."

"I know there's no way that Wohali was involved in the murder of that poor family."

"You cannot know that."

She turned her gaze on him once more, her brown eyes pleading. "Asher, you know Wohali and Noya were staying with Aunt Dolly. Do you really think he sneaked out that night to murder the Marshalls and burn down their home before returning to Nashville and slipping back into his role as a civilized man?"

"I've seen a lot of things, Rebekah. A lot of things you don't need to know about. You've been protected from some of the harsh realities of life, and it's my intent to make sure you remain that way. Trust me when I say that a man can lose his grasp on civility in the blink of an eye. Even the best man can turn into a murderer under the right circumstances."

"But there are no circumstances that would compel Wohali to murder. I know him, and I know his wife. They are good Christian people who are trying to embrace our way of living. Why would he suddenly decide to kill a bunch of strangers and put his whole future at risk?"

"I saw the evidence with my own eyes, Rebekah. I cannot give you a reason why Wohali would do anything so horrendous, but I know he did it."

Rebekah's eyebrows drew together. "You cannot know that."

Asher pried one of her hands from her reticule. "How can I make you understand the truth? Your innocence leads you to believe the best of people, but sometimes they don't deserve your trust. Do you know how scared I was when I realized that the weapon used to kill Mr. Marshall belonged to a man who lived next to you and your family? I must have died a thousand deaths on the way to Wohali's farm. I was so afraid that he might have turned his rage on you."

Rebekah jerked her hand away. "You have no need to worry about me anymore."

"Please, Rebekah, let's not start that same argument over again. You know I love you, and I know you love me. I promise you that I'm going to talk to your pa as soon as this is all—"

"Do not use that patronizing tone with me, Asher Landon. I'm not a child you can pat on the head and make empty promises to. I may have been protected by my loved ones, but that doesn't mean I'm stupid or easily misled. If anyone is being misled in this room, it's you. You are so blind you cannot see beyond your own nose. Noya has given me the only tomahawk that her husband owns."

Asher raised his eyebrows. "And you believe her?"

"Yes, I believe her. Coupled with the fact that Pa has worked side by side with Wohali for all these months and the fact that I know where he was that night, I have no doubt that Wohali is innocent. Instead of being so eager to believe that only Colonel Lewis and his daughter know the truth, why don't you ask yourself who might benefit from having Wohali arrested?"

If the situation had not been so serious, Asher would have laughed at the jealous comment she made. But it was serious. A man's life hung in the balance. "I cannot believe you think I am incapable of discerning the truth."

"And I can't believe you're not taking me seriously. Asher, I was willing to give you the benefit of the doubt. I was willing to believe that we could still have a happy marriage even if it meant I had to move to Nashville. But now I realize that you are not the man I thought you were."

"Rebekah—" Asher tried to break in, but her words struck him like blows, robbing him of breath. The expression on her face brought back his nightmare with vivid clarity.

"That's my fault, not yours. It's become obvious to me that there is a chasm between us which cannot be bridged. I was too self-centered to realize it earlier, and for that I do apologize. When Pastor Miller helped me realize that I had not been asking God for His leading, I turned to Him and asked for a sign that we were supposed to be together."

Asher had to be dreaming. That was it. That was why he couldn't make his tongue work—why he couldn't stem the flow of Rebekah's words.

"I guess the fact that you will not listen to reason is a pretty clear sign, so I want to formally release you from your promise." She stood up and walked across the room. "I pray you find your way to happiness."

❧

Rebekah rushed outside after her argument with Asher. She couldn't bear to face his parents. They were wonderful people, and they were worried about Asher, too, but she needed to be alone to get her emotions under control.

A sob nearly broke loose, but she choked it down. She climbed into Pa's wagon and grabbed the reins, turning the horse's head toward Aunt Dolly's home. As they traveled the streets of Nashville, the rhythmic sound of the wheels seemed to declare the verdict. . .over. . .it's over. . .over. . .it's over.

Her eyes stung, but she refused to let the tears fall. Was this how it was supposed to feel when one followed God's path? She could not believe Asher was truly lost to her. But since she'd left Nashville, he had gone even further down the path away from God. She could not join him there, even if it tore her heart out. She would collect Pa and go back home, and she hoped she would never have to set eyes on Nashville again.

A breeze caressed her cheek like a gentle hand, and peace settled inside her bruised heart. In that instant, she knew that their separation was necessary. Her heavenly Father knew what was best for all of them, and she would trust His judgment.

As she neared her aunt's home, a song of thanksgiving filled Rebekah's mind, and she began to pray. She prayed for Wohali and for Noya, but most of all, she prayed that God would protect Asher and lead him into a bright future.

She felt her heart begin to break as she realized that future would not include her.

Chapter 17

Asher rode from the livery stable to the jail, leading Wohali's horse. But his mind wasn't on the Cherokee. It was on the scene with Rebekah.

After she had left, he tried to convince himself that it was for the best. He would go on with his life in Nashville, and she would live out in the country like she wanted. He would marry someone else, someone who respected him as a capable provider. Not someone who questioned every decision and tried to force him to bend to her will.

He would see Rebekah every now and then—when she came to visit her aunt, or when he had business in her area. Perhaps eventually they could even reclaim the friendship they'd once had. By then, he would probably have a couple of children, even if none of them sported her golden hair or soft brown eyes. Would she marry someone else? The pain that swept through him at the thought almost made him bend over his saddle.

She couldn't marry some other man. But if she didn't marry him, she would find someone else. . . .

He pushed the thought away. If he continued focusing on Rebekah, he would not be able to see things through for General Jackson and Colonel Lewis. And then he would lose both his love *and* his position.

The city was beginning to awaken as he reached the jailhouse. Hitching both horses to the rail, he went inside and asked the sheriff to release the prisoner.

The sheriff stood up. He was taller than Asher and probably outweighed him by a good thirty pounds. "Where are you wanting to take him?"

"Colonel Lewis and I are continuing our investigation under the direction of General Jackson."

The sheriff pulled out his ring of keys and walked over to Wohali's cell. "Make sure he doesn't plant a tomahawk in your scalp."

Asher rested a hand on his holster, glad he'd thought to buckle it on before leaving his parents' home. After the scene with Rebekah, it was a wonder he'd managed to do anything practical. "There's no danger of that."

Wohali looked the same as the day before. *Stoic* was the word that came to Asher's mind. The man's face could have been carved from stone.

Asher wished he could feel as unperturbed as Wohali seemed to be. He nodded at the Indian, who preceded him to the hitching post. He kept the reins of both horses in his hand as they headed for Colonel Lewis's home. "I trust the sheriff made sure your basic needs were met."

"The sheriff is a fair man."

They rode on in silence for a few moments, but Asher could not resist trying to break through Wohali's composure. "Are you curious about where we're going?"

"Do I seem curious to you?"

"No, but if I was in your place, I would be."

Wohali shrugged and turned his black gaze to the street. "You do not hold power over me."

Asher snorted. "I wouldn't be so sure about that. I'm about the only person in Nashville who wants to be sure you're guilty. If it were up to others, you would already feel the pinch of a noose around your neck."

Wohali glanced upward. "I answer only to my Lord and Savior. He knows my heart, and He alone will judge me."

Asher felt like he'd been slapped. He looked at the tall man who swayed to the rhythm of his horse. He felt small in comparison. How had that happened? He'd been certain he held the upper hand, but this Indian had put him to shame with a few simple words.

⍦

The woodcarver was not sitting outside when Asher and Colonel Lewis arrived with Wohali. Asher dismounted and stood at the horses' heads and waited while the colonel went in to get the man.

After a few minutes, he returned with the woodcarver. The colonel pointed at Wohali. "Is he the man who bought your tomahawk?"

"Yep, yep." The woodcarver wiped his hands on his pants. "That's the same one. Tall fellow, dark hair. That's the one alright." Another swipe of his palms on his trousers. "The very Indian that bought the tomahawk you fellows showed me t'other day. Yep, he's the one alright. Yep, yep. That's him."

Asher frowned. The woodcarver was not acting the way he had when they brought the tomahawk to him. He'd been calm then—proud of his craftsmanship and secure in his abilities. Today, he was exhibiting clear signs of extreme nervousness. He hadn't even looked at Asher. Or at Wohali. How could he be sure Wohali was the one who'd bought the tomahawk when he kept his head down and his gaze trained on the ground? He was also repeating himself again and again. Something was wrong.

Asher looked toward the colonel, but the older man didn't act as if anything was out of place. A glance toward the impassive Indian told him nothing.

The woodcarver was still talking about how they'd caught the right "varmint" and he'd be proud to be present at the hanging. Asher wanted to yell at him to quit talking. Every word he uttered convinced Asher that he was lying.

Rebekah's voice echoed in his head. *"Who might benefit from having Wohali arrested?"* Was this a conspiracy? If so, who were the conspirators?

Chapter 18

Sisters were a headache.

Asher wished he had never agreed to escort Mary to the dressmaker's, but he had been trying to mend fences with his family. They had been so cold and distant since that morning when Rebekah came to see him. Did they, like Rebekah, believe he was incapable of discerning the truth?

"Why, Captain Landon, I never expected to find you visiting a dressmaker." Alexandra's sultry voice interrupted his melancholy thoughts and brought a smile to Asher's face. She was dressed in a nice outfit—not that he knew much about women's clothing, but he thought the navy blue color made her eyes shine. And it had plenty of bows and lace. He knew from listening to his ma and sister that those types of notions made a dress more desirable.

He bowed and straightened. "What a pleasant surprise."

She breezed up to him, a smile on her face. "You say the kindest things, Captain. I'm so glad to run into you. I have the most exciting news—"

"Who are you talking to, Alexandra?" The colonel's bass tones were unmistakable. "Captain Landon!"

"Good morning, Colonel."

"Papa, I was just about to tell the captain about your decision to run for office."

Asher looked from one to the other, his mind in a whirl. "Run for office, sir?"

"Well, yes." Colonel Lewis lowered his voice, even though there were no other customers in the shop. "I guess it's acceptable to tell you, but I didn't want it bandied about just yet." He pointed a finger at Alexandra. "If I thought you were going to announce it to the whole world, young lady, I never would have told you."

"I'm sorry, Papa. But Asher is not the whole world." She put her hand on Asher's arm. "He's practically one of the family."

Asher could feel heat rush to his face. His initial pleasure at seeing Alexandra was drowned in embarrassment. While he enjoyed her friendly attention, being referred to as family was something else entirely. He refused to accept that things would not work out with Rebekah. She was the only family he wanted at this point.

He pulled his arm free from her grasp. "You are too kind, Miss Lewis." He turned to her pa. "Please be assured your news is safe with me."

Mary came out from the dressing room. She sized up the situation with a speed that pleased her brother. "Oh my, we're late for our appointment, Asher." She threw a smile in the general direction of the Lewises. "Please forgive me for dragging my brother away."

The next thing Asher knew, they were out the door. He breathed a sigh of relief. "That's the last time you will get me to go shopping with you."

Mary pouted at him. "And here I thought I'd rescued you handily."

"Maybe so, but I wouldn't have needed rescuing if you hadn't dragged me into that shop in the first place." Asher helped her into the carriage and looked around to make sure Alexandra hadn't decided to pursue him. Something about Alexandra's announcement was bothering him. He looked up at the driver. "Take Mary back home, and do not let her talk you into stopping anywhere else."

"Aren't you coming with me, Asher?"

Asher shook his head. "Tell Ma I'll be back later. I need to do some thinking."

She started to say something, but he closed the carriage door on her protest. As the driver pulled out into the busy street, he wandered in the other direction, his mind in a whirl. Why had Colonel Lewis suddenly decided to run for office? And why hadn't he told Asher himself? Why try to keep it a secret? It made no sense to him at all.

Asher was surprised to look around and find himself back at the woodcarver's shop. It looked different today. All the windows had been shuttered, and the carver's bench was no longer sitting on the front porch.

Curious, he climbed the steps and knocked on the front door. It swung open as a result of his knock. "Hello? Is anyone here?"

He walked inside and looked around, his mouth falling open in shock. All the handles that had been hanging on the walls last week were gone. Not a single one remained. The only things left inside the store were a broom and a broken chair.

"What are you doing in here?"

The belligerent voice behind him startled Asher, and he spun around to find the woodcarver outlined in the doorway. "I found myself in the area and decided to stop by."

The woodcarver grunted. "I'm closed."

"I can see that. It looks like you're not planning on reopening."

"I came into some money, so I decided to close down this two-bit operation and open up a store in Philadelfy."

Asher nodded. "Do you have family back there?"

"What business is it of yours, Captain?" The woodcarver's voice was challenging.

Asher spread his hands. "None whatsoever. My only business with you concerns the Indian, Wohali. You will be here until after the trial is over, right?"

"I don't know." The woodcarver dropped his gaze and rubbed a hand on the leg of his pants. The same nervous gesture Asher had noted during his second visit. "I...I've got me a real hankering to move away."

"But without your testimony, the murderer might go free."

The woodcarver shrugged. "I don't rightly want to go swear as to selling that tomahawk to your Indian."

Asher's jaw dropped. "You told me and the colonel that you sold it to Wohali, so why would you be hesitant to testify in court? Unless you were lying. . ."

Another shrug was the only answer.

Asher's heart banged in his chest. "If you were lying, you must have a real good reason." A plausible motive occurred to him. "Were you part of the raid that killed that poor family?"

The woodcarver looked at him again, and now Asher could see his fear. "I didn't kill nobody."

Asher decided to push him a little. "And why should I believe that? Guilt is usually what makes men run away."

"You got it all wrong, Captain. I promise you I didn't kill those folks. I just make the weapons 'cause God give me a talent for it."

"If you didn't kill anybody, why would you lie about who bought the tomahawk?"

"I come in here one morning, and it was gone. Somebody stole it."

Asher blew out a breath of disgust. "Come on and try another tale. But this time, try to make it plausible."

The man cringed.

"I'm running out of patience." Asher tapped his foot. "Who bought the tomahawk?"

"If I tell you that, they'll come back and kill me."

Asher pointed a finger at the woodcarver. "If you don't tell me, I am going to drag you to jail and throw you into the cell with Wohali. Then we'll see what's what."

"No." The man looked back over his shoulder. "Look, I'll tell you, but you've gotta promise that you won't say anything until I get outta here."

"I can't make that promise." Asher strode forward and grabbed the man's elbow. "Why don't we go see Colonel Lewis? Maybe he'll convince you to tell the truth."

The woodcarver struggled to break free of Asher's hold. "No, you can't take me there. He'll kill me for sure."

Asher twisted to block the doorway. "What are you saying? Are you trying to implicate Colonel Lewis? Did you sell him the tomahawk?" His mind reeled. But it made sense. The facts lined up with military precision. The colonel was planning to grab Wohali's and the Marshalls' land. Only substantial landowners could hold public office. It didn't matter whether he lived on the land or not, so long as he held the title.

The woodcarver was sniveling, his misery plain to see. "I didn't do nothing wrong. You've got to believe me. I sold it to him, but I thought he was going to use it for some ceremony, not to kill them folks. And when I found out, it was too late. The colonel came here and told me to say I'd sold it to an Indian. He said them Indians was all guilty on account of they've killed lots of white men. And he said he'd pay me big. All I had to do was agree with him—then I could leave Nashville, and everyone would be okay."

Asher's whole world changed in that instant. Colonel Lewis, the man in whom he had placed so much faith, was pure evil. He'd been such a fool. Everything he'd thought was right had turned out to be wrong, terribly wrong.

All this time he had refused to listen to his loved ones. They had tried to warn him, but he'd been certain he was right. He'd let his ambitions blind him to the truth. He knew without a doubt that he was nothing more than a flawed sinner. Asher wanted to sink to his knees on the dusty floor and beg for God's forgiveness. But he didn't have that choice. He had to stop the colonel before Wohali paid the ultimate price for Asher's stupidity. He could only ask God to help him until he could really seek peace later. "Come on. We're going to the sheriff."

The woodcarver shook his head and tried to get through the doorway, but Asher tackled him. "No you don't. You're through running from shadows. It's time to stand up and be a man." He hustled the frightened man down the street toward the jail and dragged him inside.

The sheriff looked up when they entered. "Who are you bringing in today, Captain?"

"This man has an interesting story to tell you, Sheriff. I think you and Wohali are going to want to listen."

He tossed a glance toward the Indian, who was sitting quietly in his cell. The woodcarver faltered at first, but he told his story once again.

When he finished, the sheriff looked at Asher. "Do you believe him?"

Asher lifted his chin toward the broken man. "Look at him. He's scared to death. Too scared to lie."

The sheriff nodded. "I agree." He stood and walked to Wohali's cell and turned the key in the lock. "I guess we'd better get you out of here."

The front door flew open and banged against the wall. "Don't anybody move."

"Colonel Lewis." Asher reached for his holster before realizing he'd not strapped it on that morning. He'd never dreamed he might need a weapon on a shopping excursion.

The colonel, however, had brought his weapon, and he pointed it at Asher. "Get back, boy. I don't want to hurt you. My daughter's got a soft spot for you."

Asher's jaw dropped. "Please tell me you haven't embroiled her in this sordid mess."

"Don't be ridiculous. This is men's business. I wouldn't think of even telling her about it." He barked a humorless laugh. "Just look at the way she said too much to you today and roused your suspicions."

Out of the corner of his eye, Asher could see the sheriff easing his way back to his desk. He needed to distract Colonel Lewis if any of them were going to get out of this alive.

"Is that the way they do business in New Orleans? Murdering innocent women and children?"

The colonel shrugged. "They were in the way. I need all of that land from the river to the Taylor farm for my purposes. That idiot wouldn't sell to me. Said he'd planted roots there. So I had him planted there with his roots."

He pulled back the hammer and pointed his gun at the woodcarver. "I told you to keep your mouth shut or you'd end up like that farmer."

Asher could not let the terrified man be killed. He leaped toward the colonel and shoved the older man's arm hard. A double blast filled the jail with smoke and the smell of burned powder. The colonel let out a groan and fell dead at Asher's feet.

Asher looked down at himself, surprised to see that he was not leaking blood. He looked at the woodcarver, who was staring in horrified fascination at the other end of the room. The sheriff! He turned in time to see the tall man fold in half and land on the floor with a *thump*.

He hurried to the sheriff and turned him over to see a nasty wound a slight distance from the man's heart. Someone knelt beside him. It was Wohali.

"I can take care of the bleeding. You get the doctor." Wohali inclined his head to the body of Colonel Lewis. "No one else should die because of that man's greed."

"Wohali, I don't know what—"

The sheriff's groan cut off Asher's apology.

"Go now." The Indian pressed his hand against the wound. "We can talk later."

Chapter 19

Rebekah pulled off her shoes and stockings and thrust her feet into the cold stream. A sorrowful sigh seemed to fill her chest, and tears gathered at the corners of her eyes. "I will not cry. I will not cry. I will not—"

A chirp in the limb above her head stopped her words. She looked up to see the gray brown feathers of a mockingbird. Its song continued, full of chiding tweets.

She frowned. "Are you mocking me?"

"Perhaps. But she is more likely trying to warn you away from the babies in her nest."

Rebekah's breath caught, and she drew her legs out of the water so she could turn around. There he stood—so tall, so handsome, so much the man of her dreams. *Asher.* "What are you doing here?"

"I came to ask for your forgiveness." He reached for her hand and drew her up. Rebekah's petticoat clung to her damp, bare legs. She took one step to the right, hoping to hide her shoes and stockings from his view. How embarrassing to be caught dangling her bare feet in the water like a child. She would have liked to leave him standing beside the creek, but she could not move without exposing her undergarments.

"I forgive you, Asher." She looked down to be certain her bare toes were not peeking out.

He put a hand under her chin and raised her face to look at him. "No, not yet."

All thoughts of her feet slid out of Rebekah's head.

His blue eyes captured her whole attention. He looked so uncertain, so anxious. "Did you know that Wohali has been released? He is completely exonerated."

Rebekah nodded. Wohali had come home a week ago. Her family had celebrated the release with great joy. He'd told them about Asher's part in uncovering Colonel Lewis's devious plan. He'd described the woodcarver's confession and the gunfight, almost causing her to experience an Aunt Dolly swoon at the thought of Asher being shot down in the city jail.

Another detail he shared with them was the departure of the widowed Mrs. Lewis and Alexandra. They had decided to return to the family plantation rather than face the scandal surrounding the colonel's reprehensible actions. Rebekah could not imagine the grief and pain Alexandra must be experiencing and found herself praying often for God's comfort and peace to surround her former rival.

Asher's hand reached back to tuck a stray lock of hair behind her ear. "I cannot believe what a fool I've been, Rebekah. I should have listened to you. You saw everything more clearly than I did. You were right when you accused me of being heartless. I had let myself be misled by promises of glory and wealth. But I hope you know that I had no idea what means the colonel had in mind to achieve those goals."

"Of course I believe that, Asher. I never thought you were a criminal."

"Thank you. When I look back on my words and actions, I couldn't blame you if you didn't believe me." He paused for a moment and gazed over her shoulder. "When I discovered what really happened at the Marshall farm that night, I was devastated. This bright light seemed to bear down on me, and it made me so ashamed. I wanted to run from the truth, but there was nowhere to hide. God let me see how far from Him I'd gone. I died in that moment, Rebekah."

She put a hand on his arm. "I'm so sorry."

"No." He shook his head and focused on her again. "Don't be sorry. Be glad. I know I've been foolish, Rebekah. When I told my parents how sorry I was, Pa suggested I go talk to Pastor Miller. He's a very smart man. He and I talked a long time. When I told him how I felt, he read to me about Isaiah's vision of God. 'Woe is me! for I am undone; because I am a man of unclean lips. . . .' Knowing that one of God's prophets had felt the same gave me hope that I could change in spite of the terrible things I had done. I feel like Paul—ashamed that I have spent so much time doing the wrong things but full of joy that I can now spend my energies on pleasing Him."

Rebekah could not see him struggling so without feeling a deep pathos for Asher. Yet underlying that sadness was an upwelling of joy. Was it possible that he had changed in an instant? Yet hadn't her own views changed that fast because of the face of an Indian boy on the road from Natchez? "Oh, Asher."

"I hope you understand, Rebekah. I'm not only asking for your forgiveness for my past errors. I want you to take me back." He dropped to one knee in front of her and took her hand in both of his. "I have put God first in my life, and I feel that He has led me to this moment. Can you ever love me again?"

Rebekah laughed. She could not help herself. All the sorrow that had weighed her down for weeks was gone as if it never existed. "Although I was resigned to life without you, it was so hard to forget how much you meant to me. I kept thinking I should be doing more to reach you, but I didn't know how to accomplish it. So I prayed."

"Thank you, Rebekah. I am not worthy of such dedication."

"Please get up, Asher." She tugged on the hands that enveloped hers. "You don't need to humble yourself to me. 'For all have sinned, and come short of the glory of God.' Everyone needs God's grace and forgiveness."

"Does that mean you'll marry me?"

She laughed again. "Well, you still haven't asked Pa. . . ."

"I can take care of that detail right now. But first. . ." Asher sprang to his feet and wrapped his arms around her.

Rebekah reveled in the feel of his strong arms and sent a prayer of thanksgiving heavenward. The Asher she'd grown up loving had come back to her. His sincere remorse was plain to see in his face. She no longer had to worry that he would sacrifice her happiness or his relationship with God for fame and fortune. As he held her close, she felt safe and finally at peace. Her heart skipped a beat when he gently bent his head and kissed her.

She felt God's love surround them and give their relationship a wonderful new aspect. It was deeper and richer than before. Somehow, she knew that this was the way God intended for His children to come together, and she could hardly wait to begin their journey along His path.

Epilogue

Mid-October 1815

Donny came running into the room and pulled on the skirt of Rebekah's dress.

She pulled him onto her lap. "Yes, dear. What's wrong?"

"Ma says come on. Ev'one waiting."

Rebekah lifted her little brother off of her lap and stood. As he ran back outside, she brushed the pale yellow material of her gown. It was the first one Aunt Dolly had given her. . .and her favorite. She had known it would be the perfect choice to begin her new life.

Rebekah opened the door and stepped into the bright autumn sunshine. She sent a quick prayer heavenward, thanking God for providing such a beautiful day for the moment she would become Mrs. Asher Landon.

"Here she is." Pastor Miller's voice turned everyone's attention to her. He was standing beside Asher under the shade of the tulip poplar, which seemed to have dressed especially for her wedding, as the beginnings of fall colors showed in its leafy branches.

She walked past the grand table Pa had hewn from the trunk of a gigantic tree. When she had first seen it, she'd not been able to imagine that they could fill the table with food, but it now practically groaned underneath the weight of everything from cakes and pies to roast chicken, duck, and venison. As soon as Pastor Miller invoked God's blessing on her union to Asher, they would all sit around Pa's table and fellowship together.

She smiled at Wohali and Noya. They were being better received since the truth about the Marshall tragedy had been uncovered. The Cherokee couple's steadfast faith during Wohali's imprisonment had even won over several of her neighbors who did not normally like to associate with Indians.

Asher's family was standing next to the creek, to his right, while Rebekah's family stood on the other side of Pastor Miller.

Una Miller had claimed one of the chairs Pa had moved out from the cabin. She sat next to Rachel Jackson, who cooed over the precious baby girl Mrs. Miller cradled in her arms. Even the general was smiling as he bent over his wife. Aunt Dolly was standing next to the sheriff, whispering something in his ear as she waved a lace handkerchief at Rebekah.

Then all Rebekah's attention centered on Asher standing so tall and handsome in his uniform. It was a shame he would not don it again after today's ceremony, but he had decided to resign from the militia and take a job at his pa's bank. The only reason he wore it for the wedding was because General and Mrs. Jackson were present.

Asher had also joined her in talking with Pastor Miller about working with the Indians in the area. They would help to educate them so they would be able to adapt to the changes on the frontier. But more importantly, they would work together to tell the Indians of God's love and forgiveness, available to *all* of His children.

It seemed to Rebekah she had waited for this moment for half a lifetime, but she could not regret the delay because she knew instinctively that she and Asher had not been ready to begin a marriage two years ago—not until they put their lives fully in God's hands. She prayed they were ready now.

Together they faced Pastor Miller, who smiled as he opened his Bible. "'And the Lord God said, It is not good that the man should be alone; I will make him an help meet for him.' Friends, I give you today Asher Landon, a good man who has come to me many times over the past weeks, seeking the will of God. He has promised to cherish and care for Rebekah Taylor. . . ."

Rebekah let the words wash over her. She looked at the man who was becoming her husband and felt a great peace flow through her. Here under their tulip poplar, all of their dreams were coming true.

A BOUQUET
FOR IRIS

Dedication

To our fellow Bards of Faith. You are more than just critique partners. You are friends and family. We have shared so many things. . .both good and bad. Thank you for always being there through it all. We look forward to sharing many more special times together—including your many future contracts! God bless us all as we continue to write for Him.

Chapter 1

Nashville, Tennessee
December 24, 1835

Iris Landon bunched the soft velvet of her new gown into gloved hands as she descended from the family carriage and followed her parents up the steps to Aunt Dolly and Uncle Mac's home. Most ladies her age would be excited about the evening's festivities, but she rather dreaded them.

This was not the first of Aunt Dolly's Christmas Eve galas she had attended, and she knew what lay ahead. She would have to sit through a long dinner, listening to the latest gossip about the elite families of Nashville. There would also be the obligatory inquiries about her plans to marry. Iris had learned over the past year to smile and nod as various relatives offered advice on how to attract the interest of the young gentlemen of the area.

Eventually everyone would move to the ballroom, and she would be forced to spend hours listening to endless chatter from other young ladies when she'd much rather be discussing westward expansion or the plight of the Indian nations. She would endure the usual games, and at least one of the more enterprising young men would seek to steal a kiss from his dancing partner by maneuvering her underneath a sprig of mistletoe while it still held kissing berries. She had half a mind to pull off the berries herself just to make sure no one tried anything that silly with her.

Iris lifted her gaze to the clear night sky, and her breath caught. Against the horizon, a single star rose, and for a moment she was transported to the days of Matthew's Gospel. What a miraculous sight the star must have been on the night Christ was born. Had the wise men been weary when they arrived in Bethlehem? Or had their anticipation wiped out all the long, fearsome months of travel? She closed her eyes for a moment as the creak of a harness was transformed into noises from burdened camels. Golden light pressed against her eyelids like the torchlight from inside Mary and Joseph's humble home. Her flight of fancy ended when the opening of the front door and her great-aunt's greeting brought her back to the present.

Aunt Dolly practically glowed in the light pouring out of her foyer. She wore a rose-colored dress with crimson piping and a scattering of decorative gold bows. She might be diminutive, but from the peacock feathers perched atop her graying hair to the tips of her shiny black slippers, Aunt Dolly looked as regal as European royalty.

"Rebekah, you become more beautiful every year, dearest." What Aunt Dolly lacked in height, she made up for with enthusiasm, catching Iris's mother in a warm hug before turning to her father. "And Asher, don't you look as distinguished as ever. I'll never understand why you didn't stay with President Jackson. He certainly needs better advisers—someone to convince him that the poor Indians shouldn't be forced out of their homes."

The others might not have noticed, but Iris saw her father grimace slightly at Aunt Dolly's remark before he bowed over her hand. "I doubt anyone could change the president's mind once he has made a decision. The only person who might have done that is no longer with us."

Aunt Dolly sighed. "I really miss Rachel, too. Not only was she a gentling influence on her husband, she was one of my dearest friends." She shook her head as if to clear it of gloomy thoughts before turning to the tall man who hovered in the hallway behind her. "Look who has arrived, Mac. It's the Landons."

"So I see." Robert "Mac" McGhee raised Ma's gloved hand to his lips. He always made Iris think of a wrestler, with his widespread stance and thick chest. He didn't look very comfortable in starched trousers and a long-tailed coat. He straightened, and she noticed that the collar of his shirt was already beginning to droop a little, as though he'd been tugging at it before their arrival.

As he turned toward her father, Iris saw the glint of his pistol handle peeking underneath his coat. She wondered if Aunt Dolly realized that her husband, the retired sheriff of Davidson County, was armed.

"Iris, child, come here so I can see you." Aunt Dolly pulled her forward into the pool of light thrown by dozens of candles in the foyer. "I declare, you've grown a foot since I saw you last."

Uncle Mac tossed a wink at her. Trust the dear man to bolster her confidence. He was one of the few men who stood head and shoulders taller than she and therefore knew how awkward it felt to tower over others. He bent to kiss her cheek and helped her remove her brown wool cloak. Glad to be relieved of its weight in the warm house, Iris shook out the folds of her skirt.

"Whatever were you thinking, dressing your daughter in lavender, Rebekah?" Aunt Dolly's voice practically quivered with dismay as she caught sight of Iris's new gown. "All the young men I've invited will think she's in mourning."

Iris wanted to roll her eyes but kept her gaze firmly fixed on the floor. She did not want to embarrass her parents by showing disrespect toward her aunt. She refused to believe, however, that her choice of dress color was important to anyone but her.

"You know how our Iris loves shades of purple." Ma unbuttoned her black cloak and slipped it off her shoulders, bringing into view the golden brocade dress that reflected the rich color of her hair. The generous skirt swirled around her ankles as she handed the wrap to Uncle Mac before turning back to Aunt Dolly. "I blame it on her father, who insisted we name her after his favorite flower."

"Besides, Aunt Dolly, no matter what color I chose, it would not make me appear even one inch shorter." Iris swept one long arm in a downward arc. "Most men in attendance will want to avoid dancing with a beanpole."

Uncle Mac handed their cloaks and coats to the housekeeper. "Now Iris, don't be foolish. I'm sure all the young lads will think you are the most delightful girl in the room."

Aunt Dolly sputtered for a moment. "Men! You never understand fashion."

Iris's father cocked an eyebrow at Aunt Dolly. "I believe you have won Mac's argument for him. If men have no clue about fashion, then you need not worry yourself about the color or style of Iris's dress."

Iris held her breath, fully expecting her volatile aunt to launch into a diatribe about the fundamental importance of fashion and color. She wished for a moment that she had let Ma talk her into purchasing the bolt of green material the storekeeper had said would bring out the highlights in Iris's brown eyes. But she had never really liked the color green, except perhaps in springtime. And then only because it meant her flower namesake would soon be in bloom.

Every year since she was about five, she had waited impatiently for the irises in Ma's flower garden to begin showing their colors. Some would be dark and velvety like the night sky, while others bloomed a pale color reminiscent of early morning or late evening. The latter were her favorite blossoms and the reason she'd chosen the material for her new dress.

And why shouldn't she choose to please her own taste? None of tonight's guests were likely to go into a decline when they saw she was not wearing white or some other insipid color. It wasn't as if she would be inundated with dance partners no matter what color she chose.

As she had pointed out to Aunt Dolly, she was much too tall. And it seemed that she would never stop growing. The last time Pa measured, her height was a full eight inches above five feet. When one added her inability to make light, flirtatious conversation, the result was abysmal.

Not the type to simper mindlessly, Iris wanted to debate political issues like the discovery of gold on Indian lands, the abolition of slavery, or even popular literature or classic poetry. It seemed that most men preferred giggling, empty-headed girls. And if that's what they wanted, then she didn't want them.

Aunt Dolly stomped her foot. "I should have known all of you would join forces against me." She held her frown for an instant longer before dissolving into laughter. "And why must you always be right?"

Uncle Mac's deep laugh harmonized with Aunt Dolly's delicate notes. "I know better than to answer a question like that." He shook a finger at her. "Almost two decades with you has taught me when to agree with my adorable wife."

Aunt Dolly's ire seemingly melted completely away. She unfolded a lace-edged rose fan and tapped her husband's arm with it. "You are indeed a very smart man."

Ma nodded her agreement before turning to Pa. "Asher, while I appreciate your defense of masculine logic, you really should not encourage our daughter to rebel against fashionable dictates."

He bowed before holding out both elbows, one for his wife and one for his daughter. "I'm certain all the young men will pay enough attention to Iris to satisfy your dreams and raise my misgivings."

Iris forced her lips into a smile, although she wanted to groan, as they made their way to the dining room. This was a familiar point of contention for her parents. Pa was willing to let her wait until God led the right man into her life, but Ma was anxious for her to marry and settle down nearby. It wasn't as though she didn't want to marry and start a family. What girl wouldn't? But she knew that a marriage without God's blessing was a recipe for disaster.

And she had a good idea of the kind of man whom God would send. He would appreciate her unique strengths instead of expecting her to be an imitation of every other girl in the area. He would love her like Pa loved Ma. Until God led someone like Pa into her life, she was more than willing to wait.

Iris was not sure she wanted to live in Nashville for the rest of her life, either. Didn't Ma realize what a big world was out there to be explored? There were so many towns and settlements nowadays and people passing through the area in search of land to the west of the Mississippi River. It was not fair that single women could not join a wagon train. Iris was fully capable of taking care of herself. She had no need of a man to help her drive a wagon or fix dinner. If only she could explore the country and see for herself all the land beyond the Mississippi River. The newspapers promised land enough for all, white and Indians alike.

Some nights after all of her family had gone to bed, Iris would sit at the window in her bedroom and search the horizon for answers. She wasn't even sure what the questions were, only that God had placed in her heart the desire to leave Nashville and search for a different kind of life.

Iris stood to one side as Pa helped her ma to her seat. Her gaze drank in the long table covered with pine greenery, holly berries, and silver serving dishes.

Flickering candlelight from the large chandelier hanging over the center of the table gilded the edges of the delicate china place settings. Not only was Aunt Dolly a fashion plate, but she also knew how to create a wonderful atmosphere in her lovely home. Even with her limited interest in such things, Iris could appreciate the artistry of the formal dining room.

When they were all seated, Uncle Mac leaned forward and closed his eyes. Iris followed his lead and listened as he blessed the food, the arrival of loved ones, and the celebration of Christ's birth.

Warmth seeped through her at the thought of Baby Jesus being born. What a miraculous event that reached out to envelop all of them this evening. She added her thanks to having been raised in a Christian home. The good Lord had showered so many blessings on her and her family.

Uncle Mac ended the prayer, and Iris let her gaze drift around the table as her relatives talked about their plans for the Christmas season and the upcoming year. She could not repress a shiver of anticipation. Surely the Lord wouldn't wait much longer before showing her His plan for her life.

❧

Eugene Brown escorted Iris to a group of ladies who included her ma, Aunt Dolly, and Grandma Landon, her paternal grandmother. Iris thanked him for their dance and wondered if he realized how much relief showed on his face as he left her standing with her relatives.

Grandma Landon raised her brows at Eugene's abrupt departure. "Someone ought to teach that young man his manners. He didn't even speak, much less thank my granddaughter for dancing with him."

Aunt Dolly nodded. "Young people these days have such lackadaisical habits."

"Perhaps we should not be so hasty to judge." Ma's voice gently chided the others as she turned and watched Eugene dash out of the ballroom. "You see, the poor boy may have a valid reason to hurry."

"He probably needs to go rub his feet." Iris could not keep the mischief out of her voice. "I know I must have stepped on them a dozen times during our dance."

All three of her relatives were taken aback by her pronouncement, but then Ma smiled. "I did notice that Mr. Brown was a bit shorter than you."

Iris raised her eyebrows. "His head was at the level of my shoulder. And his steps were so short I felt I was mincing my way through our dance."

Her grandmother studied her from head to toe. "You may be a bit tall, child, but that color you're wearing is very becoming."

A sound of irritation came from Aunt Dolly. "Doesn't anyone in this family have a bit of fashion consciousness?"

Grandma looked somewhat affronted at the comment, but she must have decided to exercise her manners by ignoring Aunt Dolly's question. She turned her attention to her daughter-in-law. "Where are your parents, Rebekah?"

"They volunteered to entertain Hannah and Eli this evening so they would not have to stay at the house alone."

"I'm surprised you didn't volunteer for that duty, given your oft-repeated disdain for parties."

"I wouldn't let her stay home this year," Aunt Dolly answered for Ma. "Of course, I was hoping she would bring the children with her."

Ma shuddered. "You don't know what you're asking."

Iris could feel the corners of her mouth turning up. "Our Eli has far too much energy to behave himself all evening. If he had come, you would all bemoan his inability to mind his manners."

A flurry of activity at the door gained their attention. Several footmen were bringing a shiny washtub into the ballroom. Aunt Dolly excused herself and moved toward them to supervise the placement of the tub. Iris knew from previous parties that it was filled nearly to the rim with water. The housekeeper entered with a sack of apples that she dumped into the tub as soon as Aunt Dolly was happy with its placement.

Iris clapped her hands together. "Can I try catching an apple this year, Ma?"

Grandma looked up at the ceiling as if for guidance before addressing Iris's mother. "I hope you will not allow any such thing, Rebekah. It's not seemly for a young lady to dampen her gown or hair by taking part in such high jinks."

"I have to agree, Iris." Ma reached out and tweaked one of her daughter's curls. "Your coiffure already seems to be in some danger of coming undone. You would not want to be seen with your hair around your shoulders."

Iris reached up and patted some errant strands back into place. It was a shame her naturally curly hair was so thick and heavy. Ma had spent nearly an hour taming her unruly mane this evening before they came to the party, but she could tell it was trying to escape the dozens of pins that had been twisted into it. "Perhaps I could take it down and plait it like I used to do?"

Ma looked as if she was considering the request, but then she shook her head. "You are a grown woman now, Iris. The time for you to sport braids in public is long gone."

Iris let her shoulders droop, but then an idea popped into her head. "If I'm so grown, then won't you reconsider that advertisement in the *Sentinel*?"

"What advertisement?" Grandma asked. "And what are you doing reading newspapers? Does your ma not give you enough chores to fill your day?"

Ma tossed a warning look at Iris. "We have gone through this several times, dear. You know that your father and I prayed about your request. We simply don't think it is advisable for you to travel to some little town in the wilderness to teach youngsters."

"What?" Grandma's voice was so loud that several people looked in their direction. "This is exactly my point, Rebekah. Young girls should not be allowed to fill their minds with all types of information. It's not good for them. You see what can come of it. Now your daughter wants to travel all alone to some unknown destination."

"It's not unknown." Iris defended her position. "It's a town in Texas called Shady Gulch. Doesn't that sound like a wonderful destination? I can practically see the little schoolhouse standing in front of a field of wildflowers, all white-washed and sparkling. And it would be so fulfilling to help mold young people's minds."

"Or be attacked by marauding Indians or the Mexican army." Her grandma shuddered. "Just because a town has a pretty name does not mean it's a desirable destination."

Ma patted Iris's hand. "I know you want to teach youngsters, but there are lots of opportunities to do so right here in Nashville."

"Quite right." Grandma smoothed the front of her blue-and-white-striped skirt. "Why would you want to leave your loved ones?"

Iris wanted to argue with them, but she knew better. The look in Ma's eyes was the same one she got when she had to chase a fox away from the chicken coop—determined. Iris sighed and turned to watch the young men who were taking turns trying to bite into one of the apples floating in the tub. Some of the young ladies had drifted in that direction to cheer for their favorite participants.

Eugene had come back in, and he was standing next to Melissa Baker, a young lady who was several inches shorter than he. It looked like she was try-ing to convince him to compete in the apple bobbing. But from the way he was shaking his head, Iris had the feeling he had no desire to accede to her wishes. Poor Eugene. It seemed that things were going from bad to worse for him this evening.

Pa walked over to them and put an arm around Ma's waist.

Ma looked up at him. "Aren't you going to bob for apples this year?"

Pa laughed. "I think it's time for me to retire and leave the horseplay to the younger generation."

The others talked about past Christmases, but Iris's thoughts turned down a different avenue. She wished her expectations had not been met this eve-ning. It would have been nice if some tall, handsome stranger had appeared and whisked her onto the dance floor.

She could almost see him—dark and handsome and, oh, so tall. He would have a mustache and hair that fell just so across his forehead. He would whisper sweet compliments into her ear and make her feel graceful and beautiful. Then he would bring her back to her parents and spend time talking intelligently with them of current events and his passion to serve the Lord. After the evening was over, her parents would be equally impressed by him. Then, of course, he would ride out to the farm to see her every day this winter, regardless of the cold and snow. And then he would propose in the springtime—

"Iris?" Ma's voice intruded on her sweet imaginings. "Are you ready to leave, dear?"

Iris refocused her attention on her parents, surprised to see that Grandma Landon was no longer standing with them. The advanced hour seemed to hit her all at once. She covered a yawn with her hand.

Pa smiled at her. "It looks as if our daughter is more than ready. If we don't whisk her away soon, I'm concerned she will fall asleep standing in the foyer." He led them to the doorway where Aunt Dolly and Uncle Mac stood.

After hugs and best wishes were exchanged, Iris collected her cloak and followed her parents to the waiting carriage. Cold night air made her nose tingle, but the warm bricks at her feet kept her from shivering. She drifted in and out of sleep as her parents talked quietly of the evening. She heard her pa mention something about a meeting of the Cherokee leaders, but the words wove themselves into her dreams. Tomorrow she would remember to ask him about it.

Chapter 2

Adam Stuart balled up his left fist and shook it at the dark sky, even though he cringed inwardly at the bleak hatred consuming his heart. But how could a caring God allow such a thing to happen?

Up until this day, he'd hoped he was wrong, but today he'd been proven absolutely correct in his pessimistic predictions. He spat at the ground. The treaty had been signed in New Echota this afternoon, a few days after Christmas. This should be a season of rejoicing and celebrating the human birth of God, not a time of fear and perfidy.

Today Adam had been an appalled witness to the worst kind of travesty. A small group of Cherokee leaders had sold their people's extensive landholdings in Georgia, Tennessee, North Carolina, and Alabama to officials of the United States. They had willingly agreed to abandon their homes, move their families hundreds of miles away to a wild and unforgiving wilderness, and start all over again.

Couldn't they see this would not be the end? They had been conceding tracts of their land to white men for more than two decades. And still they were asked to move—again and again and again. If this pattern continued, the Cherokee would soon be nothing more than a memory, a footnote in the history of the United States. Why had God created these people if He was willing to let them be destroyed? And why had God given Adam this desire to protect them?

Adam looked up once more at the sky. Hadn't he given up everything to pursue his mission? And for what? The bitter taste of absolute defeat.

A harsh laugh escaped his chapped lips. Loss and defeat were his only companions anymore. What would he say to those who were depending on him back in Ross's Landing? What would John Ross, the real leader of the Cherokee Nation, say? How could he justify what had happened? Would things look better tomorrow? Or worse?

Could he have done anything to change the treaty signing? His mind saw again the hard faces of the Cherokee and the gleeful expressions of the white officers. Both sides had already made up their minds and were not willing to listen to anything he said. He'd tried everything, hadn't he? No matter what arguments he put forth, no one wanted to admit the possibility of making a terrible mistake. In the absence of Chief Ross, why hadn't he been able to make John Ridge and his followers see that their actions would affect the Cherokee people for generations to come? Betrayed by these chieftains who actually represented only a small number of the tribe, what would they do?

The night seemed to grow even darker as Adam tried to make himself face the inevitable. The God he had always worshipped was apparently a white God who cared nothing for the plight of Indians, whether they worshipped Him or not. The Bible spoke of a God who loved and protected the helpless and innocent, but Adam had learned to disregard such fanciful stories.

His horse whinnied. Adam leaned forward, feeling a little guilty to have forced his faithful mount back onto the path they'd traveled that very afternoon. "Careful, Samson. I know you're cold, but you have great strength in these—"

Samson reared up, and Adam fought to keep his seat. What was wrong with his horse?

A moment later he realized that the shadows to his right were moving. It was the only warning he had. Suddenly he was surrounded by a silent, deadly group. He fought to reach his rifle, but it was hopeless.

A noiseless adversary threw himself toward the saddle.

Adam clung to the pommel with dogged determination, but a blow to his head made him see stars. He was jerked off Samson. He crashed to the ground and tasted the cold, wet soil of the path he'd been traveling. Still fighting, Adam turned over in time to see the edge of a tomahawk sweeping toward him. A mighty roll sent him off the path and into dense brush. Thorns caught at his clothing and tore at his skin.

Grunts and stomps followed him into the forest.

With no time to get to his feet, he kept rolling. And then he was free of the brambles, hurtling downward to what would likely be his last resting place.

∼

Something tickled Adam's nose. A leaf? He reached up to bat it away and groaned. His arm hurt. He squinted to focus his vision, surprised to see dappled sunlight sparkling on dew-laced grass. Where was he? The woods? That was odd. He tried to sit up, but pain pushed him back against the cold ground.

He took a deep breath and tried to remember what had happened. He'd been going back home. Then he remembered his restive horse and moving shadows. He'd been attacked! His outspokenness at the treaty signing must have caused some in the Ridge party to think he was a liability.

Adam remembered falling under the blows and rolling away from his attackers. They must have left him for dead. Adam realized he was lucky to be alive, but his luck was going to run out if he couldn't find his way to shelter.

He decided to try rolling over. The pain was excruciating. He clamped his lips against the yell filling his chest. His assailants might still be in the area. He managed to get one elbow under him then the other. The effort had his body slick with sweat even though Adam could feel cold air against his skin.

He pushed against his elbows and managed to get his head and upper torso high enough to look around him. Wilderness was all he saw. He could hear a nearby stream, which made him realize how parched his throat was. He needed to get on his feet, get to water, and then find shelter so he could assess his wounds. He pushed again, but the pain that swept over him made Adam realize he would not be walking anywhere. His leg was either broken or badly sprained.

He lay down again and panted for a while. The world seemed to disappear as he fought the waves of pain. Anguish that was as much mental as physical racked him. Adam didn't want to die. He would not die.

He got up on his elbows again and dragged his body forward, bracing against the pain caused by moving his injured leg. Slanted ground helped him reach the stream. He ducked his head in the cold, clear water for a moment and came up spluttering. He used his right hand as a scoop and drank deeply. Renewed strength flowed through him with the water.

After slaking the worst of his thirst, Adam grabbed the trunk of a young poplar and pulled himself into a seated position to take stock. His leg was causing the worst of his pain, but his arms and face had been scratched and scraped as he fell down the ravine. He was lucky that his wounds were so minor.

Minor! He laughed at the word. He was in a tight fix, and he knew it. The chance that he would survive seemed very small, but as long as he had strength, he had to try.

He turned his head at the sound of crunching leaves. His attackers? A bear? His heartbeat tripled its thumps in his chest.

Then he saw what was making the noise. A rabbit hopped its way across fallen limbs and approached the stream a few feet away. What Adam wouldn't give for his rifle. That fat rabbit looked like a mighty fine meal.

The rabbit must have sensed the danger because it reversed course and disappeared back into the woods.

His gaze followed the path of the animal, and then he saw it. A cabin! Shelter! It was only a few yards away from his position, but he'd been so focused on reaching the stream he'd not even seen it.

"Hello the house." His voice rasped the greeting that would reassure the owner he was not an Indian brave. No one responded, but because his hoarse call might not have been heard, he tried again. "Hello the house!" This time his voice was stronger. Adam waited for any inhabitant to respond, but only the noise of the forest answered him.

Maybe whoever lived there was out setting or checking traps. This far away from the safety of a settlement, the cabin was likely occupied by a trapper. Adam hoped he would at least help him with his leg and feed him so he'd have a chance to get back to civilization.

Whatever the outcome, he knew he could not remain in the open. But before he began dragging himself to the door of the cabin, he would need something to support his leg. A good bit of deadfall lay within reach. He chose a limb that was as big around as his arm. He pulled off his grimy overcoat and turned it inside out, stopping to rest for a few moments after the effort.

Adam reached for his hunting knife, thankful to feel its reassuring hilt under his fingers. With a satisfied grunt, he went to work cutting out the coat's lining and tearing it into strips. He laid the limb against his leg and bound it with the strips from his coat. Another large limb would serve as a crutch to help him keep his weight off his injured leg.

Using the sapling and the second limb, Adam pulled himself up. The world around him lost some definition, but he managed to get to his feet. With a stilted, shuffling movement, he lurched forward. One step. Rest. Another step. Rest. Thirty-two steps and rests got him to the door of the cabin.

What he saw carved into the rough planks made him groan in despair. Three letters—GTT. Gone to Texas. The cabin was abandoned. He would find no help here.

Adam looked up at the sky. *What now, God? Are You through with me yet? Or do You have other plans in mind?*

God didn't answer, of course. Proving again that He did not exist. Or if He did, He had no concern for mortals.

Adam forced the door open and made his slow way into the cabin. It was a single room with sparse furnishings: a square table, one chair, and a straw sleeping mat. But it represented shelter. He held on to the wall and made his way to the fireplace. It was cold, of course, but a sizable log still lay in it; a few smaller logs were stacked to one side.

Adam spied a chunk of flint on the rough mantelpiece and knew he would soon have warmth. He steeled himself to ignore the pain in his leg as he worked to ensure his survival. A few of the cotton strips from his coat lining made a combustible ball, which he placed on the sooty back log. He broke smaller twigs off the firewood and tented them above the cotton. Striking his knife against the flint created molten chips that soon ignited the cotton and twigs.

With a satisfied grunt, he added a couple of logs and soon had a blaze going.

A rumbling sound filled the small room. Food was his next problem, as his stomach had reminded him. He forced himself up once more and continued his exploration. Two wooden barrels in one corner revealed dried corn and sprouted potatoes. His stomach rumbled again, and his mouth watered. He picked up a potato. It was soft but still edible.

He also discovered a pair of identical clay jugs. He picked one up, surprised to find it so heavy. He uncorked it and sniffed the contents. Moonshine. A satisfied sound escaped him. The alcohol would come in handy to cleanse his wounds.

The voice of his stern father echoed in Adam's head. *Alcohol is the devil's brew. It makes fools of wise men and drowns the morals of saints.* Well, no need to worry about that. He would only use it to cleanse his wounds. . .and perhaps take a swallow or two to dull the pain in his leg.

Chapter 3

Iris tucked a curl under the brim of her riding cap and encouraged her horse, Button, along the road. Brooding white clouds seemed to press down on her shoulders, spewing out fat, lazy flakes that clung to her mittens or melted into her horse's mane.

She pushed Button to a canter. This morning when she'd volunteered to take supplies to Grandpa and Grandma Taylor, her ma had been doubtful. But Iris had been sure she could make the trip before the roads became treacherous. She shook her head. It was far too late to turn back now.

At least she wasn't cooped up at home this afternoon. The thought replaced her concern with the exhilaration of freedom. She loved her family, but spending all of her waking hours in close quarters with them had made her as fidgety as a squirrel. It would be fun to sit by the fire and listen to her grandparents talk about the days when Ma was a little girl. And Grandma probably had something really good to eat, too.

She cantered around a curve and saw her grandparents' house tucked next to their large barn. A relieved sigh escaped her frozen lips. "Whoa, Button." Iris pulled on the reins as she reached the front yard. A curl of smoke rose from the chimney, drifting upward to mingle with the low-lying clouds. She dismounted and pulled off the heavy saddlebags her parents had packed with a ham, a roast, and some of the sugared peach chips her grandma loved.

Grandpa Taylor stomped out onto the front porch, a wool scarf tucked around his ears. His bald head gleamed in the muted light, its smooth surface reminding her of a hen's egg. He followed her to the barn and dragged the door open, pointing her toward an empty stall. "Is everything okay at home?"

Iris nodded as she unsaddled her horse and rubbed him down. "I had to get out of there, though. Eli has a cold, and Ma is making her special liniment to rub on his chest." She wrinkled her nose. "I know it'll make him feel better, but it sure makes the house smell awful."

Grandpa waited for her to exit the stall before fastening the door. "It's a wonder you made it in this weather, but I'm glad you're here." He raised an eyebrow at her. "You'll never guess who has come over to visit today. Wohali and Noya."

"Aunt Noya and Uncle Wohali!" Iris named the Cherokee couple who had been her grandparents' neighbors since before she was born. She grabbed her mittens and followed her grandpa back to the house, thinking of the days when she was younger. She had often played over at their house while Ma and Grandma pieced together quilts. They had a grandniece, Kamama, who was about Iris's age and who had visited them often. Maybe she could find out what Kamama was doing now that they were all grown-up.

Iris stamped the snow and mud off her boots before entering her grandparents' home.

Warm air and the scent of cinnamon welcomed her. Grandma and Aunt Noya were sitting in rocking chairs in front of the fireplace, while Uncle Wohali sat nearby in a straight chair, whittling at a small piece of wood. Grandma was rolling yarn into a ball while Aunt Noya held the newly spun wool in her hand to prevent tangling. They were laughing exuberantly as Iris and her grandfather entered.

Grandma leaned her head back as she laughed. Her hair had been knotted into a loose bun, and she wore a lacy shawl around her shoulders to combat any stray drafts.

Aunt Noya's dark hair had developed a few streaks of gray and reflected the light of the fire she sat in front of.

"What are you two laughing about?" asked Grandpa.

Grandma looked up, dropped her ball of yarn, and clapped her hands together. "It's so good to see you, Iris." She pushed herself up slowly and reached for the black walnut cane Grandpa had made for her last year.

Aunt Noya stood and waited until Iris and her grandma had shared a brief hug before stepping forward. "*Osiyo*, my friend." She used the Cherokee word for hello, her deep voice filled with warmth and welcome.

"Osiyo." Iris threw her arms around the older lady.

She turned to Uncle Wohali, who was awaiting his turn. "Osiyo."

Grandpa grabbed another chair from its peg on the wall and placed it close to the fireplace. "What's the news from your house?"

Even though Grandma and Grandpa had already heard about the Christmas Eve party, Iris gave them a humorous accounting for Uncle Wohali and Aunt Noya's benefit. The quizzical looks on their faces as she described apple bobbing made Iris laugh. No matter that they had lived among white people for two decades or more, some of the traditions still seemed odd to the Indian couple.

"And what happens to the apples that were missed?" Aunt Noya wanted to know.

Iris had to admit she'd never considered the question, but she guessed they went into apple pies or sauce. Whatever the purpose, they would not have gone to waste. Fresh fruit was far too precious, even in a city that bustled with traders.

Grandma finished rolling her yarn and drew out a pair of needles to begin knitting.

"What are you making, Grandma?"

Her grandmother glanced up and smiled. "A new pair of socks for your grandpa. The last time I did the mending, I noticed he had several pairs with more holes than threads."

Grandpa looked a bit sheepish, but he did not contradict her.

Aunt Noya walked to the kitchen area and began collecting dishes with easy familiarity. "Get the blackberry pie and bring it to the table, Iris."

She spotted the lidded iron pot perched on the far edge of the large fireplace. Her mouth began to water. She loved Grandma's fruit pies made in a dutch oven. They always had such flaky crusts and intense fruity flavor. "Blackberry pie is my favorite."

Grandpa removed the coffeepot from its hook on the fireplace while Uncle Wohali tucked his whittling back in his pocket and put his knife in its beaded holster. The reserved Indian stood and picked up an armful of logs, tossing them on the fire to keep it from dying. They all seemed to have their appointed tasks, and they worked together without speaking.

Iris helped move their chairs around the dining table and made sure that a pitcher of fresh cream was placed in the center of the table.

Grandma didn't move from her rocker until everyone else sat down. Then she put away her chain of stitches and joined them at the table. According to established custom, they all linked hands while Grandpa blessed the food.

Iris was so glad she'd made the trip this afternoon. A relaxing visit was exactly what she had needed to combat the fidgets that had been plaguing her for the last few days.

She poured some milk into her cup of steaming coffee and added a dollop of cream to her dish of pie. "How is Kamama doing?"

A gentle smile crossed Aunt Noya's face. "Our niece has gone back to the village where she was raised to take the message of salvation to her family."

Iris forgot all about the food on the table. "How wonderful! The last time I saw her, Kamama was more worried about clothing styles than witnessing. What changed her mind?"

Uncle Wohali, a man Iris could never have accused of being talkative, spoke up. "Her cousin was killed in a fight several months ago. He was not a Christian." His face was as hard as granite.

Iris thought of how she would feel in his place. "How awful. I know that must have hurt all of you."

Aunt Noya reached a hand to her husband. "To know that you will never again see a loved one in this life or the next is a very difficult thing."

Grandpa cleared his throat and leaned forward. "It's very courageous of Kamama to use the tragedy for good. Before she left, she told Martha and me that her desire is to make sure no other Cherokee has to die without hearing the teaching of Christ."

"Yes," Grandma agreed, a smile of sympathy deepening the soft wrinkles on her face. "I know you miss her greatly."

Iris looked at the people around the table as they talked of the Indians who still had not heard of Christ's message. She almost envied Kamama for her sense of purpose. She would much rather it had not taken such a tragedy, but at least some good would come from the untimely death of Kamama's cousin.

She thought of Paul's promise in Romans that "all things work together for good to them that love God." When she was younger, she'd thought the verse meant that only good things would happen to the people who loved God, but now she thought that Paul was trying to encourage early Christians by explaining that all things—the good events as well as the bad ones—were tools God used to bring blessings to His people.

She reached into the pocket of her skirt and pulled out the familiar newsprint advertisement. How many times had she unfolded it and read it? How many nights had she clutched it in her hands as she prayed for guidance. Iris dreamed of making her life count for something more than attending parties and bobbing for apples. Would she be able to find God's path for her life like Kamama had done? Or would she waste away here, an object of pity to her neighbors? When would her time come? Or would it? Would her family shield her from danger so assiduously that she never had the chance to fulfill her dreams?

❧

Iris bent over the buckskin breeches her young brother had torn, punching her needle through the thick hide. "I wish Eli would be more careful with his clothing."

Ma stirred a large pot of stew that smelled wonderful. "He's too busy to be careful, dear. A lot of work didn't get done while he was laid up in bed with that terrible fever last week."

"I was worried he would never stop coughing, but that nasty-smelling salve really eased his congestion."

"Thank the Lord." Ma bowed her head, and Iris knew she was repeating her thanks to God. After a moment she looked up and smiled widely. "I'm so thankful the rest of us avoided catching it. I can remember past winters when it seemed that you and your sister and brother passed sickness back and forth for weeks on end."

"That must have been hard for you, Ma. How did you cope with all three of us being sick at the same time?"

Ma moved to the table and diced a few more potatoes. "Although I spent a great deal of time worrying about you and praying for your recovery, the actual work wasn't difficult. When you have your own children, you'll understand." She added the potatoes to the stewpot and began stirring once more. "Now that Eli's fully recovered, his appetite is back. Whether he's careful with those breeches or not, he'll soon outgrow them."

"That's true," Iris agreed. She set a final stitch, tied a knot in the thread, and cut it with a satisfied smile. She held the breeches up to inspect her work. "Should I also let out the waist?"

Ma shook her head. "Those ought to have enough room for now. But I'm sure your brother will need them loosened in a month or so."

Iris leaned back in her chair and breathed in the pleasant aroma of the bubbling stew. "Is Pa going to bring us some sassafras root to boil? I've been wanting some for weeks now. Ever since Aunt Dolly's Christmas dinner, as a matter of fact. She always has the best tasting sassafras tea."

The sound of hoofbeats stopped their conversation. Ma put the lid on her pot and turned to the door. "Speaking of your pa, I imagine that's him now. He went into town early this morning."

Iris would have asked why, but the door swung open as her pa walked into the house.

"How are the most beautiful women in Davidson County doing this fine morning?" He caught his wife in a hug and placed a loud kiss on her cheek. Then he turned to Iris and grabbed her from her chair, swinging her around like she weighed only a few pounds. "I have news that both of you are going to want to hear."

When Pa placed her back on her feet, Iris put her hands on her hips and looked at him. "What is it, Pa?"

"Yes, tell us your news, Asher."

Iris wished she could stop time and savor this moment. Her ma practically glowed with love now that Pa was home. And Pa, dressed in a black suit, white shirt, and black cravat, was the very picture of the gentleman farmer. Iris wondered if he ever regretted giving up his financial career to work the soil. Of course his political aspirations had ended before he and Ma even married. Still, by the accounts of her aunt and grandparents, her pa had been poised to become one of Andrew Jackson's most trusted advisers. But he'd turned down the opportunity to travel the world with the famous and popular president.

Her pa reached into his coat and produced several folded sheets of ivory paper with a flourish. "Guess who has sent us a letter?"

Iris mentioned Pa's younger sister. "Aunt Mary?"

Ma clasped her hands and rested them against her chin. "My sister, Eleanor?"

Pa shook his head at both of them.

"Has Uncle Donny written from Philadelphia?"

"Nope. That's three guesses. Do you give up?"

At their nods he lowered the stationery so they could see the return address printed above the wax seal.

"Pastor Miller?" Ma's voice was a squeal of joy.

"Yes." Pa winked at Iris. "And there's even a separate note inside from Camie."

"Camie wrote to me?" Iris's heart leaped. She grabbed for the letter but was frustrated as her pa lifted it up over his head.

Hannah, Iris's younger sister, ran in as they were trying to grab the sheets. "Whatever are you doing?" She took the chair her sister had recently vacated and clambered atop it. With her additional height, it was easy for her to reach Pa's hand. She grabbed the letter with a triumphant squeak.

Iris was not about to tolerate her younger sister stealing the letter. "Give it to me. You don't even remember Camie."

"I do, too." Hannah stuck out her tongue at Iris. "She's that blond girl who used to come over and help us shell peas."

"That's enough, you two." Ma interrupted them before a fight could break out. "Give me the letter, Hannah. I'll read it out loud so we can all enjoy it at the same time."

Iris was chastened by her mother's admonition. "I'll do better, Ma. I promise."

She silently berated herself while her parents talked about the family who used to live in Nashville. Besides being Aunt Dolly's pastor, Reverend Miller, along with his wife, had built and managed a school for the local Indians. Iris and her family had worked at the school as she grew up, infusing her with the desire to do something important with her life. The Millers' daughter, Camie, had been one of her best friends. They had even been baptized together on a cool Sunday morning in the calm blue waters of a small stream just outside the city.

Iris had cried for days when Reverend Miller announced that he had been called to work at Brainerd Mission near an Indian settlement on the Tennessee River called Ross's Landing. She and Camie had hugged and made promises to always stay in touch. But it was hard to fulfill that promise. The years went by. Camie had married a fine Christian man, a surveyor who had come to work in the area and decided to stay after falling in love with her. Iris wished she could have gone to the wedding, but her parents had been unable to leave at that time and unwilling to send her alone. It was the story of her life. They didn't want to let her out of their sight.

Pa cleared his throat and put a hand on her ma's arm before she could start reading the letter she held. "I read the letter before coming home, and Reverend Miller mentioned something we need to discuss."

Ma folded the stationery. "What is it, Asher?"

He gazed at his hands for a moment before speaking. Iris wondered what could be wrong. She held her breath and concentrated her attention on him.

"Reverend Miller mentioned in his letter that Camie has decided to give up her job as nanny to take care of her own children."

Ma's brow wrinkled. "Wasn't she caring for some Cherokee orphans?"

"That's right. Their parents died, and they are living with their grandfather. Camie was hired not only to care for the children but also to teach them how to live in a white man's world. A house slave has been looking after them ever since Camie left several months before her babies were born. The little girls' grandfather has not been able to find a suitable replacement yet." Pa glanced toward Iris. "Reverend Miller is hoping we can suggest someone to take her place. It would have to be a young Christian lady of excellent reputation."

At first his words did not penetrate fully. Then their import seemed to explode in her mind. "Me! I can go and take Camie's place."

Her parents exchanged a long look. Iris could feel the excitement bursting out like sunshine after a week of rain. "Please, Pa. You have to say yes. You know it's right."

"I don't know, Iris." Ma's voice sounded troubled. "Your pa and I will talk about it."

"But Ma! It'll be perfect. I will be right there in the same town with Camie and her family. They live so close to Reverend and Mrs. Miller. You know they'll watch over me as closely as you and Pa do. I have to do this."

"Iris, I knew what your reaction would be from the moment I read Reverend Miller's correspondence." Pa walked to where her ma still sat with the letter in her lap. "I've been praying about what to say since I left Nashville."

Iris could feel her heart thumping in her chest. They had to let her go. It was too perfect. She pulled the dog-eared advertisement from the pocket of her skirt. "I've been reading this article nearly every day for the past three months and praying God would either find a way to send me to teach or take the desire from my heart." She paused for a breath. "The desire is still there, and I truly believe He is showing me the way."

"Although that part of Tennessee is not as settled as we are here, you wouldn't be going to some frontier town in the wilds of Texas," her ma cautioned. "And being a nanny to two young girls is not the same as a teaching position. It will only be a temporary situation at best."

Iris shook her head. "I know that, but once I am out there, God may open the way to other jobs. If not, I could always come back to Nashville. When I found out that Kamama had gone to witness to the people in her village, I began to understand that there are many opportunities to serve God by serving others. I even thought maybe one of my aunts or uncles would need to have me come in the same way that you moved to town to take care of Aunt Dolly, Ma. But no one needed me, so I went back to the advertisement in the newspaper. I thought maybe everything would work out so I could go there. But I always knew it was a remote possibility."

Ma held out a hand to Pa. "I have to admit it causes me much less worry to think of your going to be in the same area as the Millers, but there are other matters we should consider. I rely on your help here, Iris."

Hannah had been so quiet during the discussion that Iris had nearly forgotten her sister was in the room until she spoke. "I can take over Iris's chores, Ma."

Iris beamed at her younger sister. She had never expected Hannah to come to her assistance. "See, Ma? We can work it out."

"I don't know." Ma turned to Pa. "What do you think?"

Iris could see the answer in his eyes. He thought it was a good idea. They were going to let her go! She would get to see another part of Tennessee and live close to her best friend! Iris wanted to jump up and down. But this was not the time to make either of her parents question her maturity. She would have to maintain her dignity until she could get off by herself.

"Maybe Hannah and I should go out to the springhouse and get some fresh milk while you and Pa discuss it."

"Don't you want to read your note?" Ma asked.

Iris nodded. She broke the seal with one tip of her finger, careful to avoid destruction of the stationery. From now on she would be on her guard at all times and show her parents just how self-controlled their elder daughter could be.

At least while anyone was around to see her.

Chapter 4

Daisy, Tennessee
February 1836

The stagecoach driver jerked the door open, startling the passengers from various stages of slumber. "We're at Poe's Crossroads, young lady."

A blush crept into Iris's cheeks as she tried to understand why the coachman was beckoning toward her. "But I'm supposed to be going to Daisy, Tennessee."

The driver rolled his eyes, showing his disgust for her ignorance. "They're one and the same. Daisy's the name of the town, but this is the crossroads where the stage stops. Did you expect me to take you to your doorstep?"

Reassured, Iris inched forward, trying not to jostle the sleeping child on her right. Mr. Howington, the middle-aged gentleman sitting in the position opposite hers, offered her a hand. She had been miffed at Pa for treating her like a baby by asking Mr. Howington to watch over her during the overland trip from Nashville, but she had to admit that he'd made the journey much more bearable. When they'd stopped for meals, he'd been her escort. Each evening when they reached a coaching inn, he'd made sure that some other female—whether the innkeeper's daughter or a female passenger—slept in the same room with her so that her reputation would be protected. If not for his persistence, on several occasions she would not have received fresh water to wash away the day's dusty travel. He'd even shared his food with her on those days that the coachman had decided to press on rather than stop for a midday meal. But perhaps most importantly, Mr. Howington had always made sure she occupied the seat directly behind the driver. The other passengers had grumbled a bit since that position inside the coach endured the least number of bumps and jars, but they had backed down in the face of his firm insistence.

"Thank you so much, Mr. Howington." Iris allowed him to pull her forward until she could stand up, albeit with a rather hunched stance. "I can never repay your kindness."

"That's quite all right, Miss Landon. I would only hope some other gentleman might do the same favor for any daughter of mine."

In the crowded interior of the coach, Iris did not have enough room to give the dear man a hug, so she contented herself with squeezing his hand. "Godspeed."

One of the other passengers yawned while a grouchy man frowned at her. "Would you go on and get out so we can get on our way? I've got to get to Washington before Friday."

Another blush suffused Iris's cheeks. She had overheard the bad-tempered man offering a bonus to the stagecoach driver to get him to his destination early. Not only had that meant long days on the coach, but it had also meant she had a problem. Camie and her husband would not expect her to arrive tonight. As she inched her way past the feet, bags, and boxes of the passengers, Iris wondered how she would arrange transportation to their home.

She stepped to the ground with a sigh of relief and took a moment to thank God for her safe arrival. A thump to her right made Iris jump back and stumble against the outside of the coach. Her trunk lay in the dusty road at her feet. A grunt warned her just in time. Iris looked up to see her portmanteau, the large case that held her dearest possessions, sail through the air to land neatly atop the trunk. She winced, hoping the bottle of expensive French perfume from Grandma Landon had survived the coachman's callous treatment.

Iris would have complained about his roughness with her items, but the coachman had already regained his bench on the front of the large coach. He whipped up the team of four horses without a backward glance, and the equipage careened around a corner and disappeared.

"Well, I never." Iris looked around her at the tiny town that was to be her new home. What she could see in the gloom of late evening was not inspiring. Only three or four buildings seemed to make up the town of Daisy, and only one of those was lit up. There were no lights outside, of course. Not that she'd expected them. This was not Nashville, after all. It was barely a community. According to the description Camie had sent, only a few dozen families lived on this side of the Tennessee River, although more settlers were beginning to make their way here. The other side of the river was mostly Indian Territory, although it did boast a trading post, called Ross's Landing, and Brainerd Mission, where Reverend and Mrs. Miller lived.

Iris wondered if she could walk to Camie's house but realized she didn't even know which way to go. Tears burned at the corners of her eyes. Whenever she'd imagined arriving, it had been in the middle of the day, not during the gloom of night and not a whole day ahead of schedule. What was she supposed to do?

The cool night air nipped at her cheeks as she wondered if the town of Daisy boasted an inn. She drew her shoulders back in an effort to bolster her waning confidence and walked down the street in search of a likely prospect.

Raucous laughter spewed from the one lit building in town. It must be a tavern. Iris took a step in that direction. Perhaps they could direct her to the Sherers' home or at least rent her a room for the evening. Another roar of laughter slowed her. She tilted her head and listened intently. Someone played a piano, and a lady sang. It sounded like a friendly place. She pasted a smile on her face, gripped her reticule tightly, and stepped past the hitching post onto the raised walkway that ran the length of the building.

As Iris reached out a tentative hand toward the door, it swung outward. A man exited precipitously, barreling into her and pushing her down. Her teeth clacked together. "Well, I never!"

"What are you doing on t' ground?" His slurred voice indicated that the man had been imbibing. "Here." He leaned over and offered his hand.

Iris wanted to burst into tears. Maybe she was having a bad dream. But then why did the ground under her feel so solid? She put her hand in the stranger's and allowed him to help her up. Her nose wrinkled at the smell of whiskey. In their work with the Indians at home, her parents had often had to deal with Indians who had imbibed too much "firewater."

The stranger bowed, still holding onto her hand. "Adam Stuart's m' name."

Iris didn't know how to answer him. She should have been embarrassed by his casual manners. Back home she would never have considered speaking to a man without a proper introduction. And she certainly wouldn't allow him to continue holding her hand. She gave a tug and pulled free.

He pointed a finger at her. "Why are you wandering outside all alone?"

Some part of her mind noticed that Mr. Stuart was tall, taller than she. He had a square chin and even features—she might even call him handsome if he were sober. His eyes were large and appeared brown in the muted light. They shone with intelligence and something else—was it vulnerability? Pain? For a brief instant, she wanted to comfort him.

What was she thinking? Offer comfort to a complete stranger? Iris shook her head and immediately put a hand up to keep her hat from falling off. Her pins must have loosened while she napped in the coach, and then her jarring tumble had made the situation more tenuous. Now her hair seemed determined to escape captivity. She fought the heavy curls, tucking them away with little success. Finally she gave up to concentrate on her main problem. "I need to find Lance and Camie Sherer."

Mr. Stuart turned in a circle. "I don't see them."

"Of course not." Iris wanted to scream her frustration. Why did Mr. Stuart have to be drunk? "They are probably at home. I need someone to help me get to the home of Mr. Lance Sherer."

He frowned and stroked his chin with a finger as if deep in thought.

Iris waited a moment or two for him to answer. She had opened her mouth to ask him again when he dropped his hand and nodded at her.

"Lance Sherer. Nice man. Very smart. He already has a wife, y'know. And children." He hiccuped and smiled at her. A dimple appeared in his left cheek, making him appear debonair in spite of the wrinkled condition of his dark suit.

"Well, I never!" Her indignation made her splutter the words. What was the man thinking? "I am a good friend of his wife. I've come at her suggestion."

"Is there a problem here?" Unnoticed, another man had stepped through the doors of the tavern.

Foreboding made Iris's heart thump loudly. Now she faced two strangers, and both of them were likely inebriated. What should she do? Cry for help? Make a dash through the door of the tavern? Or would that land her in even more trouble?

She took a deep breath to calm her fears and glanced at the second stranger. At least he seemed to be able to stand straight without aid. And he was tall, too. Were all the men tall in this part of Tennessee? She couldn't believe that her first two encounters in Daisy were with men she had to look up to.

In appearance the second stranger was the opposite of the amiable man behind her. His hair was blond, and his shoulders were straight and wide. She couldn't tell for certain in the dim light, but Iris thought his eyes were either blue or green. His style of dress was different, too—buckskin pants and a fur-lined coat instead of a crumpled suit. He carried a wide-brimmed hat in one hand, which he swept in an arc as he bowed to her. "Nathan Pierce at your service, miss."

Iris didn't know whether she should laugh or cry. Here she was stuck in the middle of nowhere, all her worldly goods lying in the street, and presented with two different men—one a charming rogue and the other a model of propriety. Except. . . If Mr. Nathan Pierce was such an upright citizen, what was he doing coming out of the tavern?

Another wave of laughter from inside suggested that the three of them would soon be joined by other examples of the male population to be found in Daisy.

"Do you know where Mr. and Mrs. Lance Sherer live?"

Mr. Pierce inclined his head over his right shoulder. "About two miles down that road."

Two more men stumbled out of the tavern. One of them stared at her but moved past without saying anything when he caught the warning look in Mr. Pierce's eyes.

Mr. Pierce returned his gaze to her face. "I can take you there, if you'd like."

Iris wondered if the stranger was trustworthy. But what other option did she have? She couldn't stay out here in the street all night.

"Don't pay att. . .att'ntion to him." Mr. Stuart's words were still as slurred as when he'd first come outside, even though the crisp night air should have penetrated the fog of alcohol. He grabbed hold of the hitching post and leaned against it. "I c'n take care of you."

Mr. Pierce deftly inserted himself between them. He held out his arm. "Ignore him. Mr. Stuart is too. . .tired. . .to recall his manners."

Iris certainly couldn't fault Mr. Pierce's manners. Mr. Stuart was obviously not tired. But she appreciated Mr. Pierce's kindness in trying to shield her from the man's boorishness. Maybe it would be safe to allow him to take her to the Sherers' home. She was about to tell him so when she remembered her trunk and portmanteau. She glanced around him to the street. From the corner of her vision she saw Mr. Stuart make a shaky bow and stagger away. She returned her attention to Mr. Pierce.

"Don't worry about your things. I'll have someone come back in the wagon and pick them up. When you wake up in the morning, everything will be there."

"I cannot thank you enough, Mr. Pierce." She put her hand on his arm, impressed by how hard his muscles felt under the thick fur coat.

"It's my pleasure, Miss. . . ?"

"Landon."

"Miss Landon." He led her to a tall roan stallion. "May I?"

Iris nodded and found herself picked up and tossed into the Spanish-style saddle. It was a good thing she'd spent time riding bareback, or she might have fallen, since there was no place to hook her knee without immodestly displaying her ankles. Mr. Pierce mounted behind her and put an arm around her waist. Now she was safe from falling, but what about her reputation?

With a tiny shrug, she decided there was little choice if she wished to reach Camie's home tonight. And what was the alternative? Taking her chances with the charming drunk? Not a good idea. She relaxed as she realized that Mr. Pierce was not going to take advantage of the situation.

"How do you know the Sherers?" His deep voice tickled her ear.

"Camie's father, Reverend Miller, built a school for the Indians around the Nashville area, and my parents were very involved in its mission to teach English and spread the message of salvation. Camie and I worked and played together there. We were as close as sisters growing up."

"I see."

Silence grew between them, punctuated by the steady hoofbeats of his horse. Iris tried to force her tired mind to come up with another topic of conversation. "Have you seen her little girls?"

"No." He shifted in the saddle. "Children make me nervous."

"That's because they're not yours."

Whatever his answer would have been was lost as they turned off the road toward a house that stood some feet away. It huddled at the edge of a dense forest, every window dark and shuttered against the night.

"They are not expecting you?" Mr. Pierce asked.

"Not exactly." The Sherers were to meet her. But she had never imagined that her arrival would be twelve hours early.

"Hello the house!" Mr. Pierce's yell ended her introspection. She waited while he dismounted and reached up to lift her down, once again marveling at the fact that he was so tall. Once her feet were on the ground, Iris actually had to bend her head back to meet his gaze.

Mr. Pierce escorted Iris to the front door with the same easy confidence he'd shown since they met. She deeply appreciated his taking charge because she felt overwhelmed. She stood to one side as he banged on the door. At first no sound came from inside the Sherer house, but then she heard heavy footfalls on the staircase. Yellow light flickered around the outer edge of the front door as it opened.

"Nathan Pierce? What brings you out in the middle of the night?" Lance Sherer's voice was deep and authoritative.

"I'm sorry for disturbing you, Lance." Her escort was nothing if not polite. Iris admired politeness. Her parents had stressed the finer points of social niceties, saying that living in the country was no excuse for poor manners. Apparently Mr. Pierce's parents agreed with that philosophy. "I have brought a friend of your family." He glanced back to where she stood. "Miss Landon was recently delivered to us by stage."

"Iris?" Camie's husband stepped onto the narrow porch, a candle in one hand and a rifle tucked under his other elbow. "Is it really you?" He leaned the rifle against the doorjamb and beckoned to them to enter.

She nodded and stepped forward with a little hiccup of relief mixed with tiredness. "It's so good to meet you."

Mr. Sherer was not as tall as the other two men she'd met tonight, destroying Iris's earlier hope that all the men in this part of Tennessee would make her feel of normal height. Strands of dark brown hair straggled across his forehead, but her attention was caught by his wide blue eyes. They were so kind and calm, so full of welcome. She liked him immediately and could see why Camie had fallen in love with him. Everything about him, from his warm smile to his beckoning hand gestures, made her feel welcome.

"Camie, it's your friend Iris." He looked over his shoulder to address his wife, who must have been standing on the stairway. "She's come to us early."

Camie's husband turned back to look past her. "Where are your bags?"

"They're back in town, lying in the middle of the road." Iris forced the words between stiff lips. Irritation straightened her spine as she remembered the callous coachman.

Mr. Pierce diverted her thoughts by gently taking her hand and pressing a warm kiss on her gloved fingers. "I hope to see you again soon."

He was such a nice man. "I hope so, too." Iris couldn't help being flattered by the obvious admiration in his voice. She watched him stride back to his horse before stepping back to allow Mr. Sherer to close the door.

She forgot all about Mr. Pierce as she suddenly found herself wrapped in Camie's tight hug. Her irritation and exhaustion disappeared as her tears mixed with those of her friend.

Camie was all grown up. Gone was the shy girl she remembered—in her place was a beautiful young matron. She was dressed in a flannel gown of pale blue that flattered her delicate complexion. Her honey gold hair was plaited and hung down her back like a silk rope. She had thrown a cotton wrap over her shoulders before coming downstairs, and she hugged it to her as protection against the cold night air.

Camie picked up a candle that was sitting on the table next to the front door and lit it from her husband's before handing it to Iris. With the additional light, Iris could make out the wide foyer with doors off to the right and left. She guessed that one led to the parlor and the other perhaps to a dining room or the kitchen.

Mr. Sherer looked at Camie. "I wonder if I should saddle a horse and go help him with Miss Landon's bags."

"Please don't stand on ceremony, Mr. Sherer. I hope you will call me Iris."

His nod seemed to hold approval. "I would be delighted, if you'll return the favor and call me Lance."

"I doubt you should make the effort to go back into town, dear." Camie raised an eyebrow in an expression of mischief that took Iris back to their shared childhood. "It would take you too long to saddle the horse. Besides, you need to give Mr. Pierce the chance to impress our Iris with his chivalry."

Iris looked down at her gloved hands, surprised that the candlelight showed how much dirt had accumulated on the white material. She wanted nothing more than to wash up, fall in bed, and sleep for two or three days.

"Tell me all about your trip." Camie pulled her plaited hair over her shoulder. "Was it scary? Did you have any trouble on the way? Why did you get here in the middle of the night?"

"Now Camie." Her husband shook his head. "There will be plenty of time for you to catch up on the news tomorrow. Why don't you get Iris upstairs to a

152

bedchamber? I'm sure she's about to drop where she stands."

Camie sighed but nodded. "You're right, of course." She lit another candle and led the way upstairs. "I can't wait to hear all about your journey."

"And I can't wait to see your daughters." The hallway at the top of the stairs disappeared into shadowy darkness their candles barely penetrated. Iris followed Camie past two doorways to a third that was closed.

"They are adorable. Like the dolls we played with when we were little girls."

"Only better." Iris noticed a framed sampler hanging on the wall, but it was too dark for her to see its details.

"They have taught me so much." Camie's serious voice drew Iris's attention away from the wall. "I understand the love of God like I never did before." She opened the third door. "Here we are."

Iris wanted to ask about her comment, but it was late. She watched as Camie bustled over to the bed and patted the mattress. "I can ask Lance to bring up some coals so you can have a fire while you undress."

"Don't worry about that." Iris could almost feel the softness of the sheets enveloping her. "But I do need a nightgown since my bags are still in town."

"Of course." Camie clucked her tongue against the roof of her mouth. "What kind of hostess must you think I am?"

Iris put her candle on a tall dressing table that was angled in a corner to one side of the fireplace. "How could you know that I would arrive with only the clothes I am standing in?"

As Camie disappeared into the dark hallway, Iris could hear her still bemoaning the failure to anticipate her guest's needs.

While she waited, Iris pulled off her hat and let her hair cascade down with a sense of relief. She could hear pins plinking on the wooden floor where it was not protected by Camie's rug. She pulled off her gloves and placed them next to her candle. The air in the bedroom was quite nippy, but she had no doubt that she would warm up quickly once she buried herself under those inviting quilts.

While she waited for her friend to return, Iris rinsed her face and hands with water from a washbowl. It was a relief to rid herself of some of the grit from her travels, even though the cold water stole her breath away for a moment.

"Here we go." Camie reentered with a thick cotton nightdress over her arm. "Oh my! I had forgotten how curly your hair is. Would you like me to plait it for you?"

Iris shook her head, sending the brown tendrils flying in several directions. "I have lots of practice. Go on back to bed. You need your sleep. I'll be fine." To prove her point, she scraped her hair back with nimble fingers and twisted it into submission.

"Well, if you need anything else, just call out. We're right down the hall."

Camie laid the nightdress across her bed and left her.

It wasn't long before Iris was in bed, the weight of the heavy quilts pushing her into the softness of the mattress. After thanking God for bringing her safely to her destination and asking for His protection over her loved ones, Iris let her thoughts drift to Camie's statement about her little girls. Did God take the same pleasure in the birth of each of His children? What a wonderful thought.

She burrowed down into the bed, her mind filled with praise for the loving God who provided a way for showing her how wide and deep His love ran.

❧

An insistent tapping sound roused Iris. For a moment she didn't recognize her surroundings, but then she remembered. Her life was really beginning. She had made it to Daisy and to the Sherers' home. The sound was someone knocking at her door. "Come in."

"Well, Sleeping Beauty." Camie entered the room with a large wooden tray balanced in her hands. She had pulled her hair back and twisted it into a bun. Several strands had worked free already and framed her face. Her gray dress was accented with a darker gray collar and cuffs, and a starched white apron protected her skirt. She was the very picture of a matron. "I finally decided I'd have to come up here and rouse you if I was ever going to find out about all the people back in Nashville. I hope you still have a prodigious memory."

Iris sniffed the air appreciatively. "Is that breakfast?"

With a nod, Camie placed the tray on the edge of the bed.

Iris could see a stack of fluffy batter cakes, fried eggs, a small mountain of bacon strips, potatoes, and biscuits. "I'm hungry, but I couldn't eat half of all the food you brought up here."

"I'm going to help, silly." Camie divided the food between two plates and handed one to Iris. "Lance is watching the girls while you and I eat breakfast. They woke up around daybreak, but since you were sleeping so peacefully, I took them downstairs."

"It's so good to be here." Iris dug into her breakfast with gusto.

"What was your trip like?"

"Crowded and dusty. I don't know why they have to put so many people in one coach. There was always an elbow in my side and some stranger's knee pressed against my leg." She rolled her eyes. "And the driver was the surliest man you can imagine. Not only did he toss my trunk in the middle of the street, he had so little concern for me that he left me standing all alone, even though it was obvious no one was awaiting my arrival."

"How awful for you." Camie popped a strip of bacon into a biscuit and took a small bite out of it. "But it turned out well. I can't believe Nathan Pierce rescued you and brought you all the way out here in the middle of the night. How romantic."

Iris's mind went back to the evening before. What more could a girl want from a man? Mr. Pierce was tall, handsome, and a perfect gentleman who had been most accommodating and helpful. He had been a model of propriety from the moment they met until he left her at the Sherers' door. And yet, when she considered her arrival, it was not his blond hair and handsome face that appeared in her mind's eye. Instead she saw a head of darker hair, a lock of which fell forward on a wide forehead. She saw a dimple and the spark of intelligence in dark eyes. She shook her head to displace the image. Maybe the reason she remembered him was because he had been the first person she'd met after her arrival.

She decided the best way to banish the troublesome image was to concentrate on finishing her breakfast and getting dressed. "Do you have a dress I can borrow until my bags get here?"

"Of course, Iris. You know that anything I have is yours, but there's no need. Mr. Pierce delivered your trunks earlier as he promised. They're sitting right outside the bedroom door." Her eyebrow arched. "I think he was disappointed that you weren't awake so you could express your appreciation in person."

Iris slid from the warmth of the bed. "I had no idea he could really get them here so quickly."

"I think that man is smitten." Camie followed her to the hall. "Nathan's parents died when he was a young boy. His uncle, Richard Pierce, raised him. They own the dry goods store in Daisy, and his uncle is also the leader of the town council. Everybody calls Mr. Pierce the mayor. He and Nathan are the richest folks for miles around. Mayor Pierce moved here a long time ago and bought up lots of land. I guess Nathan is the most eligible bachelor we have in these parts."

"You know I don't care anything about money or land-holdings." Iris opened her trunk and drew out a brown wool dress and apron. "It's a man's heart that counts."

Camie plopped back down on the bed to watch her get ready. "He seems to have a heart of gold. He came to your rescue, didn't he?"

"I guess so. I met another man last night, too." Iris pulled her dress over her head. "His name is Adam Stuart."

"Adam Stuart?" Camie made a tsking sound with her tongue. "He's a bitter, cantankerous sort. The exact opposite of Nathan."

"I see." Iris walked over to a small mirror hanging above the dressing table to consider what might be done with her hair. She frowned at her reflection. She had to agree with her friend's assessment of Mr. Stuart's personality. So why did his dimpled smile remain so clear in her memory? Was it the pain she'd seen in his eyes? The man had been drunk. His pain was probably caused from a liverish complaint.

Iris checked herself. She was determined to banish all thoughts of Adam Stuart from her mind. Focusing her attention on the wild mane that floated around her head, Iris attacked it with impatient, rapid strokes. The more she brushed, the more her hair seemed to expand.

"Here, let me." Camie stepped up behind her and took the brush from Iris's hand. With long, gentle motions, she patiently tamed the wild curls. "You have such beautiful, thick hair. I always wanted curls like these."

"And I always wanted straight blond hair like you and my ma have."

Camie pinned Iris's hair up, allowing a few ringlets to escape at the temples and the nape of her neck. "There we go. You look perfect."

Iris looked at both of their reflections in the mirror to savor the moment before turning to give Camie a hug. "You're the best friend ever. Now, can we go see Emily and Erin?"

Camie's nod was emphatic.

They tarried only long enough to make the bed and pick up the pins Iris had scattered the night before. She was relieved at how easy it was to control her thoughts. All she had to do was concentrate on the task at hand. Gathering the breakfast tray, she began quizzing Camie about the family she was going to work for.

"You will hardly see Mr. Spencer. Since his family died, Wayha busies himself with the business of his plantation. The little girls, June Adsila and Anna Hiawassee, are adorable."

"What interesting names." Iris tried to picture the little girls with long black hair and dark eyes.

"Yes. Mr. Spencer wanted his granddaughters to have English names as a sign of their right to be American citizens, but their parents also wanted them to remember their heritage, so they insisted on adding traditional Cherokee names."

"I see. Were they difficult to care for?"

Camie shook her head. "They were little angels. Almost too quiet. Of course they were still recovering from the loss of their parents, but I can remember wishing they would laugh and run around outside like we used to do." She stopped talking as they entered the dining room.

Iris was impressed by the size of the Sherer home. The dining room was well appointed with a large table and six chairs. Her gaze was drawn to the large window that took up most of one wall, and her mouth dropped open. The view was stunning. Although the land close to the house was flat, in the distance she could see mountains rising up toward the sky. It reminded her that she was far, far away from Nashville.

Camie allowed her a minute to absorb the view before walking through a door at the far end of the dining room. "Come in here and see our little angels."

Iris forgot all about the scenery outside. As she entered the kitchen, she caught sight of Emily and Erin, the Sherers' twins. They were playing with a wooden bowl their father must have given them, beating the bottom side of it with spoons and laughing at the noise they created. Camie plucked one of them from the floor and kissed her soundly, her blond hair a shade or two darker than the white strands on her daughter's head.

"This is Emily." She smiled widely at Iris. "And that is Erin."

"They are beautiful." Serious brown eyes looked at her, and Iris's heart melted. A pull on her skirt made her look down. Erin gazed up at her. Iris reached down and scooped her up, totally captivated by her gap-toothed smile. "I don't know how you ever get any work done." She kissed the soft cheek, delighted when Erin's arms circled her neck.

Camie nodded. "I hated to leave Wayha's children without a teacher, but you can understand why I had to."

Lance walked over and put an arm around his wife. "That's why we're so glad you could come to Daisy. Knowing that the Spencer girls are being loved and taught by a kind Christian lady is an answer to our prayers."

Iris dropped another kiss on the top of Erin's head. "It's an answer to my prayers as well."

Chapter 5

Adam leaned against the bar and fingered the glass of amber liquid in front of him. He was shaking, but not because of the March wind outside the tavern. When had escape become so important to him? And why did it matter? He picked up the glass and studied it. Candlelight gleamed through it, turning it golden.

"No matter how long you look at it, that whiskey is not going to turn back into corn." Margaret Coleridge, the tavern's auburn-haired singer, took the seat next to him at the bar. "I'll take a cup of coffee, Cyrus."

The bartender nodded. As the man filled a mug and placed it in front of her, Adam tipped his glass against his lips and drank its liquid down in one quick gulp. He grimaced as the bitter taste of the whiskey filled his mouth and burned its way down his throat. He lifted his chin at Cyrus, who pulled a bottle from underneath the counter and refilled his glass. This time Adam didn't hesitate. He downed the glass without studying it, anxious for the forgetfulness it promised.

"Slow down there, Adam." Margaret's green gaze studied him, as mysterious as a cat's. "You don't want to be drunk before I start my performance."

Adam smiled and patted her arm. "I've heard you before."

"Are you criticizing my talent?"

"Not at all. I've told you many times that you should go to Washington. You're too good to stay in this backwater. You'd be in great demand. Even the imperious President Jackson would be impressed."

A frown appeared on Margaret's face. "I doubt he would let me into his house when he learned that part of my heritage is Cherokee."

He tilted his head and considered her words. "Did you know that he adopted an Indian boy who was orphaned in battle?"

"Are you trying to tell me that the man who is almost solely responsible for the removal of the Cherokee Nation has an Indian son?"

Adam couldn't believe he had put himself into the position of defending the man who had ended all of his dreams. He guessed that was one of the worst things about being a lawyer—no matter which side he argued, he could see the strengths of the other. "Yes, he had an Indian son. Sadly the boy died the year before Jackson became president."

"Yet he fights against allowing Indians to control their own futures. If not for his utter disregard for the law, the Cherokee would be safe on their land."

Adam tapped his empty glass and shoved another gold coin across the counter. Cyrus obligingly refilled his drink. He tossed it back, barely feeling the burn. With a gusty sigh, he turned around on his stool and surveyed the room.

He knew most of the men by name, but he wouldn't consider any of them a friend. He was an outsider and a known Indian sympathizer. Of course, he'd done little to encourage friendliness since his arrival in Daisy. The last man he'd been close to, his business partner, had betrayed him in the worst way. It was far easier to maintain some distance. That way he wouldn't get hurt. . .again.

All the regulars were here, some awaiting Margaret's performance while others played games of chance. It was the same every night. At one time Adam would not have joined them. But lately he felt that he fully understood Solomon's cynical suggestion to eat, drink, and be merry. No one watched out for the poor and downtrodden. Regardless of what they taught over at Brainerd Mission, he could detect no master plan. He grimaced at the bitter certainty that filled his heart. *Because there was no Master.* All of them were simply living here. Heaven and hell? Who really knew what would happen when this life ended?

Margaret put a hand on his arm. "I hope you defeat the demons chasing you, Adam." She stood and headed toward the raised stage where she performed nightly.

A couple of years ago pioneers had left a piano behind, likely trading it for supplies to see them through their journey southward. Adam wondered what the family would think if they could see it sitting in this tavern. He shrugged. Given the dangers of the trail, they'd likely died or been killed before they reached their destination. Such was the way of this world.

The men clapped and called out to Margaret, but she walked past them without a glance to the left or right. When she reached the platform, she nodded to the piano player and turned to smile at the audience, her bright gaze piercing him from across the room.

Adam leaned back against the bar and watched her sing, his foggy mind still able to appreciate the talent she displayed. A disturbance at the door drew his attention. "Our fine mayor has decided to join us tonight," he said to no one in particular.

Richard Pierce ran a thumb down the length of his suspenders and surveyed the room, a sneer evident on his face. Adam raised one eyebrow. If the man disliked the tavern, why didn't he stay home like the other "righteous citizens" of Daisy? Adam didn't disturb their Sunday morning church services, so why should they come bother him at his chosen haunt?

"If you're looking for Nathan"—Adam gestured at the rowdy crowd—"he hasn't graced us tonight." Now that he thought of it, it was odd that Nathan was absent. He was usually present to watch Margaret sing, even though he didn't drink or gamble.

"Actually, I'm looking for you." The elder Mr. Pierce shook his head at a barmaid headed his way. She shrugged and turned her smiling attention to another customer.

"I'll have the council's transcription ready in a day or two," Adam growled. His job as the town scribe was what paid for his evenings, but he was tired of everyone pushing him to finish his work. It wasn't as though anything earth-shaking had happened at the council meeting. It was always the same—the council discussed ways to attract more settlers, or they complained because the Indians were encroaching in some way on their rights. Ha! Those same men had no trouble trading at Ross's Landing on the far side of the river, the settlement that had been founded by John Ross, the chieftain of the Cherokee Nation. He wished Ross would come home where he belonged instead of fighting the lost cause in Washington. Then they could spend their time protecting the people who lived here. And Adam wouldn't have to deal with the likes of the pompous windbag standing next to him.

"No, I need to hire your services."

What an odd development. Adam straightened the collar of his shirt in an attempt to appear more professional. "What's the problem?"

"Some thieving Indians have been stealing my livestock."

Disgust filled him. Adam should have known better than to hope for a real job, a chance to be an advocate. He slouched forward again. "Sounds like you need the sheriff more than an attorney. Or maybe a gunman to teach the rustlers to respect your property."

The mayor pulled out his watch and glanced at it before answering. "You misunderstand me, Mr. Stuart. I need someone to get a copy of that treaty from Washington. It's time these Indians understood that this town is going to be run by white men."

"I can't help you." Adam tried to keep his voice neutral, but it was hard. He couldn't abide the prejudice that had been unleashed since news of the treaty had leaked out. It might be true that the American government was going to remove the Indians from their rightful land and that some of the Cherokee had turned traitor to their own people and signed the treaty, but he didn't have to support their efforts.

"You mean you *won't* help me." The mayor spat at the floor, barely missing Adam's foot.

Anger burned white-hot in Adam's chest. His fist clenched. He'd like nothing better than to plant it in the smug countenance of Richard Pierce.

Then sanity returned. He was no Arthurian knight with a sacred quest. No, he had more in common with Don Quixote, the poor deluded man who tilted at windmills. Adam knew he was nothing but a broken shell of a man waiting for his life to end. "Whether I cannot or will not doesn't matter. What matters is that you need to find someone else."

"You're a sorry excuse for a man, even by lawyers' standards." The man's voice was soft and venomous. "I must have been crazy to think you'd like to earn a respectable salary. Do you think anyone else is going to hire you? Where do you think you'll end up if you don't take this job?"

"I guess I'll end up dead whether I work or not." Adam hunched a shoulder. "The same as you."

Pierce huffed once or twice before leaving him alone.

Adam concentrated on his glass. His head was beginning to ache, a sure sign that the past was trying to resurrect itself in his mind. He took another gulp and waited for his memory to recede.

Margaret had finished singing when he struggled up from his stool. Adam made uneven progress across the tavern floor, pushing through the door and taking a deep breath. He smiled as he thought of the tall woman with flyaway hair who'd been stranded right here a week earlier. She'd looked so lost and abandoned, like a puppy looking for someone to feed and care for it. Some sentimental part of him had surfaced briefly that night, wanting to protect her and make sure nothing destroyed the innocence in her gaze. But she'd accepted Nathan's offer of help, instead. *Smart girl.* Adam wondered if it was the alcohol that had made her appear so beautiful and pure. *Most likely.*

Adam banished thoughts of her from his mind and concentrated on keeping his gait even, a challenge ever since he'd been attacked and left for dead after the treaty signing in New Echota. Although the pain in his leg didn't trouble him when he was drinking, his ability to walk suffered greatly. But he didn't have far to go. His office, one of the few commercial buildings on the main street of Daisy, was only a few feet away.

Opening the door, he shuffled past a large oak desk. A second door took him to his apartment, the room where he slept and ate. Had he locked the front door? He shrugged. He was safe even if the door was standing open. Who would want to disturb a broken-down lawyer with no future and too much past?

With a grunt, he removed his coat, boots, and pistol before falling into bed and embracing oblivion.

Chapter 6

Tell me about the Spencer family." Iris glanced at Lance, wishing Camie had been able to come with them this morning. But that was selfish on her part. Camie was at home, caring for her daughters. Little Erin had a cough, and Camie had not wanted to risk the croup.

The cold air nipped at her cheeks and made her thankful for the thick fur that covered her legs. This part of Tennessee was so different from home. Instead of gentle hills dotted with farms and streams, the ground rose up and reached for the clouds scuttling across the sky.

Lance guided the wagon down a slope toward the river that bisected the valley and formed a natural barrier between Indian land and American soil. "Well, you already know he's a Cherokee. He moved to this area before it was Hamilton County and built a home on land granted to him by the state of North Carolina. He had one daughter, who married and had two little girls, June and Anna." He paused and looked at Iris. "Everything seemed to be going well for the family until Mr. Spencer's wife, daughter, and son-in-law died."

She met his gaze, unsurprised by the empathy she saw in it. "What happened?"

"Cholera."

Iris's eyes closed briefly. The word brought nightmare images of sickness and death. An outbreak of cholera had swept through Nashville last year, leaving many dead in its wake. Iris's heart ached for the family. "What a blessing the little girls didn't die."

"They stayed home with the house slave while Spencer took the others to the village on Lookout Mountain where they became ill, not knowing that the disease was spreading through the Cherokee tribe. He was the only one who came back."

"Those poor little girls." Her eyes filled with tears as Iris considered what it would have been like to lose her ma and pa so suddenly. "How old were they?"

"Anna was just a baby, and her sister was about two."

"They probably don't even remember their ma." She turned to Lance. "It must have been hard on Camie to have to stop caring for them."

"Yes it was. She was so glad when your parents wrote to us."

Iris looked about for another topic of conversation. "Does that mountain have a name?"

"That's Lookout Mountain. It's the tallest peak in this part of the world."

It reminded her of a cantankerous old man with hunched shoulders, and the leafless trees scattered across its summit made the peak appear to be his balding head. "How far away is it?"

Lance's eyes narrowed as he calculated the distance. "It's probably ten miles."

"It looks much closer."

"I suppose so." He smiled at her. "Since you're from Nashville, the mountains must be quite different to you."

Iris leaned against the back of the wagon seat and breathed deeply. "I like it here, though."

This morning, once Lance had loaded her things into the wagon, she and Camie had tearfully hugged each other. As they pulled out onto the road, Iris had been torn by conflicting emotions. Part of her wanted to stay with her childhood friend for a few more days, but another part of her was anxious to begin her new position. Now that she had heard the story of the Spencer children, she was glad she had not tarried longer. The Spencer children needed someone to hold them and love them.

"Camie is so happy to have you living close by. I hope you will be able to visit often." Lance's words brought her thoughts back to him.

"It's wonderful to see her so hap—" The word broke off when her mouth formed an O as they drove through an iron gate onto the Spencer estate. Thick woods had hidden the large home until they turned into the lane. It was more a mansion than a house. She'd never seen such a large home except in some of the fancier neighborhoods of Nashville. It was made of dark red brick and resembled a large box. . .a very large box.

As they drew closer, she saw the house had three floors. A row of windows at ground level indicated the presence of a basement, too. Dormer windows jutted out from the sloping, gray-tiled roof that made up the third floor. Four windows per floor looked out on one side, lined up one on top of the other with symmetrical precision. The front side of the home featured a porch on the first floor, topped by an identical balcony for the second floor, each flanked by six white columns. The dark-paneled double doors that formed the entrance on the first floor were echoed by an identical doorway on the second floor. The third floor had no door or balcony, but six windows completed the balanced architecture of the house.

Iris focused on the second-floor balcony, wondering what room led to it and hoping it would be the children's parlor. Once the temperature warmed a bit, she could see herself teaching the two little girls while they sat on the balcony and listened to the cheerful gurgle of the nearby stream that wound a silvery path along one side of the property.

Lance slowed the wagon as they reached the wide set of stairs marching up to the front porch, while Iris admired the beaded detail on woodwork that separated the brick walls from the tiled roof. She hadn't realized until now just how wealthy Mr. Spencer must be.

Iris accepted Lance's help to dismount and trailed him up to the front door. He grabbed an ornate brass knocker and banged it against the polished wood of the wide front door to announce their arrival.

After a moment the door opened, and a short, rotund woman with a face as dark as a starless night wrung her hands on a white apron and smiled at them. Her white teeth shone brightly in a face wreathed with smiles. "If it isn't Master Lance come to visit." She turned her dark brown gaze to Iris. "And you must be the new nanny. I have to say it's a relief to see you. Not that I don't adore the children, but there's so much other work that needs to be done."

Iris felt a little overwhelmed as the friendly woman continued her monologue. Uncertain what else to do, she gathered her skirts and dropped a curtsy.

"Oh, you don't need to be bowing to me, missy. It's not like I'm kin to the master. I just keep the house and watch over the children."

Lance greeted the older woman. "Josephine, it's good to see you."

"Who's here?"

Josephine peered back over her shoulder. "It's Master Sherer and the new nanny."

Iris looked past her to the man who was making his slow way across the marble floor of the vestibule. His hair was mostly gray, although she could see a few strands that were as black as a raven's wings. He wore it parted in the middle and pulled back in a neat queue, which had the effect of making him look very old-fashioned. Most of the men she knew had shorter haircuts that did not have to be tied back. Mr. Spencer used a cane carved from black walnut that made her think of the one Grandpa Taylor had made for her grandma.

A wave of homesickness struck her as suddenly as a bolt of lightning. For a moment she desperately yearned to visit her grandparents' farm. She closed her eyes for a second and took a deep breath.

What nonsense! She was here because it was her dream. She opened her eyes, smiled brightly, and held out her hand to her new employer. "It's a pleasure to meet you, Mr. Spencer."

He moved his cane to his left hand and took her hand in his. "Many prayers have been answered by your safe arrival." His face was weathered, and his nose was broad and slightly crooked, as though it had been broken sometime in the past. His eyes were faded brown in color, but they held an expression of welcome that eased fears Iris hadn't even realized she held.

"Thank you, Mr. Spencer. I am thankful to be here."

"Perhaps you shouldn't be quite so thankful, Miss Landon."

Iris squinted in the direction from which Mr. Spencer had come. A man stood in the doorway, but she couldn't see his features because of the sunlight streaming into the vestibule from the room behind him. She could see that he was tall and slender, but he didn't look at all familiar to her. How did he know her name?

"Don't pay any attention to Mr. Stuart." Her host frowned over his shoulder at the man. "He is filled with doom and gloom today."

Iris looked back toward the man in the doorway. Mr. Stuart? The man who had knocked her down on the night of her arrival? She barely heard Lance's greeting as she remembered that evening.

Mr. Stuart looked completely different when he was not inebriated. His light brown hair had been styled so that it no longer fell over his forehead, and his clothing was neither wilted nor creased. He stood much straighter, too. The only thing she did not like about his transformation was the stern look on his face and the disappearance of his dimples. His mouth had a distinctive down-turn, and his brows were drawn together in a frown. How had she ever thought him charming or genial?

She turned her attention back to Lance. "Thank you so much for bringing me. I will come to visit as soon as I may."

"We'll look forward to it, Iris. You know that Camie and I are thrilled to have you so close." He nodded to the older man. "I suppose we'll see all of you again soon."

Iris tried to ignore the snort from Mr. Stuart as she assured Lance that she hoped to see him and his family at church. She glanced at Mr. Stuart. From his raised chin and downturned lips to the way he cast his gaze to the ceiling, he personified disdain. Did the man not even attend the local church? What an awful thing. She could not imagine trying to get through the week without the chance to join other Christians in worship and fellowship.

A little voice inside her head stopped Iris's thoughts. Was she being judg-mental? Perhaps Mr. Stuart attended services across the river at Brainerd Mis-sion or in some other community. Perhaps he had a sweetheart who lived nearby, and he chose to attend her church's services. A disagreeable feeling fluttered through her stomach, and Iris wondered if she was coming down with a cold. She hoped not. She didn't want anything to mar her first days with her new charges.

As she followed Josephine upstairs to the nursery, she heard Mr. Spencer invite Lance in for a business discussion. She wondered if their business would change the expression on Adam Stuart's face.

❧

Adam watched as the young woman gathered up her skirts and followed the house slave up the wide stairs to the nursery. He could not believe anyone of Miss Iris Landon's ilk would make a decent nanny, but he supposed Spencer had his reasons for hiring someone so young, inexperienced. . .and beautiful. She was nearly as tall as he and carried herself with the assurance of European royalty. And her puppy-brown eyes had been filled with innocence and hopeful expectation. She had absolutely nothing in common with the nanny who had raised him and his siblings. That woman had been older and much more fierce than he imagined Miss Landon could ever force herself to be. She reminded him more of Sylvia Sumner.

Sylvia. The name provoked a stabbing pain in his chest. It made him want a drink, but he couldn't leave. Not when work remained to be done.

Adam followed Lance and Mr. Spencer into the parlor, but a trill of laughter floating down from the upstairs landing made him want to run from the house before he made a fool of himself. He could clearly recall meeting Miss Iris Landon when she'd been dropped off in front of Poe's Tavern in the middle of the night. He had been drawn to her natural beauty even then. He could try to convince himself that it wasn't true, but something about Iris Landon made her stand out from other women. Some undaunted spirit that called to him. So he'd paid attention to what was being said about her in town.

Nathan Pierce had been the first to report on Miss Iris Landon, describing her as "that pretty, curly-haired gal staying with the Sherers." Then Adam had heard she would be moving into the Spencer household as nanny to the two little orphaned Indian girls since Camie Sherer had given up the job.

A maelstrom of discussion had taken over as the community discussed whether or not a marriageable white woman should work in an Indian household. That brought forth those who had originally been against the Indian children being cared for by Camie Sherer. Hadn't they tried to warn people at the time that no good would come of accepting Wayha Spencer's decision to hire a non-Indian female to tend his granddaughters?

It was all a part of what was wrong with this country. Adam didn't know why it still irritated him to hear the biased comments of the white settlers. He should have learned by now that the original inhabitants of this land would never be accepted as equals. Not when acceptance meant that thousands of acres of land would be unavailable to white settlers.

Miss Iris Landon's willingness to work for an Indian family notwithstanding, most white people only wanted to exploit Indians or have them removed to some inhospitable land far away. He didn't know which was worse, the greedy landgrabbers or the overeager missionaries. Miss Landon was definitely not part of the first group. She had most likely accepted her position so she could proselytize the little girls. Like most women, she had an ability to deceive herself into believing in a benevolent Creator, but why must she try to force her beliefs on others?

"You're not making your case very well." Mr. Spencer's sharp gaze brought Adam to the matter at hand. He waved Adam to a horsehair-covered settee before taking a seat in an overstuffed chair to one side of the hearth. He pointed Lance to a straight-backed chair that stood between his seat and Adam's.

"I apologize, sir. What more do you need to hear?" Adam had been all through this many times before, but he was willing to explain it again if Mr. Spencer wanted him to. All he needed to do was focus on the reason he'd come out here in the first place, a reason that had nothing to do with what was going on upstairs.

"Adam here feels I should put my house and lands up for sale."

Lance looked in his direction, and Adam could feel his ire rising in response to the man's incredulity. "It's not like I'm the one who wants to buy it. I've never pretended to have that kind of money at my disposal."

"Then why do you advise Mr. Spencer to sell? In spite of the tragedy of losing his loved ones, there is no reason he should move back to Lookout Mountain."

"Of course not. That's an outlandish idea!" Adam tugged at his waistcoat and straightened his back. "Who said anything about his going to the village?"

"You don't understand, Lance." Mr. Spencer tapped his cane on the floor to get their attention. "Adam thinks I should go to the new Indian Territory."

"What!" Lance turned to Adam. He looked confused. "I thought you were an opponent of Indian removal. I thought you believed as I do that the Indians have a right to their land."

Adam shrugged and looked out the window as he tried to organize his thoughts. How could these men be so blind to the truth? It was time to face facts. President Jackson had won. It didn't matter what they or anyone else thought. The Cherokee would never be allowed to stay in Tennessee. If he could convince his friend of that truth, then the old man would be able to see the logic in moving now—he would have his choice of homesteads in the new Indian Territory. Instead of waiting until his home and land were wrested from him by the full force of the American government, he could sell his holdings for a reasonable amount and have money when he made the move. "What I *believe* has no bearing on it. The fact is that the signing of the treaty at New Echota is a death knell to the Cherokee Nation."

"If that were the case, Chief Ross would be here gathering his belongings instead of staying in Washington." Lance's voice was calm and reasonable, but to Adam it reeked of ignorance and self-deceit. "Obviously he believes there is still a chance for the Cherokee to win."

"Again that word—believe." Adam's jaw was so tight it ached. "It sounds to me like that missionary wife of yours has turned your brain into mush."

Lance came out of his chair like a shot. "Be careful what you say about my wife, sir."

Adam also stood and sized up the shorter man in case he had to defend himself. Lance Sherer looked brawny and strong, a side effect of earning his living traipsing through the wilderness to survey property. But no matter the outcome of a bout of fisticuffs, Adam knew he had to apologize. He'd allowed his temper to get the better of him. He let his gaze drop. "I meant no disrespect."

The tension in the room did not ease appreciably. He could see the other man's hands still clenched in fists.

After a moment Mr. Spencer sighed, pulled himself out of his chair, and came to stand between them. He turned his back on Adam and addressed Lance. "As a good Christian, you will no doubt accept his apology."

Adam spread his hands. "I'm really sorry. This is a difficult time for all of us."

Lance nodded and turned back to his chair. "What do you need from me?" He directed his question to Mr. Spencer.

The older man went to the mantel and grabbed a large wooden box from it. Adam watched as Mr. Spencer maneuvered his way to the settee and sat heavily. He opened the box, and Adam saw that it contained several official documents. "Even if you're right and the Indians are forced to leave their homes, I am in a different situation. I hold an official warrant for this land." He triumphantly pulled out a parchment and waved it.

"That warrant is only a piece of paper." Adam could not keep the mockery out of his voice. "If the people who want your land set fire to this house, what would you have?"

"That is why I invited Lance into our conversation. It seems to me that his arrival could be considered God's intervention. He can keep the deed safe for me."

Adam mulled over the idea. Letting a third party hold the warranty was a good idea. He knew that Lance kept warranties of properties he surveyed, but since he had never surveyed Mr. Spencer's land, no one would suspect where the official deed was being held. He nodded his agreement. "But I still think you'd be better advised to leave while you still have a choice."

"I will raise my granddaughters in this home I built until the government of the United States forces me out."

Adam shrugged. Why should he care what happened? He should never have come in the first place. Obviously no one else had the vision to see the future that was bearing down on them.

❧

As she climbed the stairwell behind the house slave, Iris soaked up the atmosphere of the Spencer home. It did not feel much like an Indian home—at least not the Indian homes she had visited at the side of her parents. No stretched skins or animal horns hung on the walls. She saw framed oil paintings rather than charcoal drawings. The draperies were constructed of rich burgundy velvet, and she noticed a pair of vases made of etched glass. How beautiful they would be when filled with fresh spring flowers.

Josephine opened a door at the top of the landing, and both of them entered the children's parlor. It was a handsomely apportioned room, light and airy, and filled with a profusion of toys for young children. Iris clapped her hands as she looked around. It was a child's dream come true. She could imagine playing in this room as a little girl. What fun she and her friends would have had. She noticed a checkerboard and its black and red pieces, a box of marbles, several spinning tops, and a whole shelf of dolls. Some of the dolls were handmade cornstalk dolls like the ones she'd had as a little girl, but there were also several fancy dolls with porcelain faces and intricate dresses.

"Where are the children?" Iris asked once she could pull her gaze from the wall of toys.

Josephine winked at her. "They love to hide from me. I spend a large part of my day trying to discover all their hidey-holes."

A faint giggle came to her ears. Iris realized this must be a game for the girls and Josephine.

"Now where could they be this time?" Josephine put a finger on her chin and looked around. "I wonder if they're on the porch." She swept across the room and pulled the doors open, sticking her head outside and looking from left to right.

"Are they out there?" Iris joined the game.

"No luck today." Josephine came back inside. "You know, one day I found them in the secret shelf Mr. Spencer had built underneath the window seats. I wonder if that's where they're hiding today."

She advanced on the window seats. Suddenly the giggles stopped. "Yes indeed." She opened the window seats with a flourish.

Two dark heads popped up. Two mouths shrieked. Josephine threw her hands up in the air, and Iris laughed as hard as she had since her arrival in this part of Tennessee. It took several moments for all of them to calm down enough to talk.

"Come out, girls, and meet your new nanny."

A slight hesitation preceded the girls climbing out of the window seats and coming to where Iris still stood in the center of the room. She could see how much they depended on each other by the way their hands clung together. The younger child hung back slightly and plopped a thumb in her mouth. They both looked up at Iris, their big brown eyes filled with a mixture of trepidation and curiosity.

The nervousness Iris had felt upon her arrival melted away. These little girls were adorable. She could hardly wait to hold them in her arms. She knelt in front of them and smiled. "You cannot believe how badly I've wanted to see the two of you." She looked at the older sister. "You must be June."

A hesitant nod answered her.

Iris turned to the younger girl. "Now don't tell me. . . ." She put a finger on her chin and looked upward as though trying to think. "Your name is Amber?"

A headshake from both girls.

Iris tapped her chin. "Elsie? Laura? Ada?" At each guess, the girls shook their heads. "Maybe you'd better tell me then, or I might spend all day guessing."

As Iris had hoped, the younger child removed her thumb to answer. "Anna Hi'wa'se." She had a little trouble with the vowels in her Cherokee name.

"What a pretty name," Iris encouraged, eliciting a smile.

The older girl took a step forward. "I'm June Adsila."

Iris nodded. "That's a pretty name, too."

"*Adsila* is Cherokee for 'blossom.'" The older child offered the information as though seeking Iris's approval. "*Hiawassee* means 'meadow.'"

"Well, isn't that grand?" Iris laughed and lowered her voice as though she had a secret to tell them. "My name is Iris. Do you know what an iris is?" She waited while they glanced at each other. They shook their heads in unison. "An iris is a type of flower that has a pretty purple blossom and can be seen in the meadow in the spring."

"Our ma is in heaven." Anna made the statement before returning her thumb to her mouth.

Iris prayed for the right answer to give the girls. They were both watching her, their brown eyes inscrutable. "That's right. And I know she is proud she has two such beautiful young ladies here to keep their grandpa company."

"That's what I tell them all the time." Josephine reentered the conversation, warm approval evident in her voice.

Iris stood and brushed her skirts, although the floor was too spotless to have soiled it. She wanted nothing more than to wrap her arms around the precious girls who were watching her. She was so grateful to be here and sent a quick prayer of thanksgiving heavenward.

"Why don't you come with me, girls? We'll let Miss Iris unpack, and then she can join us." She glanced quizzically at Iris. "Can you be ready in an hour? I will need to get started on the day's chores by then."

"I don't think that's necessary." Iris smiled down at June and Anna. "Would the two of you like to come with me? I could use some help unpacking."

Two nods answered her. The girls turned pleading looks on Josephine, who held up her hands and laughed. "An extra hour to get more work done? That would be a great help, Miss Iris, if you're sure."

"Of course I'm sure. Maybe the girls can also give me a tour of the house. I'm sure they know every nook and cranny of their beautiful home."

"What a good idea. Then you can all come down to the kitchen. I'll make sure Cook has a snack all ready for you." Josephine disappeared down the hall with a wave of her hand.

Iris looked down. "Oh, my. I forgot to ask Miss Josephine where my room is. Do you think the two of you can help me find it?"

They glanced at each other before nodding. She held out her hands. June grabbed her left while Anna reached for the right one. Then they tugged her around and out the doorway. She had to laugh at their eagerness. This was going to be an easier job than she had ever imagined.

Chapter 7

I ris sighed as she tried to tame her hair. It was raining outside, bad news for two reasons. The first and least important was her unruly hair. The second was the disappointment her girls would face when they found that their planned picnic would have to be postponed. She pulled her hair back and wrestled a ribbon around it.

In the week since her arrival, she had grown to love the sweet Spencer girls. And they had responded to her with all the love in their dear little hearts. A clap of thunder brought another sigh. It looked like a picnic was out of the question. She wrinkled her nose at her reflection in the mirror. She didn't look overly professional, but she had learned during the past week that she would most likely not see anyone but her charges and the slaves.

She still found it hard to believe that Mr. Spencer had a house full of slaves. How could a man own slaves when his own people were fighting a battle for the right to control their futures? She understood his desire to live like his white counterparts, but not all wealthy men had slaves to work in their fields and keep their homes clean. Her pa was a good example. When it came time to plant or harvest his crops, he employed workers and paid them a fair wage. Their house was not so large that she, Ma, and Hannah could not keep up with the housework. But if it got to be too much work, she knew her parents would hire a housekeeper, not purchase a human being to do the work.

She had discovered the truth at the end of her first day. After meeting June Adsila and Anna Hiawassee, who were the sweetest little girls she could have imagined, Iris had asked Josephine how the staff managed their days off. She had neglected to ask her employer if she would be allowed to attend Sunday services in town and still take an afternoon off to visit the Sherers. Josephine had shrugged her shoulders and explained that she did not take days off except for Christmas, as she was a slave. Iris had been incredulous, but Josephine had assured her that she was happy to find herself in a good home with a kind master.

Iris wanted to ask Mr. Spencer why he owned slaves, but she had not seen the man since the day of her arrival. He had sent for his granddaughters once or twice, but she was not included in the invitations. So she had spent the time describing her new home and situation to her family in a letter. Perhaps the good Lord would provide an opportunity later. She hoped He would also provide her with the words to present her case to the man.

A knock on the door was her signal that the girls were awake and ready to be dressed. Her room was in the center of a connected suite, with June's bed in one room while her little sister's was located in the other. It was yet another indication of the wealth enjoyed by the Spencer family. A room for each of the children was a luxury where she came from. Of course, little Anna could often be discovered in June's bed by morning, an arrangement that neither girl seemed to mind.

Iris opened her door and was immediately bombarded as June and Anna barreled into her for early-morning hugs. "Good morning. Who is ready for breakfast?"

"When can we go on our pickanick?" June asked.

"Weeell," Iris drew the word out as she kissed first one child and then the other, "it seems that God has other plans in mind for us today."

"I told you so." Little Anna might be younger, but she was the more talkative and logical of the pair.

June's eyes filled with tears.

"Don't worry, little one. We will go on the next pretty day." She walked into June's room and pulled a shift from her bureau, laying it across the bed. The next hour was filled with questions and exclamations as she got the girls dressed and seated in their parlor where they would break their fasts together.

The mouthwatering smells of crisp bacon and warm bread greeted them. Iris helped the girls fill their plates before choosing a warm biscuit and coddled eggs for herself. "Whose turn is it to bless our food this morning?"

"It's June's turn," precocious Anna answered as usual. She glanced at her sister. "But I don't think she wants to talk to God today."

"Is that true, June?"

The older sister stared at her plate but nodded her agreement.

Anna was unperturbed by her sister's silence. "Do you want me to say the blessing?"

Iris considered the two girls, so much alike in looks, so different in personalities. June was a sweet-hearted little girl, but she obviously still grieved for her parents. Anna, on the other hand, had been much too young to remember her ma and pa, so she didn't feel the lack. "I think maybe we should talk to June about why she is so reluctant."

June shrugged.

Anna opened her mouth to answer for her sister, but Iris stopped her with a raised finger. "Let's let June tell us what is wrong."

They waited in silence as the food cooled on their plates. Finally June looked up. "Does God love us?"

Iris felt like she'd been punched in the stomach. "Of course He loves us. Whatever would make you think otherwise?"

"Why does He make people go to heaven and leave us?"

Iris pushed her chair back and went to kneel next to June, praying for the right words to share God's love with them. "I know you miss your ma and pa so much. I miss mine, too."

June's eyes turned into brown pools of tears. "Did Jesus take them to heaven, too?"

"No, but they live far, far away from here." Iris could feel the burn of tears in her own eyes. She needed to change the tone in the nursery, or it was going to be a miserable day for all three of them. "Do you know the story about the missing sheep?"

June and Anna both shook their heads.

"Once upon a time, a boy had the job of watching over a whole flock of sheep. There were white ones and black ones and even a few spotted sheep."

"Were there any lambs?" Anna interrupted.

"Yes, Anna. Lots of lambs. Well, one day when the shepherd was counting all of his sheep, he realized that one of the baby sheep was missing. He looked in the valleys and on top of the hills, but he couldn't find the little baby sheep."

"Oh no." June's tender heart was obviously hurting for the lost sheep. "What did the boy do?"

"He left all of his other sheep in a safe place and went to find the little lost sheep. He looked and he looked until he finally found it." Iris hoped her improvisation of the scripture in Matthew was acceptable to God. Jesus didn't tell exactly how the shepherd had found his sheep, but she was certain he would have looked high and low.

"One time, one of our calves got stuck between two big rocks." Anna lifted her arms up high to show the size of the boulders. "And it took Grandpa and two other men to get it out."

"That may be what happened to the baby sheep. Or maybe he just wandered off and couldn't find his way back home. But anyway, the shepherd boy found the baby sheep, picked it up, put it on his shoulders, and took it back home with him. He was so happy that he had found the baby sheep." Iris hugged June close. "That's because that shepherd boy loved his sheep the same way that Jesus loves you and me. That's why I'm here now. To hug you and take care of you—"

"And make sure we don't get caught in any rocks." Ever the practical one, Anna interjected her thoughts.

"That's right." Iris hugged June first then Anna. "I'll make sure you two get out of any tight spots."

Their smiles warmed Iris's heart. She stood up and returned to her chair. "How about if I say grace this morning, since I feel extra thankful to get to watch out for two smart little girls?"

They nodded their acceptance. The three of them held hands. The girls bowed their heads, and Iris followed their example. "Lord, thank You for giving us this special day together. Thank You for watching out for all the lost sheep, and help us to be good shepherds with each other. Bless the hands of those who prepared this food. May it nourish our bodies in the way You nourish our souls. Amen."

Anna and June began to eat their food, but Iris only picked at her eggs and biscuit. She wanted to make this day special even if they could not go outside for a picnic. She looked around the room for inspiration. Several framed landscape paintings—some depicted mountainous terrain while others portrayed springtime meadows—decorated the walls. One in particular had become her favorite, as it reminded her of Ma's garden back home. The artist had created a profusion of colorful flowers, including Iris's namesake. Inspiration struck, and joy filled her heart. "I know what we can do today."

"What?" June's voice held a note of hope that had been missing earlier.

"We'll have our picnic right here."

"But"—Anna looked around the room—"that's not a picnic. It's just a luncheon like we have every day."

Iris shook her head. "Not if we spend the morning decorating. As soon as we finish eating, we'll get out those watercolors and start painting flowers and trees. By the time we get done, you won't be able to tell we're still inside."

Dismay turned to anticipation as both girls finished their breakfasts quickly and urged Iris to hurry so they could begin their art project. After securing aprons from Josephine to protect their clothing, they excitedly returned to their parlor and looked to Iris for guidance.

Four hours later their aprons were liberally splattered with the colors of the rainbow. It had been a little slow at first, but Iris had shown them how to paint trees and flowers on their canvases. While their artwork would never capture the eye of a collector, the canvases were filled with bright swaths of color that seemed to brighten the dreary day.

Josephine had prepared a basket of food and helped them move the table to one corner of the room. They spread a blanket on the floor and sat in the middle of it while they munched on fresh cheese and bread.

"Anna, you may be outside in the middle of nowhere, but young ladies must still wipe away their food with napkins, not their sleeves." Iris's statement elicited giggles from both girls, and she smiled when the younger complied.

"Which painting is your favorite?" asked June.

"I don't know. They are all very pretty."

Anna stood up and walked over to one her sister had painted of a meadow ringed by mountains. "I like this one. It's the same as my Indian name."

"That's right, Anna. And wasn't June smart to think of painting something special for you?" Iris smiled at June, relieved to see that her sadness had been replaced by a look of satisfaction. "And I especially like the flowers you put in your picture. They look just like the irises that grow wild in the meadows at home."

"Do you like my river picture?" Anna wandered to a canvas that looked to Iris like a mishmash of greens and blues.

"Yes, it's very nice." She pointed to a dark blob on one side of the blue slash that was apparently Anna's idea of the Tennessee River. "What is that?"

"It's a fish. There are lots of fish in the river."

Iris tilted her head. She nodded. "I see it now. My goodness, what a great big fish. Big enough to feed this family for a week."

Anna nodded. She came back to the blanket and sat down. "I wish we were really outside though. Then we could find some real irises and give them to you."

"I have a secret for you, Anna. And for you, too, June."

Both girls leaned toward her. "What's your secret?" they asked in unison.

"No bouquet of flowers could be more beautiful to me than the two of you. You're the most precious bouquet any nanny could ever want." She held out her arms and gathered them close, so thankful for their loving arms and enthusiastic kisses.

Chapter 8

They are adorable." Iris kept her voice low to avoid waking Camie's sleeping children. "They look like little angels." She watched as Camie tucked the cover more securely around her daughters and thought about how nice it would be to have children of her own.

Happiness and anticipation made her stomach flutter as she followed her friend out of the bedroom. Nathan would be here soon to have dinner with her and the Sherers. She wondered if he was the man God wanted her to marry. He was certainly nice. She was looking forward to getting to know him better.

Camie's voice interrupted her musings. "Lance and I are going to take the girls to Brainerd Mission for Easter to see Ma and Pa. We'd love for you to join us."

"I'd love to! I'm sure Mr. Spencer wouldn't mind if I took the day off."

"Good. I know how much Ma and Pa would like to see you. They were so excited when you agreed to come."

"Me, too." Iris squeezed Camie's hand. "You know that I consider your father's letter an answer to prayer."

Camie's reply was halted by a knock at the front door. "That must be Nathan and Mr. Pierce."

Iris wondered why Mrs. Pierce was not attending and made a note to ask if Nathan's aunt was ill. She smoothed her collar with nervous fingers as the Pierce gentlemen entered the parlor. A flurry of greetings and introductions filled the room.

Nathan Pierce was as nice as she remembered, but his uncle was another matter entirely. Looking from one to the other, she wondered how Nathan could be so unassuming and have a relative who practically oozed self-importance.

Although the elder Mr. Pierce was much shorter than Nathan, she could see some family resemblance. They both shared the same cornflower blue eyes and blond hair, although the hair of Nathan's uncle had begun to thin.

"It's too bad your wife could not come for dinner tonight, Mr. Pierce." Iris folded her hands in her lap.

He cleared his throat before answering. "She died some years ago, Miss Landon." He fastened his blue gaze on her face with some interest as though he

TENNESSEE BRIDES

was considering whether she would be an acceptable replacement.

"That is a shame. I'm sorry for your loss." Iris turned to Nathan. "I know your uncle must rely on you greatly to keep him company since your aunt's death."

Nathan shifted his feet. "I don't know about that. I run the store so Uncle Richard can tend to the town's business as well as keep our accounts straight."

"I see."

"You have an expressive face, Miss Landon." Mayor Pierce thrust out his chest. "I am rather an expert when it comes to reading faces, you see."

"Is that so?" She assumed what she hoped was an interested expression as the mayor droned on about the subject of wordless communicators.

She would be relieved when the Sherers joined them. Their housekeeper was visiting family in Athens, Georgia, so Lance was helping to set the table, a chore Camie had forbidden Iris to do. Iris loved her friend, but she didn't need help in finding a husband, which was obviously the reason for tonight's dinner party. She wondered if Camie intended to pair her with Nathan or his uncle. Either way, the plan was doomed to failure. When God decided it was time, she would fall in love with a good Christian man, someone who would provide for her and their children the way Lance provided for Camie, Emily, and Erin.

Lance and Camie entered the parlor together, their hands linked. Iris could admit to herself that there would be advantages in having a husband, like the companionship and shared laughter that seemed to be a part of her friend's marriage. But she was content to wait for her own knight.

She glanced toward Nathan. He was a nice-looking man and very considerate. He nodded at something his uncle said. She could not fault his manners or his attitude toward her. He was exactly the sort of man she should be attracted to, so she determined she would keep an open mind. Perhaps she would fall in love with Nathan once she got to know him better.

"I think we're ready for you to come into the dining room." Camie sounded breathless. Iris wondered if the flush on her cheeks was caused by the preparations she had been making in the kitchen, or perhaps her husband had been stealing kisses from her as they worked. Maybe Camie's refusal to let Iris set the table had been driven by more than one consideration.

Both Nathan and his uncle approached Iris where she sat next to a console table. Iris set her teacup on the table, wondering how she should handle two escorts. The problem was solved when Camie swept forward and took Mayor Pierce by the arm. A nod to her husband had Lance leading the way to the dining room. "Mayor Pierce, Lance has been telling me all about the new fields you will be planting to our south. How exciting."

Nathan watched them for a moment before turning his attention to her.

178

"May I have the honor of escorting you?"

Nodding her head, Iris allowed him to draw her upward. They followed the others and found that Mayor Pierce was sitting in the place of honor to the right of his host's seat at the head of the table. Camie's seat, at the foot of the table, put her next to the doorway leading to the kitchen. As Nathan and Iris entered, she motioned them to the pair of places sitting side by side on her right.

Candles took up the center of the table, casting a golden glow on the room. They were ringed by pinecones and winterberries, lending a festive atmosphere to the table.

Iris murmured her thanks to Nathan for seating her and turned to Camie. "Everything looks so nice. You're a wonderful housewife."

"I'm sure you will be one, too." Camie looked toward Nathan. "Don't you agree, Mr. Pierce?"

Iris blushed at his nod and picked up her fork. A banging at the front door startled her.

She looked at Camie, who shook her head, indicating she had no idea who was visiting at this late hour. Iris hoped it was not bad news.

Lance pushed back from the table. "Please excuse me. I imagine that's some traveler who's lost his way."

Iris was not surprised when he grabbed his rifle before heading to the front door. Unannounced visitors after dark warranted a certain degree of caution.

"Should I go with your husband?" Nathan looked at their hostess.

"Don't be foolish." His uncle answered the question. "Lance Sherer doesn't need your help to answer his door."

Iris felt sorry for Nathan. His uncle's scornful answer must have stung. Nathan was a grown man after all, not some wayward child.

She picked up her fork and watched as the elder Mr. Pierce calmly sliced a piece of meat off the roast at his elbow and put it on his plate. He was reaching for the basket of rolls when the door to the dining room burst open and slammed against the back wall.

All four diners jumped, and Iris may have even let a small cry escape her lips. She clapped a hand over her mouth to avoid waking the children upstairs and watched as Adam Stuart stumbled into the dining room, closely followed by Lance.

"I told you we are having company."

Mr. Stuart stopped. He took in the scene with a quick glance and swept a bow in Camie's general direction. "Pardon me, Mrs. Sherer, for disturbing your dinner party. I have business that cannot wait."

"Adam, what are you doing here?" asked Nathan, standing up to form a barrier between the rude man and Iris.

While she appreciated his gesture, she was not afraid of Adam Stuart. But when she would have explained her lack of fear, her words were drowned out by Adam's voice.

"I was told you'd be here." Iris watched Adam limp his way over to Nathan's uncle.

Mayor Pierce was practically cowering in his seat, apparently much more frightened by a belligerent man than he ought to be.

"Get up!" Adam raised his fists into a fighting posture.

Camie gasped.

"Leave my uncle alone." Nathan's voice was as sharp as Adam's. "If you have a problem with my family, why don't we go outside and discuss it where we won't disturb the ladies?"

Adam ignored him. "I said, get up!"

Mayor Pierce shook his head. "I will not be threatened by a drunken fool."

"I'm entirely sober and extremely angry. Is it true you called a special meeting of the council this afternoon?"

Nathan reached his uncle's side. "Why on earth are you asking such a question? Have you lost your mind?"

Although he did not rise from his chair, Mayor Pierce must have gained confidence from having his nephew close by. "Who better than the mayor to call a meeting of the council? They elected me to make those decisions."

"Everyone knows the council meets at seven o'clock on the second and fourth Monday evenings of the month." The man spat the words out as though they caused a bad taste in his mouth. "A special meeting should only be called in case of an emergency. Not because you had some sneaky idea that you wanted to shove through council before the townspeople knew anything about it."

"Do you mean to tell me that you came barging into my home and disturbed my wife and guests because the mayor called a special council meeting?" Lance frowned at Adam. "I ought to march you out of here right now."

Adam pointed a finger at Iris. "I think his special meeting had something to do with her employer. I have it on good authority that he's got a resolution ordering the immediate removal of Mr. Wayha Spencer and his family from their home and lands on this side of the river."

Iris felt her jaw drop. Her gaze went to the cowering mayor. "Is that true?"

Mayor Pierce shook his head and mopped his damp brow with one of Camie's monogrammed napkins. "Of course not! This man is jumping to conclusions based on idle speculation and gossip."

Iris turned back to Adam and spread her hands in a placating gesture.

"This is obviously a misunderstanding."

Adam made a disgusted sound. "You're too naive and trusting for your own good." He reached for Mayor Pierce's shirtfront.

Nathan grabbed his hand and pulled it back. "Don't even think about touching my uncle."

"I think we've heard enough, Mr. Stuart." Lance stepped forward and stared at Adam. "Mayor Pierce has denied your charges, so I would appreciate it if you'd leave."

A pan of frying chicken would have sizzled less than the tension in the room. Iris felt herself caught by Adam's tortured gaze. Some part of her noticed that his eyes held a green fire she'd never noticed before. She'd thought his eyes were brown, but looking into their depths, she made the discovery that the man's eyes were hazel—with enough highlights to make them appear as green as grass when he was angry.

She stared at him, for once thankful for her tall frame. He seemed to be begging her to take his part, but she couldn't do that. He had to be wrong about Mayor Pierce. Why else would he deny everything? He had to know if it was true they would all find out at the next official council meeting.

A desire came over her to smile at Mr. Stuart, offer him some comfort, however small. But it was an impossible, dim-witted idea. They were in her friend's dining room, and the man had barged in uninvited.

She watched as Lance escorted him back to the front door. Their words were muffled by the closed door of the dining room, but she could still make out Adam Stuart's angry tones in stark contrast to the calm, reasonable comments being offered by Lance.

"Shall we continue our meal?" Camie sat down and began passing the plates of food as though the recent scene had not happened.

Nathan looked toward the doorway, but he was apparently reluctant to leave his uncle alone. Iris wondered if he thought she or Camie was a threat to the cowardly mayor. But then she grew ashamed at her thought. Knowing how kind Nathan was, he'd probably decided to stay behind so he could protect her and Camie in case Adam's visit was a ruse to cover some nefarious plot.

"He's gotten downright dangerous since the treaty signing." Mayor Pierce pulled on his collar. "We are going to have to lock him up one of these days."

"Well, it is a shame what happened to him that night." Nathan turned to Iris to explain. "He spoke out against the Ridge party, who signed the treaty at New Echota. He left and was on his way back here when he was attacked and left for dead in the middle of nowhere. A lot of men wouldn't have survived, but Adam found cover and managed to get himself back here alive. The injuries he suffered are what cause him to limp. When he came back, he got the council to hire him. He's been attending their meetings to record the minutes and to offer legal advice when he's asked to. Most of the council seems satisfied with his work." Nathan looked at his uncle, who at least had the grace to duck his head.

Iris couldn't help but admire Nathan even more as he defended the man whom he had every reason to dislike. She couldn't imagine being so charitable to anyone who tried to attack her relatives. The younger Mr. Pierce was a truly fine Christian who believed in turning the other cheek in the most trying of circumstances.

Quite the opposite of Adam Stuart. What right did he have to come bursting in on her friends? And how dare he call her naive? She had a lot of experience. Hadn't she traveled across Tennessee and been left alone in the middle of the night without any way to get to the Sherers' home? Perhaps she'd not been attacked and left for dead, but that didn't mean she was devoid of common sense.

Camie excused herself to go check on the girls and returned with a relieved smile that they had somehow slept through the commotion.

Lance returned a moment later and apologized to them for the disruption before sitting down to continue his dinner as though nothing untoward had happened.

Nathan smoothed the napkin in his lap. "I wonder why Adam Stuart came barging in here."

"He seemed to believe there will be an attempt to take Wayha Spencer's land." Lance shook his head.

"But how can that be?" asked Camie. "You showed me his origi—"

A warning shake of her husband's head stopped Camie midsentence.

Mayor Pierce shoveled food into his mouth until there wasn't a morsel left on his plate before pushing back from the table. "A fine meal, Mrs. Sherer. Please excuse me for a moment."

They continued discussing Adam Stuart's interruption and wild accusations as they lingered over Camie's delicious food.

Iris wasn't sure how much time passed before she realized Nathan's uncle had not yet returned. Had the man been grabbed by the belligerent Mr. Stuart? The thought had barely formed when Mayor Pierce pushed open the dining room door and rejoined them.

Nathan patted his stomach and sighed. "Everything was delicious."

"I'm glad you were able to enjoy the meal in spite of the interruption." Camie's smile was radiant.

"Camie is a wonderful cook." Lance's voice was as warm as his glance.

Iris added her compliments to those of the men. She was so proud of her friend's abilities. It was obvious Camie was thriving here.

Too bad Adam Stuart was not. His accusations had been wild and unfounded. She would not let him cast a pall on her enjoyment of the evening. Instead she would concentrate on Nathan Pierce's admirable qualities.

The rest of the evening passed quickly. Iris and Camie checked on the girls once more while the men enjoyed a lively discussion about the Texas war for independence from the Mexicans. All in all, it was a pleasant evening. Iris hoped she would one day be able to be such an accomplished hostess.

Chapter 9

Iris settled herself in the wagon next to Camie before waving good-bye to June and Anna, who were clinging to Josephine's skirts. She would miss them, but Mr. Spencer had insisted they stay with him to avoid overcrowding at the Millers' home.

Lance drove to the ferryman's hut and woke him. While he arranged for their transport across the river, Iris and Camie played with Erin and Emily to keep them from fussing. A white mist hung over the river, but Iris knew it would disappear as the sun rose.

The ferryman was short and rotund with a knitted cap covering grizzled hair that matched his shaggy beard and mustache. He wore a coat of rabbit fur and long woolen socks that covered his legs all the way up to his knees. He nodded at them and headed down to the river.

Lance climbed back aboard the wagon and guided it onto the wooden raft. It only took a short time to cross the river, but Iris held her breath as she watched the swift water slide under the edge of the ferry. Lance waved to the man as he pulled the wagon back onto solid ground, and they were off on the next leg of their journey.

The sun came up over the eastern hills and brought with it some warmth. Iris found herself dozing as they made slow but steady progress on the muddy roads.

Camie's voice roused her. "Ma and Pa are going to be so excited to see you, Iris."

Iris raised an eyebrow. "I imagine they will be much more interested in seeing their granddaughters than the child of their old friends. And rightfully so." She tickled Erin, laughing along with the girl. "You're much more interesting than an old maid nanny."

Lance's chest seemed to expand a little. "They are special, aren't they?"

"Yes they are." Iris rubbed her nose against Erin's cheek. "Children are a gift from God."

Camie pulled Emily onto her lap. "That's true, but I know my parents will be excited to see you, too."

"We're about to find out just how much." Lance turned down a lane and through a wide gate.

A BOUQUET FOR IRIS

A large sign swung between the tall posts. "BRAINERD MISSION." Iris also read aloud the words carved into the bottom half of the sign, "So that I could but gain souls for Christ."

"It was David Brainerd's lifelong dream." Camie referred to the brave missionary whose tireless work had inspired the formation of missions like this one.

"I didn't realize how large the mission is." Iris gazed at the extensive grounds dotted with comfortable homes, livestock, and cherry orchards.

As he steered the horses, Lance pointed out the mill perched on the banks of Chickamauga Creek, as well as the main house where the students resided, and the large meetinghouse where they would attend Easter services in a little while.

"Whoa." He pulled back on the reins in front of a two-story whitewashed cabin.

Iris and Camie began gathering blankets, baskets, and children while Lance secured the horses. Before they could unload all the necessary items, the front door opened and Roman Miller, dressed in black pants and a starched shirt, stepped onto the front porch.

"They're here," he called back into the house. He had aged somewhat, which wasn't surprising as nearly a decade had passed since Iris had last seen the man. Though his hair had turned white and his girth had widened a little, the twinkle in his dark eyes had not changed at all.

Una Miller stepped onto the front porch, wiping her hands on her apron. Her hair was pulled back in a tidy bun and was now liberally streaked with gray. Iris could see crow's feet bracketing her eyes and mouth as she smiled. It made Iris think of Ma and wonder where her family was spending their Easter Sunday. She shook off the thought. This was no time to get homesick.

Hugs from both Pastor and Mrs. Miller helped to brighten her mood. They were as excited to see her as their own grandchildren. As they went inside, Pastor Miller asked if she was happy at the Spencer home.

"Yes. June and Anna are so sweet and obedient."

"We would like to enroll them in the school here." Camie's mother led the way to the parlor, a chortling Erin in her arms. "But Mr. Spencer is adamant that they will attend school in Daisy."

Iris wandered around the parlor, admiring several charcoal sketches that decorated the walls. "He is determined for them to be treated the same as white children."

"I hope he can realize his dream," said Pastor Miller, "and that he can avoid being removed with the others." He reached for Emily as she toddled across the room. "You will enjoy having them as neighbors, won't you, little one?"

"Who is leading the service today?" asked Camie.

"I am." Her pa shifted Emily to his left arm, pulled out his pocket watch, and squinted at it. "I'd better put on my coat and tie."

Camie took Emily back. She turned to her husband, who had finished unloading the wagon. "Is there enough room for all of us to ride together?"

"That's not necessary, Camie," her ma said. "You know we usually walk to the meetinghouse."

"But the children—"

"Will be no trouble at all."

Iris nodded her agreement. After their two-hour trip in the wagon, it would be a relief to walk.

After Camie's father came back, they gathered their cloaks and set out. Pastor Miller insisted on carrying one of his granddaughters while his wife took the other. Camie linked one arm through her husband's and gestured for Iris to walk on her other side.

They greeted several of the other missionary families on their way to the large building where the church services would be held. The missionaries' children laughed and played with the Indian children, a sight that warmed Iris's heart. If only President Jackson could see this scene, he might understand there was no need to push for the removal of the Cherokee.

Her gaze rested for a moment on a large black horse whose tall rider stood nearby. Her heart skipped a beat. Surely she must be mistaken. Adam Stuart would not have come out here to stir up more trouble. Yet there he was. She would recognize that rumpled suit anywhere. He turned, and she caught a glimpse of his face, which he had apparently not bothered to shave. The nerve of the man. She would have walked right past him, but Pastor Miller stopped to greet him.

"I'm glad to see you here."

Adam put his hands in his coat pocket. "I am on my way to the village and thought I would stop in to say hello."

"You're just in time for our morning service." Pastor Miller turned and spotted Iris. "Come over, my dear, and meet the brightest hope of the Cherokee. Adam has been fighting for the rights of the Cherokee in Washington for years, and then he came here to attend the treaty signing at New Echota because Chief Ross had to stay in Washington. He tried to stop that travesty and on the way home was the victim of a brutal Indian attack that nearly killed him."

Iris was amazed at this interpretation of Adam Stuart's personality and goals. Had she judged him too harshly? All she'd seen was his surliness. But now his anger made a little more sense. It must have been hard for him to accept defeat. And then to be attacked by the people he was trying to protect...

A BOUQUET FOR IRIS

Adam wanted to get on his horse and race back to the other side of the river. Why had he thought a visit to the Indian village would help clear his mind? And why had his horse thrown a shoe just as he reached the turn to Brainerd Mission? He'd come to find the blacksmith and get his horse reshod so he could continue his journey. The fact that it was Sunday made no difference to him since he and God were no longer on speaking terms. He had planned to wait quietly outside until the services were done, get his horse tended to, and get on his way.

Pastor Miller continued lauding Adam's legal abilities, never realizing that his audience, Miss Iris Landon, was staring at Adam in shocked disbelief.

It was another indication of his bad luck to run into her after the scene he'd caused last week at her friend's house. What must they think of him? He didn't want to see the censure in Miss Landon's big brown eyes, so he kicked a rock loose and watched it skip across the ground and disappear under the steps leading to the meetinghouse. What right did she have to judge him? She was new to the town, and from what he'd heard, she'd grown up in the lap of luxury in Nashville. She was probably just a slightly more rustic version of Sylvia—secure in her little world and her narrow beliefs. Well, he had news for both of them. They might think they knew it all, but that was because they'd never had to brave the world beyond their safe borders. He would like to show Iris Landon what the real world was like.

Righteous anger filled his heart. He would not allow these people to judge him. "Excuse me." The words came out in a low growl. Let them think what they may; he was going to escape. Adam turned on his heel and made his way into the meeting hall. Row after row of rough-hewn pews filled the main room. He supposed the preacher would stand on the raised dais up front so he could be seen by everyone.

Several of the pews were already occupied as Adam made his way to the front of the room and plopped down in the first pew. He'd show them that he was not afraid of them or their God. Condemning voices from the past filled his head as he sat there. They blocked out the rustle of a skirt as someone sat down next to him, but they could not compete with the wonderful fragrance that tickled his nose. Roses. Someone had brought roses into the room.

Adam looked to his right. Miss Iris Landon. Only she didn't look disgusted, angry, or even scared of him. She looked. . .concerned. Her wide brown eyes searched his face even as her smile made his jaw unclench. He wanted to return her smile. He wanted it more than he wanted to maintain his anger.

She was not Sylvia, after all. She was just as beautiful but in a more natural way. His gaze soaked up the details of the long eyelashes that fluttered downward modestly, her rosy cheeks, and the generous mouth that still hinted at a smile. His fingers itched to push back the curls escaping her coiffure. He reined in his traitorous thoughts. They were what had gotten him in trouble before, and he would not allow history to repeat itself.

Pastor Miller stepped up on the dais and opened his arms to the crowd. "I am pleased to see you this Easter morning. We Christians have so much to celebrate, especially on this day. Let's start the morning in song."

Adam listened to Iris's lilting soprano join in as the pastor sang "Jesus, Lover of My Soul." He let the words wash over him, bringing some comfort to his roiling thoughts. When the next song began, "Sun of My Soul," he allowed his own voice to join in. But his throat closed up when they reached the verse about a "wand'ring child" who spurns "the voice divine." His conscience roared to life, pushing him to his feet. Well, why not. He'd entered the service on a wave of anger. Wasn't it fitting that he exit on a river of remorse?

❧

Iris shifted to allow Adam past her. She wanted to reach out and touch him, but she kept her hand at her side. Instead she sent a heartfelt prayer to God to defeat the demons in his life.

She settled back against the pew and concentrated on Pastor Miller's message, but part of her mind worried about the tall man. Pastor Miller described Adam as a tireless defender of Indian rights. Perhaps she should give him the benefit of the doubt. It was a difficult time for anyone who cared about the future of the Cherokee. Perhaps if they'd met a year earlier, she would have seen another side of Adam. A charming, irresistible side.

When the service was over, she returned to the Millers' home and enjoyed a large dinner of ham, sweet potatoes, and early peas. She, Camie, and Mrs. Miller put the girls down for a nap before returning to the parlor to overhear Lance and his father-in-law discussing a visit to the Cherokee village at the top of Lookout Mountain.

"It's been a long, hard winter, and I'm worried that some of the villagers may be short on basic supplies," Pastor Miller explained. "You would be doing me a favor to go up tomorrow, and you could show Iris here the citadel of rocks."

Lance turned to his wife. "What do you think, dear?"

Camie looked apologetically at Iris before shaking her head. "I don't think it's a good idea to take the girls up there. It's still a bit too cold, and Emily started coughing as we were putting her in the crib."

Mrs. Miller came from the kitchen carrying cups, saucers, and a silver pot filled with aromatic coffee. Iris also recognized the spicy smell of fresh maple cookies. "Why don't you leave them here with us? It's the perfect opportunity to let Iris see a little of the country from up on high. And since your house-keeper is still away, I know you and Lance could use a break."

"I concur." Pastor Miller accepted a cup of coffee from his wife. "If Emily is getting sick, she probably ought to stay indoors for a day or two anyway."

Iris turned down the coffee but reached for a cookie. She passed the plate to her friend and bit into the treat, savoring the piquant flavor.

"You may be right." Camie's voice was hesitant. "Would you like to go, Iris?"

"Of course she wants to go." Lance answered before she could swallow the mouthful of cookie. "Don't you remember your first time on the mountain? Besides, I think your parents want a chance to spoil our daughters a little."

Iris thought a trip up the mountain sounded like a grand adventure if Camie was willing to go. She relished the idea of meeting with some of the local Cherokee, as well as seeing the view from the top of the mountain. The outline of the tall peak had intrigued her since her arrival.

Soon it was settled. Lance and Pastor Miller loaded the wagon with staples—coffee, flour, and sugar—to take with them while she described the changes in Nashville and the surrounding area to Mrs. Miller. Then the men came back in, and they all sat around discussing the mission's successes and failures in this part of Tennessee.

That night, as Iris pulled her quilt to her chin, she wondered what had happened to Adam Stuart. Then she wondered why she cared. There was something about the man, something that drew her to him. Was it her desire to share her faith with him? Or something else?

Chapter 10

How far is the village from the mission?" Iris swayed with the wagon as Lance negotiated a sharp turn.

"About three hours by wagon," Camie answered. "We're almost there."

From the tall trees on one side of her, Iris heard the call of birds and the rustle of small animals. She looked toward the other side of the trail, surprised that she could only see the tip-tops of trees stirring at the touch of a gentle breeze. Dizziness attacked her vision as she tried to look down the slope of the mountain on that side, making her grip the slats of the wagon bench. "That's good."

Camie sat next to her husband on the front bench, but she must have heard the discomfort in Iris's voice. She turned around and laid a hand on her knee. "It's overwhelming at first. But wait until we get to the top. The view is awesome."

Lance guided the horses with care. "It always reminds me of how big God really is. He created so much, and we can only see the barest fraction of it."

Iris tried to make her smile less shaky for Camie's sake. She was determined to enjoy the trip.

The path opened up ahead of them, and suddenly she saw the village. The cluster of small mud-and-log houses reminded her of the Cherokee village close to Nashville. Women sat outside their homes cooking, sewing, or weaving on the looms donated by the government for their use. Several dogs ran to where they stood and barked vociferously, announcing their arrival to the tribe.

Camie waved and called out to a couple of the women as they made their way through the noisy animals. Soon they were in the middle of a laughing, hugging group. A few moments later the braves came out of the round council house, where they had apparently been holding a meeting.

Iris lost count of the names and faces as she was introduced around, but everyone was friendly and eager to learn about her. She told her story of coming to work for Mr. Spencer again and again, describing the children and their grandfather.

"If I didn't know better, I'd think you were following me."

The sardonic voice turned Iris's head. She forgot all about the Spencers.

190

Her heart fluttered like a startled bird as her gaze locked with Adam Stuart's. "What are you doing here?"

"I could ask the same question. I thought you were visiting your friends at the mission."

Iris frowned. Was the man deliberately baiting her? His tone was certainly filled with sarcasm. Was that how he kept people at a distance? But why? Why would he be so eager to alienate her? He and Pastor Miller obviously admired each other. And even Lance seemed to have a grudging admiration for him. Maybe he had a problem with women. She remembered her prayer for God to help him. Was his presence here a gentle nudge from above to encourage her to befriend Adam?

"It's a pleasure to see you, too. I was hoping we'd have a chance to talk, but who would've thought it would happen so soon." Iris congratulated herself on her answer. From the surprised look on his face, her response had not been what he expected. "I wonder if you could show me around. Lance and Camie promised me an awesome view, but he's gone back to the wagon, and she's busy renewing old friendships."

Iris held her breath and watched the expressions crossing his face. Distrust, surprise, calculation, and finally surrender. He offered his arm to her. "Why not?"

A little voice inside warned Iris that she had been too impetuous, but she would not back down now. She took his arm and grabbed her skirt in case his stride outpaced her own, but she need not have worried. Adam Stuart might be taller, but he was considerate enough to shorten his stride so she had no trouble keeping up with him.

"Where are you from?" she asked, eager to open a dialogue.

"I was raised in Virginia. My pa sent me to William and Mary. I earned a degree before going to Washington to open a business."

"My pa went to William and Mary, too, but he moved back to his parents' home in Nashville and married my ma. Did you like living in the capitol city?" She saw him glance her way, but she focused on the path before her.

"I guess it was okay. I met a lot of important people, people who are making decisions that will shape the future of our country."

"That must have been exciting. What made you come out here?"

The look in his eyes was dark and full of pain. What had happened? Had someone hurt him terribly?

He seemed to shake off the disturbing memories as he answered her. "Chief Ross asked me to set up shop out here and do what I can to help his people." He helped her slide through a narrow opening between two giant boulders that crowded against each other. "But enough about me. Tell me about your home.

Why did your parents allow you to come alone to Daisy?"

Iris allowed him to change the subject, relating the reasons for her journey to Daisy, but she couldn't help wondering about the abrupt change. Something had happened to Adam in Washington, something to alter his outlook on life. If she could convince him to tell her about it, perhaps she could help him overcome it.

Excitement filled her as he led her onto a stone plateau that thrust itself out over the valley. She forgot his hidden problem as the world spread out before her.

❧

Adam saw the view as though he was looking at it for the first time, the way Iris must be seeing it. The citadel of rocks was an awesome place, perched at the very top of the mountain and overlooking the serpentine waters of the Tennessee River as it wound its way through the large, flat valley below. The sun had not set, but the moon had already risen in the east, its face turned pumpkin orange from the reflected blaze of the sun.

"Can you see the raft traveling toward Ross's Landing?" Adam stood close behind her and pointed to a small shape in the giant U of the river. He didn't realize anything was wrong until Iris slumped to the ground at his feet.

He knelt beside her, his heart climbing up into his throat. "Miss Landon? Iris, are you hurt?"

No answer. He lifted her gently against his chest and listened for her heartbeat. It seemed steady enough. In fact he couldn't find any reason for her to lose consciousness at all. He loosened her bonnet and pulled it off, checking to make sure there was no evidence of injury to her head. Nothing. Nothing but a profusion of curls that danced around her face. He was about to loosen her collar when Iris groaned.

Her eyes fluttered open. "What happened?"

Adam shook his head. "I don't know. One minute you were standing there looking, and the next thing I knew, you were swooning at my feet."

"I don't swoon." She glared up at him and tried to push him away, but Adam would not let go of her. He was relieved that she seemed to be recovering fairly quickly.

"Well, how do you explain it then?"

He could feel her shrug. "I think I got dizzy. The ground seemed to be moving, and then darkness swallowed me up."

"Vertigo." He nodded. "It's not a common complaint, but I have read of it." Now that he was certain Iris was neither ill nor wounded, he could relax and enjoy the feeling of holding her close to his heart. "It's caused by heights."

They sat like that for a few moments, as close as a breath. Her head was on his shoulder, her curls tickling his chin. He could have remained that way the rest of the day, breathing in the sweet scent of her cologne. But then she jerked. Was she having a seizure?

His alarm eased when he recognized the giggle that bubbled up from her throat. Iris put a hand over her mouth and glanced up at him, her eyes twinkling, inviting him to laugh with her.

Here he was thinking romantic thoughts about how perfectly she fit against his chest. He was a little offended that she found their situation humorous. Was she laughing at him? "What is it?"

She shook her head, loosening more curls in the process. Soon her hair would be tumbling around both of them. He could almost imagine how delicious it would look and the silky feel of it in his hands. His thoughts were disrupted by another giggle. This one ended in a hiccup.

Adam loosened his hold, and she sat up. "What is so funny?" he asked.

"I just don't understand how anyone so tall can have a fear of heights." Her eyes danced as she looked at him, inviting him to join the joke.

He chuckled. "Fear of heights."

She nodded and giggled again.

Adam couldn't help it. He laughed out loud. She laughed with him, the noise wrapping around him like a hug. The laughter built up inside him like a volcano, rushing to the surface again and again. He would think it was gone, and he would stop. But then he'd hear her still laughing, and it would overwhelm him again. He doubled over and laughed so long that he was sure his belly would be sore later.

He'd forgotten how good it felt to really laugh. There had been so little to even smile about over the past year. Life had become far too grim. But for this one evening he would forget about all his problems. Alone with Iris on top of the mountain, Adam determined that the rest of the world and its weary troubles could fade to insignificance.

Eventually their laughter abated. He stood and offered his hand to Iris, pleased when she accepted his help.

He glanced at her from time to time as they made their way back to the village. He was glad she had not put her bonnet back on.

As if she felt his gaze, Iris reached up and pushed the curls back from her face. "What I wouldn't give for a handful of hairpins."

Adam wanted to tell her how beautiful her hair was. How he thought it would be a shame to force it into submission. But those words would take them into dangerous territory. Territory he could ill afford to explore. He tightened his mouth and kept his attention on the path ahead, helping her when necessary and releasing her as quickly as possible.

Her friends fell on Iris the moment they entered the village. As Adam hung back, she glanced over her shoulder at him and smiled.

A butterfly tickled his stomach, an echo of their earlier merriment. It brought a smile to his lips, and he bowed to her as she disappeared into a group of eager Cherokee women.

෪

Iris wondered why God had seen fit to saddle her with such impossible hair. It would not be tamed.

She let her bonnet hang down her back as she and Camie helped the Indian women prepare a meal. She peeled and chopped vegetables to go into a savory stew and then helped ladle the hot mixture into bowls and trenchers.

When everyone gathered to eat, she looked for Adam but could not see his familiar figure anywhere. She tried to tamp down the feeling of disappointment. Just because they had shared a few moments of closeness was no reason to expect him to stay around and keep her company. She sat down next to Lance and Camie and concentrated on her meal.

Lance sopped the last of his stew with a wedge of corn bread and patted his stomach. "We'd better head back so we can get down the mountain before it gets dark."

The local chief had some of the older children ready the wagon while Iris and Camie helped with the cleanup. Before long they were waving good-bye to their hosts and heading back down the mountain.

As Lance negotiated the steep path, Iris distracted herself from the dizzying views by wondering what had happened to Adam after they returned to the village. She felt like he'd shown her a side he rarely allowed others to see. The laughter they'd shared at the citadel of rocks was a memory she knew she would always cherish. It had been so good to see his anger and bitterness replaced by simple pleasure. Adam Stuart was a complicated man—intriguing, infuriating, and fascinating. Perhaps that was why she couldn't banish his handsome features from her memory.

Chapter 11

Iris reached for her cloak and pulled it on. She was glad the past week had drifted by without alarms or problems. The girls had welcomed her back with warm hugs and soft kisses, and they had all settled into a routine as the outside temperature rose and the days began to lengthen. Every time she and the girls heard a horse canter up to the house, however, Iris rushed to the balcony to see if the visitor was riding a tall black stallion and sporting a creased suit. And every time, she turned away and tried to quell the disappointment that tightened her chest. She didn't know why she was drawn to Adam Stuart. There were several reasons she should want to avoid his company. But something made her want to help him.

She pushed aside thoughts of the intriguing Mr. Stuart as she prepared to depart. She had made plans to spend her afternoon off with Camie. They were going to town to shop.

"Why can't we go with you?" June asked, her hand bunched in the folds of Iris's cloak.

"We'll be very good." Anna stood on the other side, her face upturned.

Josephine walked into the nursery. "Now you leave Miss Iris alone. It's her afternoon off, and she needs to spend it the way she wants to."

"It's too far for you to walk, my dears." Iris knelt between them. "I am going to see my friend, Mrs. Sherer. You remember her, don't you?"

They nodded.

"We're going to do some shopping. If you are very good and don't give Josephine any trouble, I'll bring each of you a peppermint stick."

Their faces brightened.

Josephine put an arm around each girl's shoulders. "I'm not sure they like peppermint."

As Iris descended the main staircase, she could hear June and Anna protesting that they loved peppermint more than anything else in the world.

Iris opened the front door and breathed deeply. Spring had finally come, and she was grateful. Warm sun kissed her cheeks as she walked along, considering what she would say if she saw Adam Stuart. Which facet would he show her the next time they met? Would he be the outlandish flirt, the angry pessimist, or would his hazel gaze and ready laughter remind her of the charming guide at Lookout Mountain?

Iris walked to Camie's house, her mood buoyed by her thoughts. The Sherers' housekeeper had returned from visiting her family in Georgia and was going to keep the twins while their mother shopped.

Camie filled Iris in on the latest news as she drove the wagon the two miles to Daisy. "Lance says that Nathan's uncle is on a rampage. He failed to get the council to go along with his latest scheme to take Mr. Spencer's farm away. He's apparently gone to the district judge to ask that the land be put up for auction."

"I cannot see how Nathan abides his uncle's attitude."

"You and I are more in the minority than you realize." Camie frowned at her. "A lot of people in Daisy don't think an Indian ought to have that nice a place."

"They're jealous of his success." Iris rolled her eyes. "Those same people are probably envious of your hardworking husband, nice home, and beautiful children."

"Jealousy and envy are strong emotions." Camie's lips straightened into a flat line. "It's why God warns us not to covet what our neighbor has."

Iris shook her head. "Well I, for one, refuse to worry about the malcontents in town. Mr. Spencer has owned that land for decades, and nothing is going to change that. Why, even President Jackson is not trying to remove Indians who own their land. The Spencers will be living in that house for generations to come."

Camie slowed the wagon as they made it to town. It was a good thing she did as a man came dashing out of Mr. Pierce's store and ran right in front of the wagon, his arms waving. "Remember the Alamo! Remember the Alamo!" He untied his horse from the hitching post, threw himself into the saddle, and galloped away.

"What do you suppose that was about?" Iris asked.

"I don't know, but why don't we go to the store and see what we can find out?" Camie climbed down and tied off the horse's reins.

From the sound of it, most of the town was there. The ladies had to push their way inside.

"Hi, Mrs. Sherer." The feminine voice belonged to a woman about their age. She was stunning, with exotic green eyes and shiny auburn hair.

Camie nodded at the beautiful woman. "Hello, Miss Coleridge."

The woman looked to Iris. "I don't believe we've met." She held out a hand, and Iris took it, instantly impressed by the indomitable spirit she saw in the woman's eyes. "Hi. My name's Margaret Coleridge. It's a pleasure to meet a friend of Camie's."

"Likewise." Iris squeezed her hand. "I look forward to getting to know you better."

"It's a small town." Miss Coleridge smiled warmly. "I'm sure we will bump into each other with regularity."

"What's going on in here?" Camie nodded toward the crowd of people clustered around the long counter at the front of the store.

Margaret's expression grew serious. "It's bad news, I'm afraid. There was a battle in a place called the Alamo in Texas Territory. They are saying that Davy Crockett, our recent congressman, was killed in the battle."

Nathan sauntered over, wiping his hands on his apron. "It's worse than that."

Someone pushed past Iris, jostling her elbow. "What could be worse?"

"They're saying Davy and several others survived the battle and were assassinated after they surrendered."

Iris covered her mouth with her hand, her eyes filled with horror.

Someone banged on the counter with the butt of his gun. "Remember the Alamo!" The cry was picked up and repeated, making Iris feel uncomfortable.

Nathan nodded his head toward the door. "I think maybe you ladies should leave." He tried to guide all three of them to safety, but somehow Iris found herself carried in the other direction by the restive crowd. Even though she was tall enough to see over most of the men in the store, she could not push hard enough to get to the exit.

An elbow jabbed her in the ribs at the same time that a booted foot trod on her shoe, and Iris could feel herself falling. Panic clawed its way up her throat. If she fell here, she might be seriously hurt by the angry crowd.

A strong arm snaked around her waist, and Iris found herself with her nose pressed into a hard chest. "It's okay. I've got you." The man twisted so that he was between her and the shoving crowd then half-dragged, half-carried her to safety outside.

Iris pulled away from the strong arm, her mouth open to thank her rescuer. She looked up into blazing hazel eyes and snapped her mouth shut.

Adam Stuart pointed a finger at her. "You need a keeper, Miss Landon. Didn't your parents teach you not to go into a mob like that? Those men are ready to riot."

"Maybe so, but no one asked you to come to my rescue." Iris wondered what had happened to the appealing man at the citadel of rocks. Adam's charm had evaporated like early morning dew. She glared at him. "Why don't you mind your own business?"

Camie ran over to where they stood. "I was so worried." She hugged Iris close. "Thank you, Mr. Stuart. I would never have forgiven myself if anything had happened to Iris."

"Well then, maybe you should keep her on a shorter leash." He strode down the street without another word.

❧

Adam wanted to avoid Poe's Tavern, but tonight he had no choice. It was his job.

He had not been there since taking Iris—Miss Landon—on that tour up to the citadel of rocks. He didn't know what it was, but something about her purity and goodness made him want to be a better man. When he looked at the faith shining out of Iris's brown eyes, he had to wonder if God existed after all. And if He did, maybe the reason for the pain and death of this life was due to man's sinful nature rather than an uncaring Creator.

"Here you go, boy." He pulled a cube of sugar out of his pocket, fed it to his horse, and left the animal tied to the hitching post.

He entered the tavern, surprised to find it so crowded. It reminded him of the scene at Pierce's this morning. When he'd seen Iris foundering in the crowd, his heart had stopped beating. And then he'd scorched her with his words the moment he was sure she was safe. He would give his good leg to erase those angry words from existence.

A place had been made for him at the round table where the seven members of the town council sat. He shook hands with the ones on either side of him and waited for the meeting to begin.

Richard Pierce banged a miniature mallet against the table to get everyone's attention.

Adam pulled out his pencil, several loose sheets of paper, and the ledger he used for transcribing council minutes. From the sound of things, it was going to be a long night.

"Quiet! Quiet! I now call this meeting of the Daisy town council to order." Pierce waited for the noise to abate before giving Adam a regal nod. "Read the minutes from the last meeting, Mr. Stuart."

Adam opened his book and went down the list of items that had been discussed at the previous meeting. When he was done, he looked back at Pierce.

"Are there any objections to the minutes as read?" asked Pierce. The silence in the room was only broken by the tinkle of glass and the scrape of chair legs against the wooden floor of the tavern. "Then let the record reflect that the minutes were adopted without change." He banged his mallet again. "Now on to new business."

Someone coughed, and a low murmur began in the room.

Pierce raised the mallet once more and banged it loudly to regain their attention. "For the first order of the day, I think this council should consider a matter that causes me great concern. Now you all know that I'm a fair man." Someone in the back of the room laughed, but Pierce continued without pause. "I don't mind the Indians who live over there at Ross's Landing. I've even been known to sell them a few things just to keep the peace. But no matter what my personal thoughts are, I have to speak out about the danger that has sought refuge in our fair town."

Adam watched the man's face twist with hatred and distrust. Why had God left such a man as Richard Pierce alive and well, while He took someone brave and honest like Davy Crockett away from them? This world needed more Crocketts and fewer Pierces.

One of the other council members stood up. "This had better not be about Wayha Spencer, Richard, because we've tabled that matter."

"Yeah, leave Spencer out of this." The voice came from a bearded man in the back of the room. "He's been here a lot longer than I have. Besides, we've got more serious matters to discuss, like what happened in Texas."

A general chorus of agreement stopped Pierce from continuing his argument. His face reddened, and he slumped back, crossing his arms over his chest.

For the next hour the men in the room suggested ways to support the Texans fighting for freedom from Mexican tyranny. Several men said they were leaving at daylight, while others pledged the support of ammunition and supplies. One of the council members proposed starting a list of men who wished to donate to the cause. His idea won support, and the meeting adjourned.

Adam gave them a sheet of paper and a pencil and then left them to figure out the rest. It wasn't part of his job to direct charitable efforts. He ambled past the men crowded around the table and sat down on his usual stool.

"Do you have any fresh coffee, Cyrus?"

The bartender nodded and walked away for a moment.

Before he returned, Nathan Pierce entered and took the stool next to him. He turned his back to the bar and faced Adam. "I know Crockett was a friend of yours, Adam. I'm sorry for your loss."

Adam hunched a shoulder and stared at the steaming mug Cyrus set in front of him.

"Are you going to Texas?"

"I thought about it." Adam indicated his bad leg. "What good is a limping soldier? What about you?"

"No, my uncle needs me at the store." Nathan's cheeks darkened with a rush of blood. "And there's another reason I don't want to leave right now, a more recent development."

A ringing sensation filled Adam's ears, and his hands clenched. Icy fingers of despair wrapped themselves around his heart and squeezed. "Does this development have a name?" *Idiot,* a dark voice taunted him. *Did you think you were good enough for the likes of Iris Landon? Much better for Nathan to claim her. He'll take good care of her.*

Nathan's face reddened further. "Yes, but I'm sure it's not necessary. You must know which lady has caught my eye."

With a swift motion, Adam took a large gulp of the coffee, feeling the sting of the hot beverage on his throat. "My congratulations. Her heart is as big as the whole outdoors. She'll never play you false."

"There's only one problem." Nathan leaned closer to confide in Adam. "I'm not sure my uncle will approve of her."

Adam watched his hands tighten on the polished edge of the bar until his knuckles turned white. The man didn't deserve a woman like Iris if he was afraid she wasn't good enough for his pompous windbag of an uncle. "She may be a bit impetuous, but if your uncle is too stupid to recognize her qualities, then he doesn't deserve your consideration." Didn't Nathan Pierce realize how lucky he was?

A small voice whispered to Adam that he could not face this loss without help. And he knew the voice spoke the truth. For a brief instant he wished he had not severed his connection to God, but then he banished the thought and raised his hand to get the bartender's attention. He needed something stronger than coffee to cope with his pain.

Chapter 12

That cannot be allowed!" Iris tried to calm her voice, but it was the outside of enough. Lance Sherer had to be mistaken. "What does Mr. Pierce hope to accomplish by filing suit against Mr. Spencer?"

"I guess he wants to make sure Wayha goes west with the other Cherokee." Lance sighed. "And his position as mayor may lend him credence in a court of law."

Iris stood up and paced the floor. She glanced at Mr. Spencer, who sat at his desk saying nothing. Didn't he realize how serious the matter was? He could lose everything.

She turned to Lance. "But I thought you said the council and even some of the townspeople defended Mr. Spencer last night."

Lance nodded. "But it was what he said after the meeting that concerns me. He swore he would have Wayha's land no matter what. He said he was going to sue Wayha. If he files his complaint, it will be heard in the Superior Court of Law and Equity in Knoxville, not by a local judge who knows the real situation."

Mr. Spencer raised his head, and Iris could see the pain in his eyes. "Perhaps I should consider leaving after all."

"Don't even think about such a thing." Iris walked to the window and looked out. "You've built a wonderful life here, and no man has the right to take it from you." She turned to face him. "Didn't the Cherokee people own all of this land at one time?"

"No." Mr. Spencer shook his head. "We did not own the land. It is the bounty of God. The Cherokee people have always lived here freely. It is only since the white man came that we have come to accept the idea of owning land."

"But this land does belong to you legally, doesn't it?" Iris asked.

A nod answered her question. Mr. Spencer looked at Lance. "You have my deed as proof."

Iris's feeling of relief died a quick death when she saw the expression on Lance's face. "What's wrong?"

"There's a problem with the deed."

Mr. Spencer's face turned as white as parchment. "What do you mean?

There is nothing wrong with that deed. It was properly executed and signed."

"The problem is not with the deed. It's with the location of the deed." Lance's cheeks were ruddy with embarrassment.

"You have lost my deed?"

Lance shook his head. "I did not lose the deed. I. . . It was stolen from my house."

Iris gasped. "You were robbed? Is Camie okay? The children?"

His cheeks grew even darker. "I don't know when it happened. Someone broke into my office. He must have known the deed was there. We heard nothing. I'm not even sure when it happened, but he broke into my safe and rifled through all the papers."

"Who could have done such a thing?"

"I don't know." Lance turned to Mr. Spencer. "I will make this right. I remember reading that your land was given to you by the state of North Carolina as recompense for your service during the Revolution. I plan to draft a letter to the land grant office in Washington, asking for their help."

Iris had never considered how old Mr. Spencer was. But after hearing this news, he suddenly looked old enough to have fought with her grandfather in the Revolutionary War. This man deserved protection from greedy men like Mayor Pierce, and she would do everything in her power to make certain he was treated fairly. "Until you hear from Washington, we need to make sure Mr. Spencer's rights are protected. He will need to be defended by someone who is familiar with the court system."

Lance drummed his fingers on the arm of the settee as he considered their options. "It needs to be a man who is sympathetic to the Indians."

All three of them sat in silence for a few minutes.

Iris wished she could ask her pa for advice, but he wasn't here. Besides, she was an adult. She could come up with solutions on her own.

"There's only one man I know of who fits the bill." Lance tugged his collar. "Adam Stuart."

Iris frowned. "We can't ask him for help."

"Why not?" Mr. Spencer asked. "Adam is smart, and he'll know how to approach the case. He's our best chance."

೨

Iris sat next to Lance in the wagon as they made their way to town and Adam Stuart's office. "I don't think this is a good idea."

"I know, but who else could we ask? Besides, Mr. Spencer trusts him."

"So does Pastor Miller." Iris wished she trusted Adam. At first she had taken him to be a libertine because of his behavior on the night she'd arrived in town. But he'd disproved that assessment when he'd taken her to the top of Lookout Mountain. He'd been the perfect gentleman, even though she had swooned in his arms. And she couldn't fault his concern for the Cherokee. If only he could shake off the cloud of bitterness surrounding him, she was sure he'd be an outstanding citizen and the perfect advocate for Mr. Spencer.

"Lance, who do you think could have taken the deed?"

His face tightened. "I have no idea. Few people knew it was there. You, Camie, Wayha..."

He left off the last name, but she heard it in her mind. Adam. Again she questioned whether or not they should turn to him for help. Yet who else was there? Adam knew more about Indian rights than any other man around. She prayed for God's guidance and felt peace settle around her like a cloak.

Adam Stuart was an intriguing man—full of contradictions. No one else had ever had the power to rouse her anger so quickly. She considered his rescue yesterday. She had to admit she had been frightened when she was separated from Camie and unable to make her way out of the crowd. But after he got her outside, his attitude had been inexcusable. And he had run off before she could express her thanks or much else. Today would be different. Now that she'd had time to fully recover her equilibrium, she would not let him annoy her again.

Lance pulled up on the reins and climbed down from the wagon. Normally Iris would have scrambled down without any help, but several curious people were watching so she waited until he tied the horses to a post and came around to assist her in disembarking. She felt the gazes of the townspeople on them as she followed Lance to the door.

Lance knocked, but no one answered. "I hope he's here." He tried the doorknob. "It's not locked."

Lance pushed the door open and waited for Iris to precede him.

"Hello," she called out. "Is anyone here?"

The office was dusty and dingy. Not at all what she had pictured for an attorney. Of course, this attorney probably worried very little about things like simple housekeeping chores.

A thump and a groan from the far side of the room answered her query. "Who's there?"

Lance shut the door behind them. "It's Iris Landon and Lance Sherer. We're here to hire your services."

A series of thumps and bumps sounded, and then a hand came up from the far side of Mr. Stuart's desk and rested atop it, followed by a second hand. They pressed against the surface of the desk. Then Iris saw a head of light brown hair that made her think of coffee with cream, followed by the pale, haggard face of Adam Stuart, attorney at law. He bore more resemblance to the scarecrow Grandpa Taylor used in his cornfield than a professional lawyer. His coat was missing, and his hair looked like it could use a thorough brushing to remove tangles, twigs, and dust. His shirt was unbuttoned and hung slightly open, exposing an indecent amount of his chest.

"This is ridiculous." Iris could feel her cheeks burning as she turned to Lance. The peace she'd felt earlier melted away. "There must be someone else who can help."

"Why don't you step out to the wagon for a moment, Iris. I'll see that he gets cleaned up."

Iris couldn't look toward Adam again. She held her chin up to mask her embarrassment on behalf of the pitiable man and swept out of the office.

The sun moved slowly toward the west as she waited. They were making a terrible mistake. Mr. Spencer would be better served if they sent for someone from Nashville or even Knoxville. Surely there were competent attorneys who could also manage to stay sober.

Finally Lance came out to collect her. "He's better now." He let her in and went back to Adam's living area behind the office.

The scent of coffee was strong in the room. Iris hoped it would have a salutary effect on the man they'd come to see. The man who might very well be Wayha Spencer's only hope.

❧

Adam's head throbbed, and his mouth felt like it had been stuffed with cotton. He wanted to slink back to his bedroom and sleep for a few days until the embarrassment wore off, but he forced himself to walk back into the office and face her. How could he have fallen asleep on the floor behind his desk? And why did Iris have to pick that particular day to visit his office?

Nathan Pierce would never have found himself in a similar situation. Which was why Nathan Pierce deserved her, and he did not.

Adam peered at the vision as Iris moved farther into the office. Did she have to be so beautiful? She was as tall as a statue and twice as lovely. A statue, however, could never capture the warmth and caring that shone from her eyes.

He dropped his gaze. It must be the alcohol still swimming around in his head that was making him so crazy. He had to get her out of here. "I can't help you."

He heard her shock in the swift intake of her breath. "You don't even know what I need from you."

He pasted a smile on his face. He'd had ample opportunity to mask his true feelings. "Lance explained about Spencer's trouble with the law. Some men would say I should not aid a slave owner."

"Let's address one problem at a time, Mr. Stuart." Her voice was strained, and he could see desperation in her eyes.

Her pain tempted him to change his mind, but Adam refused to be drawn into a battle that had already been lost. "I told Wayha weeks ago to clear out, and he wouldn't listen."

"So that's it." She huffed. "You won't even try to help us?"

Adam shook his head.

"I had planned to tell you that I was sorry for thinking you were no more than a bitter man who wanted to live in the past. It is not my right to judge you, but as a Christian I can deplore your actions and decry your cowardice."

How dare she pass judgment on him? Hadn't she said it was not her right? "I suppose it was a coward who rescued you from certain harm yesterday, too?"

That stopped her.

"You're right, of course. You did protect me, and I owe you my thanks."

"What? No more denunciations?" He stepped from behind his desk and walked toward her. She didn't shrink back like most women would have done. She squared her shoulders and glared at him through those disdainful brown eyes. He wanted to shake some sense into her. She should go back home to Nashville before she found herself on the wrong end of a lynch mob for defending an Indian. This country of his was not going to see reason when it came to the Cherokee, and the sooner everyone agreed, the better it would be.

"No, although you sorely try my patience." She took a deep breath. "I will not let anger control my words or my actions."

Adam couldn't have been more surprised if she had produced a pail of water and dashed him with it. How could she decide to not get angry? And yet he could see the calmness that entered her eyes. If he reached out for it, he could have almost caught the ire that rolled away from her, leaving her serene and peaceful.

"How did you do that?"

She looked confused by his question. "Do what?"

"How did you get rid of it? It's not like you tamped it down. I could sense it leaving you as though it were an uninvited guest."

"I get my strength from the Lord." She smiled at him, the sweetness plain to see. " 'Cease from anger, and forsake wrath: fret not thyself in any wise to do evil.' "

"I know the verse." Although it had been a long time since Adam had read his Bible, he was familiar enough with David's psalms to recognize the words. "That chapter promises that evildoers will be cut down as easily as grass, yet evil still flourishes."

"That's because of the devil's wickedness here in the world of men. It will not always be so." She leaned toward him.

Adam was the one who backed up a pace when he caught a whiff of her perfume. It was too heady a mixture for his poor head. "Then we may as well give up and get along until God decides to come back and straighten us out. He doesn't seem to be in much of a hurry."

"Don't you see, that's because of you and me. It's up to us to spread the Gospel. God is long-suffering and wants everyone to be saved. I believe it's the reason He is allowing the white man to overrun this land."

"Because He likes white men better than Indians?"

Iris shook her head. "Because we are bringing His message with us. At least some of us are."

He ignored what might have been a jab at him and attempted to ignore the inner jab that he knew came from Someone else. "So how does that fit with greedy land grabbers? And what about Davy Crockett and the others who died at the Alamo? How does that fit into God's plan?"

Adam was shocked to see unshed tears in Iris's expressive eyes. Was she sad for Crockett? Spencer? Him? He didn't have the nerve to ask.

Lance came back into the room bearing a dented coffeepot and several mugs, one of which was so cracked Adam doubted it would hold liquid. He was embarrassed all over again for Iris to see the conditions in which he lived.

He looked around at the dust and dishevelment surrounding them. It had been so long since he'd cared about the niceties of life. Lately he'd been more interested in getting through each day. Perhaps it was time for him to rejoin the living.

He could almost hear the call to arms. It was the same call that had filled him once before with the need to defend Indian rights. Suddenly he was tired of all the pretense. It was time to stop hiding from the future. Hope filled his chest and made his heart beat faster. He straightened his shoulders and smoothed the wrinkled material of his suit coat. Adam had almost forgotten how exhilarating it could be to strive for fairness and justice.

This case against Wayha Spencer was nothing but a trumped-up accusation. Who knew? He might even enjoy routing the pompous mayor in the courtroom. "Tell me about the deed."

Chapter 13

The past week had been tense as Iris waited for Adam to report on the progress of Mr. Spencer's case. This afternoon she was determined to distract the girls by teaching them a new game. She surveyed the pattern she'd drawn on the dusty ground with some satisfaction. Her ma had taught her the game of scotch-hoppers when she was a young girl. The layout she had drawn was fairly small to accommodate June's and Anna's shorter legs.

She handed a rock to each girl. "Now, what you do is toss your rock into the first square right here." She dropped her own rock to show them and waited while each girl followed her action before gathering up her skirts. "The object is to hop into each square except the one that holds our rocks, but the trick is to use only one leg."

Iris demonstrated by hopping up through the ladder of squares she'd drawn in the grassless area behind the Spencer home. "When you get to the round space here, you can rest on both feet for a moment before returning to the start."

The girls clamored for a chance to try their luck, so Iris sent June first and then Anna. When each girl had returned, she had them pick up their rocks and toss them into the second square.

The sound of someone clearing his throat nearby made Iris spin around and drop her skirts with a gasp as she recognized Nathan Pierce's broad shoulders and handsome face.

"Oh my!" Iris wondered if she would survive the embarrassment of knowing he'd seen her acting like a hoyden with her skirts around her knees. She lifted her chin in defiance. What did she care? She was doing her job, after all. "I thought it would be a good idea to give the children something energetic to do this afternoon."

He smiled and nodded. "I understand."

"Were you looking for Mr. Spencer?" she asked.

"No, I wanted to talk to you about a matter that causes me some concern." He glanced toward the girls, who were noisily arguing over whether June's foot had landed inside one of the squares. "Is there somewhere we can go?"

Iris clapped her hands. "Girls, please go to the kitchen and ask Cook if she can prepare some refreshment for our guest." She raised a hand at their protests. "If you don't go now, we won't be able to finish our game before it gets dark."

The girls looked at each other, and she could almost see the thoughts churning through their active minds before they ran back to the house, calling out to the cook.

Nathan's sigh of relief reminded her of his aversion to children, and she wondered if it was because he had no siblings. She couldn't imagine growing up without her own sister and brother. A wave of homesickness hit her as she thought of them.

"Thank you so much, Miss Landon." Nathan stepped close and took her hand in his own. "I thought it prudent to come and warn you."

Iris forgot about home as she concentrated on the man in front of her. "Whatever is the matter?"

"Everyone in town is talking about the amount of time you've been spending with Adam Stuart."

She pulled her hand free. He'd come to warn her about gossip? She shook her head. He must know that his uncle had brought a suit against her employer. Did he expect her to do nothing? "Yes, I have hired Mr. Stuart to defend against your uncle's complaint that Mr. Spencer and his family should be removed from their land."

"I know, and I hope you will understand when I say I do not support my uncle's actions. But I don't think it's necessary for you to hire someone to defend the Spencers. I cannot believe any judge would rule against them."

"That might be true if his deed had not been stolen from Lance's home."

Nathan frowned at her. "When did this occur?"

"No one knows, but it must have been taken by someone who intended to harm Mr. Spencer, since it's the only document missing."

Nathan spun around and paced toward a stand of trees, obviously considering the information she had given him. She thought of the night he and his uncle had come to dinner at the Sherers' home. Could Mayor Pierce be the culprit? He was the most obvious suspect to her because he was so determined to have the Spencers removed. She watched as Nathan turned around and retraced his steps to stand next to her.

"I know you must blame my uncle, but I cannot believe he would stoop to thievery." His earnest face beseeched her to agree. "He's an honorable man."

Sympathy filled her. Nathan was being more reasonable than she would have been in his place. And perhaps his uncle was innocent. At this point it didn't much matter what had happened to the deed. They simply had to find other evidence to prove Wayha's claim was legitimate.

Nathan took her hand in his. "You will not want to hear this, but there is a more likely candidate. The very man you hired. He has been quite vocal in his opinion that the Spencers should give up and move west before it's too late."

Iris blew out a disgusted breath. "Adam Stuart would never do such a thing."

"I believe you are right. He would not do anything dishonorable. . .as long as he was sober." He squeezed her hand. "The night he came to the Sherers' home, he was anything but."

She shook her head. "I won't believe it."

Nathan shrugged and let her hand go. "You should at least consider it before you condemn my uncle. I know he can be a bit overbearing, but he is a good man. Uncle Richard is much more likely to fight honorably than resort to underhanded means." He left her alone then, his words echoing in her mind.

Iris hated to admit it, but there was some truth to what Nathan said. Alcohol often stripped away the morals of honorable men.

Could Adam have taken the deed that night? Was she being foolish in trusting him to defend the Spencers? Yet he seemed so intent on working with her to keep the Spencers in their home. Was it all a facade? No. She shook her head. It could not have been Adam. He might not be perfect, but Adam Stuart was not a thief. . .she hoped.

Chapter 14

Adam could feel anticipation welling up as he turned onto Wayha Spencer's land. He couldn't wait to see the beautiful, courageous Iris Landon. When she had turned to him for help two weeks ago, she'd turned his whole world around. He would do everything in his power to see that Wayha kept his land.

Earlier this morning he'd gone to visit Lance Sherer about the missing deed. The paper had not turned up, so everyone had to assume it had been stolen. But who had taken it? Who could have known that it was being stored there? When Lance had first suggested that he keep it, Adam had been certain it was the perfect solution. If Iris's God did exist, He certainly did work in mysterious ways.

Adam had been about to return to town, but then he decided to ride out to Wayha's home. He tried to tell himself it was a logical way to gather more information to help the case, but deep inside, he knew he was hoping to see Iris. What was it about her that drew him? He was like a callow youth who had fallen in love for the first time. He could not get enough of her beauty and spirit.

He dismounted and handed his horse's reins to the slave who met him at the front entrance. Josephine greeted Adam, but before she could lead him to Wayha's study, he heard the clatter of feet hurrying down the staircase.

He looked up to see the granddaughters. Although they were of different ages, they looked very much alike with their dark hair and shiny brown eyes. When they spotted him, they stopped their headlong progress and looked back up the stairs.

His gaze followed theirs, and he found himself drinking in Iris's beautiful visage. No wonder her parents had named her after a flower. There was something so clean and bright and sparkling about her. She looked like a fresh blossom, especially in the lavender dress she was wearing.

She descended the stairs gracefully. "It's a pleasure to see you, Mr. Stuart."

"Likewise," he answered, wishing he could think of something intelligent to say. What was it about Iris Landon that tied his tongue in knots? "Are you taking these young ladies outside?"

Iris reminded them of their manners with a glance. "June, Anna, you remember Mr. Stuart. He's working for your grandfather."

The older girl curtsied, followed by her little sister.

He bowed. "My, how grown-up you've become. I'm sure your grandfather is proud to have such lovely young ladies about the house."

"Miss Iris, can he come with us?" June asked.

Iris shook her head. "I'm sure Mr. Stuart is here on business. We must let him meet—"

A door opened, and Mr. Spencer came into the hallway. "I thought I heard voices."

"Yes sir," Iris answered the older man. "The girls and I are going on a picnic down by the stream. We'll leave you and Mr. Stuart to your business."

Wayha shook his head. "I have matters to attend to in Ross's Landing." He turned to Adam. "I'm sorry you came all this way, and I can't stay."

June tugged on Adam's pant leg. "That means you can come with us."

Adam smiled down at her. "There's nothing I'd like better." He glanced toward Iris. "If I wouldn't be in the way, that is."

Anna, not to be outdone by her sibling, moved closer to him. "We have lots of food. And Miss Iris is going to show us how to catch fish."

He noticed a heightened flush in Iris's cheeks. Was it caused by anger or excitement? He hoped it was the latter. He was certainly anticipating an enjoyable afternoon.

The house slave handed a basket to Iris, but he took it from her. "The least I can do is carry the food, since you have been so kind as to invite me along."

Iris tied shawls on the girls and straightened her hat before they headed outside. Adam offered her his arm, pleased when she rested her hand on it. They ambled slowly down the path that led to the stream behind the house. She didn't seem to mind his uneven gait, a fact he was thankful for.

"Be careful. Don't get too far away," she called out, admonishing the girls, who had skipped ahead of them.

"Are they always this excited?"

Iris nodded. "They have a natural ability to enjoy the simplest of things. It's such a pity that their mother and grandmother died. They are starved for affection." She blushed slightly and looked away. "Not that Mr. Spencer doesn't love them. He's just. . .just reserved."

"My father was much the same." Adam looked ahead to the sparkling blue waters of the deep stream. "But I never doubted his love for me."

"I thought we could spread our blanket near that tree." Iris pointed to a tall maple. "That way we can get out of the sun if it grows too hot this afternoon."

Adam set the basket down and took the blanket from atop it, spreading it out on the ground and anchoring it on all four corners with rocks. At the same time, he picked up several smaller flat rocks and dropped them in his coat pocket. When he was done, he joined the girls, who were exploring the banks of the stream.

"Did you see that?" June pointed to a ripple in the water. "It's a fish."

Anna pointed, too. Her eyes grew round as a dark shape broke the surface once more. She jumped up and down on the sloped bank, and Adam reached to grab her before she could fall into the swiftly flowing water.

"Be careful. Miss Iris would be very upset if she had to jump in the water to save you."

Anna looked back toward the tree where Iris was setting out food for their lunch. "Miss Iris can do anything."

Adam laughed at the faith in the little girl's voice. "I'm sure she can. But let's not try swimming this afternoon. Would you like to learn how to throw rocks and make them jump across the water?"

Both girls nodded, so Adam pulled his stones out. He gave one to each child and chose another for himself. He bent down and showed them how to hold a rock between the thumb and forefinger. Then he tossed his out across the surface of the stream where it bounced one, two, three times before sinking below the water.

June bent her arm back and threw her rock with all her strength, but it only plopped into the water. When Anna tried for the first time, her rock did not quite reach the water's edge.

Adam pulled more of his rocks from his pocket, and the three of them tried again and again. After a little while, Iris wandered down to where they stood. He could feel her gaze on them and turned to catch her smiling.

"Come here and show us how well you can do it."

❧

Iris couldn't help but compare Adam's ability to entertain and charm her girls with Nathan's discomfort the day he'd come to see her. Of course Nathan had his own charm and many excellent qualities, but it was Adam who was winning June's and Anna's hearts.

She clapped her hands as Anna managed to get her rock into the water. "What talented girls you are."

"Did you see me?" asked June. "My rock bounced two times."

Anna ran to her. "Can you bounce a rock, Miss Iris?"

"Oh, I doubt it."

"Come on. Mr. Stuart can show you how. He showed me."

June added her own endorsement. "And me, too."

"Here." Adam handed her a rock. "This is a good one. I'm sure it will bounce several times."

Iris took the rock and turned it over in her hand. She had no idea how to throw the thing to make it skip. Skipping rocks was something she and Camie had never tried. She tossed the small stone toward the water, twisting her arm to add extra power. The silly thing didn't bounce a single time.

"Try again." Adam's voice was encouraging as he handed her another one.

"I don't know. We don't want to fill the stream with all these rocks."

Adam's laughter made her smile. "I don't think there's any danger of that." He moved directly behind her. "Here let me show you how to do it."

Iris's heart jumped up to her throat as she felt his arm encircling her. Her back and shoulders stiffened, but he didn't seem to notice as he took her hand and turned it sideways.

"Hold the rock loosely." His breath tickled her ear, and his nearness reminded her of the day he'd shown her the citadel of rocks.

She'd been breathless that day, too.

Iris tried to concentrate on the method he was trying to teach her. She let him manipulate her wrist back and forth. Then he snapped her hand forward. The rock flew out of her grasp and sailed out over the water. Her eyes widened as she saw it skip again and again before falling below the surface.

"I did it!" She twisted around in her excitement and came face-to-face with him. Their lips were only inches apart. If he puckered slightly, he would be kissing her. Everything seemed to slow down. As if from a distance, she could hear June and Anna congratulating her. But all she could see was Adam's face. Some shred of sanity made her pull away from him, but it took several seconds before she could breathe normally. Apparently she was no more immune to his charm than June and Anna.

Iris herded the girls back to the blanket, relieved that their chatter covered her embarrassment. She sat down and took several deep breaths in an attempt to calm her still-racing heart. Why did it beat so hard against her chest when Adam was present? And why wouldn't it even flutter when she was around Nathan?

❧

Adam took a deep breath to steady his racing heart. He'd been so close to kissing Iris. Right out here in the open and in front of her charges. What had he been thinking? If she had not pulled away, he would have yielded to the temptation. While he was thankful her reputation was still intact, a part of him longed to pull Iris back into his arms and never let her go.

He stood alone on the bank of the small stream and watched as she settled the children on the blanket and handed each of them a piece of chicken. Maybe he should leave them alone. Just then, Anna looked toward him and waved her arm.

"Come and eat, Mr. Adam."

He walked to where they sat, wondering what he could say to reassure Iris. "Perhaps I should return to town."

June's eyes rounded. "But you'll miss the best part if you leave now."

"That's right." Anna nodded solemnly. "Miss Iris promised to tell us a story."

He tried to read Iris's expression, but she had her face turned away.

"Well, perhaps I can stay for a little while." Adam sat down on the blanket. "Is Miss Iris a good storyteller?"

"The best." June looked toward Iris. "What story are you going to tell us?"

"Tell the one about the lost sheep," Anna suggested. "I like that story."

Iris placed a piece of chicken on a plate and handed it to Adam. "But you already know that story."

Anna's bottom lip protruded. "Please, Miss Iris."

"Well, if you're certain." Both girls nodded at her, so Iris took a deep breath. "Once upon a time, a young shepherd boy loved his sheep very much. . . ."

Adam munched on his chicken as Iris began to talk. This should be interesting. He was familiar with the story, but it had never held much meaning. What kind of shepherd would leave his flock to find one lost sheep? Better to protect the ones left in his flock.

Yet as Iris talked about the shepherd's concern, he felt a tug on his heart. Then she described the shepherd's joy, and he felt it, too. The excitement of finding something that was lost. The celebration of not only the shepherd but also the other sheep, as they welcomed the lost lamb back to the fold.

He was so lost in contemplation that Adam didn't realize Iris had finished the story until he felt a small hand tug on his shirtsleeve. He looked down into June's earnest face.

"Don't you like that story?"

Adam cleared his throat. "Yes. It was a wonderful story." His voice sounded gruff even to his own ears. He glanced at Iris. Could she tell how much her story had affected him? Somehow she had brought the scripture alive this afternoon. No wonder it was the children's favorite story. It was well on the way to becoming his favorite, too. Of course it was only that. A sweet story. It would be nice if the real world worked that way. But he knew all too well that it didn't.

How wonderful it would be to feel so loved, so prized. But Adam's mind balked at the idea of God trying to return him to the fold. Not when he'd been so eager to blame God for all his problems. Not when he'd strayed so far from the path. He didn't deserve that kind of love, and he knew it.

Chapter 15

The next few weeks passed in a whirl of activities. Adam rode over to Dallas, a community some miles to the north where they had a telegraph office. He sent queries out to the nation's capital as well as to Raleigh, the capital of North Carolina, where records of land grants were recorded and should be housed. The documents he was trying to find out about, however, were neither listed by location nor by owner, making his task harder.

Iris came to town to visit him at least twice each week, and they would spend hours poring over faded land grants, old deeds, and ambiguous records. He would always regret not kissing her that day by the stream. She'd been so close. If only the Spencer children had not been there, he might at least have dropped a peck on her cheek.

Since then he'd been careful to keep a discreet distance between them. He didn't want to scare her into avoiding him altogether. At first she had been stiff and wary of him, but that had eventually worn off as they worked side by side toward the same goal. She usually brought something for them to eat, and Adam made certain nonchipped crockery and clean surfaces were available for their shared meal.

The two of them created a list of dates and facts substantiated by the documents still in Lance's possession and the reports they received from Adam's queries. He would have liked to have the original deed in hand, but since it had disappeared so mysteriously from Lance's home, he suspected it would never again surface.

The court date was only a week away. It was time to pack up the evidence and say good-bye to Iris. He rolled up the last map and tamped it into a tube to take with him to the courtroom. "I will be back in less than two weeks."

"I don't know why I cannot come with you." Iris frowned at him over her plate of yams and sliced ham.

"Yes you do. Wayha will have to go with me so he can testify on his own behalf. He trusts you to watch over his grandchildren while he is away."

She rolled her eyes. "I know, but still I want to be there."

"I know you do. I'd like it, too. But you know you cannot go." He put a hand over hers and squeezed it gently.

She allowed her hand to stay there for a moment before pulling back.

"Maybe Camie could stay with them."

"No, Iris." He sat down across from her. "It's far better for you to stay here. We have a strong case. Please trust me to see that Wayha's rights are protected."

"I do trust you, Adam. Why would you do all this work and not defend him well in court?" She smiled at him. "No matter the outcome, I'll always be grateful for the effort you've put forth on his behalf."

Adam wished he had the right to lean across the table and kiss her. She had such faith in him and his ability to save her employer. He only hoped it was well placed. If he won, maybe he would tell her how he felt. He could tell her how much he admired her spirit and her positive outlook. He could tell her how he wanted to bury his face in her hair and drink in the delicate aroma of her perfume. He would explain how she'd brought him back to life and given him a reason to continue, a reason to stay away from alcohol. He'd not been tempted to go to the bar once, even when he had to attend council meetings at the tavern.

"I hope you know how special you are, Iris."

She blushed at his words. "Dozens of women are more special than I am. You should talk to my great-aunt Dolly. She'll tell you that I have never been a proper female. Parties, fancy dresses, and exchanging recipes hold no interest for me."

"Believe me, the women who are interested in such things are not worthy of consideration."

Her expression became serious, as it often did if she was concerned about something or someone. It was another of the qualities he admired in her. "Adam, I think we've grown to know each other fairly well over the past weeks."

He nodded.

"May I ask why you are so cynical about women?"

It was his turn to blush. He could feel the hot blood rushing to his cheeks. He didn't want to think about what had happened in Washington, much less explain it to Iris. But if he ever hoped to have a future with her, he had to be honest with her about his past. He took a deep breath and released it slowly. "There was a girl who I thought loved me, but it turned out she loved her comforts more."

"I'm so sorry. Did she break your heart?"

He nodded, choosing his words carefully. "Sylvia was the beautiful, sheltered daughter of a powerful attorney in Washington. And I was a radical newcomer with lots of lofty ideas. It wasn't her fault. I swept her off her feet. For a little while, everything was okay. I thought she needed time to understand how reprehensible it was to remove the Indians from their land." Adam stopped when he felt Iris's soft hand cover his for a moment. The gesture warmed him and gave him the strength to continue. "But she thought I would give up on

Indian rights, take a job in her father's firm, and escort her to all the right political galas."

"She expected you to give up your principles?"

"She thought her world would appeal to me. And when it didn't, she looked around for another candidate. Someone her daddy would approve of." Adam still remembered the shock of finding that his best friend and business partner was going to take his place as Sylvia's fiancé. But the memory had lost its sting. He looked into her eyes, hoping Iris could see the love he now felt for her. "I once thought I'd never love again, but it turns out that a heart can mend."

Her eyes widened, and she leaned away from him.

Her reaction made him clamp his mouth shut. She was not ready for him to declare his love. Maybe she never would be. That's when he realized that a mended heart could shatter again.

Chapter 16

Adam was glad to be back in familiar territory. His heart pounded with anticipation as he knocked on Wayha Spencer's front door. He had missed Daisy while he was away. Or rather he had missed one of Daisy's inhabitants, namely Iris Landon. Although Wayha would have told Iris the outcome yesterday when he got home, Adam wanted to celebrate their victory with her.

He was let in by the house slave and shown to an empty parlor. As he waited for Iris to appear, he thought about the last time he'd come here and the thrill of holding Iris in his arms as he showed her how to skip rocks. And then the time they'd spent together in his office. Nathan might be a better prospect as a husband, but no one else knew Iris the way Adam did.

In a way, he could hardly believe it had been two weeks since he'd left Iris to go to court. The time had been very busy—more than a week traveling and four days in court arguing Wayha's position. It had taken all his legal skills and Wayha's sincerity to convince the judge, but it had been worth their efforts. He paced from one end of the parlor to the other, eager to tell Iris how the evidence they had collected together had convinced the judge that taking Wayha's land would be a terrible mistake. Wayha and his granddaughters were safe.

The door opened. She stood, a vision in her pale lavender gown. He let himself savor the moment. An expectant, hopeful look filled her beautiful face. Her glorious hair was escaping from the restraint of pins and ribbons as always and framed her face.

He was drawn closer to her as a moth to an irresistible flame. "Iris, you are more beautiful than the flowers you are named after."

A becoming shade of red flagged her cheeks, and she smiled at him. "So we were victorious?"

He nodded and took three long strides across the room to stand next to her. Taking hold of her hands, he leaned back and started to spin, causing her to swing around and around until they were both breathless and laughing. Her eyes were luminous with joy, and a wide smile showed her even teeth. She looked just the way he'd imagined.

He described the twists and turns of the trial, how grasping Mayor Pierce had appeared on the stand and how well Wayha had answered every question asked by the plaintiff's attorney.

"I wish I'd been there," said Iris. "I would have loved to see you in the courtroom."

Adam had dropped her hands while talking about the trial, but now he took them in his again. "Maybe we can do something about that." He drew her a few inches closer.

Her laughter disappeared instantly. "Wh–what do you mean?" Her breathy voice, so near his ear, sent his heart soaring. She seemed as affected by their nearness as he was.

"Will you do me the honor of becoming my wife?" He knew the words were a mistake the minute they were out of his mouth. Where was the eloquence that had helped him win in the courtroom? He'd meant to start by telling her how much he admired her. She was the kindest, most endearing woman he'd ever met. Her honesty was like a breath of fresh air blowing away the doubt and betrayal of his past.

Iris's whole body stiffened, and she pushed against his chest.

Adam wanted to hold on to her long enough to say the words that crowded in his mind, but he didn't want to frighten her. So he let her go. She sprang away from him with all the force of a ricocheting bullet. In an instant she had moved to the far side of the room, strategically putting the settee between them.

"I'm not any good at this, Iris. I want you to know—"

"Please stop, Mr. Stuart."

He noticed that she had gone back to using his last name. Not a good sign. He closed his eyes, his mind going back to another beautiful woman who had broken bad news to him. Was she going to break his heart as Sylvia had done? This time he wasn't sure if he would recover.

"I blame myself for this situation. I probably led you on by allowing informality to creep into our relationship because of the hours we spent together before the trial." She stopped talking for a moment and looked toward the empty fireplace.

"You could never lead me on, Iris." He intentionally used her first name. Maybe her hesitance was an indication that she did love him. Maybe if he could prove his case to her, she would judge him worthy. "I have changed so much because of you. Look at me. I'm sober and ready to fight once again for the rights of the Cherokee to keep their lands. I have even been thinking about moving back to Washington so I can once again work with John Ross and the other Cherokee leaders to overturn the treaty signed at New Echota. My home and my whole life are clean and orderly because of your influence."

Her gaze turned back to him, and Adam could see the sadness. She opened her mouth to answer, but he knew he had lost before she uttered the first word.

"Adam. . .Mr. Stuart, while I am flattered and touched by your declaration, I cannot accept your kind offer." Her voice broke a little on the last word. She cleared her throat before continuing. "The things you mentioned are important, but I cannot link my life to a man who has not allowed God to clean him up on the inside."

Her words stung like an angry wasp. Could she not see how much he had changed? Why did she have to ask for his total commitment? God hadn't argued Mr. Spencer's case or obtained a favorable ruling. Adam had. It was the logical outcome of their hard work and intelligence, not some benevolent figure protecting the innocent.

Adam hardened his heart to keep it from breaking beyond all hope. "I am sorry you don't think me worthy. I'll take my leave now." He dropped the deed to the Spencer holdings on a convenient table. "Please see that Mr. Spencer gets that."

"Wait, Ad—"

It was the last thing he heard as he slammed the parlor door on her. Would he never learn how quickly a woman could send him from the heights of joy to the depths of despair?

Chapter 17

Iris walked into Richard Pierce's store with her head held high. She wasn't sure how Nathan would react to his uncle's loss in court. They'd all nodded to each other at church last Sunday, but the two men had disappeared soon after the services were over.

She lifted her chin as she passed through the front door. A quick glance told her Nathan was working at the counter. She wandered to the fabric section of the store, fingering several bolts as she tried to decide what would be suitable for making new dresses for the girls and herself.

"I've been saving a special bolt of material in the back, in case you came by, Miss Landon." Nathan's voice tickled her ear.

Iris jumped slightly in surprise. She turned, breathing a sigh of relief when she saw his welcoming expression. Tension she had not even realized she harbored drained away from her shoulders. "That's very sweet of you, Mr. Pierce. I would love to see it."

He smiled, showing his even, white teeth. "I'll bring it right out."

She browsed through the rest of the material as she waited for his return, wondering why Nathan did not make her heart stutter or beat faster in spite of the fact that he had startled her earlier. It wasn't fair. He was a good man. A good *Christian* man.

She'd only had to pass Adam Stuart's shuttered office to set her traitorous heart thumping. He was the opposite of all the things she held dear. She would simply have to get over her feelings for him. Why had she ignored the danger until it was too late?

She thought back to the day Nathan had come to warn her about working with Adam. A sardonic smile curled her lips. She should have listened to him and avoided putting her heart at risk.

Iris had been certain she was immune to romantic notions. No Nashville suitor had ever roused the least interest. But then, no man in Nashville had Adam's zeal for justice. No one else had invited her past his crusty exterior to see the warm, vulnerable heart underneath.

"Here it is." Nathan proudly held a bolt of lavender cotton for her inspection.

"It's perfect." Iris didn't have to feign appreciation. "How thoughtful of you

221

to realize my favorite color and hold it for me."

"I'd like to do even more for you." He glanced toward the counter and then back at her.

She looked into earnest blue eyes that had picked up some of the color of the material he held against his chest. Perhaps she could fall in love with Nathan if she tried a little harder. "I think your uncle might have something to say about that. He knows how I feel about Wayha's rights. And he is bound to be upset about the judge's verdict."

He frowned. "Uncle Richard has forgotten all about that, and I hope you will, too. Especially now that Congress has ratified the New Echota Treaty. He says it is only a matter of time until everything works out."

Iris felt her heart drop to her toes. So the treaty had been ratified. A major step toward removal, it was a blow in the fight for Indian rights. Maybe Adam knew what to do next. But that was silly. Hadn't she just been thinking about distancing herself from the dangerous Adam Stuart?

She allowed Nathan to lead her back to the counter and waited while he wrapped her material in a piece of heavy paper. His smile made Nathan look even more handsome. Maybe she did feel a flutter. A tiny one, anyway.

She was trying to decide how to answer him when the front door flew open and banged against the wall. She looked up to see the recent subject of her thoughts marching toward her, his limp more pronounced than usual. He was furious. She didn't think he'd been this angry the day he'd saved her from being trampled by the riot.

"I hope you're happy now." He slapped a newspaper on the counter in front of her.

She looked down and read the headline: TREATY RATIFIED BY SINGLE VOTE. "Nathan told me. It's a shame, but—"

"A shame? I suppose you could call it a shame." Adam's voice shook. "And the worst part of it is, I almost fell for your loving God. When the judge ruled with Mr. Spencer, I began to hope He would protect the Cherokee and stop the United States government from stealing Indian land. But I was obviously wrong. What kind of God would allow this to happen?"

A couple of ladies who'd come in to purchase sundries were staring at her and Adam. Iris wanted to sink through the floor. She could not believe Adam had chosen to air his feelings now.

Apparently Nathan agreed with her. He stepped from behind the counter and took Adam by the elbow. "This is neither the time nor the place, sir. You are disturbing my customers, and I would like for you to leave. If you must air your complaints, I will come by your office later this afternoon, and we can talk."

Adam shook off his hand. "I've had my say."

Iris watched as he stalked across the room, looking neither to the right nor the left. The door slammed behind him.

Ignoring Nathan and the other shoppers, Iris perused the article. President Jackson must know the treaty was a sham. John Ross, the elected chief of the Cherokee, had not even been present when it was signed. According to the reporter, Ross had been vocal in his condemnation of the treaty, as well as of the men who had signed the document. Yet Congress had chosen to ignore his protests. "This is so sad."

"Why do you say that?" Nathan asked. "No one forced the Cherokee to sell their land."

She folded the paper and laid it back on the counter. "The whole thing is disgraceful. Apparently, a small group of men signed the treaty without the agreement of the Indian leaders. They didn't even represent a majority of the Cherokee."

"I heard there's gold on some of that land." He shrugged and returned to the far side of the counter to pick up her bolt of material. "The Indians don't want it for themselves, but they don't want to let anyone come in and mine it. Why shouldn't they accept a fair price and move away?"

Iris stared at Nathan. She could feel her blood heating at his cavalier attitude. Had he not thought about the situation? "What if they don't want to move away? What if they love their land in the same way that Mr. Spencer does? What if they want to pass their heritage down to their children and their grandchildren?"

"I guess they can do that when they relocate." He continued tying the twine on her package as though the matter under discussion were unimportant. When he finished, he patted her hand kindly. "They'll be free to follow their own way of life without interference from white men."

Iris didn't know if he meant to sound as patronizing as he did. Perhaps he didn't realize how condescending his smile was. As though she was too simple to understand the issues involved. She wanted to ask if he agreed with his uncle's trying to take her employer's home, but she didn't have the nerve. What if Nathan confirmed her suspicions?

She suddenly felt like she had more in common with Adam than she would ever have with Nathan.

❧

The council meeting was over, and Adam was ready to go home. He wondered why he was still here in Daisy. He ought to be in Washington fighting for the Cherokee with every legal argument he could dream up. Last month's victory for Wayha Spencer had reawakened his thirst for justice.

He didn't need to worry about Sylvia Sumner, who had probably married his erstwhile partner by now. He hoped she and Jeremy were happy.

Happier than he was.

Night after night, he relived the last time he'd seen Iris. With Nathan. He supposed Nathan had overcome his reluctance to tell his uncle about his feelings for Iris. Good. Iris deserved someone nice to take care of her. Not a bitter cripple.

Pain in his hands made Adam look downward, surprised to see his fingers gripping the table so hard his knuckles had turned white. With a conscious effort, he relaxed his chest, his shoulders, his arms, and finally his fingers. Then he stood and headed toward the door, horribly aware of his unsteady gait. He passed the bar without waving good-bye. At least he didn't feel the urge to sit back down and have a drink.

Adam made his way to his office and kicked open the door with his good leg. It was dark and empty, a homecoming he should get used to. Why expect more? Wasn't life full of harsh realities and broken dreams? His life certainly was. Every time it seemed things might be turning around, something happened. Like the ratification of the New Echota Treaty. . .

And having to watch the courtship of Nathan Pierce and Iris Landon.

Chapter 18

The delicious aromas of roast pork and gravy rose from the table as Anna's childish voice blessed their luncheon.

After Iris had filled each girl's plate with food, she concentrated on her own meal. A few small bites and she dropped her fork. It was odd that she had so little appetite these days. She wasn't sleeping very well either. Ever since the day Adam had confronted her about the treaty ratification. As if it were her fault his world had crashed once again. She knew she wasn't responsible, so why did she feel guilty? Or was it something else she felt? Something like heartbreak?

"Can we go outside this afternoon?" June asked around a bite of meat.

Iris's concentration returned to the girls. She owed them her full attention, so she shook her head and dabbed at her lips with a snowy white cloth napkin before speaking. "A lady should not talk with her mouth full."

June made a show of swallowing her food. "I'm sorry, Miss Iris. May we go outside this afternoon? The sun is shining, and Josephine said there is a nice breeze."

Iris glanced at one of the windows. "Perhaps we could take a stroll after our meal. I would like to pay a visit to Camie since her parents are staying with them this week, and I know how much you two enjoy playing with her twins."

Anna whooped her delight but subsided when Iris frowned at her. "As much as we would all enjoy an outing, perhaps we should stay here and practice our deportment instead."

The two girls concentrated on minding their manners for the rest of the meal, quietly finishing their food.

Iris hid a smile. Her charges could be a handful, but they were fully capable of ladylike behavior for the right incentive, much like she and her siblings had been.

When they had completed their meal, Iris told Josephine their plans and helped the girls with their bonnets. They skipped through the door and onto the porch while Iris followed more sedately. The three of them walked briskly down the lane and reached the main road that led to town, admiring the bright colors of wildflowers dotting the landscape.

"May we pick some flowers?" asked June. "We could take a bouquet to Mrs. Sherer."

Iris nodded. "I think that's a wonderful idea."

June and Anna ran ahead of her and began gathering blossoms. Iris strolled along more circumspectly, enjoying the bright sunshine and the laughter of the girls. She soon had an armful of blossoms. "That's probably enough for today."

"Look, I found an iris!" Anna ran up with a purple flower in her hand.

"It's not an iris." June's voice was strident. "Tell her, Miss Iris. Anna thinks she knows everything."

"I don't, either."

June stuck out her tongue at her younger sister.

Iris was about to admonish the pair when she heard a wagon coming down the lane toward them.

Anna held a hand over her eyes. "Who is that?"

"I don't know." Iris wasn't concerned. They weren't far from the Sherers' farm. It was probably Lance or Camie. She watched as the wagon trundled around a curve, preceded by a man on horseback. Her heart thumped when she realized they had pulled lengths of cloth over their mouths and noses. They couldn't be worried about chapped faces at this time of the year.

"Come here, girls." The flowers were forgotten as she pulled June and Anna onto the side of the road, her arms gathering them close. She began to pray for protection. There was no way to outrun the men, even though every part of her screamed that they should try to reach the distant woods.

The horseman rushed past them on the road, but when Iris began to hope that the men had some distant goal, he pulled up and brought his mount dancing back toward the three of them. The wagon came to a stop directly in front of them.

They were effectively blocked from fleeing. Iris took a step back, drawing the girls with her. Her eyes widened when the driver of the wagon pulled a rifle from under his seat and leveled it at her heart.

☙

Adam encouraged his horse to a canter as he turned down the road toward the Spencer estate. John Ross had sent him a petition and asked him to gather signatures from Cherokee who opposed the New Echota Treaty. Wayha Spencer was a good place to start.

Adam promised himself that he would maintain his distance if he saw a certain curly-haired charmer. Iris might stir him in ways no other woman had, but she had made her feelings clear. She was too good for the likes of him.

His thoughts were interrupted by the sound of a galloping horse in the lane behind him. Adam twisted in his saddle, a groan escaping him as he recognized the wide shoulders of Nathan Pierce. From the looks of the fine suit he wore, the man was coming to see Iris. A sardonic smile twisted Adam's mouth. Iris's God must be intent on torturing him. He nodded to the man.

Nathan pulled up his horse as he reached Adam. "Where are you headed?"

"Same as you, I imagine."

The other man's cheeks flushed. "I. . .thought maybe. . .I wanted. . ."

Adam clucked his tongue to get his horse moving again. "You don't have to tell me what you plan. I can guess your intent."

Whatever the man would have answered was lost as Wayha Spencer's carriage rushed around the curve in the lane behind them. At first Adam thought the horses were out of control, but then he realized the driver was whipping the team to increase their speed. Wayha himself was driving them. He rushed past them without a pause, heading for the house at breakneck speed. Some calamity must have occurred.

"Come on!" Adam slapped his horse's reins and leaned forward, intent on finding out what had happened. His heart was in his throat.

Please let Iris be all right. The words formed in his mind and became a chant as he rushed to the house.

He swung down from the saddle and waited impatiently for Nathan to dismount. Together they hurried into the house through the front door, which stood open.

Wayha, his clothing liberally spattered with mud, was shouting at his slaves and servants. "Where are they? Have you looked everywhere?"

Josephine stood in one corner of the hall, among a group of hand-wringing women. The three manservants were shaking their heads, their faces showing varying degrees of dismay or concern.

"We must find them right away!" Wayha's voice was strident. He turned to Adam and Nathan. "Do you have news of my granddaughters?"

Adam shook his head. "No. What's happened?"

"They've disappeared."

Nathan stepped in front of Adam. "Where is Miss Landon?"

Wayha frowned. His normally placid face showed deep lines of concern. "With them, I hope. They should have been back an hour ago. They didn't show up for dinner. Miss Landon told Josephine they would be back."

"Where did they go?" Adam could feel dread tightening his chest.

"To the Sherers' home. Her father and mother have come from Brainerd Mission to visit."

"Have you gone to look for them there?" Adam asked the obvious question.

"Yes. They never arrived."

Nathan frowned. "How long have they been gone?"

Wayha looked different—old and scared. In all the time Adam had known him, he'd never seen the man show fear, not even when it looked like he might lose his home. But then, his grandchildren had never been in physical danger before.

Adam led the man to a chair and helped him sit down. "It's going to be okay, Wayha. We'll find them."

It took several minutes, but he and Nathan rounded up Wayha's manservants and slaves and sent them in different directions to scour the countryside. They were to knock at all doors and ask after the missing girls and their nanny then meet back at Wayha's home later in the day.

Adam went toward town, beating the bushes and checking every grove of trees. He couldn't find any evidence of Iris or the children. As the sun dropped lower in the sky, he headed back to the Spencer home, hoping one of the other men had been more fortunate.

His hopes were dashed as he was met by Wayha before he could even dismount.

"Have you found them?"

Adam shook his head, his heart heavy in his chest. "There's no sign of them anywhere."

Nathan was only a few steps behind Wayha. "Where can they be?"

Adam accepted a cup of water from Josephine but refused to give up. He was determined to keep looking. There had to be somewhere else for him to search. He had a feeling he was overlooking something.

Hooves sounded behind him, and Adam turned to see who was coming. It was a lone horseman. Lance Sherer, unless he missed his guess. Maybe the man had good news.

One glance at his grim face destroyed that notion.

Lance drew his horse up next to Adam's and dismounted. "I have nothing to report."

"I've been thinking." Nathan's hesitant voice seemed to come to Adam from a distance, nearly drowned out by a ringing noise in his head. "I may have an idea about what's happened."

Adam tried to lock out the emotions roiling in his chest. He didn't have the luxury of yielding to despair. "What do you mean?"

Nathan's gaze focused downward. "Earlier this morning, my uncle fixed up a big order for a couple of drifters who came into town last week. I never saw them pay anything for all the food and staples, which is odd enough. Uncle Richard has never been the type to encourage charity. And he told them to disappear for a few days."

Lance's voice was dismissive. "So your uncle gave away some food. Maybe he needed some work done on your house or the store and paid the men in supplies."

Nathan looked up. His eyes narrowed as he seemed to consider the suggestion. Then he shook his head. "No. The man said something about a concealed valley—"

"I found something." The last of Spencer's slaves ran toward them carrying a wilted bunch of wildflowers that he handed to Wayha.

Adam could hear Jospehine's moan of despair, but he ignored it as he turned to Nathan. "You think your uncle took those children?"

Nathan's cheeks reddened, but he nodded. "It makes sense. Uncle Richard was so angry about losing to Mr. Spencer in court. But then his ire just went away. I thought it was because of the treaty, but what if he was planning something more immediate?" He glanced toward Spencer. "He may demand a ransom."

Spencer shook his head. "Whatever he wants, I will give if he will release my granddaughters. But where could he have taken them?"

"Have we tried all the empty houses?" Adam searched each of their faces. "Maybe Nathan's wrong. Maybe they were scared by someone and sought sanctuary in one of the abandoned cabins hereabouts."

"But where?" Nathan asked the question, but Adam saw it reflected on all the other men's faces.

That was the real question. There were dozens of places where they could be hidden. Since the massacre at the Alamo, several homesteads had been left vacant as outraged men headed south to fight the Mexicans. Places like the cabin where he'd recovered after the attack last winter. . .

The idea burst on him like a lightning bolt. The cabin was situated deep down in a ravine, a concealed valley. It was far enough away from town to avoid detection but close enough to contact allies if needed. "I think I know where they might be."

The other men swung to look at him. "Nathan, you and Lance go get the sheriff. I'll take Wayha and find the girls, but we may need help to get them out safely."

"Let Wayha and Lance get the law. I'm going with you. If my uncle is involved in this, you'll need me to talk some sense into him."

Adam considered his words for a moment before nodding. He turned to Wayha. "I'll need some paper and a pen to draw a map."

They followed the Cherokee inside.

When Wayha produced the requested items, Adam drew a rough map for them to give to the sheriff. He hoped it was clear enough for them to find his destination. "Bring the men as quickly as you can."

The sun was setting as he and Nathan remounted their horses and took off toward the cabin. Every mile seemed to take a century as Adam's imagination kept supplying pictures of Iris cringing in fear from her captors.

He found himself praying, turning to the God Iris worshipped. The God he had once worshipped. Was He really there? Did He care about the tribulations of those who cried out to Him? Would He listen to someone who'd turned away from Him?

The questions twisted round and round in his mind, while the steady hoofbeats echoed in his head in time with his desperate pleas. *Keep her safe, Lord. Please keep her safe.*

Chapter 19

Mayor Pierce lit a candle and set it carefully on the small table in the center of the cabin. For a minute Iris thought they'd been rescued, but then she saw him handing money to one of the men who had abducted them and realized he had paid for the kidnapping to be done. He gestured to the other man, and both of the mercenaries headed outside, for guard duty she guessed.

The light flickered wildly, showing Iris the frightened faces of the Spencer children, who had been bound to chairs on their arrival several hours earlier. She tried to communicate reassurance and hope with her glance, but she doubted she was overly successful as she was also securely tied to a chair.

Iris tried to loosen the ropes around her hands as she watched the pompous man pace the floor of the small cabin. At least the children had a chance to get away from this unharmed. She knew Wayha would turn over the deed—or do anything else for that matter—to secure their safety.

Whether or not she would escape was something else entirely. Pierce seemed to blame her for the situation, and he had to know she would testify against him if she got the chance. No, there was no way he was going to let her go. A tremor shook her shoulders.

Pierce must have seen the movement. "I'm sorry for your discomfort, but it's necessary. Spencer will be ready to see reason when he finds that I hold something he values even more than his land."

Anna and June. A wave of revulsion swept through her. What kind of man threatened children? Her gag prevented Iris from expressing her disdain. She glared at the mayor.

"Wayha never should have had that land anyway. No Cherokee should be given a legal deed. Trying to act like white men." He pointed a finger at her. "I thought I took care of that when I took the original deed from your friend's house."

Her shock must have shown on her face because he chuckled.

"Yes. I knew it had to be there. I know how to read people. I saw the look that passed between Sherer and his wife the night we all had dinner with them. I burned the deed and waited for my chance to take over that pretender's claim. But then you had to stick your nose in the business."

The mayor's expression sent a cold shiver down her back. He would never release her alive. It was obvious from the way he glared at her.

She closed her eyes to pray for the girls' safety and the strength to face whatever was coming.

❧

It took longer than Adam had hoped for them to reach the valley and plan the rescue. But at least it looked like they had found the right location.

What little was left of the sun's rays could not find its way into the ravine. As Adam crouched in the shadows, a part of his mind pleaded with God to keep Iris and the Spencer girls safe. All his doubts and questions were swept away in a tide of desperation. What if they had already been hurt. . .or killed? He pushed the thought to the back of his mind. He had to believe God led him to this place so he could save Iris.

Twigs popped and branches rustled as the man guarding the west side of the cabin approached Adam. Another guard was patrolling the east side, but Nathan would take care of him.

Closer and closer the man came, until it was finally time to act. In one swift movement Adam pounced, overpowering the stranger with ease. Adam used a length of rope he'd brought to tie the man's hands and feet. As soon as he was certain the guard was secure, Adam crept forward as quietly as he could, listening for Nathan's signal.

The hoot of an owl alerted him.

He cupped his mouth and returned the signal. Then he took a deep breath and rushed the front door, shoving it open with enough force that it bounced against the wall and swung back toward him. He dropped to one knee. His gaze swept the room.

❧

Iris fought against her restraints at this new threat. Then the flickering light shone on the man's face, and hope sprang anew in her chest. Her prayers had surely been answered. "Thank You, Lord." She mumbled the words into her gag as she recognized the man who'd come for them. It was Adam!

Gone was the cynical, rumpled attorney. In his place was a crusading warrior. He surged forward and slammed into Mayor Pierce. Down they went, turning over and over as each man sought to gain control of the other. They exchanged punches, but it was clear Adam was much stronger.

"Stand down."

Iris had been so engrossed in the battle she failed to realize another man had come inside. Nathan. But was he here to rescue them or to help his uncle?

Her eyes widened as he drew his gun, and she tried to break free of her bonds once more. A moan of pain rose up as the harsh rope abraded her wrists.

"It's over, Uncle Richard."

It took a moment for his words to penetrate, but then Nathan's uncle stopped fighting. He glared at his nephew as Adam tied his hands together.

Nathan came to her. "Are you all right?"

Iris nodded. She could feel his knife sawing through the ropes that held her hands together behind the chair in which she sat. Ignoring the pain as blood rushed back into her hands, she pulled off the dirty cloth that had gagged her for the past hours. She rushed to the girls and gently removed their gags while Nathan freed them from their bindings.

Horses snorted outside, and then the little cabin was filled with people. The sheriff took control of Mayor Pierce and the drifters who had brought them to the cabin earlier. Wayha entered the cabin in a rush and hugged his grand-daughters close, joy apparent on his face.

"I'm so sorry, Iris." Nathan's face was drawn into a deep frown. "I had no idea."

She patted his hand. "How did you find us?"

"It was Adam. He realized that you might be here."

"Thank God." Iris looked toward Adam, but he would not meet her gaze. She wanted to go to him, but if she did, would she be giving him false hope? The attraction was strong in spite of the insurmountable obstacles between them. Perhaps she should concentrate on comforting Nathan, who was feeling the weight of his uncle's guilt.

❧

Adam could feel her gaze on him, but he kept his attention on Wayha and his grandchildren. If he looked at Iris, he was sure he would be unable to resist taking her in his arms and declaring his love for her once more. He could not bear the thought of embarrassing either of them again. Nathan was eminently capable of comforting her. Adam slipped outside to make sure the sheriff didn't need any help.

A little while later, Nathan brought Iris out of the cabin. She seemed un-harmed but subdued as Nathan led her to his horse and helped her into the saddle.

As though from a distance, Adam watched Nathan mount up behind her and wrap a protective arm around her waist. She never looked toward him. And why should she? She had Nathan taking care of her. Adam watched as they rode out of the valley together, taking a piece of his heart with them.

Wayha Spencer was the next to come out of the cabin. He had an arm around each of his grandchildren. Tears filled his eyes as he made his way to Adam and thanked him for reuniting them once more. The joy on the older man's face eased Adam's pain and brought a smile to his lips. Was this the same joy that Christ had described on finding the lost sheep? Was this how God felt when one of His children was returned to Him?

The thought nearly brought him to his knees. Adam pushed back the emotion in his throat. He nodded to the Spencer family and limped to his horse. An overwhelming desire to talk to someone about his revelations had him mounting up and heading to the Sherer household, the image of Reverend Miller's welcoming smile vivid in his memory.

❧

Adam slid from the saddle and tethered his horse, relieved to see light in several of the home's windows. He was glad they were not abed. He would have hated to awaken them to talk to Reverend Miller, but the fire in his soul would not allow him to wait until morning. He rapped on the front door and tapped his foot as he waited for someone to answer.

Camie Sherer opened the door. "What is the news? Are Iris and the children safe?"

Adam reassured her and her parents, explaining that Lance had accompanied the sheriff to town and would be arriving shortly.

By the time the explanations were done, Lance had arrived, his face quizzical. "Is there something else wrong, Adam?"

"No. . .not exactly. I. . .I have something to talk to Reverend Miller about. Something that can't wait."

Lance nodded and drew his wife and mother-in-law out of the room. "We'll be praying for you."

Silence permeated the room. Adam wondered where to start. "I've done so many terrible things."

Reverend Miller regarded him somberly and nodded. "So have we all."

"I. . .I thought God was against me. I blamed Him for my troubles."

"Son, God loves you more than you can imagine. He made you. He knows you, and He's anxious for you to turn your life over to Him."

Adam felt a huge pressure in his chest as his emotions threatened to overcome him. He didn't deserve such love or forgiveness. "I want that forgiveness and love more than anything, Reverend."

Reverend Miller put a hand on his shoulder. "And God wants to forgive you. All you have to do is ask."

"But how can I? I've always blamed Him for my problems."

"There's always a temptation to blame the Creator when things go wrong. Are you familiar with the book of Job?"

Adam considered. The glimmer of hope that had appeared back at the cabin became a beacon, a warm, guiding light that was leading him home. "I think I understand. Job clung to God even though he lost everything."

"Exactly." The older man smiled at him. "We have much to learn from Job's reaction when God answered his complaints." He opened his well-worn Bible and turned to the final chapter of Job. " 'I have heard of thee by the hearing of the ear: but now mine eye seeth thee. Wherefore I abhor myself, and repent in dust and ashes.'"

"Yes, that's exactly the way I feel." Adam was relieved to know Reverend Miller understood what he'd been trying to explain. He felt like a curtain had been drawn back, revealing the true nature of everything. He'd been so foolish, so blind, so arrogant.

"Would you like to pray with me?" Reverend Miller got down on his knees and folded his hands in front of him.

Feeling a bit self-conscious, Adam followed his example. He closed his eyes and listened as the preacher began speaking to God as though He was a personal friend. He thanked God for bringing Adam back into the fold, for loving them all, and for sending His Son to make salvation possible.

Lord, please forgive me for blaming You and for my many sins. Thank You. I know I don't deserve Your love, but thank You. And. . .thank You for not giving up on this lost sheep. The words signified the beginning of a new relationship, one that Adam knew would make his life worth living.

Chapter 20

Iris entered the parlor and smiled at her visitor. Nathan was such a nice man. He had been stoic in the face of his uncle's trial and conviction for kidnapping. Not that anyone blamed him. Camie had told Iris that Nathan was being considered to take his uncle's place on the town council. The community of Daisy would benefit from having such an honest, upright man serving it.

Nathan swept her a bow. "It's a pleasure to see you, Miss Landon."

"Likewise. I trust you are well." She sat down on the sofa. "How are things at the store?"

Instead of sitting down, Nathan paced the floor. He walked to the window, looked outside, then turned and came back to where she sat. He rubbed a hand against one leg of his trousers and swallowed hard. Then he knelt in front of her. "I don't want to talk about the store, Miss Landon. . . Iris. I have a more pressing matter to broach." He took her left hand in his.

Iris's heart seemed to stutter for a second before resuming its steady pace. This was her second proposal of marriage. Where was the breathlessness she'd experienced when Adam proposed? She looked into Nathan's hopeful eyes and was overcome by a feeling of sadness. She knew how she had to answer this kind man. She was flattered by his attention, but she did not love him.

"You are a beautiful and intelligent woman, and I hope you will agree to become my wife. I know you must have seen how much I care for you. I will provide you with all the luxuries I can afford."

Iris tugged her hand free. "Please stop, Nathan."

His blue gaze searched her face. "Is it because of my uncle?"

"Of course not." She took a deep breath. "You're a wonderful man, Nathan, and you're going to make some lucky lady very happy one day—" She stopped. "Please get up, Nathan. I can't talk to you like this."

He rose and settled on the straight-backed chair next to the sofa. "I don't understand. I have the store, you know. I can afford to take care of you."

"That's not it, Nathan. One of these days, you're going to meet someone special. Someone who fires your imagination and makes your heart beat faster just because she's in the same room with you, breathing the same air."

He nodded slowly. "Is that how Adam makes you feel?"

Iris could feel the blush filling her cheeks. Was she that transparent? She'd seen Adam several times in town, but he'd never looked in her direction. This, however, was not the time to be thinking about Adam. She concentrated on the man sitting next to her. "Nathan, you're a wonderful man, and you deserve a wonderful wife. Someone who loves you. While I esteem you and appreciate all your many kindnesses, I don't love you in that way."

He glanced at her, the hope in his gaze slowly giving way to acceptance.

"But I hope we can still be friends." She gave his hand a friendly pat.

Nathan sighed. "Of course we will continue to be friends. You're a warm-hearted woman. Perhaps I can eventually change your mind about us."

He was such a nice man. But what she'd told him was true. He deserved someone else, someone who would cherish each day with him, fall asleep with his name on her lips, and wake up thinking of him. Not someone who couldn't get another man's face out of her head.

❧

Adam opened his Bible and read once more about Paul's experience on the road to Damascus when he was still Saul. Like Paul, he'd been certain he knew all the answers—he'd been full of self-righteousness. But that changed the afternoon Iris was taken. He was forced to face the truth. His fear had blinded him, but when the scales fell away, he saw the truth. God was the one in control. And no matter whether Adam understood why things happened the way they did, he now believed that God would work it all out in the best way possible.

He placed the Bible on his desk and glanced at the petition lying next to it. There had been a steady stream of men coming from Ross's Landing and beyond, as word spread about the effort to stop the government from executing the New Echota Treaty. He already had more than five hundred signatures.

He looked up as the door opened. His practiced smile slipped. "Iris, what are you doing here?" He put a hand to his forehead. Where had that come from?

She drew herself up straight. "I'm sorry for disturbing you." She stepped back and started to leave.

He got up to halt her retreat. "No, Ir. . .Miss Landon, please don't go. I didn't mean to be so rude." It didn't matter why she'd come, only that she was near.

She turned back toward him, bringing a breath of freshness with her.

He caught a whiff of perfume that made him think of blooming flowers in the meadow back home. Why did she have to be so beautiful? He ached to pull her into his arms. But she belonged to a better man than he would ever be.

She wandered past him to the desk where they'd spent so much time poring over dusty law books together and ran a finger over its surface. "I. . .we. . .the girls and I. . .have missed you. Have you. . . How have you been doing?"

Was Iris nervous? The thought made him want to comfort her. But that was Nathan's job not his. "I've rediscovered a thirst for justice. Once God got His message through my thick skull, I realized how wrong I was. How could I give up when He didn't give up on me? So I've been using my legal expertise to help other Indians like you and I helped Wayha."

"Adam, that's wonderful!" Her voice lost its hesitancy. Her eyes were wide and shiny with unshed tears.

Emotion clogged his throat. He'd better change the subject before he broke down in front of her. "I've been meaning to call on you to check on Wayha and the girls. But it's been so busy. I have to save as many as I can before the removal is enforced. And then there are all the settlers moving here to explore for gold. . . ."

What was he saying? She already knew about all that. "I'm sure Nathan—" He stopped on the word. This was harder than he'd imagined it would be. He took a deep breath and asked God for strength. "I'm sure your fiancé has been keeping you informed about everything."

Her eyes opened wide. "What did you say?"

"I—" His throat seemed terribly dry. He swallowed hard and opened his mouth once again. "I haven't seen you since your engagement."

"I beg your pardon?"

Why was she looking at him like that? Like he was not making sense. "You and Nathan will make a wonderful couple." He forced the words out. It wasn't like he hadn't practiced them. Every day for the past few weeks, as a matter of fact. "I. . .best wishes on your upcoming marriage."

Her hat slipped to one side.

Adam's fingers ached to straighten it.

"I'm afraid you are mistaken, Mr. Stuart. I am not contemplating marriage with Mr. Pierce. He's not the man I'm in love with."

It was Adam's turn to stare. Hope bloomed in his chest like flowers in springtime. He pulled out a chair for her. Her perfume wafted past him once again as she sat down in the chair—the chair she had used while they worked together to protect her employer's rights. She leaned back and looked up at him. The tears in her large brown eyes had been replaced by a sparkle.

Adam pulled a chair into alignment with the one she occupied and sat down near enough that their knees almost touched. She did not demur or back away, which kicked up his heartbeat another notch. "I asked you a question a few months back."

"Yes?"

He cleared his throat. Pressed his knee up to hers. "But now the question is a little different due to the wonderful change in my life. Would you consider marrying a Christian attorney?"

"Oh Adam. . ."

Her voice was so low that Adam feared the worst. She was going to break his heart again. He stood up and turned his back on her, concentrating on his breathing. He was going to survive this. God was with him.

And then he felt her touch on his shoulder. He turned.

"Adam, I would like nothing better than working with a certain Christian attorney in his mission to save the Indians from injustice."

He drew a deep breath. "You mean. . . ?"

She smiled at him. "Yes, Adam. I'll marry you."

His breath left him in a rush. He reached up and pushed her hat back from her head. Her unruly curls fell free, cascading around her shoulders and making her look as beautiful as he'd always imagined she would. Her hands curled around his neck, and she stared at him with those beautiful eyes. When their lips met, it was like a breath from paradise. She was the most precious gift he'd ever received, and he thanked God for allowing them to be together. "I love you, Iris."

A single tear spilled over and traced the length of her cheek. "I love you, too, Adam."

THE
MOCKINGBIRD'S
CALL

Dedication

From Aaron:
To my great-niece, Hailey Brewer. Your precious life is just beginning. May you come to share that wonderful relationship with your heavenly Father and follow His call in all you do. Always know I love you dearly.

From Diane:
To the employees of the Mississippi House of Representatives, my second family. Thanks for reading my stories and for encouraging me all these years. It's an honor to work with all of you.

Chapter 1

B ut I don't want to go to Virginia." Jared Stuart's jaw clenched, and he looked at his dinner plate, ignoring the creep of his spectacles down the bridge of his nose. His stomach churned, but not because of the food in front of his blurred gaze. It was his rebellious words that made him ill. He knew his parents planned for him to attend William and Mary, the school where Pa had studied law thirty years ago.

Jared's words seemed to echo from wall to wall of the well-appointed dining room. He felt a cold hand steal into his own beneath the cover of Great-Aunt Dolly's imported tablecloth. Victoria, the sister who was only a year his senior, knew of his wish to attend East Tennessee University in Knoxville. She had been his sympathetic confidante, her tender heart torn between supporting his desire to attend a small school and their parents' stated plan to send him to William and Mary.

"I don't understand why you don't want to go there." Adam Stuart's voice was not loud, but Jared could feel the frustration behind each word. "You know it's the alma mater of many of our country's founding fathers. Your own family has a history there. Your mother and I have all the connections it would take to ensure your success—"

"That's just it, Pa." Jared looked up from his plate. He could see the flecks of green in his father's brown eyes, a sign of banked anger. Resentment rose up and pressed against his throat. "I want to succeed on my own merits, not because I'm your son or Grandpa Landon's grandson."

"Going to William and Mary won't prohibit that."

"Adam." Iris Stuart's voice was barely a whisper. She shook her head slightly at her husband, and a curl sprang from her coiffure. She brushed it back with one finger. "Not now. We can talk about this later."

Great-Aunt Dolly, imperious in her black bombazine dress and her position at the head of the table, cleared her throat. "Well, I don't see what all of the rumpus is about." She lifted a wrinkled hand to her mouth and coughed for a moment before continuing. "Young people will always insist on their own ways in things." She pointed an arthritic finger at his ma. "Why I remember when the boy's grandma and I went all the way to New Orleans in the middle of a war just so she could see your pa. Didn't take Rebekah long to convince her parents to let her have her way."

"That's a different matter," Adam Stuart protested.

Great-Aunt Dolly shrugged a shoulder and looked at Jared. "You're a grown man now, and you have a good head on your shoulders. Doesn't matter to me if you want to go to school in Williamsburg, Knoxville, or even Schenectady. All you have to do is say so. I'll make sure you have the money."

"That's very generous of you, Aunt Dolly." Ma folded her napkin and laid it on the table next to her dinner plate. "But I'm sure Adam and I can afford to send our only son to college."

Jared pushed his spectacles up on his nose, bringing Pa's glare into focus. He refused to drop his gaze this time. He noticed the gray sideburns that framed his father's face and wondered how Pa always managed to look so distinguished. His clothes were always neatly pressed, his necktie folded into crisp lines, and his shoes brightly polished. No matter the situation, the great Adam Stuart was always in control. He might have been about to make a speech at the capitol instead of sitting at the dinner table with his family.

A part of Jared wanted to acquiesce to Pa's wish, but he could not compromise on this. He had prayed about his decision before sending an application to East Tennessee University last month, prayed for a sign like Gideon's fleece, something so clear he couldn't mistake it. And last week he'd gotten his answer in a letter of enthusiastic acceptance sent by the college in Knoxville. Now all he had to do was convince his parents.

What would he do if he couldn't convince them? Take Great-Aunt Dolly's money? He hoped it wouldn't come to that. He turned his attention to the diminutive little lady. "Thank you for your offer, but I have a little money saved. It's enough to pay for a term."

Pa tossed his napkin on the table and shoved his chair back. "We'll talk about this later." He helped Great-Aunt Dolly roll her wheelchair back and out of the dining room.

Victoria, her wide brown eyes shiny with unshed tears, squeezed Jared's hand and leaned toward him. "I'm very proud of you for telling them the truth."

"I'm glad someone is." Jared felt the tension seeping from his chest, leaving a regretful heart in its wake. He pulled his hand from his sister's and stood up.

How he wished he could walk out the door, get on a horse, and be transported to the campus in Knoxville. Instead, he helped his mother rise from her seat. Her eyes, an older version of Victoria's, searched his face. Light from the candelabra caught a few strands of gray that were beginning to appear in the ringlets around her temples. He and Ma were nearly the same height, and he had been told that they favored each other strongly, even though his coloring—light brown hair and hazel eyes—came from his pa. "I'm sorry."

She patted his cheek before smoothing one of the loose curls, so like her own, that sprang from his head. "You're a good son, Jared. Your pa and I know that." She sighed. "And I am not unhappy to think of you in Knoxville instead of Williamsburg. There is so much unrest these days."

"Pa should be glad you don't want to join the militia," Victoria chimed in. She was such a sweet, unpretentious young woman. He often forgot he was her junior.

Jared offered both elbows to escort the ladies of his family to the parlor for coffee and dessert. "I'm not going to change my mind, Ma."

"I know that, son." She smiled at him. "You are too much like your father in that respect. Once he's plotted his course, few people can convince him to reconsider."

"You can." Jared straightened his shoulders, wishing they were as wide as his father's. It seemed he'd spent his whole life measuring himself against Adam Stuart. And he'd always come up lacking.

The list of his father's successes was as long as the Cumberland River. After marrying Jared's ma, Adam Stuart had spent more than two decades in the southeastern corner of Tennessee, fighting for Indians' rights in the courtroom, and he won more often than he lost. Then he and Ma decided to take their fight to the halls of state government. They'd moved in with Great-Aunt Dolly and Great-Uncle Mac several years ago, expecting to stay for a few weeks while the legislature was in session. But those weeks grew into months. Ma started teaching at the Indian school on the west side of town, even though few Cherokee lived in Nashville since President Jackson had ordered their removal decades earlier. Jared's older sister, Agnes, fell in love and married a man from Nashville. Then Great-Uncle Mac died and Great-Aunt Dolly's health began to fail. So his parents made the decision to stay in Nashville to care for her.

They'd been in Nashville now for more than four years. Agnes had become one of the leading matrons of the city, and Pa's law practice was thriving as he became the voice for his clients, bringing their issues to the notice of the Tennessee legislature. Even Victoria had gotten past her slight gawkiness and tendency toward diffidence. There always seemed to be a suitor or two lounging in the parlor, hoping to take her on a picnic or carriage ride. Jared had no doubt she would soon accept an offer of marriage from one of them and join her older sister in Nashville's highest social circles. Everyone seemed to be succeeding. . .everyone but him.

Jared missed the quiet days of life back home in Chattanooga. He missed

the tree-strewn mountains and wide plateaus. He didn't like the hustle and bustle that seemed to surround his family here. Nor did he want to follow in his
father's footsteps. The idea of testifying to a bunch of hot-tempered politicians
made him physically ill. All he wanted was to go to college, maybe find a friend
or two, and study.

Was that too much to ask?

❧

Jared caressed the paisley cover of the slender book of poetry he held. How
would it feel to see his own name printed there? Excitement raced through
him. His finger traced the name—Henry Wadsworth Longfellow—while he
imagined sending his own work to a publisher and having it accepted. Would it
be as soul stirring as this volume entitled *Poems on Slavery* or as heartbreaking
as Harriet Beecher Stowe's novel? Could he write anything as effective as either
publication in describing the horror and tragedy of slavery? Or would he find
some other school of thought to explore in the manner of Socrates or Plato?

"Jared, where are you?" His sister's voice broke through Jared's reverie.

He glanced at the ornate longcase clock standing in a corner of the library.
It wasn't time for dinner yet. What could Victoria want? Why couldn't his family allow him a little time of quiet to read? He heaved a sigh and arose from the
deep leather chair that had once belonged to Great-Uncle Mac. He reached the
door just as his sister pulled it open.

She clucked her tongue. "I should have known you'd be here. Don't you ever
get tired of reading?"

"How can I?" He swept an arm back to indicate the room behind him. "There's
so much in Great-Aunt Dolly's library I haven't read. So much to learn."

"Of course there is."

Her sigh indicated a lack of understanding. But then, most of his family
did not share his addiction to the written word. They'd rather attend a play than
spend time reading. He was the bookish one. Maybe it was because of his spectacles. Maybe it was because he understood better than they the importance of
books, poems, and biographies. "Were you looking for me?"

"Oh, yes." Her cheeks reddened slightly. "Pa has someone he wants you to
meet. They're in the drawing room." She turned and led the way down the hall.

Jared wanted to groan. Probably another politician, someone to remind him
how popular and important his father was. Well, he would give the man five
polite minutes and then slip away to the library once more. He knew from experience he would not be missed.

His father pushed away from the mantel as Jared entered the room. "I have
brought someone home who is eager to meet you, son." He nodded to the man
seated next to his mother. "William, this is my son, Jared."

Jared noticed the stranger's conservative suit, blond hair, and deep-set green eyes that seemed to be lit from within. A wide, attractive smile graced the man's face as he stood and held out his right hand. "I have heard much about you from your father, young man."

"Pleased to meet you, sir," Jared mumbled, uncomfortable as always when he found himself the center of attention.

"Your father tells me you are interested in attending my college this fall."

What new stratagem had his father concocted in his efforts to force Jared to attend William and Mary? He tossed a long-suffering glance toward his sister.

She shook her head slightly in response. Was she trying to warn him now when it was too late? Why couldn't she have said something before? Her betrayal was like a slap.

He returned his attention to the man standing before him. "I'm afraid you are mistaken, sir—"

His mother started coughing so loudly that Jared stopped in midsentence.

He glanced at her, and her eyes were full of meaning, but he had no idea what message she was trying to convey.

A look of confusion entered the shorter man's expression. "You no longer want to attend East Tennessee University?"

"East Tennessee?" He looked at his father, who was smiling broadly and nodding. He turned back to the visitor. "No, sir. . .I mean, yes, sir. . .I mean. . ." His words faltered to a halt. How could he express all the thoughts running through his mind at this moment?

"You'll have to forgive my son's confusion." Adam chuckled. "We have been having a long-running discussion on the subject, and I have always encouraged him to attend my alma mater." He turned to Jared. "I met Reverend Carnes at the capitol today. He has come down from Knoxville to talk to the legislature about increased funding while they are in special session."

Reverend Carnes? Reverend William Carnes, the president of East Tennessee University? Excitement bubbled up in Jared's chest. His father had brought the president of East Tennessee University home with him! This must mean Pa had given up his desire to make Jared attend William and Mary. He was acceding to Jared's wishes. Now his mother's silent message became clear. She and his sister had been trying to keep him from making a fool of himself.

Reverend Carnes's wide smile caused a dimple to appear in his right cheek. "Your father was kind enough to share his insights on which of our elected officials might be receptive to my appeal. After the hearing, he introduced me to several of the senators and representatives. Because of his expertise, I have high hopes that East Tennessee University will benefit from my trip to Nashville."

Their explanations had given Jared the respite he needed to collect his thoughts. "I'm glad to hear that. No one in the state is more knowledgeable than my pa when it comes to the inner workings of the Tennessee legislature."

Reverend Carnes reclaimed his seat and accepted a cup of tea from Jared's mother. "I have to agree."

Jared sat down as well; all thoughts of slipping away were forgotten. Over the next hour, he grilled the university president on all the particulars of the campus. He was pleased to have his parents made aware of the outstanding moral and educational goals of the school. From the compulsory attendance at chapel twice daily to the challenging curriculum of the faculty, it was obvious that East Tennessee demanded the best from its students. And then there were the literary societies and even a literary magazine. It was the perfect place for an aspiring writer.

By the time Reverend Carnes took his leave, Jared was practically floating in the clouds. As soon as the college president left, he approached his father and thrust out his right hand. "Thank you, Pa."

His father grasped his hand and pulled Jared into an embrace. "I love you, son. Don't ever doubt that your ma and I have your best interests at heart. We believe in you."

He felt somewhat awkward, as he and his father had not embraced since Jared had left his childhood behind. But this was a special day—one that Jared knew he would always remember. Emotion tried to overwhelm him, but he choked it back. "I won't let you down."

Chapter 2

Montgomery Plantation, outside Nashville

Amelia Montgomery's skirt threatened to halt her progress as she followed her mother through the slave cabin's tiny doorway. She reached down with impatient hands and compressed the voluminous material so she could successfully negotiate the narrow entrance. While hoops allowed a ladylike sway in one's progress, they could often be quite cumbersome.

What she saw inside took her breath away and filled her tender heart with sorrow. One rickety table stood in the center of the room with three tree stumps placed around it, apparently serving as chairs. A few tattered blankets were laid out on the dirt floor of the cabin. On one of the blankets lay a very young girl, probably only five or six years old, who was alternately coughing and moaning, obviously in the grip of some dangerous disease. A shallow bowl filled with water and a wad of rags indicated that the only other occupant of the one-room cabin, probably the mother of the little girl, had been bathing her forehead with cool water. Now she stood to one side as Amelia's mother set her basket on the table and drew off her gloves.

"Esau told me your little girl was sick, Nelly." Amelia's mother referred to the butler at the big house. She took an apron from her basket. "Amelia and I have brought some medicine for you to use that should have her feeling better in no time."

"Thank you, Mrs. Montgomery, Miss Amelia." The older woman's face was so dark that Amelia could barely make out her expression in the dim cabin.

It was a shame they could not leave the door open to let light inside, but it was much too cold and the little girl was much too sick.

"What do you want me to do, Mama?"

Amelia's mother sank to the ground next to the blanket and placed her hand on the child's forehead. "I need you to measure out a spoonful of the butterfly root tea we brought. If we can get her to drink some, it will help with the fever and coughing."

Amelia opened the medicine bag her mother had helped her prepare, withdrew the warm bottle, and uncorked it, wrinkling her nose at the pungent smell.

Mrs. Montgomery took the spoon from her as soon as Amelia filled it. She coaxed the child to open her mouth and tipped the spoon against her lips. The poor thing was so weak and sick she didn't even react to what Amelia imagined was a very bitter dose.

She took the spoon back from her mother. "Another one?"

Her mother shook her head. "We don't want to give her too much." She laid the child back down on the blanket. "Hand me a towel."

Amelia drew out a pair of snowy white cotton towels and watched as her mother arranged them under the little girl's head. "If you will keep her head up like this, Nelly, she will be able to breathe more easily." She pushed herself up from the ground and dusted her hands together.

"Thank you, ma'am. I been so worried about my Sadie. She been gettin' worse since Sunday."

"And rightly so." Mrs. Montgomery took the bottle and spoon from Amelia. "It appears your child has pneumonia. You will need to give her one spoonful of this medicine every hour until you go to sleep tonight."

Amelia's forehead wrinkled with doubt. "But, Mama, how will Nelly know when an hour has passed?"

"Don't you fret yourself, Miss Amelia. I knows how to watch the sun."

"I'm going to leave this basket with you, Nelly. There's food inside for your family since you can't work today and earn your portion. You'll need to get one of the older women to watch after her tomorrow, though, so you can get back to work. Tell her to give your girl a spoonful at a time until this bottle is empty."

The woman thanked her mother yet again for her kind Christian heart even as the child started coughing and moaning once again.

Amelia grabbed her skirts and followed her mother back outside. Cold winter air reddened her cheeks in the few steps it took for them to reach the family carriage. Once inside, she looked at her mother. "Will her child live?"

"I don't know, but we've done all we can." Her mother shivered and pulled a thick fleece blanket over her lap. "We must always take care to provide medicine and care for the slaves, Amelia. It's our Christian duty to them. And it will ensure that we'll never be troubled by a slave uprising."

Amelia nodded, but she wondered. If that had been her little girl, would she have been so thankful for a basket of food and medicine? "Can't we make their quarters warmer?"

Her mother sniffed. "They don't need warmth like we do. They are accustomed to harsher circumstances. Just as there is a danger in ignoring their needs, there is a danger in coddling them too much."

Coddling? Amelia didn't think basic comfort was coddling. She opened her mouth to argue, but the coachman pulled up at the front steps and ended their conversation. She would remember to ask Papa later. Perhaps he would be more sympathetic to his workers' needs.

❧

Amelia pushed against the pommels of her sidesaddle to get a higher vantage point and looked all around the fields. The fall harvest had begun even though it was barely September. She could see the dark heads of the field workers as they toiled in the bright sunlight to the shouts and warnings of the overseer. She winced as the crack of a whip carried to her over the hot wind. She hoped none of Nelly's family was being punished.

In the months since she had first visited Nelly's cabin with her mother, Amelia had often dropped by to see how little Sadie was progressing. It had taken the girl a long time to recover from the pneumonia, but the cough had finally disappeared as the hot summer days grew longer. Amelia had taken Sadie gifts, trinkets really—a pan of biscuits, a handkerchief made of soft lawn, and a shift she had cut from one of her old nightgowns. She thought of the gift she brought today, eager to see a smile on little Sadie's face.

Now she glanced around to make certain no one was watching as she turned her mare's head toward the group of slave cabins her parents called the quarters. Mama and Papa would skin her if they knew what she was doing. They had strict views on which slaves she could befriend.

Tabitha, her personal maid, was an acceptable friend and confidante. Tabitha was the daughter of Esau, the butler, and Rahab, the mulatto cook. As higher-echelon slaves, Esau and Rahab had been allowed to marry and lived in much nicer accommodations than those to be found in the quarters. She and Tabitha were very close in age, having been born only a month apart. She often pulled Tabitha into scrapes, like wading barefoot in the stream or sneaking fresh cream out to the barn cat after she delivered a litter of tiny, mewing kittens. But if they were caught, she was always quick to accept the total blame, aware that her punishment would always be lighter than that of a slave.

That was why Amelia had never brought Tabitha with her to the quarters. If Papa ever caught her friend out there, he'd probably sell her to one of the neighboring landowners. He had very strict rules about the house slaves keeping separate from the field slaves. The only time they were allowed to be in the same building together was on Sundays at church, and even then the house slaves had to sit with the family while the field slaves occupied the balcony on the second floor. Amelia didn't understand why the separation was so important, but she knew enough to be careful which of Papa's rules she broke.

The hot, dry wind chased Amelia into the quarters.

Sadie came running toward her before she even had time to dismount. "Hi, Miss Amelia." Sadie's slender legs showed beneath the hem of her shift as she skidded to a stop.

"I declare, Sadie, if you don't stop growing, that shift is going to be too short for you before winter returns."

The little girl glanced at her bare toes. "Yes, ma'am. But I can't he'p it. Ev'y night I ask Jesus to keep me short, but ev'y day when I gets up, my legs is longer."

Amelia laughed and reached out a hand to pull Sadie into the saddle behind her. "I've got a surprise for you today."

"A surprise?" Excitement made Sadie twist and turn behind her. "Where is it?"

"I left it in my saddlebag. To see it properly you and I are going to have to go to the creek."

Sadie wrapped her hands around Amelia's waist. "Is it a fishing line? I likes fish, Miss Amelia."

"No, it's not a fishing line. But I'm not going to tell you anything else until we get to the creek." She clucked to her horse.

It only took them a couple of minutes to reach the shady banks of the trickling stream. Sadie slid off the horse first, and Amelia dismounted right after her. Having secured the reins on a nearby branch, she went to her saddlebag and made a production of pulling out a little reed boat she and Tabitha had woven the day before.

Sadie's mouth opened in an O. "What is it?"

"It's a boat just like a reed boat that once hid a little baby boy in Egypt a long time ago."

"Who would hide a baby in a boat?"

Amelia pulled off her shoes and stockings and sat on the bank of the creek. "A long time ago, a big king reigned in Egypt, and he was a very bad man. He had lots of Hebrew slaves, so many that he decided to kill all the little boy slaves so he wouldn't lose his power over them."

Sadie sat down beside her and dangled her feet in the water.

Amelia handed her the little boat to play with. "One day, a Hebrew woman had a baby boy. She loved him so much that she hid him in a boat to keep the bad king from killing him."

"Was he in the boat a long time?"

"No." Amelia shook her head. "The king's daughter found him, and she loved him like her own little boy. She brought him back to her home and named him Moses. When he was a grown man, he used his power to free his people."

"That's a nice story, Miss Amelia." Sadie moved the little boat back and forth in the water. "I wish I had a Moses to free my family."

"Amelia Montgomery!" Her father's angry voice startled Amelia. How had he managed to find them, and how long had he been listening?

She turned to face his wrath, praying that he would not take his anger out on the little girl beside her.

Her father's face reminded her of a thundercloud. His eyes blazed, and his teeth were gritted. He pulled his hat off and slapped it against his leg. She watched the dust billow from his pants leg and swirl around in the dry air. Next to him stood one of the overseers, a heavy-jowled man with mean little eyes and a hard mouth.

"Papa, I'm sorry."

"I don't want to hear a word from you, Amelia. Get back home and await me in my study." He turned to the overseer. "Obviously, this slave has too much time on her hands. Take her out to the fields. She can start to earn her keep."

"Papa, no." Amelia put her hand out and stepped toward him. "Please don't."

"This time you've gone too far, Amelia, sowing discord with your tales of slave uprisings." He grabbed her arm and dragged her to her mare, tossing Amelia in the saddle and slapping her mount's flank. As she grabbed for the reins to keep from tumbling to the ground, Amelia heard Sadie screaming behind her.

All the way home, Amelia prayed for God to intervene. She'd never meant to encourage rebellion. It had only been a Bible story. Tears of remorse made hot tracks down her cheeks as she reached the house. She dismounted and handed her horse to a stable boy before dragging her reluctant feet to Papa's study.

Inside the stuffy room, time slowed to a crawl. The bright afternoon faded to dusk, and still Papa did not come. Just when she thought he'd forgotten her, the door opened, and he stomped in.

Amelia stood up, uncertain what to say. She watched as he went to the far side of his large chestnut desk and dropped into his chair, leaning back and gazing at the ceiling as if searching for the right words. Then he looked at her, his eyes colder than she'd ever seen them. She opened her mouth to speak, but he held up his hand.

"I've obviously pampered you too much, daughter. I learned today that you do not understand the least thing about our livelihood, our very existence. I might be able to make allowances for some young woman who lived far away and knew nothing of plantation life, but I cannot abide treachery within my own household."

"But, Papa—"

"No, not a single word will I entertain from you, Amelia Montgomery. Your behavior this afternoon was inexcusable. I have tolerated your liberal ideas for far too long, thinking you would grow out of your ridiculous beliefs once you understood the way of the world. But I was mistaken. I cannot and will not tolerate your rebellious ways any longer. I've made arrangements for you to travel to Knoxville to stay with your aunt and uncle for a year or so. They have offered to have you visit several times, but your mother and I always turned them down. We didn't know we were raising such an ungrateful, spoiled child."

"What about Sadie?" Amelia slipped the question in as her father took a breath.

"She's no concern of yours any longer." He pushed himself out of his chair and strode toward her, anger mottling his face. "You're going to be too busy getting ready for your journey."

Fresh tears flowed down her cheeks. Did her father hate her? He must. Why else would he send her away to live with people she barely knew? And what about her mother? What did she have to say about all this? Would she intervene on her daughter's behalf, or would she agree to the banishment?

"I spent the afternoon making plans with Gregory Talbot." Her father had turned back to her, his expression as unyielding as his words. "Luke wants to join up with the army, but his father has convinced him to return to school in Knoxville for his final year. He'll be leaving on Friday. His father and I agreed that Luke will escort you to your aunt and uncle's home. I will go to Nashville tomorrow to make the arrangements for your trip and to telegraph your aunt and uncle about your impending visit. I've decided you may take your maid, Tabitha, to keep you company and protect your reputation since you'll have to overnight in Chattanooga. You will board the train in Nashville two days hence. I trust that will allow you sufficient time to pack your things and say good-bye to your mother." He sat down at his desk once again and straightened a stack of papers on its surface. "I did not inform the Talbots of your views and recent indiscretion, and I expect you to keep the information quiet, also. You're excused."

Amelia put a hand over her mouth to stifle her sobs and stumbled out of the room. In the space of one afternoon, everything had changed so much that she wondered if she would ever be allowed to come home again.

Chapter 3

A melia was already tired by the time they reached the train station in Nashville, even though it was not yet midday. She, Luke Talbot, and her maid, Tabitha, had departed before daylight to ensure their timely arrival. The chaos they encountered at the crowded depot was overwhelming and frightening for someone who rarely ventured from her parents' plantation. She was glad to have the escort of an experienced traveler. Luke had made the trip to Knoxville several times and knew exactly where they should go.

Feeling like a country bumpkin, Amelia gazed on the large brick building that was the station house. It was an odd-looking building with crenulated towers and roof and two enormous arched doorways that made her feel tiny in comparison.

Off in the distance at the very top of a hill, she saw the newly completed state capitol, with its soaring central tower and tall white columns. The sight made her proud to be from the state of Tennessee. If only the North and the South could put aside their differences and come to some kind of agreement. She wished she were smart enough to figure out a solution to eliminate the need for slave labor. The barbaric practice was tearing the country apart. No matter how long she spent in exile with her relatives, Amelia knew she would never change her mind on this topic. One day, she hoped to see all of Papa's slaves set free. But that was a problem for another day. Today, she needed to concentrate on her journey.

Train tracks ran hither and yon around the station in a dizzying patchwork. She held on to Luke's arm with one hand as he threaded his way around crowds of people and piles of luggage. Her skirt threatened to tangle around her ankles, and Amelia wished she might have worn her hoops instead of five layers of petticoats. But hoops, although cooler, would be impractical once she was seated on one of the benches in the passenger car. She glanced over her shoulder several times to make certain Tabitha had not gotten separated from them, reassured when encountering the smile on her slave's face. She thanked God again for Papa's decision to allow Tabitha to accompany her during her exile. No matter how many strangers she encountered over the coming year, Amelia knew she would have one friend in Knoxville—two counting Luke Talbot.

All the noise and smoke was overwhelming. Amelia was a bit worried she might lose her grasp on Luke's strong arm and vanish in the swirling, noisy crowd. She'd never seen so many people. Young men in uniform vied for space amongst soberly clad businessmen. Importunate merchants hawked everything from newspapers to blankets. Shouts and grunts filled the air as slaves loaded cargo into crowded boxcars.

The smells of overheated bodies and live animals pushed in on her and made Amelia yearn for the country and a breath of fresh air. But she might as well put that behind her. Papa had made it clear she was not to come home before this time next year. By then, he said, the fighting would be over and things would be back to normal. He also made it clear she was to learn her place while staying in Knoxville. He wanted her to set aside reading newspapers and confine herself to novels to avoid further addling her thinking. He'd warned of dire consequences if she did not learn to conform her behavior to what was expected of a Southern lady of means.

"We are nearly there." Luke pointed to a long, black car with wide windows that vaguely resembled an iron carriage. It was one in a long line of cars attached to a locomotive that belched black smoke from a tall pipe at its front.

"Praise God." Amelia felt Luke's gaze on her and looked up at him. He was such a nice man, and she had forgotten how handsome he was. He seemed so much more grown-up now, perhaps because of the years he'd spent away at college. He sported a thin mustache and neatly trimmed side whiskers that made him appear older than his twenty years. Gone was the lanky youngster she remembered from their shared childhood. Luke carried himself well, as befitted the eldest son of a wealthy planter. His well-made clothing was fashionable, from the brim of his tall black hat to the polished toes of his leather boots.

"I am looking forward to getting back to Knoxville." He patted her hand. "I know you will enjoy yourself there, Amelia. I hope to call on you often. Perhaps your uncle will allow me to escort you about town once you are settled in."

She nodded. "It will be comforting to know I have a friend nearby."

Luke smiled, showing his even, white teeth. "You may be certain of that. But I have the feeling it will not take long for someone as pretty as you to acquire a wide circle of admirers. I only hope you will still remember me then."

Amelia reached for her fan and opened it in front of her face to cover her embarrassment. She did not know how to answer Luke. If she agreed with his compliment, she would appear conceited, but if she disagreed he might think she meant that she would no longer remember him as a friend once she became established. Uncertain of what to say, she decided to say nothing and pretended a sudden interest in a group of people who were standing a few feet away.

They appeared to be a family saying good-bye to a young man about her age. The older lady wore a wide spring bonnet on her head, its upturned bill decorated with a bunch of flowers and greenery. She might have stepped out of *Godey's Lady's Book*, with her pale yellow bodice and matching skirt. She leaned over and kissed the young man, making his cheeks redden. He pushed his spectacles up on his nose and turned to the tall, handsome man who must be his father. Amelia wondered if the older man was a politician. He looked distinguished enough to be the governor. She watched as the two shook hands and embraced in the awkward way of men. Then the young man turned to a pair of ladies who were either sisters or some other close relatives. They all had the same look about them—tall, attractive, and openly affectionate.

An unexpected jab of envy straightened Amelia's spine. She'd always wanted to be part of a close-knit family like the one she was watching. Her parents had not bothered to accompany their only daughter to Nashville. Where had she gone wrong? Must she compromise her beliefs to be loved by her parents? Or was she destined to always fight alone for what she believed was right? Another thought struck her. Why was she so certain she was right? Perhaps the young man she was watching was more humble than she. Or was he simply the type who blindly embraced the beliefs of his elders?

Amelia sniffed and picked up the skirt of her gown with her free hand. The bespectacled young man was probably devoid of principles and incapable of independent thought. She was cut from different cloth. Amelia had been brought up on the Bible, and she knew right from wrong. She would not bow to her parents or anyone else who tried to convince her to abandon her principles. So what if she had to go live with strangers for a year? She was determined to make the best of the situation. All she had to do was keep herself from getting involved in political matters and concentrate on enjoying the round of parties and social events her relatives would no doubt be invited to. Then she could return home older, wiser, and more able to persuade her parents that times were changing.

After leading her to a seat in one of the passenger cars, Luke bent over Amelia. "I'm going to take Tabitha with me to make sure your luggage has been loaded. Are you comfortable?"

"Don't worry about me." Amelia put a bright smile on her face even though she didn't much like the idea of being left completely alone. Tabitha knew all of their trunks, but she could not be sent by herself lest she be picked up by a bounty hunter mistaking her for an escaping slave. "I have Mr. Dickens's book to read. I'll be fine until you return."

❧

Jared leaned out of the doorway and waved until the train turned a bend and he could no longer see his family. He stepped into the narrow space between cars and pulled off his spectacles, which had unaccountably become blurry. The problem couldn't be connected to the burning sensation in his eyes. That would mean he was crying. Grown men didn't cry. Surreptitiously, he wiped the lenses clean and replaced the spectacles, looking around to see if he'd been noticed.

He opened the door in front of him just as the train lurched. Allowing the movement to push him forward, Jared passed several benches and chose one that was unoccupied. That's when he noticed the lovely young lady sitting on the other side of the aisle from him.

She glanced in his direction before modestly returning her attention to the book in her lap. She was the most beautiful girl in the world. The quick glance she sent his direction showed eyes as blue as a summer sky. He also noticed her delicate complexion and generous, bow-shaped mouth. Although her hair was pulled up and mostly hidden under her bonnet, he could see shimmering strands around her face that reminded him of sun-drenched corn silk. She could be the subject of poetry, perhaps the fabled Helen of Troy.

The train began to pick up speed as they moved farther away from the station, seeming to race as quickly as his mind. Where was the young lady's maid? Was she traveling alone? Chivalry filled his chest and squared his shoulders. Like a knight of old, he could watch over her and make sure she reached Chattanooga safely.

His imagination soared. Over the next couple of hours, Jared would gradually win her confidence and offer her his protection. If she was traveling beyond Chattanooga on this train, he would speak to the conductor about her and make certain a suitable replacement would help her reach her final destination. If by some miraculous chance she was journeying to Knoxville, he would guard her from all the dangers they might encounter. It was the least he could do. If one of his sisters found herself traveling alone in these dangerous times, he would hope some man might do the same.

He tilted his head to see what she might be reading. Perhaps that would be a good place to start a conversation. It was a fairly thick volume, so not a book of poetry. Jared craned his neck farther but could not see the title. He thought he saw her gaze slide in his direction, so Jared sat back and straightened his cravat. He didn't want to make her nervous.

After a moment, she returned her attention to her book and turned a page. From the corner of his vision he saw a red ribbon she must be using as a bookmark flutter to the floor between their seats. Jared reached down for it at the same time as the young woman, narrowly avoiding a head collision.

He plucked the ribbon from the floor and put it in her hand, noticing her dainty wrist and long fingers. "You dropped your ribbon." He nearly groaned as he heard the words. He sounded like a simpleton. Why couldn't he think of something besides the obvious to say?

"Thank you." Her smile was perfect, friendly but shy. Her fingers closed over the ribbon, and she settled back in her seat.

Say something! His mind screamed the words, but nothing came to him. His gaze lit on her book. She had partially closed it when she reached for the ribbon. He saw the title, and inspiration struck. "You're reading *A Tale of Two Cities*. What do you think of it? Dickens is one of my favorite authors. I was hoping to procure a copy of that novel before leaving Nashville, but with this and that, I never quite found the time to visit the bookseller. I hope to purchase it once I reach Knoxville. If I can find someone to tell me where the bookseller is located, of course." He cringed as he realized he was babbling.

She opened her mouth to answer him but was stopped by the arrival of a broad-shouldered man who looked a year or two older, and much more debonair than Jared could ever hope to be. A brother?

"Is this man bothering you, Amelia?" The newcomer's ferocious frown raked Jared from head to foot, and Jared's hope of protecting the pretty traveler withered.

"Oh no, Luke." She reached up and put a hand on the man's arm. "I was clumsy enough to drop my bookmark, and he most kindly returned it to me."

A harrumph from Luke indicated his skepticism. "You ought not speak to strangers, Amelia, no matter the circumstances." He turned to the black woman standing quietly in the aisle. "Sit down next to your mistress, Tabitha. Perhaps between us, we can keep her out of trouble."

Jared stared straight ahead, but he could see the two women settling next to each other. The hair prickled on the back of his neck, and he looked up to see the belligerent Luke standing over him and frowning.

"Would you move over?" The man's voice was filled with exasperation.

"Oh." Jared could feel his cheeks heating up. "Of course." He grabbed the tails of his coat and scooted toward the window.

Luke's frown never disappeared, even as he sat down and pulled out his watch to check the time. If this man was Amelia's brother, he must take after another side of the family. While she was fair and delicate, he was dark, with ebony hair and eyes. His mustache and side whiskers made him appear more sophisticated than his companions. Jared stroked his own face, wishing he could grow a respectable mustache or maybe even a beard. His smooth chin, coupled with his spectacles, had caused many a new acquaintance to think he was still a boy.

"I beg your pardon, sir." Jared fingered his cravat once more. "I meant no disrespect to the lady." He wanted to explain his motives but decided to leave well enough alone when he encountered another glare from the man. Instead, he settled back against the wooden seat and gazed out the window at the passing scenery. Eventually, the rhythmic clacking of the train's wheels eased his embarrassment and lulled him into a state of somnolence.

A feminine giggle roused him, and Jared looked past the broad chest of his seatmate toward Amelia and her maid. What was the latter's name? It was something biblical. His mind searched. Tabitha! That was it. Both women had removed their bonnets during the trip, and now they sat whispering together, their heads nearly touching. It was a charming sight, straight blond tresses mixing with ebony curls. He was glad to see they were enjoying their journey. He would have liked to join their conversation, but he knew the man sitting next to him would never abide such a thing.

Jared told himself it didn't matter. She was a stranger, and he would probably never see her again once he disembarked at Chattanooga, where he would have to spend the night before catching the train to Knoxville. But he still felt drawn to her, wanting to know where she lived, where she was going, what her dreams and aspirations were. Was his inclination a nudge from God? Or did it come from his own, more shallow desire?

❧

The shrill blow of the locomotive's whistle pulled Amelia's attention away from the trials of Lucie Manette and Charles Darnay in the compelling novel she was reading.

Tabitha had fallen asleep next to her, but now she awakened with a start. "Is something wrong?"

Amelia glanced out of the window and realized the day was drawing to a close. The sun had fallen below the western ridge of tree-covered hills, casting the valley they were traveling through into darkness. Smoky gray fog rose up and blurred the trees on the upward slopes of the hills surrounding them. She craned her neck but could find no evidence of a threat. "Everything seems fine."

The train whistle blew once more, and Luke leaned toward them. "We're about to reach the end of this leg of our journey. As soon as we climb out of this valley, you'll be able to see Chattanooga."

"And we'll spend the night there?"

Luke nodded. "We'll be staying at a boardinghouse where I've overnighted several times before. I think you'll find it to your liking."

"Look at that." Tabitha pointed out the window.

While they had been talking, the train had chugged its way up to the peak, and the valley was spread out below them. Amelia caught her breath. The river at the bottom of the valley looked like an ebony ribbon, its surface gleaming as it caught the light of the rising moon. The curve of the river reminded her of a bird's nest with the town of Chattanooga serving as its hatchling. "It's beautiful. So different from Nashville." She watched spellbound as the train made its descent into the valley, slowing as it reached the station.

When the car stopped, she was glad to lean on Luke's arm once more. It was so nice to have a knowledgeable guide. Over the years, her parents had encouraged her to consider him as an eligible candidate for marriage, but somehow she'd never been able to think of him that way. She supposed it was all the time they'd spent together growing up. Luke had always acted more like a brother than a suitor.

But now she was having second thoughts. Luke was capable, handsome, and smart. Perhaps she should take her parents' advice. It might even help restore her to their good graces.

❧

Jared pulled on his boots and slipped out of the room just as the sun was beginning to make its presence known in the east. He left the boardinghouse and wandered through his former hometown. Chattanooga had grown in the past four years. New businesses had sprung up, and he spotted several new houses dotting the area in the curve of the Tennessee River.

He returned to his room as the town began to come to life. Seizing the opportunity for quiet reflection, he grabbed his Bible and escaped to the small garden behind the boardinghouse. The train would not depart for Knoxville for at least two hours, which left him plenty of time for prayer before he joined the other travelers for breakfast.

A feeling of peace settled on his shoulders. These were the times he'd missed while living in Nashville with Great-Aunt Dolly. He looked up at the limbs of a tree, noticing that its leaves were beginning to turn brown with the approach of winter. Although Jared knew God was everywhere, the silence and peace of these surroundings made him feel closer to his Lord than anywhere else.

He thumbed through his Bible and finally settled on the 53rd chapter of Isaiah, where he read about the slaughtered lamb. Had Isaiah felt the horror of his prophecies? It must have been terrible to foresee the undeserved death of Christ. Or had Isaiah been comforted by the prophecy that ended that chapter? Jared read the words again, his finger tracing the lines. *"And he bare the sin of many, and made intercession for the transgressors."* For a moment, guilt threatened to crush him. He was one of the transgressors for whom Christ had gone silently to the cross. But then he allowed the Spirit to comfort him with the knowledge that he was forgiven and that his sins had been removed and miraculously forgotten.

Jared sank to his knees, thanking God for forgiveness for the sins that had separated him from his Maker. The peace he had felt earlier flowed more strongly. He could sense the risen Christ holding out His arms for an embrace. He basked in the love and wonder of that image.

Jared had no idea how much time passed before he heard someone walking toward him. The newcomer stepped into his line of vision, and Jared's breath caught in his throat. It was her! The beauty from the train, the girl who read Dickens. "Miss Amelia!" He scrambled to his feet and brushed at the leaves that clung to his trousers. "Good morning."

She stopped as soon as she saw him, standing in a shaft of sunlight that made her hair glow. "I'm sorry. I didn't realize anyone would be out here. I came to explore the garden. From my window it appeared too inviting to ignore. I didn't mean to disturb your privacy."

"It is beautiful, isn't it?" Jared couldn't imagine any setting more breathtaking than the girl who stood facing him. He cleared his throat, his mind scurrying to find the words to tell her his thoughts.

She turned slightly away from him. "I should be getting back to my room."

"Please don't leave on my account. I was just reading from my Bible. I love coming outside and talking to God."

She turned back to him, her expression showing interest. "What scripture are you reading?"

"Isaiah, the 53rd chapter."

Her brow wrinkled. "That's a hard book for me to understand. I prefer reading the New Testament. Especially Paul's letters. They are full of so much hope."

"That's the way I feel about Isaiah." He beckoned her toward a wooden bench, pulling out his handkerchief and dusting its surface to protect her clothing. "Come look at this passage."

Amelia sat on the rough-hewn bench, and Jared settled next to her. She smelled so nice, a mixture of roses and spring flowers that made him want to breathe deeply.

He put the thought from his mind and opened his Bible and read the scripture aloud. Then he turned a few pages and read his favorite verse, Isaiah 40:31. " 'But they that wait upon the Lord shall renew their strength; they shall mount up with wings as eagles; they shall run, and not be weary; and they shall walk, and not faint.' "

"Those verses are certainly full of hope," Amelia conceded. "But what about all of the admonitions directed at the people of Israel? Didn't he spend a lot of time trying to warn them about following the path to destruction?"

Jared stared into Amelia's blue eyes. They reminded him of a clear mountain stream. He almost forgot what they were discussing as he gazed at her beautiful face. "Ummm. . .yes, you're right." He shook his head to clear it. "But Isaiah tempers his warnings with these words of hope. Words that can bring us peace in the midst of our darkest days."

"I never thought about it like that." She smiled at him.

Jared lost his train of thought once more. He closed his Bible and stood up. "I better get back inside. I'll be leaving soon. I'm going on to Knoxville."

"Me, too." She clapped her hands. "Maybe we'll see each other in Knoxville."

Was she flirting with him? What could such a lovely young woman see in a bookish fellow like him? Jared couldn't even figure out how to answer her. A large part of him wished it was likely that they'd run into each other again, but he doubted it. She would be attending parties and dances while he would spend all of his time studying.

Amelia stood and took his handkerchief from the bench. "Thank you for being so gallant."

He shook his head. "Keep it." He winced inwardly at the abrupt words. Why hadn't he paid more attention to the art of conversing with young women? He felt gauche and rude, but he didn't know how to soften his words. He was much better at writing than speaking. Finally, he settled on practicality. "It's probably time for breakfast."

After a brief silence, she let her hand fall to her side and moved to exit the garden. He followed her to the dining room, berating himself for not being more of a gentleman. He should have offered his arm to her. Why couldn't he be more self-assured? Why couldn't he find the right words for the occasion? Why did his tongue have to twist itself up into knots? Even if he did see Amelia after this trip, he was sure she would avoid him like the plague. And why shouldn't she?

Jared made quick work of his breakfast before seeking a seat on the ET&G, the train that would take him to Knoxville. Although he looked for Amelia and her traveling companions, he didn't see them again, even when the train stopped for lunch. He told himself it was for the best. Her guardian, Luke, would never allow him to speak to her. And even if he did, Jared still had no idea what to say to her.

Chapter 4

Jared couldn't stop smiling. Two weeks at college, and everything was working out splendidly—well almost everything. He had a great roommate, Benjamin Montgomery, the youngest son of a local businessman. He and Benjamin had much in common, including older sisters and a love of the natural world. Of course, Benjamin was more interested in playing around than studying, but Jared was sure his attitude would change once they got into the full swing of the semester.

The only fly in Jared's ointment was a certain senior, Luke Talbot. He was the snobby fellow who'd escorted the beauteous Amelia on the train. And he'd made it clear that he had no time for underclassmen. But it would not be hard to avoid Mr. Talbot, since they shared only chapel together. The seniors went to different classrooms, practiced their military exercises in a different area than the freshmen, and ate at different times.

With a shrug, Jared dismissed Luke Talbot from his thoughts and looked down at the flyer in his hand. It was an announcement for the first meeting of the Societas Philomathesian, a literary society at East Tennessee University. The door to his room opened, and Jared looked up to see Benjamin entering.

"I couldn't believe old Mr. Wallace surprised us with that test today." Benjamin tossed his book on their shared desk and threw himself across his bed.

"It wasn't so bad. He only asked questions from the chapter on regular Latin declensions."

Benjamin made a face at him. "He might as well have asked about cathedrals in France or shipping lanes in the Mediterranean."

A laugh bubbled up from Jared's chest. "Tell me you didn't say the same thing to Mr. Wallace."

A nod answered him. Benjamin Montgomery was a charmer who had won over most of their teachers within the first few days of his arrival. He was a good-looking man with a wiry strength that served him well on the parade grounds and large, deep blue eyes that held a hint of mischief all the time. He could say the most outrageous things, and the only response he got was appreciative laughter. Jared wished he had the same talent.

"You are incorrigible." Jared shook his head. "That would be a better line of questioning from Mr. Whitsell, our geography teacher."

"Geography, history, language, mathematics. All of it is nonsense. The only part of college that appeals to me is the military part." Benjamin sat on the edge of his bed and held his arms up, pretending to aim a rifle at the far wall. "I'm only attending ETU to please my parents. As soon as I finish here, I'm going to join up and shoot me some Yanks."

"What if I join the Yanks? Are you going to shoot me?"

Benjamin dropped his stance, and his mouth dropped open. His eyes, normally dark blue, turned almost purple in shock. "Fight with the Yanks? Now you sound like Whitsell, ready to betray your own countrymen."

"Don't tell me you haven't considered it. It's well known that Knoxville is divided. No matter which side you choose, you're likely to be fighting against someone you know."

A shrug was his only answer. "What are you reading?" asked Benjamin.

Jared held up the flyer in his hand. "The Societas Philomathesian is holding a meeting tomorrow night. Say you'll go with me." Jared knew it would be out of character for his roommate to attend something as serious as a literary society meeting, but he hoped to convince his friend. "I'll help you with your Latin verbs."

Benjamin stared at him for a full minute before answering. "I'll do it, but I want something more than a Latin tutor. I need a partner in crime."

"I don't know. . . . What kind of crime?"

"It won't be too bad. I just want to cause Mr. Wallace as much confusion as he caused me this morning."

Now it was Jared's turn to study his roommate's face as he considered his options. He could go alone to the society meeting and fade quietly into the background until he made new friends with similar interests, or he could yield to the temptation to do something daring. He'd never had much chance to be boyish at home, not with all those women around. And his pa was so starchy, he couldn't imagine Adam Stuart throwing caution to the wind. "I'll do it."

"It's a deal then." Benjamin stood up. "All we have to do is wait until everyone is asleep. I'll get the necessary equipment."

Jared took a deep breath and placed his hand in Benjamin's outstretched one. He hoped he would not regret his impulse.

❧

Jared pulled the slack out of the rope he and Benjamin had tied to the professors' doorknobs. All was quiet on the hall. The other students were snug in their beds, no doubt sleeping, as he and his roommate should be doing. Instead, they had crept to the end of the floor, where their professors slept in rooms directly across from each other. Following Benjamin's instructions, he had tied one end of their rope to Mr. Whitsell's doorknob. Benjamin looped the other end around

Mr. Wallace's doorknob. He watched as his roommate tied a knot that would prevent either professor from opening his door in the morning.

"How long do you think it will take them to get free?"

Benjamin shushed him and returned his attention to their handiwork.

"What are you boys doing down there?" The whisper sounded as loud as a musket shot in the quiet hallway.

Jared gasped and jerked around to face the consequences of his actions. His whole life passed in front of his eyes in that brief moment. He would be sent home in disgrace. His parents would be so disappointed. Why had he ever agreed to such a silly prank?

His heart climbed up to his throat when a shaft of moonlight from a nearby window revealed Luke Talbot's wide shoulders and dark hair. He wished he could sink into the floorboards or disappear like a puff of smoke. Of all the people to catch them, why did it have to be a man who already despised him? "We're uh. . .we're—"

Benjamin pushed his way past Jared and stepped up to Luke. "We thought we heard a noise in the hall and came to investigate."

"Is that right?" Luke turned his attention on Benjamin. "And I suppose you have no idea who might have tied that rope to the professors' doorknobs?"

"I suppose it could have been any number of persons. Anyone with access to a length of rope who might also have a grudge against sneaky teachers who surprise unsuspecting freshmen with examinations."

"And what do you have to say to that?" Luke turned back to Jared.

He held out his hands, palms up, and shrugged. He was about to confess when Luke chuckled quietly. "Is Wallace still pulling those same old tricks? Maybe this will convince him to desist."

Jared could not have been more surprised if Luke had grown a tail and horns. This man had a sense of humor? He wasn't going to turn them in? They weren't going to be expelled?

"You two better get back to your room." Luke pointed a finger at them. "And don't think I'll be as lenient if I catch you out in the hallways after hours again."

Benjamin winked at Jared as they crept back to their room. Once they shut the door behind them, he slapped a hand on his chest and expelled a loud breath. "I thought we were done for when I heard him."

Jared undressed quickly and pulled on his nightshirt. "Me, too. I was already imagining the disgrace of being sent home before my first month had passed."

After they had both climbed into their beds, Jared lay still, contemplating the near disaster.

"I thought you said Luke Talbot was a pompous windbag." Benjamin's voice was thoughtful. "I have to disagree with your opinion. I think he's a regular sport."

Jared closed his eyes and sent a prayer of thankfulness to God that they had not been sent home in disgrace. "Yes, he was kind to let us go. But don't forget his warning." He turned over in the bed and punched his pillow. "I'm never going to give him or anyone else the chance to catch me again. From here on out, I'll be doing everything strictly by the rules."

❧

Jared could tell how much delight Benjamin was drawing from the commotion they'd caused, even though the two of them were not awake when the professors discovered they were trapped. By the time they dressed and headed for chapel, the row had died down, but the prank was the only topic being discussed. Who might have pulled such a trick? And done it without being caught?

"I hope they find out who did such an awful thing." Benjamin's blue eyes sparkled with mischief.

Jared winced, wishing his roommate was not quite so bold. "I'm glad no one was hurt."

"Don't be foolish. I heard they were set free within a matter of minutes. All it took was getting someone's attention."

The two of them entered the chapel, which buzzed like a hornet's nest. Everyone was whispering about the incident, shaking their heads and hiding smiles behind their hands.

Jared felt a little sick. He wished he'd never taken part. Perhaps if he went to the president and confessed his part, he would feel better. But what if he was expelled? And Benjamin, too? His head began to ache. He didn't know what to do.

A hand clamped down on his right shoulder, and Jared nearly yelped his surprise. He twisted quickly and looked into the frowning face of Luke Talbot. "You look a bit green about the gills, Stuart. Are you feeling sick?"

Jared shook his head but remained mute.

Luke leaned close and whispered into his ear. "If you're thinking about blabbing about what happened last night, you'd better think again. Any confession at this point would perforce include me, and I will not stand for that. I have a spotless record here, and no underclassman is going to ruin it. No harm was done. Go about your regular studies. By evening, this episode will be forgotten."

He nodded and slid into a pew. Mr. Wallace was leading the chapel service, and Jared was glad to see the man was his usual self, confident and a little pompous. His headache eased, his stomach settled down, and he concentrated on his prayer, thanking God for not getting caught and vowing to never again allow someone to drag him into another such incident.

The rest of the day passed without incident, for which Jared was thankful.

After dinner, he and Benjamin went to the Societas Philomathesian meeting, taking seats on the back row and listening as several members stood and read poetry, stories, or essays they'd written. His imagination was ignited. This is why he'd come to ETU—to be a part of such academic pursuits. He only wished he could think of a good subject to write about. His mind went to the Indians his parents worked so hard to protect, but that was their cause, not his. He listened to one fellow get up and read about the obligation of Southern men to join the Confederate Army, and Jared wondered why he was writing about his beliefs instead of fighting for them.

So caught up was Jared in the evening that he didn't realize how bored Benjamin was until he heard a soft buzzing sound. He looked over in horror to see his friend slumped down in the chair, his face dropped so far forward his chin rested on his chest. He elbowed Benjamin.

"Wha. . .what's the matter?"

"Shhh!" Jared put a finger across his lips in warning. "You fell asleep."

Benjamin frowned. "And you woke me? Is it time to go?"

Jared expelled a breath. "No."

"Okay then." Benjamin slouched once more and closed his eyes.

What had he expected? For Benjamin to suddenly gain an interest in literature? He sighed again. Benjamin raised one eyelid and peeked at him. He looked so innocent, so longsuffering. It was hard for Jared to hold on to his indignation. He could feel a grin teasing the corners of his mouth. How did Benjamin do it? He never seemed more than half serious about anything, but still he managed to charm his way through every circumstance. Jared wished some of that charm would rub off on him.

The meeting broke up, and he watched as Benjamin complimented each of the readers on his work, listening and nodding his head as one or another expounded further on his ideas. Jared chuckled to himself. If only they knew the truth.

"Did you enjoy the evening?" Benjamin asked as they made their way across campus to the dormitory.

"Very much. I want to write something and present it at the next meeting."

"Do you really?" Benjamin's voice was full of scorn. "I cannot imagine a duller group. But I guess it depends on your interests. My taste runs to more exciting pursuits, which puts me in mind of a favor I need to ask."

"Oh no." Jared opened the door of Southern Hall. The hallway was dimly lit, as most students had already retired for the evening. "You're not going to get me involved in any more mischief."

"No," protested Benjamin. "It's nothing like that. Even I know when it's time to lie low. This has to do with my parents. Next week they're throwing a birthday party for a cousin of mine who recently came to town. She's from your part of the state—Nashville, or near to it. Anyway, my parents thought it would be nice to have a gathering of young people to help her feel more welcome."

"I don't know. Debutantes and parties are not my favorite pastimes. Besides, I have a lot of studying to do."

Benjamin's face took on the betrayed look of a heartbroken puppy. "You don't mean to make me go alone. I even told Ma I'd be bringing you with me."

"You told your mother without consulting me?" Jared shook his head. He really didn't want to go and didn't appreciate feeling manipulated. This was the perfect time to take a firm stand and refuse his roommate.

"We'll have a great time. We can skip the dinner and show up in time for the dancing." Benjamin bowed to an imaginary partner. "You'll have a great time. We'll make certain Cousin Amelia has sufficient dance partners to make her feel accepted, and then I promise to bring you straight back to your studies."

Jared's heart missed a beat and then compensated by doubling its speed. Amelia? Surely not the girl he'd seen on the train all those weeks ago? Was it possible? Knoxville was a large town, but how many young women had recently arrived there from Nashville? Curiosity and hope, a heady combination, filled his thoughts. How he would enjoy another opportunity to talk to her. He glanced at Benjamin and nodded. "I'll go."

"Great!" Benjamin slapped him on the back. "I knew I could count on you."

Chapter 5

O uch." Amelia reached up and grabbed Tabitha's hand. "That's the third time you've pulled my hair. What's wrong?"

"Nothing. I'm sorry. I'll try to do better."

"Don't try that on me, Tabitha. I know you too well." She took the brush from Tabitha's hand and laid it on the dressing table, then turned to face her friend. "Tell me what's on your mind."

Tabitha's eyebrows drew together in a frown. "You need to go down soon. Turn around and let me finish your hair."

"Unh-unh." Amelia shook her head. "I'm not going down until I find out why you're acting so strangely."

"I. . .I can't talk about it." Tabitha turned away from her and faced the window.

Amelia said nothing. She and Tabitha had grown up together, even though Tabitha was a slave and she was the master's daughter. She had shared her dolls with Tabitha, and then when she learned to read, she'd shared her lessons with the young slave. Papa would skin both of them alive if he knew. It was illegal to teach a slave to read and write, but neither of them had considered the law when they were younger. As long as they never divulged the truth to anyone else, they would not get in trouble. Amelia's conscience pricked her a little at the thought. Was it wrong to lie to others for a good cause?

"It's. . .the c–cook's son." Tabitha's words were slow, as if she was carefully considering each one.

"The cook's son." Amelia clapped her hands together. "Is he handsome? Smart? Does he make your heart beat faster?"

"No, no." Tabitha turned to face her once again. "It's nothing like that. Nothing romantic. He. . .he's an escaped slave."

Amelia could feel a lump rise in her throat. She didn't like the sound of this, but she couldn't back out on her friend now. "Go on."

"He. . .he's a conductor."

The word fell between them like a boulder. A conductor. That meant he was part of the Underground Railroad. He was helping other slaves make their way to freedom. It was a noble cause, and one that Amelia would like to support, but she knew better. Hadn't she already paid a high enough price for her dealings with slaves? She looked at Tabitha's troubled face. "I see."

"He's got a group out in the barn. One of them's been shot. A young boy."

The blood drained from Amelia's face as she considered the pain and fear the child must be feeling. "What happened?"

Tabitha knelt on the floor in front of her. Tears ran down her cheeks. "You know there's safe places where runaways can hide out."

Amelia nodded. No one knew exactly how many slaves had found their way to freedom in the past decade. Or how many had died trying. People caught harboring runaway slaves were breaking the law. It was a scary choice to make, especially since Tennessee had seceded from the Union last spring.

In the short time she'd been here, Amelia had discovered Knoxville was a town divided over the issue of abolition. Some believed each state should have the right to decide whether or not to outlaw slavery, while others were staunchly opposed to allowing slavery at all, and still others depended on slave labor to run profitable businesses. Even though she had found her aunt and uncle to be a little more liberal in their attitude toward slavery, she would never have dreamed of this possibility. "Are you saying my aunt and uncle are helping slaves get free?"

"Oh my, no." Tabitha placed her hands over Amelia's. "They'd have a fit for sure. But it's the cook's son. He's in a bad fix. The station where he was supposed to hide was found out, and the escapees were almost captured. So he brought them here and asked his ma to help."

A knock on the door made both girls jump.

"Stand up," Amelia whispered. Then more loudly she called out, "Who's there?"

"Amelia, honey, it's about time for you to come downstairs." Aunt Laura's voice was bright and cheerful. She was obviously looking forward to the party, having no idea that disaster could strike the whole family at any moment.

"I'll be right down," Amelia tried for a light tone to match her aunt's. "Tabitha is putting the final touches on my coiffure."

"All right, dear. Your uncle and I will be waiting for you."

Amelia held her breath until she heard her aunt's receding footsteps. She turned to Tabitha. "I can finish my hair. You go and help the cook's son. I won't need you any more tonight."

A slight smile turned up the corners of Tabitha's mouth. "You'd look a sight for sure. You don't know anything about fixing hair."

The clock on her mantel ticked away the minutes as Tabitha expertly twisted the hair up off Amelia's neck and fastened it into place with jeweled pins. A few tendrils escaped on either side of her face and at the nape of her neck, giving her a soft but sophisticated look.

"You look real nice. You're going to be the prettiest girl at the party." Tabitha's words did not match her expression, which was still drawn in a frown.

"Thank you, Tabitha." A few days ago, Amelia had been so excited about her new gown. It was one of her fanciest, a daring style that bared her arms and nipped in at her waist before expanding outward to form a wide bell that swayed as she moved. Now she was more concerned with the dire straits of the people hidden out back.

She stood and went to her bureau, thankful she had thought to bring her medicine bag, and pulled out strips of bandaging and forceps. "I don't know exactly what you may need, but this should help."

"Thank you." Tabitha tucked the forceps into the belt at her waist and dropped the bandaging into her pocket. Then she walked to Amelia's bed and picked up the Spanish lace shawl she'd laid across it earlier. "You need this." She arranged the soft material over Amelia's arms to fall just below her shoulders, then pushed her toward the door. "Go enjoy your party and don't worry none."

"Please be careful." Concern made Amelia's throat tighten. She would rather have helped Tabitha than go downstairs and play the part of an empty-headed debutante. "Promise you'll come get me if you need help."

Tabitha nodded and shooed her out of the room.

Lord, please protect my friend and those poor souls she's trying to help. Her prayer brought Amelia a feeling of peace as she descended her aunt and uncle's narrow staircase, but she wished she could do more.

She took a deep breath and concentrated on the designs on Aunt Laura's flocked velvet wallpaper. It was a new pattern, forest green in color with small birds perched on wide oak leaves. Aunt Laura had glowed with pleasure when Amelia had complimented it.

Amelia's skirts brushed both the polished balustrade and the wallpaper as she descended. Her heart was pumping hard by the time she reached the first-floor landing, and she pinned a wide smile on her face. She pushed her worries about the slaves to the back of her mind. It was very thoughtful of her relatives to have planned this party for her, and she was determined to enjoy it. . .or at least appear to.

Her aunt and uncle were a sweet couple, both somewhat rounded from their comfortable lifestyle. Uncle Francis, a canny investor with an eye to the future, had made a fortune by purchasing stock in such inventions as a machine for drilling through rocks, boilers for use with the new steam engines, and Elisha Otis's hoisting apparatus that moved cargo vertically. Uncle Francis had explained to her the uses for such a contraption, but Amelia could not understand his enthusiasm. Whatever its purpose, the device had earned her uncle an ample income, enough so he could spend most of his days enjoying the company of his peers at a gentlemen's club downtown.

Aunt Laura was a collector. She loved filling her home with fancy furniture and stylish knickknacks. Nearly every surface held some interesting object that her aunt loved to talk about. She was like one of the birds on her wallpaper, collecting leaves, twigs, and bits of fluff for her nest. Together, her aunt and uncle made a charming couple, quite different from what she expected when Papa banished her. She had thought she'd find herself in a prison-like atmosphere, surrounded by sour jailors who resented her presence. How wrong she had been.

"There she is." Uncle Francis's booming voice was as warm as a summer breeze. He chucked her under the chin. "You're as pretty as a picture, m'dear."

"Thank you, Uncle." Even though Amelia only stood some three inches above five feet, she was as tall as he, although his girth easily outstripped hers. Dark blue eyes, a Montgomery family trait, twinkled at her above his beard and mustache. He was dressed in a brown cutaway coat with a gold vest underneath, his attire showing that he kept abreast of current fashion. "You're looking quite handsome yourself."

She turned to her aunt, who was resplendent in a gown of rich puce satin. Tiny pearl buttons decorated the bodice from the collar to her waist. The sleeves were wide at the shoulder and elbow and tapered to a narrow cuff fastened with more pearl buttons. The skirt, made of the same material as the bodice, was full and boasted a deep flounce. "And you are also looking lovely this evening, Aunt Laura."

"What a sweet child." Aunt Laura wrapped her in a perfumed embrace. "Always saying the nicest things to your old aunt and uncle."

Amelia emerged laughing. "It's easy when I am staying with such kind, handsome hosts. How many guests do you expect to have this evening?"

"Only a small, intimate group for dinner," her aunt answered. "Our son, Benjamin, will be here, along with some new friends of his from college. And a few friends of mine from around town will be coming, with their sons and daughters."

Uncle Francis cleared his throat. "Our dinner table will only accommodate forty guests, so we were quite limited in our selection. But never fear, many more will join us after dinner for the ball."

Aunt Laura nodded. "I wouldn't be surprised if we had upwards of two hundred guests."

"I see." Amelia tried to keep the trepidation from her voice. Forty guests for dinner? And many more later? She hoped she could find enough unexceptional subjects to discuss. Growing up on a remote, self-sustaining plantation had not prepared her for fancy parties or witty dinner conversation. She prayed she would not embarrass her hosts by saying or doing something to mark herself as provincial.

She prayed even more for Tabitha, as she knew what occupied her mind most were those attempting to gain their freedom. . .and her inability to tamp her desire to help.

&

It was easy to see which house belonged to Benjamin's parents from the number of carriages lined up in front, waiting to disgorge their passengers onto the brightly lit stoop. An unexpected feeling of homesickness swept over Jared as he was reminded of parties his own parents and great-aunt had hosted for one or the other of his sisters.

A slave hurried to take their horses. He slid from the saddle, ready to be free of the tired mount he'd rented from a livery stable near the college. His horse had been only slightly faster than walking across town. Benjamin's sleek roan, a stallion he'd raised from a colt, had fought his rider all the way, trying to move at a gait faster than amble.

Jared brushed his coat and straightened his cravat. "I was beginning to think we wouldn't arrive until after the party was over." When he received no response, he looked up to see that Benjamin was halfway up the front steps. With a sigh, he hurried after his friend.

At the front door, he had a moment to take in the scene before being introduced to Mr. and Mrs. Montgomery. He could see no sign of the cousin who was the guest of honor. His gaze lit on a tall, thin girl with curly brown hair who was standing slightly behind Benjamin's mother. That must be her. His dreams of renewing his acquaintance with the girl on the train died a quick death. He could feel his smile slipping, but his sympathy was roused by the obvious discomfort on the young lady's face. He shook hands with Benjamin's parents when introduced then turned to the poor uncomfortable girl.

"This must be the sweet cousin I've heard so much about." He smiled down at her, hoping to ease her discomfort. "Hello, I'm Jared Stuart, Benjamin's roommate at East Tennessee University."

The young lady's mouth dropped open in shock. He wondered at her surprise. She was the guest of honor, after all. She dropped a stiff curtsy as he bowed.

She said nothing, so he cast about in his mind for something to say. "I understand that you are also from Nashville, where my family now resides."

"N–no, sir." Her voice was so low he had to bend forward to make out what she was saying. "I. . .my. . .fa–family is fr–from Knoxville."

Jared frowned. Had he been mistaken? He looked around for Benjamin and spotted his friend some distance away, standing on the edge of a circle of guests. He turned back to the girl, who looked like she'd rather be anywhere than standing next to him. Her hands picked at the material of her skirt, and her gaze flitted from one place to another in the room.

"There you are, Faye." A round-faced woman in a white dress more suited to a debutante than a matron advanced on them. Her brown hair was pulled tightly back from her face and disappeared under a fancy lace kerchief. She turned a smile on Jared, making him feel a little like a rabbit about to become dinner for a mountain lion. "And who is your new friend?"

The girl swallowed twice and shook her head.

Irritation was evident on her mother's face, but she pushed it back and smiled at him. "Hello, I am Beatrice Downing. I see you've already met my daughter."

So this was not Benjamin's cousin. Jared introduced himself again and made his escape as quickly as possible without appearing rude. As the orchestra began tuning up in preparation for the dancing, he strolled over to the knot of people to find Benjamin. Why had his roommate deserted him amongst all these strangers?

The thought was swept away when he saw the person Benjamin was talking to. It was Amelia, his Amelia, the girl who'd captured his imagination and appeared in his dreams with regularity. The girl who'd intrigued him from the first moment he saw her. She was standing at the very center of the group, which he now realized consisted only of young men. These men were acting like idiots, vying for her attention, offering her outrageous compliments, and begging her to dance with them.

Benjamin elbowed his way past a few of them. "I'm afraid I must claim precedence." He bowed over her hand. "It's nice to see you again, Cousin Amelia."

Several of her admirers groaned, and one of them complained loudly that Benjamin was not giving the rest of them a sporting chance.

Her laughing blue eyes made Jared catch his breath. She was adorable. It was no wonder all the young men crowded around her. Even now, he could see a blush of innocence cresting her cheeks. She turned to the young man who had complained. "I am sorry, sir." Her voice held a note of sincerity. "You and your friends have been very kind, but I must give precedence to my family."

"May I call on you tomorrow morning?" The young man's disappointment of a moment ago seemed to have disappeared. "I have a nice carriage. Perhaps I can take you for a ride in the park."

"I appreciate your kindness, Mr. Castlewhite, but I already have another commitment."

A chorus of groans came from the others standing near her, but before they could begin to importune the young lady, Benjamin put her hand on his arm and pulled her away.

"I have a very special friend I'd like you to meet, cousin." He pulled her toward Jared. "Jared Stuart, please meet my cousin, Amelia Montgomery."

"It's you." Her eyes, so deep, so mysterious, shone in the light of the candles. "I never got to say good-bye."

"You two know each other?" Benjamin's shocked gaze met Jared's sheepish one. "Have you been keeping secrets from me?"

"We rode the train together, but we were never properly introduced." Jared raised his spectacles to the bridge of his nose. "Luke Talbot made sure of that."

Benjamin's laughter turned heads in the room. "So that is the reason for—"

"Did you finish *A Tale of Two Cities*?" Jared interrupted Benjamin.

"Yes. I found it very thought provoking."

"Oh no. Spare me." Benjamin looked from one to the other. He rolled his eyes. "Please tell me you are not as bookish as Jared."

"I hesitate to disappoint you, cousin." She answered Benjamin's question, but Jared could feel her gaze on him. "I must confess that Mr. Stuart and I share a love of Charles Dickens."

Jared felt as invincible as a conqueror. "If you're not going to dance with Miss Montgomery, perhaps you will allow me to?"

Amelia glanced at her cousin, a question in her gaze. Benjamin's lips curled slightly. "It doesn't look like I have much choice." He bowed and left them standing on the edge of the ballroom floor.

Jared was finally thankful for the dancing lessons his parents had insisted on. He could partner Miss Montgomery without fear of appearing gauche. He placed one hand at her waist and held out the other for her to grasp before sweeping her into the midst of the other dancers. The feeling of holding her close was heady, but it also caused him to lose the ability to converse. He could feel tension tightening his shoulders as he searched his empty mind for something to say to her. Should he compliment her gracefulness on the dance floor? Or her pretty dress?

"Have you found time to read Mr. Dickens's book, Mr. Stuart?"

"Yes, it was one of my first purchases when I reached Knoxville." Jared felt his tension easing. He could discuss books all day long. "Tell me, were you as horrified as I by the marquis' brutal treatment of those in his power?"

"Yes." Amelia shuddered. "I was not at all disappointed by his demise."

They spent the rest of the waltz discussing the themes of sacrifice and justice explored by Charles Dickens in his novels. So lost was he in their discussion that Jared was surprised when the orchestra stopped playing. He escorted her from the floor, reluctant to give her over to one of her other admirers.

"Good evening, Miss Montgomery."

The deep voice brought Jared's head up. He nearly groaned as he recognized Luke Talbot. He should have known the man would be here.

Talbot's dark eyes were fixed on Amelia. Jared doubted the man had even noticed him. "It's such a pleasure to see you tonight, Amelia."

"Hello, Luke. I'm glad you were able to come." She took her hand from Jared's arm and held it out to Talbot. "You remember Mr. Stuart, whom we met on the train."

"Ah, if it's not the midnight wanderer." Luke's voice was full of mockery. "Where is your nefarious partner?"

Jared could feel heat rising to his cheeks. His ears grew so hot he thought steam might be rising from them. "Mr. Talbot."

Amelia's brow wrinkled. "Must you talk in riddles, Luke?"

"I'm referring to a small matter that occurred at the college last week." Luke's confident smile was turned to Amelia. "It's nothing to concern your pretty head about."

Somehow, Luke had managed to once again place himself between Jared and Amelia. Jared watched helplessly as the self-assured man skillfully drew her away from those who were vying for her attention and led her to a corner of the ballroom next to a large plant.

The next hour passed slowly. Jared partnered several young women, but they all seemed shallow and grasping in contrast to Amelia. He was relieved when Mr. Montgomery sent the orchestra on a break and announced it was time for his niece to receive her special birthday gift.

It took two servants to bring in the tall, sheet-draped gift. They put their burden on the floor at Amelia's feet.

She tugged the covering off to reveal a gilded birdcage hung from an ornate stand. A small tree had been wound around the bars of the cage on one side, its branches providing a perch for the small, black-tailed, gray bird inside.

"It's a mockingbird," explained Amelia's aunt. "We thought you would enjoy hearing its songs. It is quite the mimic, you know, and should fill your room with the most delightful sounds."

Jared watched Amelia's expression as she cooed to the frightened bird. Did she feel as sad as he did to see the poor thing trapped in a cage? She seemed satisfied with the gift. But maybe she was only being polite. He knew politeness was bred in young ladies from an early age. Amelia would never be ungracious about a gift.

Yes, he nodded to himself. That must be the explanation. A wonderful idea came to him. He would come to visit her tomorrow and offer to set the poor bird free for her. Together they could come up with an acceptable excuse to appease her aunt and uncle. He would ask her tonight about visiting and perhaps even hint at his plan. He would have to be careful, but Jared felt he could summon the requisite amount of delicacy and depend on Amelia's astuteness to grasp his intent.

Chapter 6

Amelia laughed, but the sound seemed brittle to her ears. The brightest spot in her evening had been meeting Jared Stuart once again. He was such a fascinating young man. She would like to know him better and wondered if he would come by to visit. Probably not. University students did not have much free time.

But even meeting the interesting Mr. Stuart could not completely turn her mind from the drama occurring in her relatives' stable. She was worried about Tabitha and wondered if she could escape the party for a few minutes to check on her. But the orchestra was still playing, and she still had to dance with one callow boy after another.

Her current partner, Reginald something or other, reeked of pomade and citrus cologne. He had the beginnings of a mustache that unfortunately emphasized his overlong nose and did nothing to hide a mouthful of crooked teeth. He had asked her about the weather and was currently going into great detail about winter and his hopes for an early spring planting.

She wanted to pull away from the poor fellow and escape, especially when she saw Luke Talbot taking his leave of her aunt and uncle. She would have liked to spend more time with him and find out what he'd meant by calling Jared Stuart a midnight wanderer. But it looked as if even that would be denied her. As Reginald pulled her around the floor, she saw Luke's tall form exiting the ballroom. Finally, the dance came to an end, and she escaped her partner.

Aunt Laura was showing off Amelia's birthday gift to a couple of matrons while Uncle Francis bid good night to an older couple. A red-haired young man bearing down on her position at the edge of the dance floor had Amelia turning away quickly. She pretended to trip and faked a groan. She told the approaching suitor she had to repair her dress and hurried to the nearest exit, proud of her quick thinking.

The narrow hall leading to the back door was cool and quiet. The crisp air felt good for a few minutes in contrast to the overheated ballroom, but as she reached to open the door, Amelia wished she'd brought her shawl with her. It was lying across the back of a chair in the ballroom, so she would have to do without it.

The back door opened, and Amelia caught her breath, releasing it all at once when she recognized Tabitha's high cheekbones and simple hairstyle.

"What are you doing here?" Tabitha glanced over her shoulder before stepping into the hallway and closing the door. "You need to get back to your birthday party. Someone will come looking for you."

"I thought you might need help. How are they?"

"Scared, as you can imagine. But safe for the moment." Tabitha looked down at her apron, and Amelia realized it was streaked with dirt and blood.

"Are you hurt?" Amelia looked for signs of a wound.

Tabitha shook her head. "I had to bandage the child."

"Was there a bullet? Did you get it out?" Amelia fired the questions out in quick succession. "Was anyone else hurt?"

Tabitha's smile showed her weariness. "Yes, no, and no."

"You didn't remove the bullet?"

"It went straight through the little boy's arm." She sighed. "It broke a bone on the way."

Amelia winced.

"I've seen worse back home during the harvest." Tabitha's voice sounded weary.

Amelia knew it was true. Accidents and sickness occurred, even on a plantation that was as progressively run as Papa's. She and Mama had spent many an afternoon patching up machete injuries and setting broken bones. But they'd never had to deal with a bullet wound. Mama had showed her how to treat such wounds this summer after Tennessee seceded from the Union. Who knew when the need to treat bullet wounds might arise? Mama believed it was their duty to be prepared for such an eventuality.

"Infection is the biggest danger then." Amelia took Tabitha's hand in her own and squeezed. "I know you did a good job, but I'd like to see the child for myself."

The back door opened again, and the cook and some of the staff filed in one by one. Amelia registered their surprise and fear at her presence.

Tabitha took a few minutes to reassure them before leading Amelia to the stable out back.

The wooden structure was dark and quiet since Uncle Francis had hired a public livery stable down the street for the guests' horses. Amelia stood still for a moment, waiting for her eyes to adapt to the darkness. The night air seemed to absorb sounds and made Amelia feel miles away from the music and dancing of the birthday ball.

Tabitha pursed her lips and whistled, moving her mouth and tongue so that the sound imitated the call of a bird. Another bird warbled some feet ahead of where they stood.

"It's Tabitha. I have a friend with me."

The darkness near the stable door seemed to thicken and became a short, stocky man whom Amelia recognized as the Montgomerys' senior coachman. He waved them inside the stable. Not a word was spoken as he led them to the rear of the building and opened the door of the room used to store saddles and bridles. A kerosene lantern flickered in the corner of the tiny room, highlighting the frightened, dark faces of half-a-dozen occupants.

A muscular man pushed himself from the floor and stood to face Amelia and Tabitha. "What are you doing here?"

His smooth, dark skin stretched across high cheekbones, and intelligence shone from his coffee-brown eyes. His dark clothing looked tattered, but he held himself with all the self-assurance of a prince—chin up, shoulders straight, and legs wide. He crossed his arms across his broad chest and stared at her.

Tabitha bit her lip and looked toward Amelia. "This is Melek, Cook's son. Melek, this is Amelia. She's a friend who knows medicine. She's come to look at Nebo's arm."

"You trust her?" Melek's voice was deep and full of suspicion.

Amelia understood his doubt. Someone who accepted strangers easily would soon be caught by bounty hunters and sold back into slavery or hung for treason. She stepped forward. "I would never betray you or those you are trying to help." She lifted her chin and refused to back down as Melek glared at her. Her heart thumped so hard she thought the people in the room might be able to hear it. What was she doing here? She could be inside dancing the night away instead of standing in a dark barn confronting an angry man. Yet something compelled her to her present actions.

No one spoke for a moment, and the tension built. But then one small sound changed everything. A quiet moan.

Amelia remembered why she had come. She followed the sound to a mound of what she'd taken to be rags. This must be the child.

"Nebo." She whispered the word and was rewarded when a dark head raised up from the ragged coverings.

The other people in the room faded as she knelt next to the young boy and checked his arm, then placed a hand on his hot forehead. "You're a very brave boy."

Amelia pushed herself up from the floor and faced the cook's son. "I have some willow bark in my room. I can send it down to your mother to make a tea for the child. It should bring him some ease and may reduce his fever."

He inclined his head slightly. "Thank you."

She nodded to the others in the room. "Do you need anything else?"

"Only that you will not speak of our presence here."

She straightened her shoulders and stared directly into his eyes. "I would never do such a thing."

"I hope your words are true, not the changing songs of the mockingbird."

A laugh broke out as she thought of the gift she had received for her birthday. "Your secret is safe with me."

❧

A blush heated Amelia's cheeks as she hurried down the hall to a mirror to check her appearance before returning to the ballroom. She groaned at the bedraggled woman who stared back at her.

Tabitha had fixed rosebuds in her hair earlier this evening, but they had slipped toward her right ear. She poked and prodded at the silly things until they once again perched across the center part in her hair. Pulling a pin from another part of her head, she affixed the flowers and nodded briefly. She opened her fan and waved it in front of her hot cheeks. It wouldn't do to return to the guests flushed.

Amelia glanced downward and groaned. Her skirt was a mess. She smoothed it as much as possible without help and picked off a couple of strands of straw that had clung to the material when she knelt to care for poor little Nebo. Amelia would have liked to escape upstairs, change clothes, and go back to the stable to watch over the child. But that option was out of the question. She squared her shoulders and practiced a smile before turning from the mirror.

The orchestra was taking a break, so the people in the ballroom were standing in small groups talking as she made her entrance. She glanced around to find Jared, eager to resume their conversation about Mr. Dickens and his novels.

"Where have you been, cousin?" Benjamin's deep voice tickled her ear.

Amelia jumped slightly. She'd not realized anyone was behind her. She spun around and opened her fan, waving it briskly in front of her face. "I had a slight tear in my flounce." The lie slipped easily between her lips, and guilt made her heart beat faster. She hadn't had much practice at telling untruths. "It took me awhile to get it mended."

Benjamin nodded. He spread a hand to indicate the ballroom. "It seems your ardent swains have given up, and I must say I'm relieved. This is the first time I've gotten to talk to you without being elbowed by a dozen eager suitors."

"Your mother and father have been very kind to introduce me to their friends." Amelia glanced around the room, hoping to find Jared Stuart, but she could not spot his slender figure. "I'm sure everyone was being kind to me because I'm a newcomer."

Her cousin raised an eyebrow and started talking about her taking the town by storm, but Amelia didn't pay him much attention. She wasn't interested in making a splash in Knoxville society.

Where had Jared gone? Had he left for the evening? Disappointment pulled her lips down, but then she straightened her spine. She would not allow the absence of one guest to disturb her. She had more important things to worry about. Like how little Nebo was doing. Amelia could hardly wait for the party to end so she could return to check on the child.

Momentary regret for her involvement with the Underground Railroad was pushed to the back of her mind. What choice did she have? She would never be able to live with herself if she didn't do what she could to make the slaves' flight successful.

Even as she smiled at her cousin and pretended to be flattered by his compliments, part of her mind made a list of necessities to smuggle to the hidden refugees.

Chapter 7

As he walked across the campus, Jared pulled up the collar of his great-coat. The rough wool scratched his chin, but the material kept cold air from reaching his neck. He waved at one of the freshmen as they passed each other but did not stop to talk. It was far too brisk out this morning, and he wanted to get to class in plenty of time to hear the lecture. He lowered his head and trudged onward through the cool, morning air.

"Wait up." Benjamin's deep voice drew his attention from the frosty ground.

Jared looked over his shoulder and let out an exasperated sigh. "I thought you were going to march with the early parade and go to Whitsell's makeup class since you performed so poorly on that last geography exam."

A shrug answered him. Benjamin's mischievous grin appeared, raising Jared's suspicions. "Maybe I wanted to hear the infamous newspaper editor."

"I wish William Brownlow had been able to come." Jared turned back to the pathway leading to North College, the name given to the northernmost building of the university.

Benjamin caught up with him and slung an arm over his shoulder. "I know. But after all the strife he was igniting with the anti-secession views in his newspaper, it's no wonder he had to run for his life. If the people of East Tennessee had gotten their way, you and I would be Unionists instead of Johnny Rebs. Since the occupation of the Confederate Army, things have been tense between the two groups, and his inflammatory pieces weren't helping much."

"Inflammatory pieces?" Jared shook off his friend's arm. "Didn't he have the right to print what he believed?"

"Don't get angry with me." Benjamin raised both his hands as if he was preparing to ward off a blow. "I didn't say there wasn't some truth in his articles, but you read them. In fact you read several of them to me. You have to admit Parson Brownlow doesn't know the meaning of tact."

"It's not a newspaper's job to be tactful. Every newspaper has a duty to inform its readers of the facts. Don't you remember studying Thomas Carlyle's reference to reporters as the Fourth Estate? He believed it was more important than the church, the nobility, or the middle class. Although I disagree with his putting journalists above the importance of the church, I do believe they hold

great power and even greater responsibility, especially now that we are at war."
Jared realized he'd stopped walking. He was going to be late. And he'd wanted
to be early. "I don't want to debate this with you, Benjamin. I'm going to class.
I'm sure Martin Stone has a lot to say about the importance of newspaper publishing. He is the editor of the *Tennessee Tribune*, and it's become the largest
publication since Brownlow's *Whig* was put out of business." He started walking
again.

"You're right." Benjamin matched his pace. "Why do you think I decided to
tag along this morning?"

Jared didn't answer. He reached the steps of North College and bounded up
them two at a time. He pulled open the heavy door and held it open for Benjamin to precede him. "I don't really know why you're here. You've never shown
the least interest in writing."

Benjamin pushed his chest out. "I'm turning over a new leaf. I'm going to
concentrate on writing." He linked his arm through Jared's as they climbed the
stairs to the second floor. "Maybe we can open a newspaper of our own. Isn't
that how your hero Brownlow got started? Then we can publish our own beliefs
and change the world."

A snort escaped Jared. "Don't you remember how you struggled over that
essay last week? I doubt you are eager to become a writer."

"Maybe you could do the writing." Benjamin grinned at him. "And I can
manage the other aspects of the business. Think of how famous we'll be when
our efforts end the war."

Benjamin's words seemed to echo in the wide hallway. Jared was reminded of his belief that words really could make a difference. Excitement buzzed
through him. "The pen is mightier than the sword, right?"

"I don't know about all that," Benjamin answered. "But it's certainly much
lighter to wield."

❧

Amelia sneaked down to the barn before joining her aunt and uncle at the
breakfast table. Little Nebo's forehead was hot, but that was to be expected. She
coaxed him to drink another draught of the willow bark tea Melek's mother, the
cook, had prepared. When she pulled away the bandage covering his arm, she
was relieved to see it was not swollen or draining. She glanced at Melek, who
watched her from one corner of the tack room.

Melek asked, "What is your opinion, little mockingbird?"

"I think he will recover."

"Can he travel today?"

She shook her head as she replaced the dressing. "He needs sleep to fully
recover."

"If he is caught here, his captors will not be concerned about his rest."

Amelia's lips straightened. "Would you rather kill him yourself by moving him too soon?"

Silence was her only answer. She finished her work and looked around. At least six people crowded in the little room. "Does anyone else need my help?"

Declining whispers and headshakes answered her. Amelia pushed herself up from the pallet holding Nebo and closed her bag of medicines.

Melek escorted her from the room. "Thank you."

"I will check back later."

"No. You must stay away, or your family may become suspicious."

His warning echoed in her mind as Amelia hurried to the breakfast room. She seated herself and bowed her head briefly over the plate that was set in front of her. When she had finished blessing her food, she listened to her uncle's latest diatribe.

"I'm afraid women simply don't understand these things." Uncle Francis's comment was not intended to irritate Amelia, but that's the effect it had. Her mouth dropped open, but he continued on, oblivious to her consternation. "Tennessee had no choice but to secede from the Union when Lincoln called for troops to fight against our brothers at Fort Sumter."

A thousand emotional retorts filled her imagination, but Amelia opted for logic. "Then why did Kentucky refuse to follow our lead?"

Uncle Francis shook his head and glanced toward Aunt Laura before answering Amelia's question. "My dear, suffice it to say Kentucky has many reasons to declare neutrality. Politics are often convoluted. Better to ask whether our brothers in Kentucky wish to abolish slavery. The answer would be a resounding no." He folded the newspaper he'd been reading and slapped it against the table for emphasis. "I have little doubt Kentucky will bow to the inevitable before the end of the year and join the Confederacy."

"I'm sure you're right, my dear." Aunt Laura washed a bite of toast down with her cup of tea. "If the war lasts that long. I pray every night it will end before any more young men are killed or wounded. I'm so concerned about our son's eagerness to join the fighting."

"I don't want to see him enlist any more than you do, but Benjamin is a grown man. We raised him to take pride in his heritage." Uncle Francis reached a hand across the table, palm up. "We must allow him to make his own decisions, even if we'd prefer to keep him safe at home."

Aunt Laura placed her hand in his. The look that passed between them was full of love and tenderness.

A rush of empathy filled Amelia. Her aunt and uncle were good people. They were obviously worried about their son's future. And hadn't they welcomed her with open arms? They'd made sure she was introduced to all the right people. She appreciated the lavish ball they'd thrown for her birthday and felt more than a little guilt over helping the escaping slaves when she knew her relatives would never approve of her actions.

Aunt Laura pulled her hand away and turned her gaze to Amelia. Her eyes were suspiciously bright, but she cleared her throat and forced her lips into a shaky smile. "What do you have planned for today, my dear?"

Amelia was thankful for the change of subject. "Luke Talbot is supposed to come over later this morning. We are going riding in the park."

"That Talbot fellow is getting to be a regular visitor." Uncle Francis raised his eyebrows. "I don't know when he has time for studies."

A blush crept up Amelia's throat and heated her face. "Luke has always been like an older brother to me."

"Yes, I thought at first that was his reason for coming over, to make sure you were comfortable in your new surroundings." Aunt Laura's smile widened. "But you have been with us for almost two months now. He must have some other compelling reason to continue his attentions."

"Why would he not?" Uncle Francis winked at his wife. "Our niece is as pretty as a picture and sweet natured to boot. Half the young men in Knoxville are trying to turn her head."

Amelia pressed a hand against her hot cheek. "You're the one turning my head, Uncle. I'm sure the only reason they are interested is because I am a novelty."

"Has your new riding habit arrived, dear?"

"Yes, ma'am. It's lovely." Amelia poured her enthusiasm for the new ensemble into her voice. "I can hardly wait to wear it." She thought of the short braided jacket and white garibaldi shirt that lent the riding outfit a militaristic appearance. The skirt was long and full to allow her freedom, whether she was seated on a horse or walking.

"I'm sure you'll cut quite the figure." Uncle Francis's voice was warm to match his smile. "The other young ladies had better look to their swains, or they are likely to lose them."

Amelia pushed back her chair and ran to hug her uncle. "You are undoubtedly prejudiced, but I appreciate your kind words."

"Go on, child." He laughed and shooed her out of the room.

Her conscience, which had been temporarily silenced by the affection of her aunt and uncle, roared once again as she saw the front page of the paper lying on the table. It was full of advertisements seeking information on runaway slaves and promising huge rewards for their return. As she trudged upstairs, Amelia wondered how she would ever reconcile her world with her morals and her faith.

THE MOCKINGBIRD'S CALL

Tabitha was waiting for her in the bedroom and helped Amelia don her new riding habit. Her admiring gaze met Amelia's in the mirror. "You do look a sight."

A heavy sigh filled Amelia's chest and escaped her in a rush. She was the most hypocritical creature on the planet. Here she was concentrating on new clothes when there was so much she ought to be doing instead.

"Whatever is the matter with you today?"

Amelia turned and faced Tabitha. "How can you stay here with me?"

"I. . .I don't know what you mean."

"Don't be ridiculous, Tabitha. I know you too well. You're smart and pretty. You must have thought about running away."

Tabitha turned away and busied herself with folding Amelia's nightgown and wrapper before storing them in the cedar chiffonier next to her dressing table.

"Don't you want to leave this household and taste freedom for yourself? Don't you want to use the Underground Railroad? Meet someone special? Start a family and know that your children and your children's children will grow up safe and able to determine their own futures?"

Tabitha turned to look at her, a frown marring her wide brow. "Of course I've thought of it." She paused as if considering her words. "Not everyone is as brave as you."

"Brave?" Now it was Amelia's turn to frown. "I'm not brave at all. In fact, I have been wondering all morning why I do nothing to fight against a system that I abhor."

"It was brave of you to risk your reputation to help Melek and the others last night."

"Yes, I risked my reputation. But that's nothing compared to you and the others. You risked your very lives. If I had been caught, my aunt and uncle would have been scandalized—they might have even returned me to my parents. I can understand Cook helping her son. But you and the other slaves will most likely be hung for your involvement if you're discovered aiding Melek."

"We all risk a great deal." Tabitha walked to the birdcage and pulled off its cover. Amelia's mockingbird hopped onto its perch and opened its beak. A song as bright as the sun outside filled the bedroom. "But it was worth the risk to know they will soon live free."

Amelia's breath caught. "That's what I mean. Don't you want to go with them? Don't you want to experience freedom and not live in fear?"

Tabitha giggled. "I don't fear you. Aren't we friends? Didn't you teach me to read? I am content to stay where I am for now."

"I wish I could find my own way to contentment."

Tabitha laughed.

"What?" asked Amelia, hurt that her friend was making light of something that bothered her so.

"I don't know. It seems funny to me that you have so much and yet complain that you are not content." She stopped and looked at Amelia. "We are both blessed. We live in a beautiful house, we have full bellies, and we're surrounded by friends."

"Yes. I know I should be counting my blessings. And yet how can I when I am part of a culture that treats human beings as property?" She pointed to the wide four-poster piled high with feather mattresses and quilts. "Slaves have no more right to demand consideration than that bed over there."

Tabitha's eyes narrowed. " 'Who knoweth whether thou art come to the kingdom for such a time as this?' "

The biblical quote shocked Amelia into silence. Was God planning to use her as He had used Esther? Could she be instrumental in the deliverance of slaves? Hope blossomed in her chest like an early spring. A little voice, her conscience perhaps, whispered that she could not be chosen. People who were chosen were not so riddled with doubt. "I don't have the ear of President Jefferson Davis. I can do very little."

"You may be right." Tabitha looked toward the mockingbird, who was singing through his litany of calls. He whistled, tweeted, squawked, and chirped, mocking the songs of birds from the Acadian flycatcher to the whip-poor-will. "But God can do anything. And He will, whether it is through your efforts or through someone else's."

Amelia pondered Tabitha's statement as she put out some dried fruit and seeds for her pet. She watched the bird pecking at its food and thought about how it was able to imitate so many sounds. Perhaps she *had* been placed in this area for a specific purpose. If that were the case, she needed to be ready to answer God's call, whenever and wherever she could.

Hope bloomed anew, and she smiled as the mockingbird finished eating and began its song once more.

Chapter 8

Jared tapped the end of his pen on his notebook and considered how to end his exposition. He wanted it to be perfect. He would be presenting it at the meeting next week.

He glanced out the window toward the Tennessee River and watched as a boat floated swiftly past the college. Traffic had dwindled over the past months, not because of the weather but because of the war. He didn't know of any blockades along the river, but the Unionists were curtailing trade with Europe by blockading ports along the East Coast. Many cotton growers were already concerned as they watched the demand for their goods diminish. Cutting off funds for the Confederacy was a solid strategy and one that he applauded, as it minimized bloodshed and the need for neighbors to continue fighting and killing each other.

The door to his room swung open, and Benjamin stomped in, so covered by a woolen scarf that Jared had to look twice to identify his roommate. "Is it getting colder?"

"It feels like the rain might turn into snow at any minute." Benjamin pulled off his scarf and shook it several times to remove excess water.

"Hey." Jared held up his arm to shield his paper. "Be careful with that. You're going to ruin all my hard work."

"What are you working on there?" Benjamin pulled off his greatcoat and laid it across the back of a chair.

Jared carefully mopped up the stray droplets threatening his paper. "It's a treatise on the barbarity of slavery."

Benjamin whistled. "I hope you're not planning to give that to Mr. Whitsell. He's not partial to Union sympathizers."

"It's for the Philomathesian Society meeting." Jared stood up and yawned, stretching his arms to work out the kinks from sitting stooped at his desk for too many hours. "Remember I told you I joined and I've been placed on the program. You are still planning to attend, aren't you?"

"Of course." Benjamin slapped him on the back. "I wouldn't miss it for the world."

"And you promise not to laugh, right?"

"Now, I don't remember agreeing to that." Benjamin ducked a fake punch that Jared threw. "Hey, save your moves for the war."

"Where have you been?" Jared sat back down and held his cold hands close to the oil lamp on their shared study desk. The steam pipes bringing heat to their room clanged and hissed, but they did little to dispel the chill in the room.

"Artillery practice."

"Aren't your hands freezing?"

Benjamin nodded. "Why don't we go downstairs and sit by the fire for a while. A bunch of fellows are down there right now. One of them has a brother who's a member of the Fighting 8th." His voice was filled with reverence for the Georgia regiment that had fought hard in the battle of Manassas plain and suffered the loss of many of its veteran soldiers. "His brother has written a long letter, and Tom's promised to read it to whomever wishes to attend."

"I don't think so." Jared was interested in hearing about the war, but he really needed to concentrate on his project. It had to be the best thing he'd ever written. When he read this out loud to his peers, he wanted to see the fire of righteousness enter their eyes. He wanted them to stand and cheer. He wanted to be the hero, challenging their preconceptions and conquering their stubbornness. In short, he wanted to win the war without firing a single shot. "I have some more work to do."

He could feel the weight of Benjamin's gaze on the back of his neck, but Jared refused to turn around. After several seconds, he heard the door open and close.

He breathed a sigh of relief and reread his last sentence. He needed something extraordinary for a rousing finish. In his mind's eye, he could see the scene. The president of the society had told him ladies would be present. Hopefully, none of them would swoon over the power of his words.

He wondered if the editor who'd been at last week's lecture would attend. His heart beat faster. Maybe the man would offer him a job on the spot. How exciting it would be to use his talents to educate and awaken the population. Everyone knew the city had many Union sympathizers. If he was hired on by Mr. Stone, he could really make a difference. It had always been his dream to use his talents for good. This might be his chance.

Jared leaned back in his chair and closed his eyes. He would send a copy of his first newspaper cover to his parents. The great Adam Stuart would be impressed by his son's achievements. And Ma would tell all her friends about her famous son.

He would be working for the downtrodden without having to spend all his time with his nose stuck in dusty law books. He would be the voice of the oppressed, the man whose uncompromising honesty brought peace to his countrymen—all of them, regardless of the color of their skin.

He smiled. All he had to do was finish. He opened his eyes and dipped his pen in the inkwell. The words flowed again.

☙

Amelia glanced over at Luke Talbot, sitting so straight on his stallion. The sunlight made his dark hair shine. She put a hand to her own head and tugged on the red cap that matched the braided coat of her riding habit. "Do you think my kepi is too daring?"

Luke's smile eased her fears. "You look dashing. I'm sure all the other ladies are quite put out that their own hats are so old-fashioned. They will probably rush out to purchase an ensemble exactly like the one you're wearing."

"You are very kind, Luke. You always know just what to say."

"And you are a delightful companion." He tossed her a look full of meaning but was interrupted by someone calling out from a carriage traveling toward them.

The bright yellow landau was occupied by a pair of ladies who looked familiar, although Amelia couldn't quite recall their names. The older lady waved her lace handkerchief at them as the coachman brought the carriage to a stop.

Amelia and Luke also brought their horses to a halt as Amelia searched her memory. She put on a bright smile and waited for the lady to speak. Perhaps it would come to her, or maybe the passengers themselves would give her a clue as to their identities.

"Good day, Miss Montgomery. What a pleasure to see you about." The lady pointed her fan at the young lady sitting opposite her. "Faye was only this morning asking if we could pay you and your sweet aunt a visit."

"My aunt and I would be delighted to receive you Mrs."—Amelia dredged the name up from her memory—"Downing. And I look forward to renewing my acquaintance with Faye."

Mrs. Downing nodded and turned her attention to Luke. "Mr. Talbot, isn't it? I trust you are enjoying your studies."

Luke bowed over the lady's proffered hand and murmured an agreement. "How kind of you to remember me."

"Oh yes." Mrs. Downing glanced toward her daughter. "Faye never forgets a face. And her father and I are staunch supporters of the university you are attending. We have a son who will most likely go to school there one day."

Luke assumed an interested expression and nodded. He did not seem eager to continue the conversation.

Mrs. Downing looked from him to Amelia and smiled. "I should be letting you young people get back to your ride. Faye and I will be stopping by this afternoon. I have something of great import to discuss with you, my dear."

Amelia didn't know how to take the woman's statement or the meaningful look that accompanied it. Perhaps she wanted Amelia to befriend her daughter. Maybe Faye wished to secure Benjamin's attention. She smiled at the younger woman and was rewarded by a smile that made her think of an eager puppy's. That must be it. She watched as Mrs. Downing sat back against the cushioned seat and gestured to the driver.

"The park is growing crowded." Luke's voice brought her attention back to the present. He loosened his horse's reins and moved forward.

As she followed her escort, Amelia took note of the dozen or so carriages trundling along the pathway that wound through tall trees and along the banks of the Tennessee River. They moved slowly to allow for conversation. "Yes. It's amazing. I didn't realize quite how popular this park would be."

Luke glanced at her. "There's no reason why you should. It's not like you've spent any time in society."

Amelia didn't know whether or not she should be offended by his remark. Was Luke calling her a rustic? Yet how could she take offense when that's exactly what she was? The safest thing to do would be to introduce a new subject. "Have you seen my cousin lately?"

"He was on the parade ground yesterday evening." Luke's chin rose a notch. "He's going to make a fine soldier."

"Please don't say anything about that to my aunt. She's fearful he will join the campaign and end up wounded or dead."

"Would she rather he take the coward's way out by not enlisting? I think his parents should applaud his patriotism. He and I both share the desire to fight for our principles. Someday I hope we will be comrades in arms. Your aunt is not a traitor to the Confederacy, is she? I know many such reside in Knoxville, but I had not thought to find them within your family."

Amelia's face grew hot under his stare. She didn't know which way to look. What if Luke knew the truth? She was the one who was helping slaves escape north. Would he also condemn her and the actions she took? The answer was obviously yes. He might even feel it his duty to report her to the authorities.

"I cannot imagine anyone in my family sympathizing with the abolitionists." The lie tripped off her tongue easily, and her conscience stung her for a brief moment. Then the thought came to her that she had to deceive Luke or lose her ability to help those poor men and women. "Uncle Francis supports the rights of states to make their own decisions without federal interference."

"Quite right. As do I." Luke reached over and captured her hand in his. "And I know you and I agree on the issue of slavery."

Luke had no idea how she felt about slavery. He had just confessed his desire to fight for the South in support of his principles and expressed his disdain for "traitors to the Confederacy." He must believe she viewed slave labor with the same complacency as her father. Was it wrong for her to be relieved he had accepted her lies? Again her conscience prodded her, but this time, Amelia easily smothered it. She hadn't meant to become involved with the Underground Railroad, but since she had, it was essential that she mask her true feelings.

Luke's mount reared onto his hind legs. Amelia watched in admiration as he kept his seat and brought the horse under control. He looked so capable and strong. She might not agree with him in all areas, but she knew Luke Talbot was a good man. Her heart warmed as she saw her lifelong friend in a different light. He was no longer the mischievous young man who'd teased and played with her while their parents visited in the parlor downstairs. Luke was a grown man, and one who could probably set female hearts fluttering all over Knoxville. Gratitude for his attention warmed her.

She sent him a challenging look as he subdued his horse. "Perhaps we should try a gallop." Without waiting for an answer, she clucked at her mare.

Luke was only a second behind her, his stallion's longer legs eating up the distance between them. Then they were riding neck and neck, their horses straining to reach the line of trees in the distance.

Amelia's kepi caught the wind and lifted from her head, so she had to draw in the reins and drop out of their impromptu sprint. She turned her mare's head around and spotted the red cap on the ground some feet back. She would have to remember to ask Tabitha to secure it more tightly in the future.

Hooves thundered behind her. Amelia looked over her shoulder to see Luke racing to the rescue. The wind teased at her hair as he raced past her and dismounted with alacrity. He scooped up the cap and tucked it under one arm. Then he reached for her and swung Amelia out of her saddle, his hands encircling her waist.

Luke was ever mindful of decorum and released her as soon as her feet touched the ground. So why did she feel so breathless? She gazed up into his brown eyes and wondered if the gleam was caused by his usual kindness. Or was there something warmer in his expression? And if there was, how did she feel about that development?

She and Luke had grown up as close as siblings, but if she was reading him right, the emotion he was currently feeling had nothing to do with brotherly affection. Unsure of herself, Amelia stepped back and lowered her gaze to the ground.

"I. . .Amelia, I must admit to an ulterior motive in bringing you out today."

That brought her gaze up again. He looked normal now, the Luke she'd grown up with, the Luke she felt comfortable with. "What is it?"

He cleared his throat. "There is a function at the college next Saturday evening, and I wondered if you would like to attend. . .with me."

"I would be most flattered to have you as an escort, Luke, as long as my aunt and uncle agree."

"Of course." He ran a finger under the collar of his shirt. "It's a rather special affair, a meeting of the university's literary society."

"That sounds nice. Will there be dancing?"

He nodded. "But before that, several writers will take turns reading their works to the audience. My name is on the program."

Amelia clapped her hands together. "That's wonderful. I never knew you were a writer. You must be quite talented."

"I don't know about that. But my literature professor has been very encouraging." Luke's humility was as unexpected as it was pleasant.

Amelia had always thought of him as being self-assured, as in control of his life as he'd been over his mount a little while ago. She was beginning to see the man in a whole new light. One that opened her eyes to possibilities she had never imagined before.

Chapter 9

J ared checked his appearance in the mirror one last time.

Benjamin slapped him on one shoulder. "You look quite dapper."

"How does my cravat look?" He patted the starched cloth and turned so his roommate could judge. He held his breath as Benjamin's gaze traveled upward from his feet, checking every detail.

"Not too shabby." Benjamin nodded. "You'll do well."

Jared let his breath escape in a *whoosh*. He was ready if Benjamin pronounced him satisfactory. He reached for his papers. "Are you ready?"

Silence answered his question. Jared returned his attention to Benjamin. His roommate had discovered a sudden interest in his bed pillow.

"Benjamin?"

"I can't come." Benjamin looked up, an unreadable expression on his face.

Jared wanted to protest. His closest friend wouldn't be there? "I thought you wanted to open a newspaper with me."

"I know, I know." Benjamin jammed his hands into his pants pockets. "And I do. But I just don't feel like getting out. It's been a hard afternoon."

"What do you mean?" Thoughts about the evening were whisked away as Jared considered Benjamin's words. Several things that he'd ignored while working on his magnum opus came to mind now. The amount of time his roommate had spent on the parade grounds. The studies he was ignoring.

As he'd wrestled with phrasing and grammar, a part of Jared had wondered how Benjamin ever expected to catch up with his classwork, but he'd been far too busy to ask many questions. Now guilt attacked him. What kind of friend was he?

"I've been down to Gay Street."

Benjamin's words did not sink in at first, but then he knew. His friend had visited the enlistment office.

"Did you enlist?" The three words fell between them.

Benjamin pulled his hands from his pockets. He went to the window and stared out at the bleak winter evening. Jared walked over to him and gazed at the bare limbs of the trees scattered across the campus. The silence in the room was broken as a loud banging came from the steam pipes that brought heat into the room. Jared waited. However much time it took, he would wait to hear what

Benjamin needed to tell him.

"No. I didn't enlist." Benjamin's voice was so hushed that Jared had to lean toward him.

"You didn't enlist? Why did you go there then?"

"I wanted to enlist. But I kept hearing my ma's sobs and seeing the look of disappointment on Pa's face. So I just hung around for an hour." He looked up, a deprecating grin turning up the corners of his mouth. "How's that for a lame story?"

Jared punched his upper arm. "Sounds more like a son who honors his parents' wishes."

"Trust you to put a good face on it." Benjamin glanced at him. "You don't think I'm a coward?"

"You? A coward?" Jared didn't have to fake the shock he felt. "I think your biggest problem is a tendency to leap before you look. You and I are only freshmen. We should stay in school as long as we can."

"But what if the South wins the war before we graduate? What if we miss our one and only chance to fight for our country?"

Jared could have made several answers. The words burned his throat. Words about the evils of slavery and the overwhelming odds aligned against the Confederate states. But now was not the time to go into that. They could debate the reasons for secession at some other time. They had discussed the subject in the past and would undoubtedly do so again. "I don't think that's going to happen. President Lincoln seems determined to keep fighting for quite some time."

"Well in that case, maybe I do have time to come to your poetry reading." Benjamin pushed an elbow into Jared's side.

Instead of protesting Benjamin's characterization of his serious paper, Jared laughed. "That's good. But you'd better get dressed. There's not much time, and I want to—"

"Get there early." Benjamin finished the phrase for him, and his laughter joined Jared's.

Optimism buoyed Jared. It was going to be a great evening.

❧

Amelia settled into the carriage and touched the fur collar of her pelisse with a gloved hand before burying her cheek into its softness. She smiled at Tabitha, her chaperone for the evening with Luke. "Are you warm enough?"

Tabitha nodded and helped Amelia arrange a blanket over both of their laps. Amelia was so excited she could barely contain herself. She'd never been to a literary society reading and wondered if she would make any new friends this evening. She hoped so. She loved literature and would appreciate having friends with similar tastes.

Luke clambered in and settled in the opposite seat, his back to the coachman. He looked especially handsome this evening, his dark hair curling onto his high forehead. She would be the envy of the other women in attendance.

"You look lovely, Amelia." His deep voice filled the tiny space. He reached forward and took one of her hands in his. "I am so glad you were able to join me."

"Me, too." She pulled her hand free when Tabitha cleared her throat. The coach moved forward, and she settled back for the ride across town. "Please tell me what to expect tonight, Luke."

She sensed rather than saw his smile in the dark carriage. "It should be interesting. Several of the freshmen have written essays. They were visited by one of our local newspaper editors, and I understand that he inspired the whole class."

"Will my cousin be there?"

"His name is not on the program, but I believe he may attend since his roommate, the young man we met on the train, will be presenting a work. And I've already told you that I'll be reading a poem."

Amelia heard the rustle of paper.

"Would you care for a preview?"

"I would be delighted, but how can you read in this gloom?"

A chuckle answered her. "I have been reading it again and again ever since you agreed to come with me. I wanted to impress you by reciting it from memory."

"Then perhaps I should wait and be impressed with the rest of those in attendance."

"As you wish." The paper rustled once more as Luke apparently tucked it into his coat pocket.

"Are you going home for Christmas?" Amelia was excited about the upcoming holiday even though it was still two months away. She and Aunt Laura had already begun to consider the decorations. Of course, it was too early to bring in a Christmas tree, but they had already begun stringing berries and raisins for garlands and stitching bits of lace and ribbon to baskets that would be filled with fresh fruit for the holiday. They had pored over decorating ideas from previous issues of *Godey's Lady's Book* and discussed several intriguing projects.

"I don't know. There's talk of the school closing early because of the war."

Amelia could feel her eyebrows rising. She had not heard of this. "I didn't know. But the atmosphere in Knoxville does seem to be getting more tense. Yesterday when Tabitha and I were shopping for holiday ribbon, we saw soldiers marching through the streets. They seemed so serious, all stepping in time and holding their weapons on their shoulders. I am planning on attending a rally tomorrow."

"I don't know if that's wise, Amelia." She could hear the hesitation in Luke's voice. "It might be a good idea for you to plan to return to your parents. I don't think things are nearly so unstable in Nashville. Knoxville is a target for both sides because of the two rail lines that intersect here."

She didn't know how to answer him. She doubted her papa would welcome her return. He'd made it very clear that she was to stay in Knoxville for at least a year. She was saved from coming up with a reply by their arrival at the college.

Luke opened the door and disembarked before turning to help her as she followed him. She stepped aside, expecting him to offer the same assistance to Tabitha, but Luke slipped a hand under her arm and led her away from the carriage. "What about our chaperone?" Her voice gently chided him for his insensitivity.

"She'll be fine."

Amelia halted, forcing Luke to do the same. "I insist."

An exasperated sigh answered her, but he let go of her arm and turned back to help Tabitha alight. His grip was not as gentle when he returned to her, but Amelia didn't care. She would not stand for her friend to be treated with disdain, and if Luke didn't like it, he was not the man for her.

❧

Jared rose from the folding chair and bounded up the steps to the stage. He cleared his throat and looked at the sheet of paper in his hands. His palms were sweating, and his spectacles slipped. He settled them more firmly on the bridge of his nose and cleared his throat again. A quick prayer for courage resulted in a measure of confidence. It was time for his star to rise.

He began to read, his voice rising and falling as he described the injustices of slavery—the horror of being owned by another, the tragedy of losing children and spouses who were sold to other owners, and the indignity of having no control over the least aspects of one's daily life. The audience grew restless as he described life from a slave's point of view. He was not surprised. Most of the people in attendance tonight, if not all, owned slaves. But he would not apologize for his words. They were true. Harbingers of the future. He prayed some of those in the audience would be open to his message.

When he finished, the applause could only be described as sparse. He returned to his chair and relaxed, glad to have his public reading finished. Now he could look forward to some lively dialogue about the issues he'd raised.

The next student headed for the stage, but Jared was still energized from his experience on the stage so he barely heard a word. He considered the audience. He had not been surprised to see Luke Talbot in attendance. The man was a member of the society. But his companion had shocked Jared.

Amelia Montgomery. He'd spotted her as soon as he reached the stage.

Who could not see her effervescent beauty even in a roomful of people? She would stand out in any crowd. Yet she seemed so kind and unassuming. He thought of their conversation during her birthday celebration. During that admittedly brief interlude, she had managed to make him feel as if he was the very center of her attention.

Did she and Luke have an understanding? It seemed likely since he was her escort once again.

As he was about to turn away, she glanced up and their gazes locked. Jared could hardly remember to breathe. Then Luke leaned over her and whispered something in her ear. The distraction made her look away, and Jared realized in that moment that he had better stay far away from Amelia or risk losing his heart.

The readings ended. An orchestra took over the stage, and the audience began to mill around, renewing acquaintances and discussing the presentations. The floor was cleared of the chairs for dancing.

Jared didn't plan it, but somehow he ended up shoulder to shoulder with Amelia. He knew it when her perfume tickled his senses. He tried to move away, but the press of the crowd prevented it.

"Good evening, Mr. Stuart." Her voice was calm, self-assured. "I enjoyed your essay immensely."

Jared could feel his ears heating up. They were probably as red as hot coals. He noticed Amelia's fuchsia-colored dress. Several satin ribbons scattered across it, along with rosettes that matched the color of her velvet gown. He noticed that the sleeves were wide and full at the elbows but wrapped snugly around her slender wrists. She was wearing a double strand of pearls, and a pearl comb was perched at the crown of her head.

"Hello." It was the only word he could squeeze out of his tight throat. Again, he wondered what she was doing here. Benjamin hadn't mentioned anything about her attendance. Why hadn't he warned Jared about the possibility? Hadn't he visited with his family last weekend? Jared could distinctly remember turning down an invitation to join him for Sunday dinner. Perhaps he should have accepted, as he would have at least been prepared to see her tonight.

"Yes, who would have thought of taking the viewpoint of the slaves?" Luke Talbot's words had a rough edge that bespoke his disdain.

Jared could feel his ears again. They were going to burst into flame at any moment.

"I thought it was inspired." Amelia's eyes, as blue and clear as the summer sky, caught his attention and held it. "You are a talented writer." He felt her hand on his arm.

He wished he was as good with the spoken word. "Thank you." Jared knew he needed to get away from this corner of the room. Get away from her so he could think again. "Would you care to dance?" Had those words come from his mouth?

Apparently so, as Amelia nodded. "I'd love to."

Jared led her to the center of the dance floor. "I didn't have any idea you would be in attendance this evening." He winced. He sounded callow. Next he would be talking to her about the weather.

"I am so glad I was able to hear your piece especially, Mr. Stuart." Her smile warmed his ears once more.

"I cannot imagine that you agree with anything I wrote."

She bit her lip for a moment, looking adorable as she considered how to answer him. "Whether I agree is not the point. I doubt you intended your words to be heard only by abolitionists. Wasn't it your intention to make all your listeners think of slavery in a different light?"

She understood. Jared could no longer feel the floor beneath his feet or hear what anyone else said. The whole of reality shrank down to the two of them. They might have been standing in the middle of a busy street or on the moon. Her expression told him she was speaking from the heart. He would have been happy if the moment could have continued for an eternity. Just the two of them, so close in body, mind, and spirit.

The orchestra ended the song, but Jared did not want to let go of her. He hated to surrender Amelia to her escort, but the rules of society demanded it. She stepped back from the circle of his arms. Was she blushing? His heart pounded. He opened his mouth to say something but halted when Luke walked up and whisked her away. She glanced over her shoulder at him once before being swallowed up by the crowd.

He had no memory of leaving the dancers, but he must have because he found himself standing in a group of his classmates. They were discussing the war, of course. It was the topic that seemed uppermost in everyone's mind. Jared smiled or frowned as necessary, but his thoughts were still on the way Amelia had reacted to him, the way she had fit so well in his arms.

"It looks like the evening met your expectations." Benjamin clapped him on the shoulder. "I saw you dancing with my cousin. Should I inquire as to your intentions?" A laugh followed his teasing remark.

Jared shook his head. "I doubt she remembers who I am."

"I don't know about that. She seemed content to let you lead her around the dance floor, yet I noticed that few others of our friends got the same honor."

"Luke danced with her several times." Jared could have bitten his tongue off as soon as the words were out of his mouth. He escaped the ballroom, Benjamin's knowing laughter trailing him. As he gathered his hat and coat, he wondered how he could have been so foolish as to let anyone know he'd been watching Amelia that closely.

Lanterns from the guests' coaches lighted the pathway to the dormitory. Jared relived the evening in all its glory—the applause, the accolades of his classmates and professors, and the admiration in a certain pair of blue eyes. Had he found his calling? Had God given him the talent and opportunity to make a difference?

Pushing back his confused feelings about the beauteous Amelia, words of thanksgiving and praise filled his heart, and his feet seemed to have grown wings. He could hardly wait to get back to his room and begin writing his next opus.

Chapter 10

Amelia gathered her medicines together and headed downstairs. Tabitha had told her that another group of slaves had been brought in and were resting in the barn as before, and she knew she would not be able to get a wink of sleep until after she checked on them. She pushed her bedroom door open and crept down the stairs, thankful for the dim glow of a lantern that showed her the way to the kitchen.

All the dishes and leftover food had been stored, and the fire was banked for the evening. She shivered and pulled her cloak tighter around her shoulders. A squeaky noise behind her made Amelia freeze and hold her breath. After a moment passed without further noise, she eased forward once again.

She opened the back door and slipped through it, picking her way along the path to the barn. She'd been out here several times in the past weeks, even though she had originally hoped her work with runaway slaves would be done after Melek took that first group out of town. But that had only been the beginning for Amelia, the agent Melek now referred to as the Mockingbird.

She stopped outside the door and pursed her lips. Her first attempt at a whistle failed miserably, sounding more like a hissing snake than a bird. Amelia licked her lips and tried again. There! That was more like it. She was quite proud of the liquid sound she produced.

After a moment, the barn door opened, and the old coachman, whose name she had learned was Tom, grinned at her and beckoned her inside. He led the way to the tack room. "We've a tired group tonight. They been running for days without much sleepin'."

Amelia went inside, and her heart melted at the sight that met her eyes. A couple about her own age cowered against the wall. The young man had a protective arm about the girl. He watched Amelia with wary eyes.

"I came out here to help you." She set her bag of medicines down on the floor and dropped to her knees beside them. "Let me see your feet."

She unwound several layers of dirty cloth from the young woman's feet, dismayed to see the cuts and bruises on them. It was a good thing she had found a merchant who sold tincture of iodine. She soaked a clean length of cotton in the solution and gently cleaned the young woman's feet. Tearing several new lengths from a discarded sheet she had rescued last week before it could be thrown away, she rewrapped the slave's feet before turning to her companion.

"You have a gentle touch." The young man's eyes were not nearly as wary as they had been before.

"I need to do the same for you."

He nodded and stretched out his feet, and Amelia began the process again. When she finished, she drew out some of her precious willow bark. "If you chew on this while you are walking, it should ease your pain."

The young woman reached out her hand and took the bark from Amelia before settling back into the curve of her husband's arm.

"Where are you from?"

"Al—"

"It's safer if you don't know too much, miss." Tom the coachman interrupted the girl before she got more than the first syllable out.

Amelia's cheeks heated as she glanced at the old man. "You're right. It's not the time for polite conversation."

Amelia gathered up her supplies, pointing to the bloody rags she had removed. "Those should be burned. They are too dirty to be of use to anyone."

"I'll take care of it." The old man held open the door to the tack room. "It's time for you to get back to the big house."

It was nearly dawn by the time Amelia divested herself of her clothing, her mind on the frightened pair hiding out back. They had so far to travel on their poor feet. She hoped her ministrations would help speed their journey. As she drifted toward sleep, Amelia prayed for their safety and for the courage to continue helping those like them.

&

Sunshine warmed Amelia's face as she stood amongst the crowd. She was frustrated at not being able to see the foot soldiers, but at least she could hear the cadence of the drums and the reedy notes of the fifer. The mounted cavalry looked smart in their matching, double-breasted frock coats, gray in color with gold buttons and red silk sashes. Given the way Luke had talked last week, he would soon be one of them. She could imagine him sitting proudly astride, his shoulders straight and his red forage cap, so like the one that went with her own riding suit, perched on his dark hair.

The people around her seemed to be caught up in the patriotism of the day. They cheered and waved. Some of the ladies even blew kisses to the men in the parade. The horses were barely past her location in the crowd when Amelia spied two flags—the first was the Bonnie Blue flag, a single white star in a field of brilliant blue. Following it was the official flag of the Confederacy, a bright white stripe separating two red stripes and a circle of stars inside the blue corner on its upper left side. Luke had told her a different flag, the Southern Cross, led soldiers on the battlefield. The colors of this flag reminded her of the Union flag, but the differences it symbolized opened a pit of despair in her stomach.

She supposed the soldiers must be marching behind the flags, but all she could see were the tips of their bayonets. A young boy wove in and out of the crowd, following the progress of the soldiers. A miniature drum was slung over his shoulders, and he beat a tempo to match that of the parade drummers. She wondered where his parents were. If they were not careful, the child was likely to become the youngest member of the army, judging from his fervent expression.

"Miss Montgomery, Miss Montgomery." The sound of someone calling her name took Amelia's attention away from the youngster. She turned and recognized Mrs. Downing.

"I am so happy to find you, Miss Montgomery." Mrs. Downing was out of breath from pushing her way through the crowd of onlookers. "Your aunt said you had planned to attend the parade."

"Hello, Mrs. Downing." She looked behind the older lady, searching for Faye, but could not spot the tall, spare girl. "Where is your daughter today?"

"She is. . .indisposed this morning." Mrs. Downing looked around them. "Can we go somewhere to talk?"

"I am sorry to hear that." Amelia gestured Tabitha toward them. "Where would you like to go?"

"There's a house about a block from here which is being used as a church and for other, more important purposes." Mrs. Downing's glance was pregnant with a meaning that escaped Amelia. She grasped Amelia's arm and began pulling her away from the other spectators.

Mrs. Downing loosened her grip as the crowd thinned. The soldiers were more than a block away by now, the sound of their marching feet fading into the distance. Finally Mrs. Downing, Amelia, and Tabitha came to a street corner. A two-story frame house stood there, its windows boarded up, its doors scarred as though from fire or assault. Their guide hesitated before going up to the door, and she looked around once more before turning and gesturing for Amelia and Tabitha to follow her. "Come on. We'll be able to talk inside." She pushed open the front door.

Amelia heard it squeal in protest. "Whose house is this?"

"The original owners are not important. The only thing that matters is that it was donated to the free blacks they had employed and now has new life as a church." Mrs. Downing led them past an empty parlor and several closed doors toward the back of the house where the original kitchen would be. She pushed open the door.

The sight that met Amelia's eyes caused her to halt. Several battered trunks sat on the floor, their lids open. They were filled with clothing—skirts, trousers, shirts, and hats. The far wall was lined with shoes and boots, neatly arranged in order of size. Jars of preserved foods lined the shelves, and a pile of blankets lay neatly folded on a large table. Nothing was new, but the room held more items than any mercantile she had ever shopped.

Her gaze met Tabitha's in wonder before she turned back to Mrs. Downing. "What kind of place have you brought us to?"

The older woman's wave encompassed the items. "It's a storeroom. It has been filled by people who disagree with the position of our great state, people who are sympathetic to the plight of slaves, people who believe slavery must end if our country is to survive."

Amelia could feel Mrs. Downing's gaze on her. "How do you know I will not turn you in to my aunt and uncle?"

"Because you are the Mockingbird, the person responsible for helping more than one group of slaves escape capture."

A tall black man stepped through the servants' entrance into the kitchen. He was dressed in a loosely cut, brown frock coat, fawn-colored trousers, and a brown silk brocaded waistcoat.

Amelia did not recognize him until Tabitha breathed his name. "Melek!"

He nodded to her before turning to answer Amelia's question. "Mrs. Downing is a friend of mine. I asked her to bring you to me." He then turned his smile on Tabitha. "You are surprised to see me, little one?"

Tears pooled in Tabitha's eyes as she nodded. "You look so. . ."

He tugged at the cuff of his sleeve. "*Civilized* is the word I think you seek."

"I was going to say handsome." Tabitha put a hand to her mouth, apparently as shocked as Amelia at her forwardness.

Amelia watched as his smile broadened. He bowed over Tabitha's hand. "These clothes are what I wear when I am not in the South. But when I leave this church, I will once again don the ragged clothing of a slave."

"It matters not to me what clothing you wear."

Feeling like an eavesdropper, Amelia cocked her head toward the front of the house, and she and Mrs. Downing left the couple alone.

"I'm sorry there's no furniture." Mrs. Downing stepped into the parlor and looked around. "It's been sold for clothing, food, and money for the railroad."

"Tell me what you do."

Mrs. Downing chuckled. "They call me a stationmaster. We take all of our terms from the railroad business. Melek is a conductor. He infiltrates plantations and talks to the slaves, offering them his guidance if they wish to escape. I find safe shelter for groups who come through this part of Tennessee."

Amelia watched her closely, admiration overcoming her for this kind woman with unsuspected depth of purpose. "But how do you do it? How do you hide your true nature all the time? Does your family know what you're doing, or do you have to lie to them?"

"I was raised to believe people were equal regardless of the color of their skin, but the man I married does not share my views." She turned from Amelia and walked toward the empty fireplace. "He's a good man, but he does not understand his wife's liberal ideas. So we agree to disagree. I do what I can, provide money and shelter when necessary. He may have some idea about what is going on, but he doesn't ask questions."

Was Amelia looking at her own future? Her heart was heavy. She could not imagine such a thing, yet what was the alternative? Was she destined to be like the mockingbird Melek compared her to, changing her tune all the time to hide her true feelings? She could not turn a blind eye to the injustices around her, but what did God expect of her? What was a conscientious Christian supposed to do?

"I've been working with the railroad for almost two decades now." The older woman sighed. "It's become a way of life for me. Sometimes it does become a heavy burden, but then I receive a message from a grateful family who has been reunited through the railroad's efforts, and I realize how important this mission is."

Amelia listened as Mrs. Downing described the people, young and old, who had passed this way over the years. How could she begrudge sacrificing a few of her comforts for such a worthy goal? The answer was simple. She could not. No matter what it cost, the Mockingbird would have to continue her work.

❧

Jared's stomach grumbled as he sat and listened to the professor droning on and on about Latin declensions. As much as he enjoyed language arts, he could not find anything of value in learning a language that was seldom used for anything other than scientific purposes. Most classical texts had been translated to English, so why should he bother to fill his head with unnecessary drivel? His conscience pricked him at the thought. The university president didn't think it was drivel. Who was Jared to decide which classes were useful?

Another grumble. He glanced around to see if anyone else could hear his protesting stomach. He should have found time for breakfast this morning. But after chapel, he'd been struck with inspiration and hurried back to his room to jot the ideas down before classes started.

Finally, Professor Wallace pulled out his pocket watch. "If there are no questions, we will end today's lesson."

Jared gathered his papers, careful not to let the professor see the drawings he'd created when he should have been taking notes. He folded them into his textbook and put his pencil in the pocket of his waistcoat.

"Be prepared for a test on Friday," the old man continued, raising his voice above the noise of the students who were preparing to leave.

A collective groan answered his announcement. Mr. Wallace grimaced and turned toward the blackboard, erasing his work in preparation for his next class.

Jared hurried out of the room with the other students, intent on reaching the dining hall and appeasing his stomach.

"Mr. Stuart." A voice called his name, halting Jared's headlong descent down a flight of stairs.

His eyes opened wide. He recognized the short, large-bellied man who stood on the second-floor landing. Martin Stone! The editor of the *Tennessee Tribune*. And he had called Jared by name! Excitement replaced his hunger.

"Mr. Stuart," the editor repeated. "I'm glad I found you." He held out a pudgy hand and grasped Jared's, pumping it enthusiastically. "I have a proposition for you. Actually a job, if you're as talented as your professor tells me."

Jared's stomach clenched. A real newspaper editor wanted to talk to him? It was a dream come true. The answer to a prayer. He could feel the grin that stretched his mouth wide. "You want to hire me?"

Mr. Stone returned his grin. "Is there somewhere we can go to talk?"

"I was on my way to the dining hall. Would you care to join me there?"

A shake of his head made Mr. Stone's chin wobble. "We need some privacy."

Jared was torn. His belly was as empty as a pauper's purse. But he desperately wanted to hear whatever it was Mr. Stone had to say. His stomach protested loud and long, warming his ears.

Mr. Stone clapped him on the shoulder. "It sounds like you do need to eat. Perhaps you will let me take you to a small establishment a few blocks from here."

They exited the building and walked briskly away from the college. Jared tried to start a conversation, but Mr. Stone was winded from the exercise, so he contented himself with waiting. They reached the restaurant and took off their coats as they were enveloped in warm air and delicious scents. The restaurant was busy, but Mr. Stone managed to procure them a table tucked away in a far corner.

"I recommend the stewed beef with macaroni." The older man tucked a napkin into the collar of his shirt and beamed at Jared. "Not only is it delicious, it is a prompt meal."

Jared nodded to the waiter, who complimented them on their selections before marching toward the kitchen.

"Mr. Stuart," the man began, his voice hushed, "your literature professor forwarded to me a piece you wrote recently."

"Do you mean my treatise—'The Pernicious Effects of Enslavement in the United States'?"

"Yes, it was an outstanding work." Mr. Stone continued for several minutes. "Almost on the same level as Harriet Beecher Stowe's book."

Pleasure at the man's compliments filled Jared's chest. "Thank you, sir. My parents have always been avid protectors of the rights of others. They taught me to put myself in the place of those less fortunate. When I began to consider how it would feel to be owned by another human being, the words seemed to flow."

"If only more people could share your vision."

The waiter returned with two steaming plates of food and a loaf of dark bread. As soon as Mr. Stone blessed their food, Jared dug in with gusto. Silence reigned at the table while both men satisfied their appetites.

"I'd like to offer you a job." Mr. Stone held up a hand to stop Jared from responding immediately. "You need to understand exactly what I'm talking about before you make your decision. I'm not talking about the *Tennessee Tribune*. This is a different paper, one my conscience has prodded me into starting. I have named it *The Voice of Reason*. It will be distributed throughout the city, and I hope it will garner attention from those who oppose the institution of slavery. The work is sometimes dangerous, as it does not support the Confederate mandate. I am too old and unfit for soldiering, so I want to use the strengths God blessed me with to make a difference."

"I want to do it." Jared inserted his statement when Mr. Stone stopped to untuck his napkin and lay it next to his plate.

"The pay will be negligible," Mr. Stone warned. "Probably not even enough for room and board."

"The university feeds and houses me."

Mr. Stone smiled. "Ahh, the enthusiasm of youth. It is exactly what my new venture needs. But make no mistake, this is serious business. If we are caught, you will likely be arrested or fined."

Jared heard the warnings, but his mind was busily crafting a new article for Mr. Stone's newspaper. The opportunities were endless. He wanted to get a message across to the families of Knoxville. His fingers itched for paper and his fountain pen. He could see the title spread across the front page of the newspaper. Like Benjamin Franklin, he would write stories that he prayed would live on long after he died. "I'm your man, Mr. Stone."

"That's wonderful news, my boy. Can you have something for me next Wednesday? If that's too soon, I can see about delaying the next edition until the following week."

Jared took a deep breath. "I will have something written by then."

"Excellent."

He wrung Mr. Stone's hand with enthusiasm, realizing he had finally become a man.

Chapter 11

Bumps and thumps pulled Amelia from her dreams. She tried to ignore the noise, snuggling deeper into the warmth of her quilts and squeezing her eyes shut.

She could make out the sound of Aunt Laura asking someone a question. A deeper voice answered. Then footsteps on the stairs. What was going on?

Giving up on slumber, she pushed back the covers and slid her feet into the slippers at the edge of the bed. She pulled her wrapper on and went to the fireplace, reaching for the bellows used to coax heat from the dying embers.

A soft knock on the door was followed by Tabitha's entrance. "I thought all that noise might have woken you up."

"What's going on?"

"It's Master Benjamin. They say his school has closed on account of the war, and he's come home to stay."

Amelia's heart dropped as she realized that Tabitha's news likely meant Jared Stuart would be leaving Knoxville. Would he think to stop by and visit before going home? "I have to get dressed right away, Tabitha."

Tabitha went to one of the clothing trunks and drew out a red and black plaid dress while Amelia bathed her face and hands from the washbowl. The cold water on her cheeks chased away the last remnants of sleep.

It seemed like hours before she was fully dressed from head to toe, but the pendulum clock hanging next to the window indicated only some forty minutes had passed. Finally she was ready, her hair pulled back in a simple knot Tabitha secured with a red ribbon. She checked her collar and cuffs to make sure they were spotless and flew down the steps to the breakfast room. One glance inside, however, and her heart fluttered inside her chest like a startled bird.

He was here! Sitting at the table and partaking of breakfast like a member of the family. Jared must have ridden with Benjamin.

Amelia drew in a deep breath, clasped her hands in front of her, and entered with all the aplomb she could manage. "I see we're entertaining guests this morning." Amelia addressed her aunt, who was sipping a cup of tea.

"Yes, my dear." Aunt Laura put the delicate china in its saucer and waved a hand toward Jared and Benjamin.

Uncle Francis emerged from behind his newspaper. "It seems the university ended their semester early because of the war." He frowned at Benjamin. "Not that I liked your attendance there anyway. The place has turned into a hotbed for Unionist sympathizers and abolitionists."

"Now, Francis." Aunt Laura raised an eyebrow. "Don't get yourself upset. The school is closed, and the boys are here safe and sound."

Amelia sat down opposite Jared and Benjamin. "Hello, cousin, Mr. Stuart."

Benjamin rolled his eyes, apparently inviting her to share his disdain for his father's pronouncement.

She bit back a giggle and turned her attention to Jared. "How long will you be staying with us before you must return to Nashville, Mr. Stuart?"

"It's likely to be awhile. The trains are not running presently."

"What?"

Jared glanced to Benjamin, who confirmed his statement with a nod. "Someone burned all the railroad bridges around town. I assume that's the reason for the increased military presence. I hear General Zollicoffer is fit to be tied. He's increased patrols around town. It won't be long before he finds the perpetrators."

"In the meantime, you're welcome to stay with us." Aunt Laura inclined her head toward Jared. "I'm sure we will enjoy having some company."

Uncle Francis nodded his head, but whatever reply he might have made was lost as a house slave entered the dining room.

"Mr. Luke Talbot is asking if you are at home, madam."

Aunt Laura dabbed at her mouth with a napkin before answering. "Show him in. He must have a compelling reason for visiting this early."

One of the slaves put a plate in front of Amelia, but too much was happening for her to pay attention to food. First Benjamin and Jared, and now Luke. If any more unexpected guests arrived, they would have to move to the formal dining room to accommodate them.

"Now that's a boy who has his head on straight most of the time." Uncle Francis pointed a finger at his son. "You would do well to emulate him."

The door opened once again, and the first thing Amelia noticed was the uniform Luke was wearing. His double-breasted frock coat was belted at the waist and gray in color. A sword was fastened to the belt, and he carried a black hat under his arm. He bowed to the family and took the empty chair next to Amelia. "Thank you for seeing me this morning." His easy smile encompassed the whole room, but somehow Amelia felt it was directed at her. He shook his head when a slave offered him a plate but accepted a cup of steaming, black coffee.

Amelia looked at Jared when he cleared his throat. "When did you enlist?"

"I purchased my commission this morning." He glanced down at the uniform he must have ordered several weeks earlier. "But as you can see, I've been planning to join for some time now."

"Have you received your assignment?" asked Benjamin.

"Yes." He took a sip of coffee before continuing. "I am to be part of General Zollicoffer's senior staff. Even as we sit here this morning, plans are being made to turn our college into a hospital for the wounded and ill. My squad will be moving the wounded from the battlefield to Knoxville for treatment."

Concern put a lump in Amelia's throat and made her stomach churn. "That sounds like a dangerous task."

Luke reached over and patted her hand. "Might I hope your words mean you will be praying for me?"

She pulled her hand away as if it had been burned. Luke was a dear friend, but she had not yet decided if she wanted him to be anything more than that. "I pray daily for all the soldiers—the brothers, sons, and fathers who make up both sides of this dreadful war."

"Your sentiments do you justice," Uncle Francis spoke up, redirecting her attention to the head of the table. "But perhaps you should confine your prayers to the Confederacy and pray that we will soon succeed in our quest for independence from Northern tyranny."

Out of the corner of her eye, she could see Luke and Benjamin nodding their agreement. Jared, however, did not. He took off his spectacles and buffed them against the sleeve of his jacket. By the time he returned them to his nose, the conversation had veered in another direction.

Admiration for him grew stronger within Amelia as their glances collided. Instead of the anger she was expecting to find, given his opposition to slavery, his gaze held a deep sorrow. A sorrow she instinctively understood. It made her think of the sadness Christ had described when He encountered spiritual blindness and ignorance. Regardless of her blood ties, in that moment, she felt closer to Jared than anyone else in the room.

❧

Jared set his Bible down and looked outside. A slight figure in a dark cloak hurried past the library window. Amelia! He wondered what errand had her outside at this early hour. He shook his head. It was not his business to monitor her routine. He had enough to do—like composing riveting articles for Mr. Stone's new paper.

A thrill passed through him as Jared considered God's timing with his new vocation, a vocation that gave him purpose and direction. He had written to his parents to explain why he had not come home now that the school term was over and most of the burned bridges had been repaired. They had encouraged him to keep his job even though he was missed in Nashville. Although Jared missed seeing his family, he was relieved they did not insist on his immediate return since he was not in any hurry to leave Knoxville.

Not only did he love his work for the *The Voice of Reason*, but he also enjoyed being in the same household with Amelia. The more he was around her, the more he admired her grace and humility. She was always patient and kind with others and worked hard at such tasks as mending, knitting, and even rolling bandages for wounded soldiers. She never complained even though few social outings for her to attend were held now that the city was under martial law. Her good qualities reminded him of Solomon's description of a good wife in the book of Proverbs. Amelia was, in short, exactly the type of girl he hoped to one day marry.

Jared took a deep breath and turned his attention back to his Bible. In the past weeks, he had formed the habit of starting his day with quiet meditation in his host's library. Generally, Benjamin slept late, the Montgomery ladies went on calls or errands, and Mr. Montgomery left early for his club or work, not to return until the midday meal or even later.

Lord, thank You for watching over this kind family. Help me to show them gratitude and respect for offering me a place to stay during these difficult days. Create in me an encouraging spirit to bring about a softening of their attitudes toward the bondage of other human beings. Help me to speak out for what is right while still respecting their beliefs. Show compassion on the men who have taken up arms for both sides in this war between states. And Lord, please show me how You would use me—should I fight or not? And if You wish for me to bear arms, which side should I champion? Lord, how can I take up arms against my Southern brothers? But I cannot ignore the plight of those enslaved people the Yankees champion. Please give me a clear answer. I want more than anything to follow Your plan for my life. Thank You, Lord, for the blessings in my life. Please watch over my family and protect them from harm. In the name of Christ, Your Son and my Savior, I pray. Amen.

God's peace saturated the very air around him. Jared breathed deep, awe and love filling him. These moments were so special, and he treasured them. He might have sat still in worship for a minute, an hour, or a day. Time had no meaning.

Voices in the hallway were an intrusion, indicating his private time had come to an end. With a reluctant sigh, he left the special corner he had come to consider his own and walked toward the hall. Before he could reach it, the carved door swung toward him and Amelia Montgomery, divested of her cloak, stepped inside.

"Oh, excuse me." Her hand went to her mouth when she saw him in the library. Her beauty nearly overwhelmed him. She was wearing a forest green dress with a wide skirt that swayed gently even after she stopped walking. "I was looking for Benjamin. Have you seen him?"

Jared took out his pocket watch and glanced at it. "At this time of the morning, I would guess he's still abed."

A frown wrinkled her brow. "You're probably right. Perhaps I'll borrow something to read and wait for him to make an appearance."

"Mr. Montgomery has an excellent selection." Jared dragged his gaze from her and glanced over his shoulder at the floor-to-ceiling shelves that lined three walls of the room. They were full of an impressive collection of books—from furniture making to lyrical poetry.

"Yes, this is my favorite room in the whole house." She clasped her hands in front of her and looked down demurely, her whole posture one of sweet innocence. "But I don't get to spend as much time here as I'd like."

Jared nodded, but his mind was more occupied by her beauty than her comment. Amelia's golden hair reflected the sunshine streaming through the library window. If she'd been dressed in white, she would probably have been mistaken for an angel.

Her blue eyes, sparkling with the depth and beauty of a perfect diamond, bathed him in appreciation. He felt like a bird soaring above the earth. He reined in his emotions with an effort. "Were you looking for anything in particular?"

She shook her head. "Do you have a suggestion?"

It was no wonder Amelia was so popular. Who could resist her beauty and grace? And she seemed to value his opinion.

The door to the library had been slightly ajar, but now it swung open farther, and Benjamin entered. He was dressed for an outing in a brown suit, his pants tucked into his boots and a low-crowned felt hat in his hand. "Good morning, Amelia. Have you seen Jared this morning?"

"Yes." She made a quarter turn and swept her hand back toward where Jared stood near the bookshelves. "You have found him."

Benjamin's eyebrows climbed toward his hair as he looked from Amelia to Jared. "Am I interrupting?"

Jared's face warmed in response to the speculative glance. "No. In fact your cousin was searching for you and found me instead."

"I see." Benjamin bowed to Amelia. "Did you have an errand for me?"

She dropped a curtsy. "I was wondering if you would escort Tabitha and me to a few stores in town."

His smile disappeared, and Benjamin's brows drew together. "I'm afraid not. I have a pressing appointment that will keep me busy for most of the day. Perhaps tomorrow."

Now it was Amelia's turn to frown. "Or maybe we'll just go alone and not wait for someone to accompany us."

"That's not a good idea." Jared's heart thumped as he stepped between the cousins. Since the burning of the rail bridges, the Confederate Army had increased its presence in the city. "There have been stories in the newspaper of confrontations between soldiers and ordinary citizens. Even the promenades in the park have been halted."

"I will avoid the park." She raised her chin in defiance and continued before either man could remonstrate. "I need to purchase several items for Christmas gifts and decorations. Aunt Laura doesn't feel well, Uncle Francis is at work, and if you are not available, I don't see another choice."

Jared glanced at Benjamin, whose chin was as high as his cousin's. It was easy to see the family resemblance. They both had stubborn streaks as wide as the Tennessee River. "I would be happy to escort you, Miss Montgomery."

Her pert nose lowered a smidgen. "But you are a guest in my uncle's home. I would not presume to impose on you."

"It's the perfect answer." Benjamin grinned at them. "Jared will see you come to no harm, and you can buy all the gewgaws you want." He jammed his hat on his head and hurried out the door.

"If you're sure you don't mind. . ."

Jared thought for a minute of the article he had promised to have finished by this evening. His editor had asked for a piece applauding the brave men and women who risked life and limb to resist the Confederate takeover of Knoxville. It was complete, but he had planned to go over it once more before sending it to his editor. Yet how could he disappoint Amelia? "I'm at your service. When would you like to leave?"

"It will only take me a few moments to get my wrap."

Her open appreciation made him feel like a conquering hero. "I will call for the carriage and meet you in the foyer in fifteen minutes." He followed her out of the library, his feet barely touching the floor as he anticipated the time they would spend together.

఼

"I don't know if the carriage will hold much more." Jared pointed at the small mountain of boxes lashed to the roof and piled in the boot. "We may have to send Tabitha home separately and then get the coachman to come back after us."

"Perhaps you're right, but I am not finished." Amelia reviewed her mental shopping list. She still lacked several items. "There is at least one small purchase I must still make."

He did not groan or even sigh at her pronouncement. Jared Stuart was obviously a patient man. They had visited five different establishments. He had been polite and attentive at each one, but he had grown noticeably more animated while they were at the bookseller's. He had perused the inventory with great interest and discussed several titles with the proprietor. She was glad he'd been distracted there, as it had allowed her to make a special purchase, but she wondered how many more stops he would allow before rebelling.

"What if we send the carriage home and stop for a luncheon before continuing our raid on the local merchants? I know of a quaint establishment not far from here."

She smiled and squeezed his arm. "What a wonderful escort you have been. Far better than Benjamin."

"I have two older sisters who taught me the intricacies of shopping from an early age." He left her for a moment to instruct the coachman. As the carriage rattled off, he returned to where she stood, a warm smile on his face. She liked his smile. It was strong yet gentle, the look of a man of strong principles. And although Amelia wouldn't admit it to anyone, his smile caused a flutter in the center of her stomach.

There was so much to admire about Jared, not the least of which was his willingness to fall in with her plans. As they joked and laughed the morning away, she learned that they shared many of the same convictions.

Walking with Jared to the restaurant he had mentioned, Amelia noticed the gleam from the storefront of a local jeweler. She inclined her head slightly. "What is in that display window?"

Jared drew her closer so they could both see a beautiful display of ladies' brooches, some encased in gold swirls, others surrounded by silver or pearls. Each oval depicted a different subject, although most were portraits of ladies. But Amelia was drawn to one in particular. Its frame was jet black and shiny, but it was the bird painted on the porcelain center that made her look more closely. It was a slender bird with dark gray wings, a white throat, and a light gray head with a sharp black beak. "Look, it's my mockingbird!"

She felt Jared's arm stiffen and looked away from the brooch to see why. He was looking at her like she had grown a second head or something. She had never seen Jared looking so. . .so disgusted. She had thought his eyes were more brown than green, but the sunlight seemed to catch on the green flecks behind his spectacles. Or maybe that was anger. "What has upset you?"

The green in his eyes faded somewhat. "I. . .it's nothing. . .only a difference of opinion."

"What? You don't like the mockingbird brooch?"

He shook his head and pulled her away from the window. "Don't you ever feel sorry for the bird caged in your home?"

She pulled her hand away from his arm. "Sorry? Why should I? The bird seems quite content. He is fed regularly and does not have to worry about being attacked by a hawk or another predator."

Jared sighed. "But does he have the freedom to fly through the forest or watch his nestlings first take wing?"

The question struck her like a runaway carriage. "But if he was so unhappy, would he continue to sing?"

Holding his arm out to her once more, Jared shrugged. "Perhaps he sings to keep his spirits up."

Amelia allowed him to lead her down the street, her mind chewing on the question Jared had asked. Did she have the right to deny her bird its freedom? Was she as bad as her parents? She accused them of treating others as less important than their own comfort. A small voice whispered in her ear that she was no different. She had caged up one of God's creatures for her own pleasure.

So lost was she in her contemplation that Amelia didn't realize they were being hailed until the Montgomery carriage pulled up beside them. "Whatever is wrong?"

Their coachman, a young man whose shoulders were not nearly as wide as his uniform, looked scared. "They stopped me just up the road, miss."

"Who stopped you?" Jared pushed at his spectacles and glanced back the way the carriage had come.

Amelia looked inside the carriage to make certain Tabitha was not hurt, but it was empty. "Where is Miss Tabitha?"

The coachman raised his arm and pointed behind him. "They said she had no papers—" His voice cracked. "They said she was a wanted woman and they was taking her back to her master in Georgia."

Panic-laced energy flooded Amelia, making her light-headed. "We must rescue Tabitha. She is not an escaped slave." She gripped Jared's arm. "Please, we have to do something."

"Don't worry." Jared's face had turned white, but he managed a quick smile. "No one is going to take her." He helped her into the coach, but instead of joining her on the inside, he climbed up next to the coachman. "Let's find Miss Tabitha."

The coach sped through the crowded street. Amelia grabbed the hanging straps to keep her seat as they bounced through mud holes and swerved to miss oncoming traffic. *Please keep Tabitha safe, Lord. Help us reach her in time.* The two phrases echoed over and over again as they searched for the men who had abducted her friend. Stories persisted of bounty hunters who searched for runaway slaves in free states and returned them home to their masters. But Tennessee was not a free state, and Tabitha was not a runaway. If she'd had any idea that bounty hunters were a problem, Amelia would have insisted that Tabitha carry papers of identification on her. But this was the first she'd heard of such an incident. Of course, advertisements for missing slaves were placed in the newspaper on a daily basis, but no one ever seemed to pay them much heed. Especially lately. With the increased military presence, it was terribly ironic that personal safety had lessened.

The pedestrians passed as a blur, but still Amelia searched for Tabitha's face. The cloak she'd worn today was an old one of Amelia's, dark blue in color, with black braiding and large buttons. Amelia's eyes searched frantically. More soldiers than civilians occupied the street, but she still could not spot Tabitha's cloak.

A cry from above alerted her. She prayed one of them had found Tabitha. The carriage lurched to a sudden halt and rocked as Jared leapt from it.

Amelia pushed open the door of the carriage and climbed out clumsily since no one was there to help her alight. She rushed forward to catch up with Jared, her breath coming in gasps.

Two burly men held a frightened Tabitha between them. One was well over six feet tall with bulky arms and a thick chest. The other's weight was almost all contained in his round belly. Both had long, scraggly beards that hid most of their facial features.

"She is not a runaway." Jared was speaking to the taller man. "She belongs to a friend of mine."

"Well, and ain't that lucky." The shorter man spat on the ground and gripped Tabitha's arm more tightly.

"Let go of her!" Amelia flung herself at him and raised her leg to kick him, but she was pulled back by a strong arm. She hit Jared's chest hard enough to see stars.

"You'd better hold on to your little missy." The taller man pulled on his beard with one hand and stared at them. "I wonder how much your wife thinks this gal is worth."

Amelia opened her mouth to correct him but was fore-stalled when Jared somehow moved her back behind his right shoulder. "Tabitha belongs to this lady."

"I see." The taller one shook Tabitha's arm. "Ya got papers to prove it, missy?"

"My word is good enough, and you know it." Jared's voice was a low growl. "You will release her to me, or we will go to General Zollicoffer and see if he can sort this out."

All the bluster went out of the tall man. He tossed a look at his companion. "I guess we was mistook, Orin. This gal must not be the one we's lookin' fer."

Orin scratched his beard before nodding. He let go of Tabitha's arm.

She pulled away from the taller man and stepped toward them, nearly falling into Amelia's embrace.

"Can you walk, dearest?" Amelia forced the words past the lump in her throat.

A nod answered her.

Then Jared's arm came around both of them, and he guided them back to the carriage. He put Tabitha in first before giving a hand to Amelia. "I'll ride up front and let you two have some privacy."

Amelia touched his cheek with a gloved hand. "Thank you. I don't know what we would have done if not for your fast thinking." She smiled as his face reddened. He was such a good man—kindhearted, strong, smart. If only he had any interest in her. . .

On the way home, Amelia held Tabitha close and stroked her back as she cried into a handkerchief. It was time to send Tabitha north. Jared's words about Amelia's mockingbird came back. Tears came to her own eyes as she considered losing touch with her friend. But it was time to do the right thing. She would make contact with Mrs. Downing and arrange for Tabitha to leave as soon as possible.

Perhaps this was the reason God had let her become embroiled in the Underground Railroad in the first place. Once Tabitha was gone, the Mockingbird would disappear. She would stick to her role as a vapid debutante and sever all ties with the abolitionists.

Chapter 12

Jared dressed carefully for the Christmas celebration. With all the time and energy the ladies had put into it, he had no doubt the evening ahead would be a memorable occasion. A glance in the mirror told him his cravat was straight. He slipped his arms into the navy blue frock coat and tucked a small package into the pocket of his blue silk waistcoat. Satisfied with his clothing, he brushed his hair toward his face, using a bit of pomade to hold it in place. Then he retrieved his spectacles, carefully wiped them clean on a damp cloth, and placed them on his face.

A sigh left his mouth as his reflection became clearer. He would never be as handsome as Luke Talbot or as charming as Benjamin Montgomery. His only talent seemed to lie in writing strong articles. Another sigh filled him. Not a talent to overwhelm the ladies. But perhaps that was best. He had the feeling he would soon be forced to choose a side in the war, and then there would be no time for romance.

Jared left his room and headed down the hall. Anticipation made his steps light. Did Amelia have a gift for him? But why would she? His inability to resist purchasing something special for her did not mean she would have anything to give him.

"Come on down, man." Benjamin beckoned him with an impatient gesture. "We are anxious to see what Amelia and my mother have wrought in the parlor."

Jared hurried down the stairs. "I'm sorry to keep everyone waiting." A quick glance took in Amelia's ruby red gown. White lace fell from her shoulders to her elbows in three scalloped layers, caught up in the center with a silk carnation. She was standing close to Luke Talbot and conversing with him.

Jared wished he could draw her attention away from Luke. He longed to hold her close and protect her from harm. He remembered how terrified he'd been the day Tabitha had been abducted. If any harm had come to Amelia, he would never have forgiven himself. But even in the tense situation when he'd stopped her foolhardy attack on the bounty hunter, a part of his mind had registered and memorized the feel of her in his arms.

He wondered if she remembered it at all. Sometimes he believed she was warming to him, but then Luke would drop by in his eye-catching uniform and whisk her away to an outing or party. When did the man find time to serve the Confederacy? His eyes narrowed as Luke put a proprietary hand at her waist. Had things progressed so far between them?

Jared grimaced and caught a surprised look on Mrs. Montgomery's face. He stretched his mouth into a smile and bowed in her direction. "Happy Christmas."

She inclined her head. "Happy Christmas, indeed."

"Shall we go in?" Mr. Montgomery offered his hand to his wife.

Jared wished he could escort Amelia into the parlor, but at least Luke had to take his hand away from her waist to offer her his arm. It was small comfort for Jared's envious heart, but his displeasure faded as he and Benjamin followed the two couples into the parlor. The room was awash in the golden glow of candles and the fresh smell of pine. His gaze went to the tall tree that took up the front corner of the room. The angel perched on top of the tree nearly scraped the ceiling. He stepped closer, captivated by the ribbons, candles, and fruit garlands that decorated it.

"Do you like it?"

Jared nodded and turned to Amelia. Her eyes twinkled in the candlelight. "Beautiful." Did she realize he was not only referring to the decorations?

"Yes, indeed." Luke's voice was an unwelcome intrusion. "But I'm not surprised. Your talents have always included making a home cozy."

"It was Aunt Laura's idea." Her voice chided Luke gently, and Jared hid a smile behind a hand.

Mrs. Montgomery joined them beside the tree. "Your modesty becomes you, Amelia, but you are hiding your light under a bushel." She smiled at Luke and Jared. "My niece was the designer. I could never have achieved all of this without her."

Jared shook his head. "Your home is too beautiful and welcoming for me to believe you were not both equally responsible."

"I agree." Amelia linked arms with her aunt. "It took all of our talents to complete this."

Mr. Montgomery poked at the fire and soon had a cheerful blaze going. "Shall we pass out the gifts?"

"Yes, dear." Mrs. Montgomery settled herself on the sofa and patted the space next to her. "Jared, why don't you sit here and tell me about your family's traditions. I'm sure you must miss them very much."

Benjamin and Amelia began sorting the gifts that were piled under the tree and handed them out to the occupants. Everyone had at least one thing to unwrap, even Luke. Jared fingered the sharp corners of the box in his pocket. Would Amelia like his gift? Was it too personal?

THE MOCKINGBIRD'S CALL

"Here is a little something for you." Amelia held a rectangular package in her hand.

Jared stood up to accept the gift. It was obviously a book. He unwrapped it with a flourish and gasped. It was a first-edition copy of *A Christmas Carol*.

"Do you like it?" Her voice was hesitant.

"Yes, very much." He opened it, his eyes widening when he saw Mr. Dickens's signature. It took him back to the day he'd first met Amelia. "I will treasure it always. It is the perfect present."

"I'm glad." Her stunning eyes twinkled like one of the trinkets on the Christmas tree. "I purchased it that day you took me shopping."

"I have something for you, too." He drew out the small box he'd been carrying and offered it to her.

Her mouth formed an O of surprise as she accepted the box. "What is it?"

"Why don't you sit down and open it?"

He watched a blush rise up to her cheeks. She sat down and carefully pried loose a corner of the brown paper wrapping. Anticipation quickened his pulse. It seemed to take forever, but finally she lifted the top of the velvet box.

"Oooh." Her eyes widened and she looked upward, a wide smile on her face. "Thank you."

Mrs. Montgomery bent toward her. "What do you have, dear?"

"It's a mockingbird brooch." She held the box so her aunt could see it. "One I admired last week when Jared took me shopping."

Luke elbowed him out of the way and bent over Amelia. "I have a Christmas gift I think you'll like." He handed her a large box.

Amelia put the box in her lap while she fastened her new brooch to the collar of her dress. "Thank you, Jared."

Jared felt ten feet tall. He had pleased her. The soft glow in her blue eyes made them appear deeper than ever. He could fall into their depths—so warm, so mysterious. Then she turned her attention to Luke Talbot. She opened her gift, a furry muff, and thanked him sweetly. Jared tried to gauge her pleasure with the second gift. He thought she liked the brooch more.

Soon the other gifts were all opened. He had received socks, a muffler, and a special cleaning solution for his spectacles. He was grateful for the Montgomerys' generosity, but nothing could compare to the book Amelia had given him.

Mrs. Montgomery clapped her hands to get everyone's attention. "Why don't we sing some Christmas carols?"

Her husband grumbled a little, but soon they were all gathered around the large piano. Mrs. Montgomery played, Benjamin turned the pages for her, and the rest of them sang. As his tenor melded with Amelia's soprano, Jared thought maybe this was the best evening of his life.

Luke stood directly behind Amelia, but he was not singing with the rest of them. What was wrong? The other men were singing, although she had to acknowledge the Montgomery men could not carry a tune very well. She wished Luke would relax and enjoy the family entertainment. Out of the corner of her eye she saw Jared singing his heart out. What a difference between the two men.

Her thoughts came to an abrupt halt when Luke tapped her on the shoulder. He inclined his head toward the door and sent her a look. She wondered what he wished to say to her in private. When the song ended, he drew her away with a laughing promise to return her to the festivities after a few moments.

He sandwiched one of her hands with his own. "I am concerned about the closeness growing between you and Stuart."

Amelia's mouth dropped open. He had brought her out here for a lecture? "I don't know what you're talking about."

"Amelia"—his frown was terrible to behold—"he gave you jewelry. And you accepted it."

She fingered the brooch. "My aunt and uncle didn't seem to find the gift improper."

"I'm sure your father would not be as tolerant." He paced the hall with long strides before returning to her side. "I'm not even certain he would approve of Jared staying here with all of you. He's practically branded himself a traitor."

"He's done no such thing." The words rushed out of her mouth in Jared's defense. "You can't believe he's a traitor just because he disagrees with you. He is expressing his beliefs, which I must say come closer to my own than to those of the slave hunters. Don't we have the same freedom of speech as we enjoyed when we were part of the Union?"

Luke spread out his hands, palms up. "I didn't mean to upset you, Amelia. I wanted to warn you to be a little more circumspect."

He wanted what? "My father gave you the responsibility of escorting me to Knoxville, but he didn't give you the right to dictate my behavior."

Instead of answering her right away, Luke reached into his pocket. "Please don't be so angry. I only have your best interests at heart. And to prove it, I have something I want to give you."

With a sense of impending doom, Amelia watched as he dropped to one knee in front of her. He took her hand in his and pressed a warm kiss on it. She had read about such gestures and knew they should cause a tingle in her spine, or at least in her stomach, but she felt nothing. Nothing but apprehension.

She tried to listen to what Luke was saying. He had an earnest look on his face, and he was going on about his feelings and his duty. "Please say you will agree to marry me before I leave. You'll make me the happiest man in the

Confederacy." He stopped talking and lifted the lid on the velvet box.

How she wished it might have been another brooch or a hatpin. . .anything but an engagement ring. But there it was, a golden circle topped by a lovely blue sapphire. "I don't know—" Amelia swallowed hard. Her mind raced around like a mad bee, unable to light on the appropriate response. She knew what her father and mother would say. It was what they'd hoped would be the outcome of her stay with Uncle Francis and Aunt Laura—marriage to someone of Luke's caliber. But could she agree out of a sense of duty? Could she bind herself by oath to a man she did not love?

Or was love something that formed after the wedding? What if she was looking for some giddy happiness that was only a myth? And she had to consider the man kneeling before her. If she didn't agree to marry Luke, would he pine away for her? Hadn't she just heard him say he was leaving? What if she turned him down and he got himself killed for lack of her love? She couldn't bear the thought of being the cause of his death. She found herself nodding her head.

"Really?" Luke pulled the ring from its box and placed it on her finger. "I hope you like the ring. It reminded me of your beautiful eyes."

He stood and pulled her into his arms. Feeling numb, Amelia allowed the embrace. But when she felt him plant a soft kiss on her forehead, she pushed him away. Luke frowned for a moment before relenting. "Let's go in and tell your family."

Her heart thumped unpleasantly in her chest. Did they have to disrupt the festive evening? But delaying the inevitable was senseless. She took a deep breath and nodded.

Luke threw open the parlor doors and pulled her inside. "Excuse us, everyone, but I have an important announcement to make."

Amelia wished she could match his wide smile, but all she could manage was a feeble imitation.

"Amelia has agreed to become my wife."

Aunt Laura squealed and pushed away from the piano. "What wonderful news!" She clapped her hands. "And on Christmas Eve. The two of you will always remember the occasion of your engagement."

Uncle Francis moved forward and slapped Luke on the back. "Well done, my boy. Well done. You've chosen a lovely bride and a good family."

Benjamin echoed his father's sentiments and enveloped Amelia in a brief hug. "You will make a handsome couple."

When she emerged from his hug, Amelia glanced toward Jared. He wasn't saying anything at all. Was his face pale? And what was the flicker of emotion she saw in his eyes before he looked down at the floor. Surely it had not been pain. What did he expect of her? To turn down Luke's offer?

She could not do it. It was fine for Jared to seek a rebellious path—he was a man. She had to live within society's strictures. Her parents had taught her that when they banished her to Knoxville. She was determined to be a dutiful daughter and please them. They had her best interests at heart. Besides, it was not like anyone else appeared interested. For all the men who visited her, Luke was the only one who had asked for her hand in marriage.

Amelia raised her chin and managed to form a slightly more enthusiastic smile. If a certain fastidious student thought she was making a mistake, she would prove him wrong. What did he know about such things, anyway? She would live her life as she thought best.

Her hand reached up to caress the brooch. She was free to make her own decisions.

A small voice whispered a warning in her mind. *You also have the freedom to regret your decisions for the rest of your life.*

Chapter 13

Amelia stared at the silver tea service, her mind a long way from the chatter in her aunt's parlor. A rustle of skirts brought her head up, and she smiled at Mrs. Downing. The lady and her daughter had become regular visitors to the Montgomery home, although there seemed to be little action on the Underground Railroad. Things had been quiet since the Christmas holidays. Perhaps the January weather was too harsh for runaways to attempt escape.

"You are looking lovelier than ever, Amelia." Mrs. Downing leaned over and patted her hand. "Your betrothal to the handsome Lieutenant Talbot must be putting those roses in your cheeks."

The ladies around her twittered as hot blood rushed to her face. They probably attributed the sight to maidenly modesty. How could they know the true reason behind her discomfiture? Ever since that night, Amelia had felt like a drowning victim. With each congratulatory or teasing remark, the weight of her feelings had dragged her under. She wanted to claw her way to freedom, to give back the sapphire ring on her hand and explain her mistake to Luke. He would understand, wouldn't he?

As if her thoughts had conjured him, the door opened, and Luke stepped into the parlor. Her cousin was close behind him. In the two weeks since Christmas, Benjamin had begun spending most of his time with Luke. It was a development that disturbed her somewhat, but she could do very little about it. She wished Benjamin would spend more time with Jared. Not only were they of an age, she knew she could depend on Jared's common sense to keep Benjamin from joining the fighting.

Luke bowed to Mrs. Montgomery before making a beeline toward Amelia. Just before he reached her, Amelia felt something slide under her hand. A note from Mrs. Downing could only mean one thing—the abolitionists needed her help. She slipped the paper behind the cushion of her chair and rose to meet Luke.

Mrs. Downing sighed and put a hand over her heart. "Ah, young love. How wonderful to see it in the midst of these dreary days."

Luke smiled at the older lady before turning his dark gaze on Amelia. He was every inch the Southern gentleman, from his neatly trimmed mustache and side whiskers to the polish on his boots. He took her hand in his own and raised it to his lips. "I trust you are well, my dear." He squeezed her fingers before letting them go, an indication of his happiness to see her.

Amelia knew her heart should be racing at the display of his affection, but it remained stubbornly calm. "It's nice to see you, Luke."

Behind him, Benjamin cleared his throat to get everyone's attention. "We have news."

"What is it, dear?" Aunt Laura set her cup next to the serving tray.

"Well, you already know the army has taken over East Tennessee University and established a hospital there."

Amelia nodded. Luke had kept them abreast of the activities at the university, and she had read a blistering article in *The Voice of Reason*, an underground newspaper Mrs. Downing had slipped to her just last week. She suspected Jared might have been the author. The article's frank style and uncompromising position matched Jared's personality and reminded her of the paper he had presented during the literary society meeting. She had wanted to quiz him about it, but with the exception of family meals, she had seen little of Jared since Christmas Eve.

She missed the sound of his voice and the way he pushed his spectacles up on his nose when he was thinking. He always listened to her opinions, often engaging in a lively debate.

It would be nice if Luke had time to discuss important issues with her, but he generally treated her like an empty-headed debutante. He was attentive, but if she tried to bring up a serious subject, he told her not to worry about such matters. Perhaps when the war was over, things would be different. They would have more time together, and Luke would pay proper attention to her ideas.

"Luke's skills and knowledge have come to General Zollicoffer's attention. The general is leading his brigade north into Kentucky, but he took time to give Luke here a promotion to captain, and"—Benjamin paused for effect—"the general has given our newest captain a special assignment."

The ladies all crowded around Luke, each clamoring to congratulate him and find out about his new assignment. Amelia hung back. She was worried his promotion would mean he would soon be going into battle. It was bad enough when he was responsible for transporting wounded soldiers to Knoxville. That had been after the battles were fought. This new assignment probably meant he would be in the thick of the fighting. She might not be certain they would make the perfect couple, but she didn't want him to become another casualty.

"The general has put me in charge of finding the traitors who work with runaway slaves. One in particular has been causing a large stir. We recently caught some of the renegades who know him only as the Mockingbird."

Luke's words made her jaw drop. Now her heart was thumping so loud and fast she felt light-headed. She had to get her emotions under control or risk being caught right here in Aunt Laura's parlor.

"Aren't you happy for your brave fiancé?" Benjamin sauntered toward her. His eyes lit on the brooch she often wore, the brooch Jared had given her for Christmas. "Well, look here, Luke. Maybe you should start your investigation with your betrothed." He pointed to Amelia's chest. "Perhaps my cousin is the culprit you seek."

Shocked silence greeted his words. Everyone looked toward her and Benjamin. Amelia did the only thing she could think of. She laughed. It started out somewhat stilted, but the sound immediately eased the tension in the room.

Her cousin's louder and more natural guffaws at his joke reassured the rest of the ladies, who joined in as they realized the improbability of his suggestion.

Aunt Laura shook her head at her son. "You should apologize to your cousin."

"It's quite all right." Amelia was relieved everyone was laughing. It had been a close thing there for a moment. How disastrous it would have been to be unmasked in her aunt's parlor, to be arrested by her own betrothed. She pushed the frightening thoughts back and smiled widely. "I don't mind Benjamin's attempt to bring some lightheartedness to us. We must all learn to take ourselves less seriously if we are to survive this war."

Even as her face showed relaxed mirth, her heart beat a nervous staccato. Was this how her future with Luke would be—always hiding her true self? She longed to allow her heart to fly as free as those she helped escape slavery. . .but she despaired as a door clanged shut on the cage holding her heart.

⌘

"What have you done?"

The commotion outside Jared's bedroom broke his concentration. Was that Mrs. Montgomery's voice? He had been answering the letter he'd just received from his parents, but he put down his pen and walked to the door. Then he hesitated with his hand on the knob. He didn't know if he should interrupt or not. It might be a family problem, and no matter that the Montgomerys had opened their home to him, he was not a member of their family.

The voices had moved down the staircase. It sounded like someone was crying. Was it Amelia? Was she hurt? Chivalry filled his chest. He twisted the knob and strode to the head of the stairs.

The Montgomerys—all four of them—were standing in the foyer. Benjamin had his arms around his mother, who was the one weeping. "I am a grown man, and it's about time you stopped treating me like a child." His voice was angry, but he continued patting his mother's back as if to comfort her.

327

In an instant, Jared grasped the situation. His friend was no longer wearing street clothes. He had donned the gray uniform of the Confederate army. He would be going to war. A stab of concern penetrated Jared's heart. He wanted to add his protest to that of Benjamin's family.

"If you had only come to me, son," Mr. Montgomery's voice was gravelly with pain, "I would have purchased an officer's commission."

"I can stand on my own two feet, Pa."

"As a foot soldier, you'll likely be used as cannon fodder."

Mr. Montgomery's grim pronouncement produced fresh wails from his wife. "Please stop him, Francis. You have to do something."

Jared was about to retreat to his room to keep from intruding, but he must have made some noise because Amelia looked up. Her troubled blue gaze pierced him. She seemed to be pleading with him. But what could he say? No words could undo Benjamin's actions. He had committed to serve the Confederate army. All they could do was pray for his safety.

"Perhaps Mr. Stuart can convince you."

He pushed his spectacles up and took a deep breath before heading down the stairs. "I'm sorry, but I heard a commotion."

Mrs. Montgomery pulled slightly away from her son's shoulder and sent a wobbly smile toward Jared, her eyes red and puffy from her tears. "It's okay, Jared. We consider you part of our family."

"Yes." Mr. Montgomery nodded his agreement. "I never thought I would say this, but I wish my son were as liberal as you. At least your parents don't have to worry about your going off to fight."

Jared wanted nothing more than to return to his room. He felt the same call to arms as his friend. It was hard not to. Most males between the age of fourteen and forty were needed to assure the South's freedom. Freedom. How ironic that Southern leaders sought freedom to determine their own destinies, destinies that relied upon withholding freedom from their slaves.

Benjamin snorted. "You don't have to drag Jared into this. It's my decision. Besides, I probably won't be gone for long. The officer at the recruiting station has a Bible verse on the wall behind him that reads, 'Five of you shall chase an hundred, and an hundred of you shall put ten thousand to flight.' By this time next month, I'll have whipped so many Yanks, they'll be in full retreat."

Mrs. Montgomery moaned and pulled a handkerchief from the sleeve of her dress.

The words were sheer bravado. The Confederacy could not claim victory based on the Lord's promises to the Jewish people. Jared knew the South was badly outnumbered and had few resources to rely on. Their best hope was to inflict enough pain on the Union so President Lincoln would withdraw his troops and allow the secession to stand. It was a forlorn hope. Allowing the Union to split would make both sides weaker. The whole nation might disintegrate into dozens of independent countries. The vision of the Founding Fathers to create a cohesive power would be lost.

His lack of belief must have shown on Jared's face. His friend turned away from him. "Fine. If you're all against me, I'll get my things together and leave." He took a step back from his sniffling mother and pushed his way past Jared.

Amelia tossed an angry glance at Jared before leading her aunt away. What had *he* done? What did she expect of him? Did she want him to chain Benjamin to keep him here? She would do better to blame her betrothed. Luke Talbot had taken Benjamin under his wing in the weeks since the school closed. Her cousin's decision to join the fighting was probably inevitable. No doubt Luke's influence and success had hastened the event.

Perhaps she blamed Jared for not spending more time with Benjamin. It was true that he'd not spent much time with the Montgomery family since Christmas, but the fault for that lay at her door as much as his. He could not abide the thought of Luke and Amelia together, cooing like doves. So he found reasons either to be out of the house or to be closeted in his bedroom. He felt bad to lose the closeness that had developed between him and Amelia. Her insight and intelligence challenged him to think, but their budding relationship shattered when she chose to link her future to another man.

Mr. Montgomery clapped him on the shoulder. "I'd better go to the bank and buy some of those Confederate notes. Since my son has taken the bit between his teeth, I'll need to make sure he has money for provisions." The man walked away, looking as if he'd aged a decade since last night. His shoulders drooped, and his head hung down.

Jared's heart hurt for him and for the whole Montgomery family. Thumping noises from over his head indicated Benjamin's continued anger.

The door to the library beckoned him, offering a quiet interlude. His heart heavy, Jared sought out its peace and the wisdom he knew he could glean from reading God's Word.

Chapter 14

Amelia met Tabitha downstairs, her dark cloak pulled tightly about her. It was well past midnight, and the rest of the household was slumbering peacefully. The day had been eventful, starting with Luke's promotion and her near exposure and ending with Benjamin's decision to join up.

"I don't know if I can leave you." Tabitha's wide eyes shone with tears.

Amelia hugged her and sniffed a little. "Don't be silly. Think how wonderful it will be to control your own life. You are going to be free the way God intended you to be. You and Melek will settle down in Canada and start a family of your own. After the war is over, Luke and I will come visit you." She handed Tabitha a small leather pouch. "This contains some money. It should help smooth your path and make sure you have something to get you started in your new life."

Tabitha nodded and placed the pouch inside the meager bag that held her most precious belongings. "I don't know how to thank you."

"You can thank me by leading a happy life." Amelia led the way to the door. She had memorized the instructions on the note Mrs. Downing had passed to her in the parlor. It had said to meet at the same location the lady had taken her to during the rally. The most perilous part of their journey would be avoiding Confederate patrols. They were to approach the church on foot and give the call of a mockingbird. Then they would be met by Melek and his current group of escaped slaves. Tabitha would go with him, and Amelia would return home.

Amelia wished they could use horses for the trek across town, but they would be less detectable on foot. It would take them an hour to walk across town in the dark—their progress would be slowed by having to avoid patrols.

They made their way down the dark streets, barely daring to speak for fear of being caught. Amelia had to stop from time to time and study the map that had been included with Mrs. Downing's instructions.

They were only a few blocks from the church when disaster struck. She turned a corner and nearly walked right into a mounted patrol. For a brief instant, she froze and her entire life seemed to flash in front of her eyes. Then Tabitha grabbed her elbow and pulled her into the recesses of a shadowy doorway. Amelia held her breath, trying to hear if they'd been seen. But neither of the men raised an alarm. They seemed to be half asleep as they walked their tired horses down the street, passing scant feet from where Tabitha and Amelia were hiding.

The two of them waited for several minutes before moving forward.

"That was close." Tabitha's whisper sounded loud in the quiet street.

Amelia placed a finger over her mouth and nodded. Then she gathered her courage and stepped out of the shadows, half expecting to hear a shout from one of the soldiers. No one, however, pursued them, and they made the rest of the trip without incident.

When Amelia recognized the rendezvous, she pointed it out to Tabitha. Then she tightened her lips and whistled.

After a moment, the hoot of an owl answered. A tall figure materialized out of the darkness. Melek.

They were safe. Tabitha fell into his arms with a cry of relief. Even in the dim light Amelia could see the tenderness on his dark face. It was a poignant moment for her—saying good-bye to her closest friend. But she could do no less. The hope they would see each other again in the future—on earth or definitely in heaven—would have to sustain her.

Melek looked over Tabitha's bowed head at her. "Thank you."

"Take good care of her."

"I will." He smiled down at Tabitha for a moment before returning his attention to Amelia. "Will you be okay by yourself?"

Amelia nodded. "I'll be fine."

"We need to get started, little flower."

Tabitha nodded against his shoulder. She pulled away from him and threw her arms around Amelia. "God bless you."

"He already has." She felt the words in her heart. Seeing the two of them together was a blessing. Their love was apparent in every glance, every gesture. It was so much deeper than what she felt for Luke. The thought hit her like a blow. The affection she felt toward Luke was a pale shadow of what Melek and Tabitha had. Was it enough to base a marriage upon?

The question seemed to chase her all the way back to her aunt and uncle's home. She didn't know what to do. Should she marry Luke and hope to develop the kind of love Tabitha and Melek had? Or should she end the betrothal and continue looking for the right man? And what about her parents? They would tell her she was being foolish to pine for romantic love. Luke was a good man. He would see to her needs. But was that enough?

The sky was lightening as she snuggled under the pile of quilts on her bed, but sleep still escaped her. She had no idea what to do. Amelia closed her eyes and prayed for guidance, unsure of exactly what answer she was seeking.

Eventually peace settled over her, and she drifted into slumber.

☙

Early the next morning, Amelia was awakened by a pounding at her bedroom door.

Before she could answer, Aunt Laura pushed the door open and hurried in. She was dressed in a flowing wrapper, and the long plait of her hair was draped over her shoulder.

Amelia's heart skipped a beat. "What's wrong?"

"Have you seen Tabitha this morning?"

Amelia rubbed her eyes and tried to arrange her thoughts. She glanced about the room as if expecting Tabitha to appear in one of the corners. "No, why?"

Aunt Laura clasped her hands in a prayerful gesture. "It seems your slave has run away."

"Run away? Tabitha? Are you sure?" Amelia was proud of the confused tone in her voice. She ought to be an actress. "Perhaps she's gone on an errand and will be back in a little while."

Her aunt considered the suggestion then shook her head. "Someone would know if she'd been sent on an errand. No, I'm afraid she's escaped. You'll likely never see her again."

The poignancy of their good-byes came back to Amelia full force. "I hope she's safe."

"Safe? You hope she's safe? I wish that were my only concern. I don't know how we'll tell your parents that their valuable property has disappeared."

Amelia slid her toes out of the bed. "Don't worry about that. I'll tell Papa when I return home. Perhaps I'll say she ran away during our journey back to Nashville. That way he can't blame you at all."

A calculating look came over her aunt's face, but then she sighed. "No, we can't do that. It's not Christian to lie, even to protect one's self." She shook her head. "I'll send one of our slaves up to help you dress. Do you have a preference?"

"No." Amelia forced the word out. She could barely focus on her aunt's dithering for the truth the woman had just uttered. Lying, even to protect one's self, was not acceptable behavior for a Christian. She knew that, but somehow she'd forgotten it. She opened her mouth to confess her part in Tabitha's disappearance, but shouts from outside stopped her.

Amelia ran to the window to see what was going on. "It's Captain Talbot. I wonder why he's here."

Her aunt hurried over to where she stood. "You're not expecting your betrothed?"

Concern swept Amelia. "No. Something must have happened." She urged Aunt Laura out of the bedroom and made short work of her toilette. Her stays were not as tight as usual, her skirt felt slightly askew, and her hair was a mess, but she was downstairs at the door to the library in less than fifteen minutes.

She stood still for a moment to catch her breath and heard Luke's accusing voice, punctuated by her uncle's angry questions. She knocked briefly and entered, stopping all conversation.

Jared was sitting in his usual spot next to the window. Luke was leaning over him, his fist balled as though he wanted to beat the truth out of Jared. Uncle Francis was ensconced behind his desk, and she had never seen him looking so grave, even on the day Benjamin joined the army.

"What's going on in here?" Amelia walked over to Luke and placed her hand on his arm. The muscles in it were as hard as granite. "Luke? What's wrong?"

He glared at her. "Treason."

Fear raked her spine. Amelia could almost feel the noose tightening around her throat. "What do you mean?"

"Someone in this household has been helping slaves escape."

This was even worse than she had imagined. "Why would you think such a thing?"

"We captured a runaway slave last night. Most of his group got away, but we did learn the identity of at least one of them." Luke's gaze clashed with hers once more. "Tabitha."

She could feel the blood draining from her cheeks. "Aunt L–Laura said she was missing, but I. . .I thought she was on an errand."

"Only if her errand is in Canada."

"Did you catch her, too?" She squeezed the question out of her tight throat.

"No."

Amelia sat down on the sofa with a thump. At least Tabitha had gotten away. A prayer of thanksgiving filled her. "I see."

"It's not your fault. Tabitha should have been grateful for her easy station." He turned and pointed a finger at Jared. "She would still be here if not for the Judas in your midst."

A glint caught her attention and Amelia gasped. A pair of handcuffs dangled from Luke's hand. "You're arresting Jared?"

Luke nodded. "Don't look so upset, Amelia. You should be congratulating me. Jared Stuart is the Mockingbird."

She sprang from the sofa and watched in horror as he fastened the cuffs around Jared's wrists. "This is absurd, Luke. He cannot be the Mockingbird."

Luke's eyebrows rose. "I know you feel sympathy for Jared, but you needn't try to protect him. The man we caught told us the leader of the group was connected to this household. And Jared is the only one with abolitionist leanings."

Amelia knew his logic was faulty, but she couldn't tell Luke that without exposing herself. "It can't be Jared. It has to be someone else."

Uncle Francis put an arm around her shoulders. "There is no one else, dear."

She shook her head. "No." What could she do to stop Jared's arrest? Her mind couldn't come up with a plan. She had to do something, but she had no idea what.

Luke marched Jared out of the house as she watched helplessly. Everything was spiraling out of control—like an unstoppable spring flood.

"I know you're as shocked as I am." Uncle Francis shook his head slowly. "Remember, I'm the one who recently told my son he should be more like Jared."

Amelia wanted to run after the two men, but what would she say? If she confessed the truth, she would be arrested. And her guiltless relatives would face suspicion and disgrace. "Where is Luke taking him?"

"To the school. Our friend General Zollicoffer has already filled all the jails. It seems many traitors reside in our fair city."

But Amelia knew this time Luke had the wrong person. She was the *real* traitor. . .to Luke, to her parents, to her aunt and uncle, and now to Jared. But most importantly—and tragically—to God.

Chapter 15

The new maid assigned to her in Tabitha's absence smoothed Amelia's cloak over her shoulders. While they were waiting for the carriage to be brought around, Uncle Francis emerged from his study to discover where she was going. She mustered a bright smile and told him she had promised to make a morning visit to the Downing household. Another lie. Her conscience hammered her all the way to Mrs. Downing's home, but Amelia didn't know what else she could have done. Everything was in such a mess.

Mrs. Downing's butler, a grizzled black man with a pronounced limp, announced her. Amelia was relieved no other ladies were visiting this morning. Faye was sitting next to the fire, a basket of mending beside her. Mrs. Downing, seated on a horsehair sofa, wore a pale pink morning dress that was covered with bows and laces. Her outfit reminded Amelia of a profusion of azalea blossoms. She dropped a curtsy and nodded to Faye.

"Come in, dear, and tell us why you are about so early this morning." Mrs. Downing waved her to a nearby chair.

"A train accident occurred last night."

"I see." Mrs. Downing shook her head in warning before turning to her daughter. "Faye, would you go upstairs and fetch my wrap? I am feeling a little chilled."

Her daughter put down her mending. "Yes, Ma."

"And check in the kitchen for some of those tarts I like."

As soon as Faye was gone, her mother turned to Amelia. "Tell me what happened."

Amelia recounted the story Luke had told her and ended with Jared's arrest. "I cannot bear the thought of his spending even one night in jail for something he did not do."

Mrs. Downing stood up and walked to the fireplace. "I'm afraid it cannot be helped."

"Yes, it can. I can tell them who the real Mockingbird is. I am tired of all the subterfuge anyway, and I've been having serious doubts about whether I'm following the Lord's will in all of this."

The older lady sat down again, an intense look on her face. "Think of all the poor souls who may lose their freedom if you step forward now. We have only

335

recently begun to see success with our work, and a lot of it is due to your efforts. You cannot quit now."

"The railroad will continue without me. That is its strength. The loss of a single agent may cause some hardship, but it will not be shut down."

"Consider this, Amelia. Your friend, Jared, is a known abolitionist, right?"

Amelia nodded.

"Then he probably doesn't mind spending some time in jail. He might even be glad to be imprisoned if it means the real Mockingbird can continue working."

The argument was tempting. It would be so easy to simply remain silent. "But I cannot continue to lie. To tell you the truth, I am almost looking forward to confessing."

Mrs. Downing tapped her chin with one finger as she considered Amelia's words. "At least wait a few days until things quiet down. Give me time to find someone to take your place."

Faye reentered the parlor at that point and their conversation halted. As the three women discussed the latest news, part of Amelia's mind considered her hostess's request.

She took her leave of Mrs. Downing and Faye and climbed back into the carriage, having decided to honor Mrs. Downing's request. Halfway home, however, she changed her mind. She could not remain quiet. Not even one more minute. Jared could not suffer for her transgressions.

⌒

Jared looked around the empty room in West College that had once housed his fellow students. How carefree those days seemed. In the two months since the closing of the school, everything had changed. He supposed he should have returned to his parents' home in Nashville, but he could not bring himself to regret the time he'd spent here, even though it had led to his imprisonment. A temporary condition—or so he hoped. Once they found the real Mockingbird, Luke Talbot would have to release him.

He briefly considered offering to help Talbot in his search for the Mockingbird, but then he dismissed the idea. He might not agree with the lies and deceit involved in keeping the Underground Railroad in operation, but he could not fault the men and women who used it to escape the tyranny of slavery.

The kernel of an idea formed in his mind for a new article. He could write about the railroad. But what new slant could he give it?

As he was considering possibilities, one of the guards came and unlocked the door to his room. "Captain Talbot wants to see you."

Jared searched the soldier's face for any hint of what was going on. He looked to be in his midtwenties. His uniform was well worn and bore the evidence of several patches, but it was worn with evident pride. He gestured toward the hallway with his chin.

Jared nodded and preceded him. The hallway was filled with the moans and groans of the wounded soldiers who were housed here. Jared's heart hurt for them. So much pain.

They climbed the steps to what used to be the president's office and entered the room. He was not surprised to see Captain Talbot sitting behind the president's desk, but the other occupant in the room made him halt in his tracks. What was Amelia doing here?

"Sit down, Stuart."

Jared sat down in the wooden chair facing the desk. He glanced at Amelia out of the corner of his eye. Had she been crying? She looked pale, and her eyes were red.

"I have a couple of questions for you."

"What is she doing here?"

"Never mind that."

Jared bit his lip to keep from responding. It wouldn't do his situation much good to antagonize the captain.

"You have some loyal friends in Knoxville who insist you are a man of your word. Is that true?"

Jared nodded slowly. "My parents raised me to believe that honesty is of paramount importance."

Luke leaned forward and stared directly into his eyes. "Then I ask you to give me your word that you are not working with the Underground Railroad and that you are not the agent called the Mockingbird."

Knowing he had nothing to be ashamed of, Jared held the captain's gaze as he answered. "I am not, nor have I ever been, involved with the Underground Railroad. Nor have I ever been known by the name Mockingbird. The very idea is ludicrous. I use words, not lies, to fight injustice."

"You see?" Amelia spoke for the first time. "It's as I've said. Jared is innocent. If you want to arrest someone, you know who it must be."

Jared could feel his brows drawing together. What was she talking about? Who should be arrested?

Luke's chair scraped the floor as he pushed himself away from the desk. "I suppose you're right."

Amelia stood as he approached her and held her hands out. A roaring sound enveloped Jared as he watched Luke fasten handcuffs around her dainty wrists.

"I'm so sorry, Jared."

Their gazes met, and the truth slammed into him. Amelia Montgomery was the Mockingbird.

Jared was speechless. How had she done it? And why? Why hadn't she come to him? She must have lied over and over again, deceiving all of them. He slumped back in his chair.

"You'll let him leave?" Her voice was drained of emotion. Her whole attitude was one of resignation.

Jared wanted to be angry with her, but it was impossible. How could he maintain anger when she was sacrificing her freedom for his own?

"Yes, but that is the least thing that should concern you now." Luke's face was frozen as if to hide his pain.

Jared felt an unwelcome empathy with the man. Amelia had betrayed both of them.

Luke turned away from her and approached Jared's chair, a master key in his hands. He unlocked the shackles and waited until Jared stood up. "You may have escaped justice this time, but you'd better watch your step."

Jared was glad to be exonerated, but at what price? His gaze lingered on Amelia's bowed head and slumping shoulders. "What will happen to her?"

"That will be up to the general." Luke's harsh tone took Jared's attention from Amelia.

"You can stop her from being. . .executed, can't you?" He stole another glance at her and saw a tear drip from her chin and land on her shackled hands. His heart broke. Jared took a step toward her, wanting to comfort her.

Luke stepped between them. "Stay away from her. You've done enough harm."

"Don't blame Jared." Amelia's voice was thick with her tears. "What I did has nothing to do with him."

"You have to protect her." Jared adjusted his spectacles so he could see Luke more clearly. "She is your betrothed."

"That's right. Her fate is in my hands." Luke's mouth twisted into a sneer. "Not yours. You should escape while you have the chance, before I change my mind and have you arrested for fomenting rebellion in the Montgomery household. If you hadn't filled Amelia's head with your unrealistic notions, she probably wouldn't be here right now."

"It's not his fault." Amelia raised her head, and Jared saw the streaks her tears had left on her cheeks.

"Is that so?" Luke's dark gaze raked both of them. "You're not the same girl I grew up with. And don't think I haven't seen the closeness between the two of you."

Jared wanted to dispute the angry man, but he couldn't come up with any words. He watched as Amelia was taken away by the same soldier who'd escorted him.

Heartbroken, he shook his head at Luke and stumbled from the room. He made his way across the campus by instinct. A part of his brain noticed the differences since the soldiers had taken over the school. Long, deep trenches defaced the hillside sloping to the river, and military tents had sprung up like mushrooms after a spring rain. Soldiers milled about, but no one seemed to pay much attention to him.

Where should he go? What should he do? Jared had no idea. He buried his hands in his pockets and wandered the streets of Knoxville, feeling like a rudderless boat tossed by high waves.

How could he have missed the evidence? He was supposed to be a reporter. He was supposed to be aware of what was happening around him. How had Amelia managed to hide her double life from him?

Jared thought back over the past months. Had he been blinded by her beauty? The answer was a resounding yes. He felt like he'd been an idiot. He ought to feel betrayed, but he could not summon up that emotion. Not when her goal had been freedom for slaves. And when it really counted, she had dropped her subterfuge and come forward to free him. What would happen to her now? A shudder passed through him, but it was not caused by the cold winter air.

He could not leave Amelia imprisoned, but what could he do? He considered going to her aunt and uncle, but that would mean he'd have to confess what their niece had done. He didn't want to do that. They should get that information directly from Amelia.

If this had happened a few days earlier, he could have enlisted Benjamin's help. He thought of the scrapes his friend had dragged him through. But those days were behind them. Benjamin was a soldier, and his superiors would not look kindly on his helping a confessed traitor.

If only his father were here. Adam Stuart would know exactly how to handle the situation without resorting to illegal schemes or outlandish ploys. Thinking of his father made Jared realize what must be done. He needed to secure Amelia's freedom and leave Knoxville. It was time to go home. In Nashville, he would find wiser counsel. Perhaps he could convince Luke to release Amelia into his custody or at least talk Luke into taking her back to her parents' remote plantation home where she would be kept far from involvement with runaway slaves and the Underground Railroad.

Unaware of his surroundings, Jared stumbled on a rock. He would have fallen but caught hold of the rough brick exterior of an empty building. He looked around and recognized the area. He was only a block from Mr. Stone's home—the current office of the *Tennessee Tribune*. He thanked God for leading him to the very place he needed to be. Telling Mr. Stone about his plans to leave was the first step in breaking ties with Knoxville, and his employer would have to find another reporter to write articles for *The Voice of Reason*.

With a new sense of purpose, Jared strode to the house and knocked on Mr. Stone's door. He was ushered into the living room, where he stood in front of the welcome warmth of a roaring fire. He spread his hands out and sighed slightly as they began to thaw out. The door opened, and he turned to greet the man who had hired him.

A smile creased Mr. Stone's face as he entered the room. "This is an unexpected pleasure, Mr. Stuart. Have you come on business? I have already received your latest piece. It's excellent as always. Your talent grows stronger with each article you produce."

Pleasure warmed Jared's heart. On a day so filled with difficulties, the complimentary words were a balm to his soul. "Thank you, sir. You don't know how much it means to me to hear you say so."

"Do you have another article for me? Or is there some other reason you dropped by?"

Jared pushed his spectacles up. "I don't have a new article. In fact, that's sort of the reason I'm here." He stopped and blew out a puff of air. "I mean to say I've decided to go back home, so I won't be able to continue writing for *The Voice of Reason*."

"I see." Mr. Stone sat down on a convenient chair. He stared at the dancing flames in the fireplace before turning back to face Jared. "I cannot say I am surprised. I have been expecting something of the sort since your school term ended. Young men must always throw their energy into fighting."

"I don't know about that." Jared walked to the window and looked out. The pale winter sun, almost completely obscured by lowering clouds, had barely passed its zenith. What was Amelia doing right now? Was she sitting in the same room he had occupied before Luke released him? Was she frightened? Cold? His heart seemed to absorb some of the chill from the other side of the window. "I. . .something has come up that demands my attention."

"I hope it's not bad news?" Mr. Stone's voice invited Jared to expound.

He didn't yet feel he could bare his soul about the events of the morning. The pain was still too fresh. "No. I trust my abrupt departure won't inconvenience you."

Mr. Stone pushed himself up from his chair and came to stand next to Jared at the window. "Don't worry about me. It's been a pleasure to watch you grow as a writer. God has given you a great talent, and I'm sure He will lead you on to loftier heights."

Jared thanked the man before taking his leave. It had been reassuring to hear Mr. Stone's confidence in him and to be reminded that God had not deserted him. . .or Amelia. A plan began to form in his mind, and he strode through the streets of Knoxville with renewed determination. He knew exactly how to unlock the bars of Amelia's prison.

࠴

It was nearly two o'clock by the time Jared made his way back to his former campus. He talked the sentry into letting him pass and made his way to the place where he'd last seen Luke, praying that the man would still be there.

"Come in." Luke's voice answered his knock.

Jared sent a wordless plea to God before entering the room. He would need the Lord's help if he was to succeed.

Luke was sitting behind his desk, a stack of papers in front of him. He looked up as Jared entered, and his features registered his surprise. "What are you doing here? I thought I'd seen the last of you."

Jared ignored the question. "You love her, don't you?" He watched the other man's eyes closely. There it was. Pain. And fear. Luke was afraid Amelia didn't love him. That was the answer. It gave Jared the bargaining chip he needed. "Of course you love her. You asked her to be your wife."

"I don't see what my feelings have to do with anything. Amelia has committed some very serious crimes that would bring imprisonment even if we were not at war."

"What if I promise never to see Amelia again?"

A frown brought Luke's eyebrows together. "How will that change things?"

At least the man was curious. It gave Jared the courage to continue. "You suspect Amelia and I have feelings for each other. I cannot vouch for her, but I can tell you that I love her. Even after learning how she has deceived me, I cannot find it in my heart to condemn her actions. She was trying to help people who needed her."

"She has confessed to treason."

Jared refused to be deterred by the man's cold tone. "I know you love Amelia, too. As your wife, she would be protected from the consequences of her actions. You are probably right that my influence is what led her to rebellion. I will return to Nashville immediately. I can board the next train out of Knoxville and leave this part of Tennessee for good. You won't have to wonder if Amelia is being influenced by me or my feelings for her. I will never contact her again. Once I'm gone, she will be totally committed to her marriage to you. She'll be more interested in setting up her household than altruism."

"What if she doesn't agree?"

Jared sighed. "It's up to you to convince her. I know she cares for you, or she never would have agreed to marry you. Amelia somehow got caught up in working for the Underground Railroad. But you saw her a little while ago. Her

341

remorse was obvious. She knows she's hurt those who care about her. She will listen to reason."

Luke took a turn around the office as he considered the proposal. Jared saw his expression move from despair to hope, from confusion to certainty. Finally the man walked over to him and thrust out his hand. "I have your word on this?"

What other choice did he have? He would do everything possible to protect Amelia. Jared's heart would not let him do any less. He shook Luke's hand. He would gladly pay the price of giving her up—knowing he would never see her again—to free the woman he loved.

Chapter 16

The guard had left Amelia in a large room cluttered with chairs and desks that must have been removed to make space for the rows of wounded soldiers lying on cots in the former classrooms. She wondered if it was the same room that had held Jared.

She took a handkerchief from her reticule and blew her nose. No more tears, no more weakness. Even if the general decided to execute her. She was not proud of the pain she'd caused, but she was glad to have been a part of setting Tabitha and the others free.

A knock on the door interrupted her thoughts. She glanced at the untouched tray of food a soldier had brought her earlier. She'd not been able to swallow a single morsel. Her stomach was too unsettled, and her throat still seemed full of tears. Even the smell of the roasted chicken made her feel queasy. It would be a relief to have it removed. "Come in."

Luke's broad shoulders filled the doorway. Why was he seeking her out? He'd been so angry once she convinced him of the truth.

Then his purpose dawned on her. "I suppose you came for your ring." Amelia fumbled with the golden band.

"No." He stepped into the room and closed the door behind him. "I'm not ready to release you from your promise."

"But won't it hurt your career when the truth is known?"

"Your friend, Jared, has proposed a solution."

Amelia's heart doubled its speed. Jared had argued on her behalf? "I thought both of you were scandalized by what I've done."

"Both of us have strong feelings when it comes to you, Amelia. And we have reason to be disappointed with your choice to deceive both of us, but it's time to move beyond what's past and make plans about what has to be done next."

So this was it. Amelia wondered if she would be hanged for her involvement with the Underground Railroad. She prayed for the fortitude to face her death with equanimity. After all, her own decisions were what had brought her to this.

Luke cleared his throat to get her attention. "I can't say that I blame Jared for falling in love with you, but at least he has the sense to put your safety above his feelings." He leaned against the door and watched her.

"Jared loves me?" As soon as the words slipped out, she gasped. Even she could hear the longing in her voice.

Luke's face changed. His eyes darkened and his mouth twisted. "Honesty? Do you have to be so transparent now? What happened to the woman who lied to everyone for her own reasons?"

"I'm sorry, Luke." She twisted the engagement ring off her finger and held it out to him.

"I could keep you here, you know."

"I'm resigned to stay for the duration of the war if that's what you decide."

"Please don't do this, Amelia. Don't throw away what we have. We can still have a life together."

She shook her head and looked down at the ring still in her hand. "I didn't mean to hurt you, Luke. I love you like a brother."

"I see." He took the ring but then caught her wrists in his hands. "My feelings are strong enough for both of us. Won't you reconsider? I'm sure I can make you happy."

She pulled her hands free and took a step back. "You're a wonderful man, Luke, and you deserve a wife who returns your feelings."

Luke's shoulders slumped. "Would it make any difference if I told you Jared has promised to have nothing more to do with you?"

Amelia closed her eyes as the words burned through her like poison. In that instant she knew the truth. She loved Jared. Not with the tepid feeling of friendship she felt for the man in front of her. She loved Jared Stuart with her whole heart, and she always would. That was why her betrothal to Luke had felt more like a cage than a promise. It was sheer willpower that kept her from sinking to her knees. "I told you Jared had nothing to do with the Mockingbird." She forced the words through clenched teeth.

"He'll soon be on his way back to Nashville."

Amelia tried to force her lips into a pleasant smile, but her muscles betrayed her. She looked into Luke's dark eyes, unable to say anything.

"I hope one day to find a woman who cares as much for me." The muscles in his face tightened, dragging his mouth downward. "But it is evident to me you are not that woman, Amelia. Everything you said to me and Jared this afternoon will remain between the three of us, so I have no reason to hold you any longer."

"You're letting me go?" Her eyes stung with unshed tears. Regret filled her heart. Luke deserved so much more than she could ever offer him.

"Who would really believe that you, a gently bred heiress, are the Mockingbird?" His laughter had a sardonic ring. "But I must have a promise from you."

Was he going to tell her to stay away from Jared? She could not make that promise. Not now that she knew the truth of her feelings for him.

"You must never tell anyone else the truth about the Mockingbird, or I will be blamed for abetting a criminal."

Her eyes searched his. "You have my word, Luke."

"Good. Then you are free to leave. I've ordered a carriage to return you to your aunt and uncle's home. I hope you will have the good sense to stay away from the abolitionists in town. I don't ever want to repeat this day's events."

"Thank you, Luke." She reached up and placed a chaste kiss on his cheek. "You're a good friend." Amelia followed him to the front door and allowed him to help her into the carriage. "I'll never forget this."

"Be happy, Amelia." He closed the carriage door with a soft click. "God bless you."

❧

Cold rain pelted the roof of her carriage, and Amelia wondered if it would turn into sleet. Her heart went out to the poor soldiers like Cousin Benjamin who likely had little shelter from the weather.

She watched anxiously as the driver guided the conveyance through the streets to her aunt and uncle's home. Was the trip taking longer than normal? Or was it her anxiety that lengthened the distance?

Finally the driver pulled up the horses, and she saw the familiar front door. Her foot tapped a rapid beat as she waited for him to let down the steps so she could disembark. She barely noticed the umbrella he held above her head as she hurried out of the carriage and up the steps to the front door, but she did have the presence of mind to thank the man before disappearing into the hallway.

Amelia hurried to the parlor, wondering how Uncle Francis and Aunt Laura had received Jared when he returned home. Had they been suspicious of him? Or had they been relieved to learn he was not the Mockingbird. And what had he told them about her disappearance?

She pasted a wobbly smile on her lips as she pushed the door open. Part of her was anxious to confront Jared about his feelings, but another part of her dreaded having to face him since he'd found out about her work with the Underground Railroad. Would he be cold? Or had he forgiven her? There was only one way to find out for sure. She took a deep breath and stepped inside the room.

Aunt Laura was sitting in her favorite chair on the right side of the hearth, her needlework in her lap. She jumped up, heedless of the sampler's falling to the floor. "Oh, there you are. We were really beginning to worry."

Uncle Francis was ensconced in the chair on the opposite side of the fireplace and held a book, which he closed abruptly as he looked up. "We wondered where you were, niece."

Amelia bent to kiss her aunt and then turned to her uncle. "I apologize. I was unavoidably detained and didn't think to send you a note."

"After the unpleasantness this morning, I told your uncle you had probably sought out your betrothed to ask for his help in recovering your slave." Aunt Laura nodded and settled back into her chair, retrieving her sampler and once again plying her needle with speed and accuracy.

"Speaking of notes, we did receive one from the Stuart boy." Uncle Francis snorted. "Your aunt and I went to Benjamin's encampment north of town earlier today to make certain he had everything he needed. When we got back, we were informed Jared had slunk in here during our absence and left a note thanking us for our hospitality. His note also claimed he'd been exonerated of the charge of treason. Said he had nothing to do with that Mockingbird fellow who's been helping slaves escape."

Amelia wanted to ask where Jared was now, but Aunt Laura interrupted her husband's dialogue. "Speaking of slaves, did you find Tabitha?"

"No." Amelia sat down on the sofa across from her aunt and uncle and twisted her hands in her lap. "I. . .I have a confession to make about Tabitha." She took a deep breath to steady herself before continuing. "I'm the one who helped Tabitha escape."

"You what!" Uncle Francis dropped his book.

Amelia cringed at the angry tone but would not let her gaze fall from his shocked one. "I'm sorry. I didn't mean to cause so much trouble. My. . .Tabitha has fallen in love, and I wanted her to be happy."

"Have you lost your senses?" Aunt Laura asked. "Her freedom was not yours to give."

"Tabitha is more like a sister to me than a slave." Amelia raised her chin. "I could not bear to see her unhappy."

"I don't know what this world is coming to." Uncle Francis sounded more puzzled than angry. He shook his head. "Your father is going to be very disappointed that you freed his property."

A rueful smile bent her lips upward. "You're right, but I hope he will eventually forgive me."

After folding her needlework and placing it in her basket, Aunt Laura moved to the sofa. "Of course he will forgive you. He loves you, Amelia. You are his daughter." She put an arm around Amelia and hugged her close.

Uncle Francis rolled his eyes. "Yes, yes. My brother may be hardheaded, but he will forgive you once you settle down and start providing him with grandchildren." He pointed a finger at her. "He's bound to be pleased with your engagement. Luke Talbot is a fine man."

"Yes, well, that's another thing I have to tell you about."

"What's wrong?" Aunt Laura pulled back a little and looked at her.

"Luke and I have decided we will not suit." Amelia told them about her interview with Luke and how she had confessed to helping Tabitha get away, but she avoided mentioning the Mockingbird, in deference to her promise to Luke.

"I'm sure your young man will reconsider his decision once he has time to cool off." Aunt Laura patted her hand.

"He must have been shocked by your confession," her uncle agreed. "And also embarrassed to have to set Jared free. But he'll probably change his mind once he catches the real culprit."

It was time to change the subject and broach the question she most wanted answered. "Did Jared's note say when he would return?"

Aunt Laura frowned at her. "Return? I thought you understood. Jared is gone. He is probably already on his way back to Nashville."

"His note said he wants to do his part to end the war." Uncle Francis shook his head. "Who knows what that means?"

The words echoed through Amelia. Who indeed? Certainly not her. She didn't know why she'd expected him to be here, anyway. Luke had told her about Jared's promise. One of the things she admired about Jared was his integrity. He would not linger here, knowing she would be coming back before too long.

All her hopes of being reunited with him died. It was too late.

One of the slaves came in to announce dinner, but Amelia knew she could not eat a single morsel. With a mumbled excuse, she went upstairs to her bedroom. Heartbroken, she threw herself across her bed and wept bitterly into the softness of her pillow. A maid came in, but she waved her away. She was too distraught to change into her nightgown. Who cared about such mundane things when her whole world had fallen apart?

Nothing penetrated her grief until the soft sounds of a birdcall drew her head from the pillow. She glanced toward the corner of her bedroom at her mockingbird trapped in its ornate cage. She pushed herself up from the bed and wandered toward it, her bruised heart somehow lightened by the lovely sounds it was producing. Their sweetness seemed like a promise from God.

Her breath caught as an idea took form. "I know just what we need to do so we can both be free, my friend." She moved to her dresser and picked up the mockingbird brooch Jared had given her. It was the first thing she put into her valise, followed by hastily folded clothing. Hoping she had packed enough necessities, Amelia changed into her nightgown and slipped between the covers. She would need a good night's sleep if she was going to rise at first light.

Chapter 17

The sun was beginning to push back the ebony texture of the night sky when Amelia arrived at the train station. She could barely contain her anticipation as the coachmen assisted her from the carriage. She only hoped she had guessed correctly that Jared would make the return journey by train.

The busy station had changed considerably in the months since her arrival. The civilian crowds had disappeared, replaced by young men in gray uniforms who guarded crated supplies with weary eyes. The ticket window was deserted, so she asked one of the passing soldiers where she could board the train to Nashville.

He raised an arm and pointed to a long line of boxcars. "The conductor should be able to help you."

Amelia thanked him and turned to the train. She looked for Jared's familiar face among the men she passed, her heart threatening to burst from her chest. She had almost reached the metal steps when a shrill whistle sounded and the cars began to move.

She gasped. The train was leaving! She had to get on board! Her future depended on it.

The train began picking up speed. Without a thought to her dignity, Amelia raised her skirts and ran forward. But it was no use. She was too late. Jared had left Knoxville without her.

∾

Jared slumped in his seat and tried to convince himself it was right to leave Knoxville. He had spent a restless night at a nearby boardinghouse, his mind plagued with grief and doubt. He was looking forward to seeing his family, of course. Missing them had been the hardest part of going to school so far away. But he was leaving a large part of his heart here.

To be more specific, he was leaving a big portion of it in Amelia's hands. And the ironic thing was she had no idea. She would marry Captain Luke Talbot and start a family. Maybe one day, some year in the far future, he would run into her on the streets of Nashville, a brood of young children in her wake.

He shook his head to empty it of the depressing picture and looked out the window as the train pulled from the station. His eyes slowly adjusted to the darkness as the train began to gather speed. He pushed his spectacles up and looked around, noticing only a couple of other passengers sitting on nearby benches—a far cry from the dozens who had traveled north only a few short months ago.

The war was changing everything. Now the trains were needed to move troops and supplies from battlefield to battlefield, and few private parties were on board. Of course most people didn't want to be traveling in such difficult times, either. Jared had been warned by the stationmaster that the train might not get all the way to Chattanooga, much less to Nashville. The destruction of tracks and bridges was growing more common each day, and it was becoming harder for the Confederacy to replace damaged rails and crossties.

The car lurched, suddenly and Jared barely managed to keep himself on the narrow bench seat as the train halted. Three gray-uniformed soldiers ran through the car toward the engine, their rifles pointing forward. What was going on? Had the train been attacked? Jared looked outside, but he could see nothing wrong.

"Can you hear anything?" One of the men he'd seen earlier pushed himself into the aisle.

Jared shook his head. "No. Maybe it's only livestock."

"More likely to be destroyed tracks," said one of the other passengers.

The man who was standing pointed his finger in the direction the soldiers had gone. "They're coming back." He slipped back into his seat.

Jared could hear the soldiers now. His shoulder relaxed as he heard them laughing at something. The problem must be minor. Perhaps they would soon be on their way.

A pair of soldiers opened the door and ushered in a woman who was holding a birdcage aloft in one hand.

Jared's eyes widened as he recognized the wheat-gold color of the woman's hair. His heart skipped a beat. "Amelia?"

"There he is." She pointed at him.

What was going on? He pushed himself to his feet. "What are you doing here?"

One of the soldiers clapped him on the shoulder. "You're a lucky fellow. Miss Montgomery here stopped the train by running her carriage across the tracks. She says she couldn't let you leave her behind in Knoxville."

Jared could do nothing but stare at Amelia as the soldiers continued on their way through the car.

"Can you forgive me?" She set her birdcage on one of the empty benches and stepped toward him.

Forgive her? He'd forgiven her almost instantly. In fact, while he could not condone her methods, he found himself impressed at the way she'd put her own safety aside to help slaves escape. "I think you're the bravest woman I've ever met."

"I'm not brave at all. I never intended to get involved with the Underground Railroad, but how could I ignore their plight?" She glanced up at him, her wide blue eyes swimming with tears. "But I hated deceiving my family. . .and you."

Jared cleared his throat. This was madness. He had promised Luke to have nothing to do with Amelia. Yet here they stood. He turned from her. "You should not be here."

A soft sound of distress answered his words.

Jared spun back to Amelia. "I'm sorry, but I made a promise to Luke."

Amelia's hurt look changed to hope, and she shook her head. "But you don't understand, Jared. Luke has released you from your promise. I am here with his blessing." She stepped closer and put a hand on his arm.

The words rolled around in his head for a moment before their meaning became clear. The love and tenderness in her expression made him feel like he was flying. The train lurched forward, and Jared quickly put an arm around Amelia to keep her from falling. Or maybe it was to keep himself from floating through the roof.

He could hardly believe it. He had lost all hope, but God had provided a way for them to be together. The sorrow that had filled him since boarding the train transformed into thankfulness, peace, and joy.

The forgotten cage behind her rocked slightly with the movement of the train, and its occupant began to chirp.

"Why did you bring the mockingbird with you?"

She glanced up at him, her face only inches from his. "I'm going to release him as soon as spring comes." Her voice was barely above a whisper. "How could I let my poor bird remain caged when my imprisoned heart has been set free?"

Jared looked down at Amelia, transfixed by the smile on her face. Heedless of the other passengers, he leaned forward and pressed a gentle kiss on her lips.

Love rushed through him as she put her arms around his neck. She was a special blessing, one he did not deserve. But Jared wasn't going to argue with God for giving him the opportunity to create a life with Amelia as his bride. On the contrary, he knew he would spend the rest of his life thanking God for removing the obstacles between them.

Jared kept his arm around her as he drew her to an empty seat. "I love you, Amelia."

"I love you, too, Jared. I couldn't bear the thought of a life without you."

"It won't be easy." He dropped a kiss behind her right ear. "I got a letter from Pa yesterday. He's been working with a group of state senators who opposed secession, and he wants me to join them."

"Will you have to fight with the army?"

Jared shook his head. "I cannot take up arms against other Tennesseans. Yet I cannot fight with those who would continue the institution of slavery. Pa is working with both sides to try to find a solution that will end the fighting. He's read some of my articles, and he thinks I may be able to sway some of those whose minds are closed."

"Your articles?" A look of satisfaction crossed her beautiful face. "I knew it. I knew you wrote those articles in *The Voice of Reason*. They were so well written, and the tenor of them reminded me of the piece you wrote for your literary society."

His cheeks reddened in a mixture of surprise and pleasure. "I'm glad you liked them."

"How could I not when the author has held my heart for so long in his grasp?"

Another thrill passed through him at her words. The song in his heart would undoubtedly rival the most beautiful call of any mockingbird.

A Letter to Our Readers

Dear Readers:

In order that we might better contribute to your reading enjoyment, we would appreciate you taking a few minutes to respond to the following questions. When completed, please return to the following: Fiction Editor, Barbour Publishing, Inc., P.O. Box 719, Uhrichsville, OH 44683.

1. Did you enjoy reading *Tennessee Brides* by Diane Ashley and Aaron McCarver?
   ❏ Very much. I would like to see more books like this.
   ❏ Moderately—I would have enjoyed it more if _____
   _____
   _____

2. What influenced your decision to purchase this book?
   (Check those that apply.)
   ❏ Cover   ❏ Back cover copy   ❏ Title   ❏ Price
   ❏ Friends   ❏ Publicity   ❏ Other

3. Which story was your favorite?
   ❏ *Under the Tulip Poplar*   ❏ *The Mockingbird's Call*
   ❏ *A Bouquet for Iris*

4. Please check your age range:
   ❏ Under 18   ❏ 18–24   ❏ 25–34
   ❏ 35–45   ❏ 46–55   ❏ Over 55

5. How many hours per week do you read? _____

Name _____

Occupation _____

Address _____

City_____ State_____ Zip_____

E-mail _____